"Joanna Elm brings new and exciting twists to the murder mystery genre. Her debut novel is fresh, original, and unpredictable. A highly entertaining and engaging mystery; great locales, smooth and fast narrative, and high-power characters."

—Nelson DeMille, bestselling author of *Plum Island*, on *Scandal*

"The plot's the thing here as Elm hurls one curveball after another at both Kate and her readers."

—*Publishers Weekly* on *Delusion*

"A plot full of twists and high technology observations."

—*Bookman Book Review* (Nashville)

"In *Delusion*, [Elm] writes an engrossing, page-turning police procedural set in the world of TV news. The plot has many fibers skillfully twirled into a cohesive yarn."

—*The Mystery Review*

"A well-crafted novel with that unmistakable ring of authenticity. Suspenseful."

—Barbara D'Amato, author of *Killer.app*, on *Scandal*

By Joanna Elm from Tom Doherty Associates

Scandal
Delusion

DELUSION

JOANNA ELM

TOR®

A TOM DOHERTY ASSOCIATES BOOK
NEW YORK

This is a work of fiction. All of the characters and events portrayed in this novel are either fictitious or are used fictitiously.

DELUSION

Copyright © 1997 by Joanna Elm

A Tor Book
Published by Tom Doherty Associates, Inc.
175 Fifth Avenue
New York, NY 10010

Tor Books on the World Wide Web:
http://www.tor.com

Tor® is a registered trademark of Tom Doherty Associates, Inc.

ISBN: 0-812-56480-4
Library of Congress Card Catalog Number: 97-16740

First edition: October 1997
First mass market edition: January 1999

Printed in the United States of America

0 9 8 7 6 5 4 3 2 1

Acknowledgments

Writing a novel sometimes demands more of loved ones than it does of the writer and I am indebted, forever and always, to those I love most, my husband, Joe, and my son, Danny. Without their continued patience, understanding, support, and the highest levels of tolerance I would never be able to indulge my own delusion.

I am especially grateful to my friend and editor, Camille Cline, for her insight, guidance, good humor, and exceptional eye for detail, and to my friend and agent, Robert Diforio, for keeping me—and *Delusion*—on the right track, and always coming through for me when it counts.

For his abundant help and time, and for saving me hours of legwork, I thank Det-Sgt. Mark Keenan of the Investigations Unit of Lower Merion Township Police. My thanks also to Mitchell Wagenberg for making the technical details of videoprocessing comprehensible. Any inaccuracies that remain are mine alone.

My love and warmest thanks to my mother, Alicja Ewa, and stepfather, Zbyszek Zagaja, for their wholehearted encouragement and support.

My sincerest thanks to my dearest friends, Judy Calixto Goldman for jollying the spirit, and to Mary Ellen Burke and Pam Tully for sustenance of the home-baked kind.

My love and thanks, also, to my terrific in-laws, Mary and Ray Bauer, John and Marie Elm, and Jim and Joan Elm for their enthusiasm and support and for agreeing to let me name the heroine of *Delusion* after the mother-in-law I never knew but wish I had.

Finally, my everlasting love and gratitude to Marian Henry Patyna, the best father in the world.

Delusion

Prologue

It was almost time. Jennifer would be home soon.

He had spent all evening thinking about her, wondering if she would wear the sexy nightie for him. This time he'd brought a lace-trimmed one in a pretty shade of rose—with little panties to match.

Would she? Wouldn't she? It was the only thing he wasn't sure about. The rest of it was inevitable and had been since early afternoon, when he had broken into her house.

It had not been difficult. On Mondays the cleaning woman came. He had watched her in action the week before and had seen her throw open all the windows and atrium doors as soon as she arrived. So, today it had just been a matter of waiting for the right moment when he could slip in unnoticed to hide out in the basement till the woman left, setting the alarm and securing him inside Jennifer Reed's house.

After that he'd had plenty of time to scope out everything. Now he padded surely across the tiled kitchen floor towards the seven black handles jutting from the beech-wood storage block on the kitchen countertop. Nestled between the ceramic double sink with its fancy Kohler faucet and a Saeco espresso machine, the knife set had caught his attention immediately.

Like everything else in Jennifer's kitchen the knives were top of the line. Jennifer had expensive tastes. The espresso machine had almost certainly set her back some fifteen hundred bucks. The coffee carafe that stood beside it had a gold-plated finish. On the little shelf above the countertop, a slim Steuben vase held a single red rose. He had expected the classy little touches. Jennifer had exquisite taste in everything except men.

He gripped one of the black handles and drew out the knife. Six inches of nasty, unevenly serrated stainless steel glinted in the light. The bold black lettering on the blade told him it was a Henckels knife made in Bollingen, Germany. An excellent knife. He nodded and tested the tip with his index finger. Satisfied, he retraced his steps across the kitchen floor, heading for the circular staircase that led to Jennifer's bedroom.

He picked his way through the dark to the windows to draw the drapes before flicking on the light switch. It was probably an unnecessary precaution. The bedroom was at the back of the house and screened by clusters of tall poplars. There was little chance of any neighbor seeing anything or hearing anything when Jennifer came home.

Bad for Jennifer, good for him, he thought, humming softly and tunelessly to himself, as he paced over to the TV monitor mounted on the wall facing her bed. Stabbing at the power button, he clicked through the channels till he found Seven.

Just in time.

Jennifer was signing off for the night. With a little shake of her golden curls, her full glossy lips parted in a wide smile to reveal perfect white teeth. "Thank you for being with us. Join us again tomorrow night on Seven for the ten o'clock news. I'm Jennifer Reed. Do have a good night."

He shook his head, grimacing as he waited for the little thrust thing she always did with her boobs when the camera pulled out to a wide-angle closing shot.

Her predecessor, Diane Lamont, had always swiveled around to smile at her co-anchor, leaving viewers with the indelible image of her Barbie-like chest in profile. Janey Sumner had aimed for a more professional demeanor, shuffling the pages of her script and looking demure in high-necked blouses and severe little suits. But underneath she'd been just like the others: They'd all screwed their way into the anchor chair. It was what passed for paying one's dues in Jack Kane's newsroom.

"See you soon, Jennifer," he mouthed at the monitor, as her image faded. It would take her about four or five minutes to leave the studio. Another three or four to take the elevator to the garage. The drive from Center City along the Schuylkill out to the Main Line should take no more than twenty, twenty-five minutes tops, at this time of night. Jennifer would be home by eleven-thirty at the latest.

His eyes glanced over the framed pictures on the shelves above the TV. There were about a dozen of them. He had surveyed them once already earlier this afternoon, but now he found himself drawn again to the most prominently displayed photograph: the eight-by-ten of Jennifer Reed and Jack Kane at a local Emmy awards dinner. He recognized it as a photo taken by an *Inquirer* photographer. He had a copy of it in his own files. But his wasn't signed by Kane. There was no silly little message from the station's news director, reading: You had my vote . . .

Vote? Try another four-letter word, he thought as he stared at the grin on Kane's face. Then abruptly he turned away, switched off the lights, and strode towards Jennifer's huge walk-in closet.

It was twenty to midnight when the noise of the garage door jolted him to his feet. He reached into his bag for the black silk ski mask and slipped it on over his head. Then, he brought out the knife. He was aware of his pulse racing with anticipation as his ears picked up the sound of her footfall on the stairs. Suddenly the bedroom was bathed in the rosy glow of the lamp on the nightstand, and he knew Jennifer had arrived.

He pressed his face up to the slats of the louvred door and watched her sweep the careful arrangement of pillows and shams off the bed and onto the floor before she turned down the bedspread.

She kicked off her shoes and unhooked the back of her skirt, letting it slide to the floor. Then she took off her jacket and flung it onto a big chair by the window before slipping out of her pantyhose.

He gripped the handle of the knife as he watched her walking in his direction and took a step back, waiting for the door to be flung open. But seconds passed and then he heard water running in the bathroom. He returned to the louvred slats and watched for her to return. When she finally walked back into the room, he saw she was naked and toweling her wet hair.

He pushed open the closet door with a force that sent it crashing against the wall and stepped into her full view, staring at her through the narrow slits of the mask.

He knew what would come next. It had happened with the others: The hands would move to her breasts in a vain attempt to cover them while the initial gasp of shock would precede a fuller intake of breath for the scream of fear as her eyes focussed on the long blade.

"No." He shook his head, holding up the knife with the blade pointing at her. "No, Jennifer, you mustn't scream. No one's going to hear you, anyway. Okay?"

She nodded but stepped backwards as her eyes darted to the raised knife. Without moving towards her he motioned for her to sit down on the edge of the bed. He saw that she was shaking. He reached for his black bag and rummaged inside it for the silk nightie and panties, then held the flimsy garments out to her.

"You can wear these if you like."

The expression in her eyes registered bemusement. The others had looked at him the same way, too—as if they had all read the same script—and they had all hesitated, no doubt wondering whether they were just going to turn him on more by slipping into the sexy little outfit.

He had allowed each of them to decide for themselves, curious about the different reactions: Diane Lamont had ignored the offer. Janey Sumner had grabbed at it angrily. Jennifer Reed finally nodded her head and held out her hand for the garments but just sat there holding them in her lap.

"Go on, you can put it on." He transferred the knife into

his left hand. "If you do exactly as I say, I'm not going to hurt you. Okay?"

She nodded quickly, and then slipped the nightie over her head but ignored the little panties.

"Okay." He motioned to her across the floor. "Now, put those pillows back on the bed and slide up there. I want you to get comfortable."

She scooted across the floor and picked up the cushions and pillows. When she turned back to face him he saw tears streaming down her cheeks.

"Please don't do this to me. Don't hurt me." Even as she pleaded, her eyes fixed on the blade, she scrambled onto the bed and sat stiffly against the pillows as he'd ordered her to do.

He walked to the side of the bed. "I told you this isn't going to hurt."

"Then please put the knife down. It's not necessary. I'm not going to scream."

He ignored her plea. "Try to relax. Don't look so stiff. Here . . . Bring your knees up a little . . . That's it. Now chin up . . ."

He used the tip of the blade to rearrange the folds of the nightie then stepped back to admire his handiwork. Without another word he walked back to the foot of the bed, reached into the black bag again, and then stood up to face the anchorwoman.

He stared at her from the foot of the bed, enjoying the moment as her eyes widened in a silent anguish. He saw the beads of sweat glistening on her upper lip as her eyes focussed on what he'd brought out of his black bag.

"Come on, Jennifer." He spoke softly. "You'll love this. I know you will."

He came towards her again and brought the tip of the blade down to her thighs. The anchorwoman didn't flinch at the touch of steel. She seemed unaware of the blade. Her eyes were riveted on the object he held in his right hand, and he saw her lips moving but couldn't quite catch what she was saying.

It sounded like "Oh, no. Please, no." Over and over again.

1

Kate was just hitting her stride, getting into the steady, rhythmic pounding of Nike soles on blacktop, when the police patrol car sped by her, lights pulsating, no siren, heading in the opposite direction on Old Ford Lane. Whipping around to follow its progress, she jogged in place and watched it swing into a driveway some hundred yards down the road.

Where the hell are they going in such a hurry?

She stopped and hesitated only a moment before retracing her route to the spot where she'd seen the patrol car turn. The long driveway bordered by elegant, slim poplar trees led to a rambling wood-and-glass multilevel contemporary, which she immediately recognized as the home of Gladwyne's highest-profile celebrity.

Kate had seen a picture of the house in *Philadelphia Magazine* a few months after Channel Seven anchorwoman Jennifer Reed had moved to the city's most exclusive suburb. Weeks later a similar picture had appeared in *Main Line Life*—this one with Jennifer turning cartwheels on her front lawn.

It had come as no surprise to Kate to read, in a subsequent gossip column, that Jennifer had been turned down for membership by the local country club: The upper-crust Main Line was one of the few places in the world where Jennifer Reed's type of high-profile, glitzy fame just did not impress.

She stared down the driveway. From where she stood, she

could see the lone police car but not much more. It was probably nothing but a faulty alarm that had been activated by mistake.

She shivered suddenly, feeling the chill of the early morning air for the first time. Then she turned and broke into a slow jog along the main road, deciding to circle around Old Ford Lane. It would take her about twenty minutes to make the arc. She would double-check on any further activity then.

Oh, come on, McCusker. Get over it. She chided herself for her Pavlovian-like response to the flashing police lights. But she knew it wouldn't do any good. Lawyers chased ambulances and crime reporters chased police cars. And old habits died hard. As she'd explained it once to Steve, it was a simple chemical reaction. Flashing police lights made the blood pump harder and the adrenaline soar. Steve had laughed and said she made it sound like sex.

She clenched her jaw and picked up her pace, forcing her long legs to pump harder, pounding her soles into the blacktop till she felt little slivers of pain shooting up her calves. She welcomed the distraction. It was better than thinking about Steve. Or sex. Or the even more painful combination of the two.

Abruptly, she turned off the main road, taking a shortcut through the woods. The dirt path brought her directly to the back of Jennifer Reed's house, where she slowed to an amble, picking her way through the poplars along the property line. Then she stopped, her eyes narrowing at the sight of Harry Holmsby's gray Chevy parked right behind the police patrol car. The detective-sergeant was a friend—and the top gun in the investigations unit of the Lower Merion P.D.

"Hey, miss . . . you can't walk through here." A uniformed police officer suddenly materialized across the path from where she was standing.

"Okay." She stopped. "Just tell the sarge that Kate McCusker's here."

The cop eyed her quizzically, his eyes darting from her lilac leggings and leg warmers to her hooded sweatshirt. She stood tall with her hands on her hips. At five feet six inches, she could look imposing when she wanted to. Finally, the cop stepped aside. "Excuse me, I didn't realize he was expecting you. Go ahead."

Kate gave him a little salute as she bounded across the lawn and in through the etched glass double doors. The stench hit her immediately, its stomach-heaving quality reminding her of the time when the exterminator had gassed a nest of field mice under her living room floor and had left the rodents to drain and dry up instead of tearing up the floorboards to remove the bodies. She backed up rapidly.

The body was lying on the gray flagstone foyer floor. A black pump lay a few feet from where Art Johnson, the deputy coroner, was crouched, obscuring most of the corpse. An elegant maroon leather briefcase lay on the other side, and papers had scattered from it. Harry was hunched over them.

She caught his eye as he straightened up.

"Kate! What are you doing here?"

She shrugged. "I was out jogging and spotted your Chevy." She grinned. "Thought I'd stop and say hi."

She inched forward into the foyer, holding her breath, her eyes darting past Harry's shoulder as she tried to catch a glimpse of the woman's face.

"What happened?" Out of the corner of her eye, Kate thought she saw a flash of dark hair as Art Johnson shifted to his left, and a momentary doubt made her hesitate. "That is Jennifer Reed, isn't it?"

Harry Holmsby grimaced, loosening his tie as he stepped towards her. "No, Kate. It isn't."

"It isn't?"

Harry shook his head. "No."

Kate tugged at some stray wisps that had escaped the rubber band holding her long blond hair back in a ponytail, realizing that her ready, and maybe overzealous, assumption placing Philadelphia's most popular TV anchorwoman at this death scene had obviously not escaped Harry Holmsby.

But then, not much did.

She had first met him five years before, when she'd been assigned to cover the sensational Basinger case for the

Philadelphia Daily News. Harry had been the lead investigator on the case of a serial killer who had stalked and slaughtered four rich young Main Line wives. Her initial relationship with the detective-sergeant had been somewhat adversarial as she'd hounded him for tips and information. But after the arrest of the suspect (a meek-looking bank loan officer by the name of Richard Basinger) and during the course of the trial it had mellowed into a friendship based on mutual respect. By the time the trial was over Harry had agreed to open his files on the case for her. Kate had secured a fat advance from a New York publisher and had taken a sabbatical from the *Daily News* to write a book about the stalkings.

When *Root of All Evil* hit the bestseller charts she had extended the sabbatical from the *Daily News* permanently. She had also married Harry's partner, Steve.

Harry eyed her now, with a teasing glint. "Let me guess . . . you had the title for a new book all picked out, right?"

Her face flushed. *Fade to Black* had actually popped into her head as she'd bounced in through the door. Maybe Harry knew her too well.

He laughed and she saw his attention drifting back to Art Johnson. "Anyway," she said, recovering quickly, "if it's not Jennifer Reed, who is it?"

Harry peered at her over the top of his bifocals, as if debating whether to be drawn any further into Kate's quizzing. Then, he shrugged. "Anna Mae Whitman."

"The realtor?" Kate's interest perked again as she recalled that Anna Mae Whitman's disappearance a week before had made the front page of the *Philadelphia Inquirer*'s Metro Section. Kate had clipped the item, feeling it was the sort of story that might have potential since Anna Mae Whitman had not only worked for a top Main Line real estate firm but had also served on the boards of several local hospitals and charities. A wealthy divorcee who specialized in the sale of multimillion dollar Main Line properties, she had been a familiar sight in the area, tooling around in a maroon Bentley with a license plate that stated simply, I SELL.

Kate looked around, noticing now that there was no furniture in the entrance foyer. She looked to her left into a spectacular living room with high cathedral ceilings, a fire-place with a stone hearth, and sliding glass doors that gave a view of the wooded backyard. There was no furniture in that room, either. A short, balding, well-dressed man stood by the hearth.

Kate nodded in the stranger's direction. "Who's he?"

"Stan Nixon, her partner. He found her."

Kate raised an eyebrow. "He's also the one who reported her missing, according to what I read. How come he didn't look here earlier?"

Harry Holmsby shook his head. "He doesn't know why she was here. They only just got the listing. Jennifer Reed moved out about ten days ago. He thinks Whitman stopped by to check on the cleaning job."

"And what? She was followed here by some disgruntled client?"

She broke off as Harry Holmsby started to shake his head. "You're jumping the gun again, Kate. I didn't say anything about foul play, did I?"

Kate stared at the circular staircase. "You think she fell?"

"It's a possibility. The cleaning crew did a terrific job waxing that staircase. And the bruising on her body appears to be consistent with a fall."

"Which would be consistent with being pushed, too, wouldn't it?"

Harry shrugged. "More or less." Then he sighed. "Come on up here . . . and mind your step."

She followed Harry to the top of the landing. "Take a look," he said. "That's one nasty-looking staircase. No railing, no bannister. You trip on this baby and there's nothing to grab for. That's a straight header to those flagstones down there."

"All the more reason to be careful, wouldn't you say?" Kate grinned at him, knowing she was baiting him—and knowing that it wasn't going to get her very far, either. Harry Holmsby was a good detective, with twenty-five years of experience behind him. If there was anything suspicious about Anna Mae Whitman's death he would be the first to see it.

Now he was looking at her with the same teasing glint in

his eye. "Let's just say I don't think Sharon Stone is going to be picking up the movie option on this one."

"Ouch!" Kate pretended to look hurt at his reference to the blond actress who'd starred in the movie based on her bestseller. Then she turned to saunter along the landing leading to what she guessed had been the master bedroom suite. She found herself in a small sitting room with sliding doors out to a wooden deck. Through an archway Kate saw a larger room. An open door at one end of the room revealed a large walk-in closet and beyond it a short corridor leading to a bathroom. Kate noted the glimmer of pink-and-gold marble and stepped through the archway into the bedroom to take a closer look.

"Well, well." She stopped suddenly, staring at the only piece of furniture left in the room: a big antique four-poster bed. She whistled softly under her breath and reached out to touch the hand-carved bedposts, marveling at the texture of the rough-hewn oak under her fingertips. Then she shook her head. "Steve and I traveled all over Bucks County looking for something like this. I can't believe it. Why the hell would she leave this behind?"

"Maybe it's got carpenter ants." Harry gave her a withering look.

"Wait!" She gripped Harry's arm. "Do you think it would be tacky if I called and asked her if the bed is for sale?"

The detective-sergeant narrowed his eyes. "You want to buy the bed?"

"Maybe. If the price is right. It's a unique piece." She paused and ran her hand over the wood again. "I'd really like to know why she left it behind."

"Jeez, Kate!"

She shrugged. "It just seems so odd. She took everything—except the bed."

Harry laughed out loud and walked out of the room. "Come on, let's go. I need to talk to the associate. You want to play second badge while I grill Stan Nixon?"

Kate heard the facetious note in his voice but nodded and followed him back downstairs to the living room, where the realtor was now slumped down on the stone parapet by the fireplace, ashen-faced and picking nervously at some invisible lint on his jacket sleeve. He got to his feet as Harry approached.

"So, Mr. Nixon." Harry paused to retrieve a notebook from his back pocket. "Tell me, what brought you out to the house this morning?"

Nixon cleared his throat. "I was planning to show it later today. I wanted to check that everything was in order. When I walked around back, to the garage . . . that's when I saw Anna Mae's car . . ."

"And?" Harry prodded.

The realtor shook his head. "I called nine-one-one immediately from my car phone."

"You didn't go into the house?"

The realtor shook his head. "No, I was . . . Well, I wasn't sure what I might find."

"You thought she might be dead?"

He nodded. "I guess. I just didn't know . . . I mean Anna Mae was missing several days. No one had heard from her. I knew it couldn't be good."

"You reported Mrs. Whitman missing last Wednesday," Harry said. "When was the last time you actually saw her?"

"The day before that. On Tuesday. It was just so unusual for her not to show or call—"

"What time, Mr. Nixon?" Harry interrupted briskly.

"I saw her around noon on Tuesday. She was in the office with a client. She had three or four properties lined up to show."

"But not this one?"

"No. This is a terrific property but not in the same class as the ones she had lined up. Those were more like miniestates like the Bateman estate out on Highsgrove Road and the Kane house on Cherry Lane."

"Kane?" Kate interrupted suddenly. "You mean as in Jack Kane, the president of WorldMedia News?"

Stanley Nixon nodded as Harry turned to stare at Kate.

Kate shrugged in apology. "Before he went to New York he was the news director at Channel Seven. Same station that Jennifer Reed anchors at . . ."

Harry's mouth twitched at one corner as if to say, so what? Then he seemed to think better of it and turned his attention back to Stan Nixon. "Can you get us a name for Mrs. Whitman's last client?"

The realtor hesitated. "I'll do my best." He gestured to the foyer. "It's probably in Anna Mae's briefcase." He hesitated again. "It was a woman, I remember that. A very elegant lady." He moved towards the foyer. "I'll look through Anna Mae's papers."

"No, not now." Harry stopped him. "We're going to have the crime lab technicians here soon and they'll need to take prints. We'll turn over the briefcase and papers to you as soon as they're done."

"Crime technicians?" Stan Nixon's face paled. "Why?"

"Standard procedure . . . just in case." Harry paused. "Is it possible she had another client? Someone she brought here?"

"Yes, I suppose." Stan Nixon nodded. "But it's more likely she just stopped to check that the cleaning crew did their work. Anna Mae was very thorough, you know."

Harry nodded and Kate jumped in to break the short pause that followed. "Why is Jennifer Reed selling the house? She wasn't here very long."

Stan Nixon looked at Kate with a blank expression on his face. "I'm not really sure. I know she moved back to the city and she's willing to take a loss for a quick sale, but I didn't take the listing. I never spoke to her." He paused and shook his head before adding, "I suppose I'll have to now."

"Okay, Mr. Nixon, thank you." Harry wound up the conversation curtly. "We'll be in touch." Then he turned away and Kate followed him back into the foyer where Art Johnson was ready to roll the body.

"I'll give you a fuller report later, Harry," the deputy coroner said. "Right now, though, I don't see anything that causes me any real concern here."

Kate found herself following Art and the body bag out of the house. She stopped and took a deep breath of fresh air, noticing that the sun had just broken through the clouds. Then, she checked her watch. It wasn't yet nine. But most likely Tommy would already be up. It was only on school mornings that he wanted to sleep late. Maysie would be up, too. Her mother-in-law was a light sleeper and generally got up to start breakfast when she heard the front door close behind Kate. Now she'd be getting anxious, for sure. Kate was never out jogging for this long.

"Come on." Harry came up behind her, checking his own watch. "Let me give you a ride home." He held the door of his Chevy open for her, and she slid into the passenger seat.

"By the way . . ." He paused to slam her door shut then walked around to the driver's seat and started the engine before picking up where he'd left off. "Ray Foster's retiring and we're throwing him a party tomorrow night. Piccolina's at eight. Why don't you come along?"

She didn't answer immediately but pretended to think about it, although she knew she was going to turn down the invitation, the way she'd rejected all of Harry's other efforts to introduce her to new friends over the last couple of months.

"Come on," Harry persisted. "You've got to start getting out of the house. It's bad enough you don't have a job that gets you out among people, you should at least take the few opportunities that come along."

"Opportunities for what, Harry?" She laughed softly. "To meet people? You mean men, don't you?" She patted his arm. "I wish you'd stop worrying about me. You and Maysie are going to drive me crazy. What is this? My one year of mourning is up? Now I've got to get back into the social whirl, is that it?" She paused. "I don't recall you getting back into the swing of things so quickly, either."

Harry shook his head. "I was a fifty-year-old grandfather when Nina died. That's a bit different, Kate. Anyway, all I'm saying is there'll be a good crowd there: old friends and some new faces. As a matter of fact there's a new guy, Mike Travis. He just joined the DA's office as an investigator. He'll be there. I think you'd like—"

"Harry," she held up her hand to interrupt him. "You're not listening. I'm not concerned about my social life. What I do need is to get back to work. I need a good story, not a man."

"Need?" Harry raised an eyebrow.

She laughed at his comical, quizzical expression. She knew what he was thinking. *Root of All Evil* had stayed on the bestseller list for thirty weeks in hardcover. The movie had ensured her the number-one spot on the paperback bestseller lists for forty weeks, as well as a cool half million in the bank.

Then, just two months after Steve's death, an heir to the DuPont fortune had gunned down an Olympic champion wrestler on his Delaware County estate. Kate had jumped right on the story and had churned out a quickie paperback about the eccentric multibillionaire. It was now being made into a TV movie. .

So okay, she wasn't exactly struggling to make ends meet, but neither was the money going to last forever. She and Steve had sunk thousands of dollars into renovating a big stone Victorian house they'd bought on two very desirable Main Line acres. Now, property taxes and maintenance ate alarmingly into her assets on a monthly basis. But she did not want to explain that to Harry. As dear a friend as the detective-sergeant was, she suspected he would find it difficult to sympathize with crippling landscaping bills. Glancing sideways at him, she realized he was still waiting for an answer. "I just need something to work on," she said finally. "I want to be writing again. My agent calls me all the time with ideas and projects, and there's good stuff out there. The trouble is, I'd have to travel and I can't leave Tommy. Not right now."

Harry grunted and nodded knowingly as he turned into her driveway. "How's all that going, anyway? The Belinda situation, I mean?"

She grimaced at his choice of word. *Situation* was a diplomatic way of putting it, considering the turmoil that Steve's ex-wife had caused by her sudden reappearance, with new husband and child in tow, after five years in Rio.

She let out a long sigh as Harry pulled up in front of the porch steps and killed the engine but made no move to get out of the car. "Maybe you're worrying unnecessarily," he said gently. "Maysie tells me that Tommy's handling it well enough."

Kate laughed. "Well, sure. *He* is. But he was hardly out of diapers when Belinda walked out on him and Steve. Tommy doesn't even remember her. Now he's a nine-year-old. You invite him over to a house with a puppy and buy him a skateboard and a dozen video games and all the latest CDs. What's not to handle?"

"Yeah," Harry broke in. "But Belinda seems to be handling it sensibly, too. I mean it's not like she waltzed in and demanded her son back, pronto."

Kate glanced sharply at the detective-sergeant. "It doesn't mean she's not going to, though, sometime down the road when Tommy's gotten more comfortable with her. And then what? She's his natural mother; I'm a mere guardian in the eyes of the law. How do you think a court would—" She broke off, unable to continue with the thought of losing her stepson.

"Whoa!" Harry patted her hand. "You're getting way ahead of yourself there. If she's only half as bad as Maysie says she is, she'll probably take a hike again, soon enough. You'll see, it'll work out." He grinned and opened his door, seeing Maysie appear on the wide wraparound porch. He waved to her and got out of the car.

Kate shrugged and followed him. "Maysie!" she called. "Where's Tommy? Isn't he up? Belinda will be here any minute."

Her mother-in-law stopped at the side door. "He already left, hon. *She* picked him up early. *She* said she had a busy weekend planned." Maysie grimaced, the way she always did at any mention of her former daughter-in-law. Then, she shrugged. "Come on in, I made pancakes."

Kate nodded but hung back, making an effort to shake off the empty, frustrated feeling that had descended on her at the first mention of Belinda. The woman's sudden reappearance at the end of summer had come at the worst time—just when Kate and Tommy had found themselves adjusting to life without Steve.

Kate had spent all summer helping Tommy work through his grief. She had kept him distracted and occupied. She had organized tennis lessons, horseback riding, and Rollerblading. She had taken him and his friends on trips into the city to the art museum and the zoo and the movies. She had rented a beachfront villa on the Jersey Shore for a few weeks and invited two of his classmates to join them.

She had taken them swimming and sailing and watched them surfing—her heart stopping every time one of them disappeared for a moment into the pounding white waves.

She had done her best to show him that his life was not going to change or fall apart. She had promised that he would still go to the same school and have the same friends and live in the same house. No matter what it cost she was determined to keep the upheavals in his life to a minimum.

Now, Kate wasn't sure she'd be able to keep the promises. And it wasn't all just because of Belinda either. If she didn't come up with a good idea for a book soon, then for one thing, she'd have to think about moving to a smaller, more manageable house.

No. No way, she thought, clenching her fists and throwing her head back as she raised her eyes skyward, Scarlett O'Hara–style.

"No, I will never go hungry again." She mouthed the words dramatically, punching her fists into the air, the way she thought she remembered Vivien Leigh doing in *Gone with the Wind*.

Then she laughed, feeling silly but suddenly a whole lot better. All was not yet lost. She would find something. There had to be one good meaty story out there, somewhere. There had to be things happening in Philadelphia. It was a city of almost two million people, after all. She would drive into Philly later and visit the *Inquirer* library . . . maybe even meet for lunch with Pat Norris, her onetime rival and the *Inquirer*'s chief crime reporter.

She took the porch steps in one leap, filled with fresh resolve. And when she'd done all that, she would track down Jennifer Reed at Channel Seven. She'd ask about the bed. See if it was for sale. And while she was on the phone, maybe she'd prod a little to find out what it was exactly that had driven the anchorwoman out of her own modern-day Tara on the Main Line.

2

M olly Heskell's house presented him with his biggest challenge yet. The elegant three-story brick colonial, which the TV newswoman had shared with her husband till he'd moved out a couple of weeks ago, overlooked Three Bears Park. It was a pretty spot in the heart of Society Hill, the city's prime residential area. But a major headache for him: On a sunny fall Sunday afternoon the pleasant little square with its swingsets and slides was filled with kids and their parents.

He had faced the challenge head on, realizing there was only one way to gain entry into Molly Heskell's house—and that was to do it openly and in full view. A couple of days devoted to some serious thought and planning had culminated in a trip to Home Depot, where he'd purchased paints, brushes, drop cloths, and a ladder.

He set up the ladder now in front of the first-floor window, and hitching up the pants of his white overalls, climbed up to ascertain that the windows were secured with old-fashioned catches. No surprises there. He would use the spatula to ease back the catch. He could be inside in a jiffy.

But he took his time. Molly had left fifteen minutes before with a big Toys "Я" Us bag in one hand and a bottle of wine in the other. She'd probably spend the afternoon with whomever she was visiting.

He raised the window and returned to the truck for his brush and paint can. A half hour later he was done with painting the frames around both windows on the ground floor. Gently, he raised the left window and climbed in.

He found himself whistling as he walked through into the hall and opened the front door. Leaving it ajar, he gathered up his ladder and drop cloths from the sidewalk and placed them inside his truck. Then, retrieving another can of paint and his black bag, he walked back into the house, swinging the can in his right hand, till he closed the door behind him.

He noticed his hands were shaking slightly as he retrieved a plastic trash bag from inside the tote, then took off his overalls and put them into a plastic bag, along with the paint can. He zipped up the bag and took a deep, steadying breath. The hardest part was done. He was in.

Molly Heskell's house was narrow, like many of the old colonial homes in Society Hill, where taxes had once been determined by the frontage of the house. But it was deep and three stories high. On the ground floor, he found the kitchen at the back of the house, overlooking a small walled-in courtyard.

It was a cluttered room. Newspapers lay piled up on one of the kitchen chairs. The Sunday edition of the *Inquirer* lay scattered on the small round kitchen table and on the tiled floor. A stack of unopened mail lay on the counter next to a coffee pot, which was plugged in and still half-filled with a dark, sludgy-looking brew. A small plate with a half-eaten croissant stood in the sink. It was the sort of kitchen where he'd have to rummage around in the drawers to find a knife. He wasn't worried. There was always one good, sharp knife in any kitchen. In Molly Heskell's kitchen he found it in the dishwasher—a long Hoffritz carving knife with yellow crumbs from what looked like pound cake still caked on the blade. Disgusted, he threw it back and flung open another drawer. It seemed to be a catch-all drawer filled mostly with junk and he was about to close it when he saw the box cutter. Grinning, he dropped it into his bag and carried it upstairs.

The master bedroom took up the entire front of the house on the second floor. A master bathroom connected the bedroom to a room that overlooked the courtyard at the back of the house. He figured it could have been used as a sitting room or little office. But it was empty. There was no furniture in the room and someone had started to rip off the wallpaper. Making a sloppy job of it, too, he thought. Big patches still clung in random spots, showing fluffy white clouds on a pale periwinkle background.

A sudden thought jolted through him as he recalled the *Inquirer* story about Molly Heskell's tragic loss: a baby girl, stillborn, less than a month ago. Now, taking a closer look at the damage in the room, he wondered if Molly had ripped off the wallpaper herself in some sort of uncontrollable fit of rage and grief.

He backed out of the room abruptly. He had not considered this problem before, but if Molly had gone nuts over the nursery wallpaper, then it was possible that she could totally freak out on him.

He paced across the bedroom to the window to scan the street below. Delancey was not the busiest street in Society Hill but it was historic and there was plenty of tourists in Center City at this time of year. Anyone strolling in the street below—or even crossing the little park—would surely hear screams coming from the bedroom.

Did he really need Molly Heskell?

It was a stupid question. Of course he did. She was central to the project. She had been Jack Kane's favorite, probably because until she'd frizzed her hair, Molly Heskell had borne such a striking resemblance to Jessica Savitch.

So, of course Molly had to be part of the project because that's how it had all started—with Jessica, the original Golden Girl of TV news.

Back in the days before Jess had gone network and she was still Philadelphia's number-one newswoman, he'd had a future, too. Jessica had been his ally. He had shared his dreams and ambitions with her and she had encouraged him. She was the one who had suggested that he change his name to Lewis. It was a stronger name for an anchorman than Louis or Lou, she'd said. They had discussed TV news endlessly and Lewis had taken every opportunity to learn from Jessica—even giving up his days off just to hang out and watch her in action.

Later, he would recall how Kane had always been hovering around them . . . watching them . . . walking in on them . . . But Lewis had not, back then, put two and two together. Not even that day when Kane had called him a little creep right in front of Jessica. He had not considered the possibility that Kane was jealous of Lewis' special relationship with Jess—and he had underestimated Kane's deviousness and determination to get rid of all rivals.

His jaw tensed, his teeth clamping together in a bitter resolve as he looked around Molly's bedroom. There were no photographs of her and Kane in this room. He figured she'd cleared those away when she'd married Sam Packer. But Lewis didn't need pictures to retain the image of Kane's hateful face. He stared at Molly's bed and he could picture Kane propped up against the pillows and shams. He could picture him groping and sliding around on the peach satin sheets with Molly.

There had been a time when these sorts of images had played themselves out to a final bloody scene: where he stepped into the picture like some dark avenging angel and Kane went down on his knees and begged for mercy.

But he'd refined those fantasies a long time ago. Killing Jack Kane would not settle the score. Kane had inflicted long-lasting damage on him and his career, and as hard as Lewis had tried to get over it, the scars had never quite healed. An eye for an eye required Jack Kane's downfall to be as humiliating and degrading as his own had been.

He dropped to one knee and brusquely unzipped the bag. His right hand tightened round the handle of the box cutter. Check.

Then he let it go abruptly, his fingers rummaging around for the ski mask. Check.

And the soft chemise. A gauzy white one, this time. Check.

Finally, he let his fingers rest on the black plastic casing, which held his most important accessory. Check.

He let his fingers tap idly on the casing as he considered the problem once more. If Molly Heskell freaked out on him he'd have to deal with her swiftly. He reached once again for the box cutter. Releasing the blade, he ran his index finger along it lightly.

The sudden fast flow of blood shocked him. He'd barely felt the cut. Then he took a deep breath and shoved the finger in his mouth to stem the flow.

Check.

He could proceed as planned.

3

Walking across the brick patio, Molly Heskell balanced a tray of dirty paper plates, cups, and the leftovers from the afternoon barbecue on the palm of one hand and reached out with the other to open the screen door into her sister's big, cluttered kitchen.

Vickie was on her knees, her head stuck under the sink. She emerged as Molly came up behind her. "Damn garbage disposal's jammed—again." She shook her head and got to her feet, taking the tray from Molly's hands and dumping the dirty plates and cups into the trash can.

"My, we're getting extravagant," Molly teased. She'd once caught her older sister rinsing off a set of plastic plates and cups.

Her sister laughed. "Well, now that Jerry's made it to partner, I've decided to live a little, okay? Coffee or tea?" she asked Molly. "Or another glass of wine?"

"It had better be coffee." Molly sighed. "I don't want to go back to work, first day, with a hangover." I don't want to go back to work, period, she thought. Leaning on the countertop and staring out of the kitchen window across the big backyard she watched her brother-in-law show Josh, the younger of her two nephews, how to pitch. The boy's laugh-

ter in response to Jerry's good-natured teasing drifted in
through the screen door.

"You're so lucky, Vickie," she said, abruptly turning her
back on the happy scene.

"Wanna trade places?" Vickie paused with a coffee scoop
in her hand and grinned, and before Molly could reply,
added: "But you'd have to trade bodies, too." Her laugh
pealed out across the kitchen and Molly laughed with her.
Her sister had gained about seven permanent pounds for
each of her three pregnancies.

"Come to think of it, you could use a few of my extra
pounds." Vickie stared at her sister with a critical eye as she
switched on the percolator.

"Maybe." Molly shrugged and walked over to the decorative mirror that hung by the kitchen door. She'd had her
straight blond hair permed the week before. She thought it
looked good, and a little like Farrah Fawcett's in her
Charlie's Angels period. But her face was still too thin and
drawn. There were shadows under her eyes and deep hol-
lows in her cheeks, and she knew that from the back, her
shoulder blades, protruding sharply under her cotton
sweater, made her look like some anorexic model girl.

Vickie's face suddenly appeared in the reflection and she
felt her sister's arm around her shoulders. "It's going to be
okay, Molly. You'll see . . . You and Sam can try again in a
little while. The doctors said so, right?"

Molly shrugged, then shook her head and walked away
from her sister to sit down on a bar stool at the other end of
the counter. Try again? Vickie was surely joking. The thought
of another nine months of waiting and wondering . . . of
doing all the right things, just to have it all turn to nothing
was unbearable.

In the last nine months she had focussed all her energies
and her attention on the baby. Consumed as she was with
planning for the new little life, she had coasted at work,
accepting the fluff pieces that the new news director had
thrown at her instead of fighting to be assigned the lead stories.

It had been a long, difficult haul for someone who was
used to instant results. But producing a baby was not like

producing a TV report for the ten o'clock news. The closest possible analogy was more like working on an in-depth documentary—spending weeks and weeks on an Emmy-quality feature—only to find that it was never going to make air.

"There's no way it's going to happen, Vickie—not with Sam." She stared at her sister, her mouth setting in a firm, determined line. "Didn't you read Gail Shister's column the other day?"

Vickie laughed shortly, a look of disbelief in her eyes. "You think I have time to read a newspaper? What are you talking about?"

"Sam's moved out. We're separated. Finished."

Vickie shook her head and reached for a couple of mugs, pouring the coffee slowly as if to give herself time to digest this new information.

She set one mug in front of Molly, pushing cream and sugar and a slice of Bavarian chocolate cake across the Formica countertop. "Your idea or his?"

Molly shrugged. "Oh, you know, kind of mutual . . ." She was not about to describe the final blowup to Vickie. How she'd exploded at Sam, beating her fists on his chest, accusing him of ruining her life, and screaming for him to get out of the house.

Vickie sighed. "When did this happen?"

"Two weeks ago. I was going to tell you but . . ."

"But what?" Vickie raised an eyebrow.

"I don't know. Somehow it didn't seem like such a big deal."

"Molly! What the hell is wrong with you? Sam's the best thing that happened to you." She paused. "It wasn't his fault, you know."

Molly stared defiantly at her sister.

"Well?" Vickie prodded.

Molly shook her head. "Listen, Vickie, you can't possibly understand. It's just too . . ."

"Too what?"

"Too messy, complicated, whatever." Molly sipped her coffee. "It's not just about the baby." She hesitated and focused on folding a paper napkin into meticulous little squares. "Sam and I just shouldn't have gotten married in the first place."

"Of course not." Vickie laughed abruptly. "Why get married just because you're pregnant?"

"No," Molly interrupted sharply. "I mean we should never have . . . I should never have started with Sam. I did it for all the wrong reasons."

"Oh, please!" Vickie stood up and walked over to the sink and started rinsing out her coffee mug. Molly could tell by the way her sister banged the dishwasher closed that she was annoyed. As she expected, there was more to come.

"Listen, Molly, you're supposed to be the smart one in the family, so why is it you have this huge blind spot when it comes to Jack Kane?" Vickie paused and reached across the countertop for Molly's hand. "Jack Kane never did you any favors. You still can't see that, can you? You were wasting your time with him. If you'd gone to New York with Jack Kane, he'd still be married and you'd still be single—and still worrying about your biological clock—"

"Like I don't have to worry about it anymore?" Molly jumped in, her tone laced with sarcasm.

"Don't be deliberately obtuse." Vickie shook her head. "You know exactly what I mean. Sam was as ready to settle down as you were. He was thrilled about the baby. Jack Kane was just dangling you on a string—"

"No, that's not true," Molly interrupted, her face reddening. "It would have worked out with Jack, I know it would. If I'd been more patient."

"Oh, come on!" Vickie laughed just as Melissa started crying in her playpen out on the porch.

Molly was relieved for the interruption. Through the screen door she watched her sister pick up the baby and rock her, but her thoughts were elsewhere. In the last month she'd found herself wishing more and more that she could turn the clock back. She wished Jack Kane was still news director at Channel Seven. She wished she could just wipe out the last twelve months and go back to the day when Jack had called her into his office to tell her about his new job at WorldMedia News.

"They want me to take over as president. They want to do a lot of new things, turn around the news division, launch a twenty-four-hour cable news network. They've had a lot of problems. Now, they've finally come to the right guy." He'd grinned at her, his eyes crinkling at the edges. "What do you think, Molly? President of news for the biggest media conglomerate in the country? Am I ready for it—or what?"

She had not known what to say until he'd kicked his office door shut and swung her up in his arms. "And you're coming with me."

Then she'd let out a whoop of delight. "Damn right, I'm coming with you. Just say when."

He put her down and she stepped back to lean against his desk, her heart thudding with anticipation as he put his finger to his lips. "But not a word to anyone, just yet. You're the first person I've told."

"What about Emma?"

He shook his head. "I'm taking the job, Molly, whatever Emma says. And, I'm leaving in the next two weeks." He'd paused and loosened his tie. "This is going to be a twenty-hour-a-day, seven-day-a-week deal to start with. There's no point in Emma rushing to New York with me." He reached for her fingers and stroked them gently. "But I do need you."

"You've got me, Jack."

Any way, anywhere, anytime, she'd wanted to add, her thoughts racing wildly ahead. She pictured herself and Jack Kane in New York. The two of them, working together, spending time together. A lot more time. Because, for one thing, Emma would not be around and Jack would no longer have to race from Molly's bed in the middle of the night to get home.

This was something that hadn't bothered her in the beginning. She'd entered into the affair with her eyes open, knowing that Jack Kane had a reputation for charming his favorite female reporters into bed. But increasingly, as their affair had progressed, she'd found herself wanting more. Something more permanent. Not marriage necessarily. But she did want children—and time was slipping by, after all. She was almost thirty-five.

She figured that in New York they stood a chance of

cementing their relationship and maybe Jack would even make the final break from Emma . . .

"Hey!" He'd jolted her out of her thoughts that day. "Let's go celebrate. I'll introduce you to another member of the team."

"I thought I was the only one who knew about this."

"You are. But Sam Packer's about to find out. He's just returned to the States from CNN's Rome bureau, and he's looking for something back here. Come on, I want you to meet him."

The screen door slammed loudly as Vickie came back into the kitchen, holding the baby in her arms. Melissa dozed contentedly, her sleep undisturbed by the slam of the door, but the sound made Molly jump.

"Jeez, talk about edgy." Vickie laughed. "What were you thinking about?"

Molly shrugged. "Sam . . . and the first time I met him." She uttered the little lie, knowing it was what her sister wanted to hear.

Vickie nodded approvingly. "That's more like it. You'll see; you can work it out."

"Oh, maybe." Molly pushed back from the kitchen counter and walked over to the sink to rinse out her own mug, not wanting her sister to pursue the subject any further.

In truth, Molly's first meeting with Sam Packer had been less momentous than the way she'd later recounted it to Vickie.

The evening Jack had introduced them, she had enjoyed his company and accepted him as an old friend of Jack's. She had also, in an objective way, acknowledged his dark good looks, and she'd been flattered by the way he'd paid her so much attention. In his six years in Italy he'd obviously picked up the best of European ways. He was polite and soft-spoken with a laid-back, easy charm.

When Jack had left that night to drive home to the Main Line, Sam had suggested she show him more of the city's night life. She'd declined and had not given Sam Packer much thought in the week that followed. There had been too much going on.

The news of Jack Kane's appointment had been announced in New York by Seth Reilly, the chairman of WorldMedia, and immediately rumors about her own move had rippled through the Channel Seven newsroom. Everyone expected that Jack would take her with him—and she waited for him to give her the go-ahead to put in her own notice.

But another week later he still had not said anything. She had cornered him at his farewell party at La Buca, his favorite Italian restaurant. "Just give me an idea," she'd pressed him. "A month? Two months? I know you're going to announce Sam's hire next week."

Jack Kane had barely been able to look her in the eye. Instead he'd stared across the long mahogany bar to where Sam was standing by himself. "It's easier with Sam."

"Why?"

"Emma hasn't got a bug up her ass about him."

"What does that mean?"

Jack had looked around cautiously. Emma was expected at the party but had not yet arrived. "It means Emma got wind that I intended to hire you and she went ballistic."

Molly's heart sank. "So, what's that mean?"

"It means she's threatening all sorts of things from slashing her wrists to telling Seth Reilly that I'm using my new position to hire all my slutty mistresses."

"Oh for heavens' sake! She's not serious?"

"She may be. She met Reilly and his wife last week in New York. Reilly was very taken with her." Jack had paused, shaking his head in frustration. "Everything you've read about him, the conservative, born-again Christian bit, the whole nine yards is true."

Molly's face flushed with a quiet anger. "So, now suddenly she's dictating who you can hire?"

"I didn't say that. What I'm saying is, now isn't the right time to rock the boat. Trust me, Molly. It'll all work out, just let the dust settle."

Molly had become aware of a strange sort of muted quiet in the restaurant at that moment and had turned around to find herself facing Emma Kane. Her face flushing a deeper red, she'd stuttered something about saying her farewells to a great boss.

"Well, make it good-bye rather than au revoir, dear," Emma Kane had retorted coolly, and without missing a beat had moved on into the restaurant, leaving Molly standing, suffused with embarrassment and anger, and loathing Emma Kane with an intensity that scared her.

"Care for another here, or would you like to move on?" Sam Packer suddenly materialized beside her and placed a steadying hand on her arm. She sank down on a bar stool, aware that she was shaking visibly. "Sure, I'll have one here." She glanced across the room, and saw that Emma Kane was looking in her direction. She placed her hand over his and gave him a dazzling smile. "And then maybe we can find a quieter spot."

Molly leaned in closer to Sam Packer, and then heard him laugh softly just before his lips brushed against her cheek.

"Hey, relax," he whispered as she stiffened. "I'm just following your script. We are center stage here, aren't we?"

Sam had sympathized with her dilemma and had dissipated her anger with Jack.

"He's right, you know. There's no point in rattling Emma's cage at this point. Let Jack make the move to New York, let him settle into the job. Don't worry, Jack's not going to abandon you. He's just playing it cool."

"How did she find out about me?"

Sam had laughed again. "Wives have antennae for that sort of thing. But we can mix up the signals here a bit, if you want." His arm snaked around her shoulders and Molly had not resisted that time. Five minutes later, when she was sure Emma Kane still had her in her sights, she had turned to Sam and suggested they leave. It had seemed like a good idea at the time.

Molly glanced across at her sister who now had Melissa in the high chair and was spoonfeeding the baby something yellow and mushy. If Sam were here, she thought, he would be at Vickie's side volunteering to help. Sam had enjoyed visiting her sister's family. "Family's everything," he'd said the first time she'd brought him to Vickie's. "Who wants to die with nothing but a shelf of dusty old TV tapes to their credit?"

Sam had finally seduced her with talk like that—and

with his determined pursuit of her. Even after joining WorldMedia he had made time to return to Philly to see her as often as he could. Somewhere along the way, Molly had found herself looking at Sam Packer in a new light, not just as a name that could be linked with hers in a smattering of gossip items, which she hoped would get Emma Kane's attention and allay Emma's suspicions about her.

She had believed she was in love with Sam when she told him she was pregnant, and she had not minded when he'd jokingly reminded her about the way their relationship had started. "Well, that should certainly put Emma Kane's fears to rest. She can't very well object to Jack hiring you now, can she? Especially after we're married."

Molly had laughed out loud at the thought. "I guess not," she'd said. "Except I don't want the job."

She shook her head as Sam started to protest. "No, Sam. I've thought about it. I can't get stressed out with a new job. It's not important anymore. It'll be better for me to stay in Philly. I can muddle through here; Channel Seven will give me a decent maternity leave, and Vickie's here. I'm going to need her, especially if you're involved with the new job yourself.

"The baby's the most important thing now," she had assured him honestly. And Sam had fallen right in with her plans, even offering to make the daily train commute between their home in Philadelphia and the WorldMedia offices in New York.

But that was all back then, she thought with a sudden viciousness. Now she was back to square one: There was no baby and no husband. And no TV future in New York. Gabriella Grant had her job. Gabriella was in New York, anchoring the new hit show, working with Sam and Jack. Molly had made a big mistake, she knew that now. She should have trusted Jack Kane to work things out. He had never let her down before.

She strode across the kitchen and picked up her jacket off the back of a chair. Then reached for her purse.

Her sister paused with the mush-laden spoon in her hand. "Do you need to rush home so soon? I was going to relax with a glass of wine after I finished with Missy here."

"I told you, Vickie, I'm due in on the early shift tomorrow." Molly knew she sounded snippy but the thought of going back to the Channel Seven newsroom depressed her. The news director who'd replaced Jack had hired his own people and took a special delight in freezing out the old-timers.

Molly had let it all roll off her back, refusing to complain about getting less airtime than newer hires. Less airtime had meant less work and therefore more time to spend on planning for the baby. But now her job would just serve to remind her that she'd screwed up in every area of her life.

Vickie must have sensed the turmoil inside her because she gave her a big hug in the doorway. "Will you be all right?"

"Of course." Molly put on a brave face. But it took her a few moments to get going down Vickie's driveway, and her eyes were teary as she followed the entrance ramp onto the Schuylkill.

On the highway she blinked the tears away furiously. She could not start a crying jag on the Schuylkill. She had to make it home, where she would take some of the antidepressant medication her doctor had prescribed for her. She had wanted to get off the medication before returning to work. She hated having to rely on feel-good pills, even though the doctor had said that a month was barely any time in which to recover. Her emotions, he'd said, had taken a bigger beating than her body.

Molly had not liked the sound of that. She had always thought of herself as strong-minded and in control. But every time she tried to make it without the pills she'd found herself engulfed in a new wave of depression.

To hell with it, she thought suddenly. She'd take the pills. She'd pour herself a glass of wine, too. What could possibly make things any worse than they already were? Not getting fired, that was for sure.

She pulled into a parking spot behind a dark truck halfway down her block, and the thought of a glass of wine cheered her more with every step—until she walked into her hallway and the pungent smell of fresh paint hit her.

4

She stood in the hallway, leaning against the front door, waiting for the paint smell to dissipate. It was so strong that for a moment Molly thought it might be for real. But that wasn't possible. The last time fresh paint had been used in the house was almost four months ago when Sam had painted the nursery. It had smelled exactly this way.

She covered her nose with the palm of her hand and ran upstairs, darting straight into the bathroom and slamming the door closed behind her. Her hands shook as she fumbled to open the cabinet above the sink and reached for her pills. I'm losing it, she thought, throwing the pills down her throat. I'm really losing it. It's not getting any better at all.

Her mind just wasn't working properly. If she'd been functioning normally she never would have exploded at Sam. When she didn't take the pills strange things happened: like the smell of the nursery paint coming back to her so strongly. Like seeing the woman and baby in the park across the street.

The first time she'd seen the woman she had not realized she was hallucinating. It had happened a couple of days after she'd thrown Sam out of the house and she'd glanced out of the window as she drew the drapes in the bedroom. It had been no more than a cursory glance because she did not like to dwell on the happy scene anymore. The swings and slides and in particular the stone sculpture of the three bears just reminded her that she would not be out there with other mothers who wheeled strollers into the park on sunny afternoons. But the woman holding a tightly wrapped little bundle had caught her attention, and Molly had watched as she placed the baby in one of the swings, holding it as she gently pushed the swing back and forward. Then her throat had tightened and she'd crawled into bed and down under the covers.

She'd seen the woman again last week. This time she'd forced herself to watch a little longer. She could not go through life avoiding babies after all. So she stared through the darkness for a while before reaching to draw the drapes. Suddenly, to her horror, she'd seen the baby slide out of the swing and fall to the ground.

Without stopping to grab a robe she'd gone racing downstairs and into the street in her nightdress, bracing herself for the wails and screams she expected to hear.

She was halfway across the street when she realized it was quiet, and then stopping abruptly in the center of the park, she'd realized she was alone. There was no one else in the park. No woman. No baby.

The chill that had swept through her had nothing to do with the cool late summer evening, and she'd found herself shivering violently and uncontrollably a long time after she was back in the warmth of her bed.

In the morning, she'd wondered if she'd dreamt the whole incident and when Sam had called her later that week—for what, she couldn't remember—she'd mentioned the incident to him. He'd tried to explain it away by saying she'd stopped taking her medication too early. "That's why the doctor prescribed it, Molly. It's supposed to calm you down and let your mind rest and heal."

"I wasn't seeing things, Sam. She was there and the baby fell out of the swing."

"So late at night? That doesn't make any sense, Molly. Why would anyone bring a baby to a playground in the dark?"

The fact that she had not thought of this as odd in the first place made her realize that, indeed, she was not thinking clearly or rationally and she had abruptly stopped trying to argue about it with Sam.

"Do you want me to come home?" Sam had asked, breaking the silence.

"No, I'll be okay. You're right. It was probably a dream or some sort of half dream. Maybe I was seeing myself out there and the baby falling out of the swing was—" She stopped and cleared her throat. "I'm sure there's some good Freudian explanation."

"Take the pills, Molly. You'll get better quicker."

Yes, the pills helped, all right. Molly stared at her reflection in the bathroom mirror and forced a smile to her lips. Already the paint smell seemed fainter.

Taking a deep breath she opened the bathroom door and walked through into her bedroom. She slid off her jacket and yanked open her closet. Her hand reached in for a hanger and hit something solid.

Then she saw it. A grotesque, black-hooded image. She stumbled backwards, a scream catching in her throat at the sight of this apparition of death. But the hood moved towards her and the realization hit her: This, at least, was no apparition or hallucination. This was real. There was an intruder in her closet and he was stepping out towards her with a box cutter in his hand.

"Don't even think of screaming or you're dead." The blade hovered dangerously at her eye level, then the intruder took a step back. "I'm not going to use this if you do as I say, all right?"

Molly nodded, her head jerking up and down, her heart hammering against her ribs, her thoughts threatening to spin out of control.

"Now move back, over there against the bed."

She stood rooted to the spot, unable to move.

"I said move back!"

The blade flashed before her eyes again and she stumbled backwards, hitting the backs of her calves on the lower bed rail.

He's going to rape me . . . then kill me. She thought about Sam. She hoped that Sam wouldn't blame himself. She started to cry.

"Hey, none of that. You'll wreck your face." Molly thought she heard his voice soften. "I'm not going to hurt you, so there's no call for any histrionics, okay? Relax, get comfortable . . . Take your clothes off."

"What?"

"I said take your clothes off." He stepped towards her, raising the box cutter. "You don't want me to do it for you, do you?"

Her hands jerked upwards, clumsily yanking her sweater up and off over her head. Then she hesitated, trying to avoid the staring eyes in the slits of the mask.

"Go on." His voice was just a harsh whisper now. She reached for the zipper of her wool pants, focusing on the way he'd spoken to her: There's no call for histrionics, he'd said. He sounded well-spoken. Maybe this wouldn't be too rough. Maybe she'd get through it.

She kicked aside the pants and reached behind her to unhook the clasp of her bra.

"Wait! Get up on the bed. Kneel and look this way. That's it; now hold that pose while I get ready."

Molly sank back onto her heels and wondered if all rape victims felt the way she did, if the sense of disassociation was a survival mechanism that kicked in after the initial shock wore off. She felt as if she were no longer part of the scene but merely watching with some kind of morbid fascination as he stepped back and brought out a black bag from her closet.

The bag looked like it was made of leather. It looked expensive. So did the video camera. She watched him take it out of the bag, focusing on the letters on the side. It was a Panasonic. A bigger model than the tiny things everybody carried around these days. This one looked as if it used a regular VHS tape.

A video camera? She did a mental double take. He was getting to his feet holding a video camera.

"Okay, Molly." The eyes in the slits bored into her. "I know you can do this. You're a pro. So let's try it in one take, okay?"

She bit the inside of her lip. Dear God, he was going to videotape the rape? She stared as he took another step backwards, hoisting the camera onto his shoulder.

"Now you can take off the rest of your clothes, but look

as if you're enjoying it . . . as if you're teasing a lover into bed. You know how to do that, don't you?"

She stared at the steady red light just below the lens. The tape was running. But she couldn't move.

"Come on, Molly." The angry pitch in his voice startled her. And her arms thrust behind her involuntarily. Just get it over with . . . Just get him out of here . . . She repeated the words inside her head like a mantra.

"That's a girl . . . That's lovely. Now hold your arms out to me and smile." He sounded as if he was smiling behind the mask, too. "Good girl . . . Think about your lover, Molly. He's going to be with you any minute . . . Now lie back and wiggle out of those panties."

She clenched her teeth together suddenly and looked away, shaking her head. She could not do it. This was worse than what she'd ever imagined a rape to be.

"I can't." She could hear herself whimpering. "I just can't do it."

She heard the click of a button and the red light disappeared. Now you've done it, she thought, seeing him put the camera on the floor and grasp the box cutter again. Now, he'll kill you.

He perched on the edge of her bed, and she heard his rapid, shallow breathing. "You can do it, Molly. I know you can. Jennifer was nervous, too, but she did just fine in the end."

"Jennifer?"

"Jennifer Reed."

Molly shook her head. He'd raped Jennifer Reed? When? She'd seen Jennifer on the ten o'clock news on Friday night.

"You don't believe me? Ask her. Ask her why she moved to a doorman building in the city two weeks ago."

Two weeks ago? Molly stared at the hooded figure on the end of her bed. That just couldn't be true. If Jennifer had been raped two weeks ago why hadn't Molly read about it in the papers? A story like that would have made the front page.

He leaned forward and laughed softly as if he'd read her thoughts: "Jennifer's been a really smart girl. I hope you're going to be smart, too. Keep all of this just between us. It'll be our little secret, okay? Now lie back and do as I say, and you'll come out of this just fine."

She sank back against the pillows.

"That's a girl." The intruder got to his feet and picked up the video camera again, and Molly closed her eyes, hoping she could control the anger that swirled together with despair inside her. Now she understood what was happening, and why Jennifer had not reported the rape. He'd videotaped Jennifer in the same way—undressing for him, holding her arms out to him. Who would believe a story of rape?

A hysterical bubble of laughter forced its way to her lips.

"That's beautiful." The intruder's voice broke into her thoughts. "Now, get those panties off. Nice and slow and sexy."

He didn't kill Jennifer. He's not going to kill me . . . and then we'll go to the cops together. They'll have to listen, videotape or not.

Her thumbs hooked into the elastic of the panties, and she slowly slid them down her legs.

"That's it. You're doing fine . . . that's perfect."

She kept her eyes closed even when she heard the click of the camera's power button. She heard the rustling as if he was putting the camera away in his bag. She heard him zip it up. Of course. He would not videotape the rape itself. No way could he hope to get away with that. She felt her heart pounding against her ribs and she steeled herself.

She thought she heard him creeping into the bathroom. She heard a door close. She wondered if she had time to open her nightstand drawer. She opened her eyes. Was Sam's .38 in the top or bottom drawer? How much time did she have to rummage around?

The sound of a thud downstairs made her sit up suddenly. It sounded like the front door. She listened again. There were no sounds coming from the bathroom. What the hell was he doing?

The noise of a car engine revving up outside the house suddenly shattered the silence in the room. She stared at the bathroom door. Was he in there or had he gone? Had he been scared off by something?

She eased herself quietly off the bed, careful not to rustle the sheets. Then, she saw the box cutter lying on the floor, just outside the bathroom door. Her heart thudded. What kind of a game was he playing?

She stared warily at the bathroom door. Was he waiting for her to reach for the weapon? Was he going to pounce on her as soon as she lunged for it? Or could she get to it before he got to her?

She whimpered softly, suddenly aware that it didn't matter. Her legs were trembling so violently she couldn't get them to move. She couldn't even put one foot in front of the other.

Fear had rooted her to the spot.

5

Piccolina's was a small but popular restaurant in Ardmore's famous Suburban Square. Even though it was Sunday evening, there was a knot of customers waiting for tables when Kate breezed through the doors around nine.

Checking her coat, she slipped into the ladies' room and stood in front of the mirror nervously studying her reflection as she fussed with her hair. It didn't really need fixing. Tonight she wore it off her face and swept back in a tight French braid. She knew that the style, together with the tailored black pantsuit, made her look a little prim and severe. But that was okay. She certainly didn't want anyone in this crowd thinking she was ready to whoop it up or worse, that she was out on the prowl.

She had come primarily to collar Harry and discuss her idea for a book proposal with him. After lunching with Pat Norris and spending some time in the *Inquirer* library, she had come up with a small nugget. It was not a blockbuster idea but it could work quite nicely, she'd thought. All she needed was Harry's cooperation. She had tried to reach him at the unit first thing in the morning, but had been told he was unavailable because something had come up with the Whitman investigation. The reference to an "investigation" had piqued her curiosity, and in turn settled any remaining reservations she had about attending Ray Foster's retirement party.

She had even planned to arrive on time, hoping to catch Harry before he'd downed too many beers, but Belinda had returned with Tommy just as she was about to get in the shower.

"Mom! I'm home." She'd heard Tommy's voice and welcomed the three words she listened out for every weekend when he returned from Belinda's—and she'd run out into the hallway to grab him for a big hug and kiss. But he'd ducked her, giggling, and run for his room.

She had run after him. "Oh no, you don't." She laughed. "I missed you and I want my hug and kiss."

He held his arms up in surrender but continued to edge his way around the bed. Tommy believed hugs and kisses were only for babies and went to the greatest lengths to avoid them. "Wait, Mom. Wait. I gotta question for you: Why does a glow worm glow in the dark?"

She walked towards him, laughing. "I don't know. Tell me."

"Because it eats light meals . . . get it? *Light* meals." Then he'd dived onto his bed and rolled off the other side, shrieking with laughter at his successful evasion of the hug and kiss.

"By the way," he said as she retreated out of the room, "I'm not going to Belinda's next weekend."

"Oh?"

He shook his head. "They're going to the shore."

"And she's not taking you?" Kate had barely managed to mask the surprise in her voice.

"She wanted to." Tommy nodded. "But they're going for the whole week and she knows I can't miss school."

"Well, she's right about that."

"I don't care, anyway. This weekend was kind of boring."

"It was?" Kate stopped in the doorway. "Why's that?"

Tommy shrugged. "We just looked at a whole bunch of boring old houses."

"You did? Whatever for?"

He shrugged again. "Beats me. Belinda wants a bigger house." Then, losing interest in the conversation, Tommy had grabbed his Walkman off the bed and adjusted the earphones on his head.

But his words had stayed with Kate as she walked back to her room and stepped into the shower. A bigger house? Belinda wanted a bigger house? Why?

She had gotten into the habit of dissecting everything Tommy told her about Belinda, suspicious of her intentions and true motives. Despite Belinda's assurances that she had not returned to cause havoc and disruption in Tommy's life, Kate could not rid herself of the uneasy feeling that Belinda was eventually going to want more than just weekend visitation with her own son.

She had put herself in Belinda's place. If she had returned to find her ex-husband dead and her son being cared for by another woman, wouldn't she go all out to get him back?

Then again, it was pretty pointless trying to superimpose her own emotions on a woman like Belinda. If she were Belinda, she could never have walked out on her own child in the first place. Certainly not in the way Belinda had.

According to Steve, she had left with little warning a few days after Tommy's fourth birthday. Returning from her shift as an operating room nurse at Jefferson Hospital one night, she had announced that she was leaving her husband, son, and America to go to Rio with a plastic surgeon she'd met at the hospital.

Kate had felt a chill run up her spine the first time she'd heard Steve tell the story. She felt it again, now, staring into the mirror. How could she even begin to guess what went on in Belinda's head?

She squeezed a smidgen of Vaseline onto a lipbrush and

traced it over her lips, dabbing off the excess with a Kleenex.

C'mon, McCusker, she prodded, taking a final check on her hair and makeup, this isn't the Academy Awards.

Emerging from the powder room, Kate stood for a moment in the doorway of the back party room, which was an enclosed veranda off the main dining area, her eyes scanning faces until she found Harry's. He was ensconced in a corner with the guest of honor and a couple of other detectives. The minute he spotted her, he was on his feet and wending his way to her across a handkerchief-sized dance floor.

"Hey Kate." He grinned, throwing his arm around her. "You look terrific. For a moment, there, I thought I was hallucinating." He squeezed her shoulder. "But no, you're real . . . and real late—"

"And thirsty." She interrupted his banter, raising her voice so that he could hear her over the thumping music emanating from the loudspeakers.

Harry led her to the bar and ordered her a Scotch on the rocks. Pressing the cold, heavy glass into her hand, he said, "Now, push your way through the crowd. I want to introduce you to someone."

"Wait just a moment, Harry, I've got something to show you."

"Yeh? What?"

"The proposal for my new book. I want you to take a look at it. I'm going to need—"

Harry interrupted her with a dismissive wave of his hand. "Later, Katey. Come on, this is a party." She felt the pressure of his open palm in the flat of her back, steering her towards the far end of the bar. "I'm going to introduce you to Mike."

The knot in her stomach tightened suddenly. "Hold it, Harry. Which one is he?"

"The one standing right at the end of the bar . . . looking at you."

"The one in the blazer?" she asked, her eyes meeting the young investigator's. "Dammit, Harry! Wait! Why's he staring at me like that? What did you tell him about me?"

"Jeez, Kate! Could you just come and say hello?" He gave

her a sharp nudge forward and in the next moment she found herself shaking Mike Travis' hand.

"Kate . . . Mike." Harry grinned from one to the other, winked at Mike Travis, pulled out a bar stool for Kate, and then abruptly moved away.

Kate gripped her glass in both hands. Then suddenly found herself laughing out loud. "Harry's so subtle, isn't he?"

Mike Travis smiled lazily. "Don't worry about it. Harry was just speeding up the inevitable . . ." His dark brown eyes reflected a hint of amusement. "At least for me."

"Really." Kate didn't know how else to respond to his directness so she sipped her Scotch and stared at a spot somewhere above his stylishly cut dark hair. Then she realized that he was staring at her, looking for some response to a question she hadn't heard. "I'm sorry," she said, swallowing quickly. "I didn't hear what you said." She leaned forward.

He leaned in closer, too. "I asked if you're working on a new book. I heard you're a writer."

"Oh. Yes." She nodded. "As a matter of fact, I just put together a proposal this weekend."

"Well, then I guess you're not ready to talk about it just yet."

How perceptive. She nodded. Then as if she'd voiced the thought, he added, "I know how writers are. I used to live with one."

"Really." Another pause. *Come on, McCusker, you can do better than that.* "Would I know her name?"

"Only if you read romance novels. She used to churn them out—three a year."

"How long did you know her? How did you meet?"

"I'd rather not answer that."

Kate's face flushed. Had she really forgotten how to make polite small talk without getting personal and intrusive?

"Hey, I'm only teasing." She felt his fingers brush against hers as he reached for his drink. "I don't mind sharing my deep dark secret with you . . ." He paused. "But you'll have to dance with me first."

"Oh, I don't think—"

"Come on," he urged, reaching for her hand.

"Wait!" She hesitated as the music suddenly changed to a slower beat. "I don't know if this is a good idea. I'm really . . . I mean, I've been out of circulation for a while."

"I know," he said, guiding her firmly onto the floor. "But it's like riding a bike." He placed her left hand on his shoulder and took her other hand in his. "See, you just have to hang on," he added as his right arm encircled her waist.

Like riding a bike? I don't think so, thought Kate, taking a deep breath as a sudden, distant memory flashed through her mind. This was more like her first high school dance. Like she was fifteen all over again. She felt adolescently self-conscious about their closeness and the pressure of his right thigh against hers.

Except that here no one gave them a second glance. There were no chaperones aiming laser-beam looks at her from the edge of the dance floor. And Mike Travis certainly had a better sense of rhythm than Frankie Gilligan . . . She took another deep breath and allowed herself to relax against his lean, muscular chest.

"Well?" she said finally.

"Well," he mouthed, "you're doing just great. See?"

She laughed. "I meant, what about that deep dark secret? You were going to tell me how you met the romance writer."

"Oh that . . . I posed for the covers of a couple of her books."

"You're kidding." A picture of Mike Travis, bare-chested, flashed into her head. "You mean like Fabio?" she added quickly.

The look of surprise on her face made him laugh out loud. "Yeah, but without the long hair. I did it for the money, working my way through college in New York, okay?"

"Oh. So that was a while back?"

"Yeh, quite a while," he agreed, letting a few beats pass in silence before placing her right hand on his shoulder so that he could put both his arms around her, drawing her closer still to him.

She looked up at him and caught the hint of a smile in his eyes as he realized she wasn't going to fight the intimacy. But what the hell, she thought. She was a grown woman now. Not fifteen anymore and she was actually enjoying the moment. A little slow dancing with the best-looking male in the room wasn't going to kill her.

He held onto her as the music faded, gripping her hand. "Don't run away now," he said softly. "We're only just warming up here."

"Maybe." She smiled. "But if we don't take a break, I'll be walking around with the imprint of your belt buckle on my belly for the rest of the week." Then she pulled away from him and walked off the dance floor, heading back to the bar. As she reached out to retrieve her glass, she felt a hand tap her on the shoulder and swiveling around, found herself facing Linda Barnwell, the youngest prosecutor in Montgomery County.

"Hey, Linda, how are you doing?" Kate threw her arm around the woman's slight shoulders.

"You'd know if you called more than once a year," the other woman replied in mock sternness. She turned and nodded at Mike Travis, who'd followed Kate reluctantly off the dance floor. "Am I interrupting something important here?"

Kate thought she detected an edge to Linda's voice. But Mike didn't seem to notice as he stepped away, smiling graciously. "Not yet. I'll catch up with you later, Kate. Maybe we can move on to somewhere quieter."

"Yeah, like his apartment," Linda muttered out of the corner of her mouth as he walked out of earshot, then she raised her glass. "Lucky you. He's quite something, isn't he?"

Kate shrugged. "A fast worker, that's for sure."

Linda nodded. "Well, enjoy. But be warned: Fast in, fast out. He's strictly hit—and run."

Kate raised an eyebrow.

"Of course that's hearsay, dearheart." Linda laughed but her cheeks reddened as she added quickly, "I'm only telling you because it looked to me like things were moving very swiftly out there." She inclined her head towards the dance floor.

Kate rolled her eyes. "It was only one dance, Linda. Don't worry. I certainly don't intend to get involved with another detective." She shook her head, smiling. "Even if he does wear the same aftershave as Steve did."

Linda grinned. "Old Spice, right? Must be a macho detective thing. None of them would be caught dead in any of that wussy, designer-name stuff." She paused. "But that's probably where any similarity to Steve ends. I hear Travis was a bad boy with the NYPD. He had to resign."

"Why?"

"Some off-duty incident." Linda lowered her voice a notch. "The way I heard it, it involved a woman he was going with at the time."

Kate laughed suddenly. "That's an awful lot of hearsay, Linda, but I think I get the point. Thanks for the warning," she added as Linda backed away from the bar. In the same moment, Kate caught Harry's eye across the room and raised her glass to him, beckoning him over.

"Come on, Harry." She made room for him by her side. "I need just five minutes of your time." She paused and reached into her purse, retrieving the one typed page of her proposal. "Please read this."

"Okay, okay." Harry sighed and took his bifocals out of his breast pocket, placing the page on the bar in front of him. "Where did Mike go?"

Kate waved off the question as she pushed the page at him. "Just read." She leaned against his shoulder, skimming over the neat double-spaced lines. *The rich are different from you and me*, she had written, plagiarizing the line and doodling it over and over on her yellow legal pad before typing it and adding *. . . and so are their crimes*.

The idea had taken root there and blossomed, and she had found herself at her computer at one in the morning, fleshing out the idea:

> *Det-Sgt. Harry Holmsby knows both sides of the story. At his desk he'll sometimes look through the society pages of* Main Line Life *and recognize the faces: He points to one suave, tuxedoed Main Line resident as a child molester under investigation. Another is a wife beater . . .*
>
> *On the other hand he recognizes some as victims. Only last year Harry Holmsby tracked down a ring of master jewel thieves who were reverse commuting between Palm Beach and the Main Line, spending summers in Florida*

*and winters on the Main Line burglarizing the vacated
mansions of the wealthy.*

*Harry has spent more than twenty years on the Main
Line as a detective. He knows where all the skeletons are
buried. He knows the dirty little secrets of upper-crust
society.*

*Main Line P.D. will look back at some of the more sen-
sational cases of the past as well as at current files of the
detectives who work among the richest, most powerful people in the country. The Main Line has one of the highest
per capita incomes and some of the grandest estates in the
country . . .*

Kate waited while Harry read to the end. "Well?"

Harry shrugged but looked interested. "Looks good," he
said. "So what do you want from me? Access to the files?"

"More." She grinned. "That guy who wrote *Homicide*, you
know that book that was turned into the TV series, spent a
year following one squad of the Baltimore P.D. around.
You've got to let me be your shadow, Harry."

"For a year?"

"No. Four, maybe six months. I'm going to need that kind
of access. Be there at the crime scene with you. At interviews of witnesses . . . the whole ball of wax."

Harry hesitated, taking another swig of his beer. "Well,
I'd have to clear it with Jim, and probably even the super. I
mean you're not exactly an outsider, but I'm sure Kilgore
would want to set some guidelines, especially on current
cases and on what you could publish. We'd have to have
some sort of approval on that."

"No problem, Harry. We can iron all of this out with Jim,
but could we do it tomorrow?"

Harry grinned and patted her hand. "Sure. Sure. Now,
put that away and get back to enjoying yourself."

Kate pushed away her glass. "I think I've had enough
excitement for one evening." She grinned. Across the
room she spotted Mike Travis talking to a couple of county detectives. He seemed engrossed in the conversation.
Just as well, thought Kate. She could probably make a
quick, unobtrusive exit. As flattering as his attention had

been, she wasn't sure she could deal with a man like Mike Travis just yet.

Minutes later Harry was retrieving her coat. "I guess I'll see you tomorrow morning, then," he said. "If you're really set on this idea."

"Oh, I'm set on it." She nodded. "Just one more thing, Harry. What kept you so busy on the Whitman case yesterday? Whoever answered the phone called it the Whitman investigation. What's going on?"

Harry shrugged. "I was just poking around. Can we talk about this in the morning? Let me walk you to your car."

"Just give me an idea of what it's about."

Harry sighed, pushing open the door of the restaurant for her. "The toxicology report showed an alcohol level consistent with about two glasses of wine. Which certainly means she could have stumbled down that staircase but . . ."

"But?"

"Like you said, she could have had help."

"What changed your mind?"

"We haven't been able to trace where or with whom she had the drinks. Stan suggested she had a late lunch with the woman client she took to look at the estates. The only problem is there's no reference to any name or client in her diary or appointments book and so far we haven't been able to reach the owners of the properties she allegedly took the client to see."

"So no one actually saw her with the woman?"

"Correct."

"You think Stan's lying?"

"Could be."

"Has he got an alibi?"

"For the afternoon and early evening, yes. For the morning—no."

"Motive?"

Harry shook his head as he held the car door open for her. "Jesus, McCusker, you're scary, you know that? I don't know if I can handle having you as a shadow."

Kate leaned over and kissed him on the cheek. "You'll be just fine, Harry. Oh, and for what it's worth, I spoke to Jennifer Reed. She said the house has bad karma."

"Really." Harry sounded bored. "That's a big help. What's it mean?"

"It means she was scared away by a break-in. She's living on the penthouse floor of an apartment building in Center City—and the bed doesn't fit in with the decor, she said."

"That's interesting."

"Oh, you think so?"

"I mean about the break-in. I went back several months checking the police reports for the area for any complaints about vagrants, intruders, strangers trespassing, just in case there was anything that might tie into Whitman's death. But there was nothing, definitely no report of a break-in at Jennifer Reed's digs."

"Well," Kate paused. "She said nothing was taken. It sounded like she was talking about neighborhood kids. But if it was serious enough to send her scurrying back to the city, you'd think she would have reported it."

"Yeah, you'd think," Harry echoed, and then slammed her car door closed.

Kate's thoughts returned to Jennifer Reed as she turned into her driveway some ten minutes later. Approaching the house, she tried to imagine how Jennifer had felt coming home alone, returning late at night to her own secluded home to discover that someone had gotten inside. It seemed strange that the anchorwoman had not called the cops immediately.

I know I would have, thought Kate, glancing at her dark house and shivering. The first time Tommy had seen the house at night he'd described it as horror-movie house, and Kate had to agree there was an eerie element about it at certain times of the evening. But she had fallen in love with the mock-Victorian monstrosity at first sight. She had especially loved the turret room on the second floor, overlooking the back yard. The separate staircase to the room had made it a perfect place to turn into her office and den. On the other side of the house, Steve had renovated a separate apartment for Maysie. Steve had redone a lot of the interior, sanding floors and staircases, uncovering original moldings. Together they had explored antique shops all over Bucks County to find unusual objects and items to decorate the house.

The couple of life-size dummies that looked like Ma and Pa Kettle and sat on a wrought-iron bench by the front door had been one of their first and most unusual finds. She and Steve had unearthed the pair in a garage sale at an estate in Bryn Mawr and had not been able to resist the ultimate in Main Line kitsch.

She shivered again, reflecting that even Ma and Pa looked a little spooky tonight—but she stood on the front porch for a few seconds longer, holding her face up to the chilly night air, enjoying the still and quiet and the smell of damp leaves around her. Then she walked to the front door, giving the couple a cheery wave goodnight on her way in.

As she closed the door behind her, she heard Maysie call out from the kitchen and went to join her mother-in-law, who was already dressed for bed in a warm woolly robe over thick plaid flannel pajamas. Kate grinned at her. "Aren't you glad I didn't ask Harry back for a nightcap?"

Maysie responded with a half smile. Then her lips tightened into a thin, angry line. "Belinda called for you just after you left. She wanted to know if she could pick up Tommy from school one night this week since she's not going to get the weekend with him."

Kate slumped down on a chair at the kitchen table as Maysie pushed a cup of aromatic tea towards her. "What did you tell her?"

"I said I'd pass on the message and hung up." The older woman looked at her questioningly. "I hope you're not going to agree to it. It's not right for Tommy to have to run over there anytime she wants, you know."

"No, it's not," Kate agreed, staring into her cup morosely as she recalled her first meeting with Steve's ex-wife. Belinda had seemed rather cool and dispassionate as she'd assured Kate that she didn't expect Tommy to welcome her back with open arms—and she didn't want him to hate her for turning his life upside down again. "But I'd like to get to know him now that we're back, and I'd like him to get to know his half-sister," she'd said, adding that Ivo, now her husband, had returned to Jefferson as head of reconstructive surgery.

What choice did she have? Kate had thought back then

when Belinda had asked if she could have weekends with her son. What choice did she have now? "I don't want to be unreasonable," she said finally, staring at her mother-in-law's unhappy face. "I'd rather work things out amicably with her than have her storming into court to demand her son back."

"Why?" Maysie looked defiant. "You don't honestly think you'd lose?"

Kate sighed. "I'd play my best hand, Maysie, and I'm sure the last five years would count for something. But she's got all the aces. She's his natural mother—"

"She's a schemer—and a bad woman," Maysie interrupted vehemently, getting to her feet and walking to the doorway. "She may sound reasonable now but all she's doing is testing the waters. You'll see; she'll be worming her way in, step by step, pushing for more, little by little. And you won't know what she's up to until she's ready to drop the ax. Then it will be too late."

With that, the older woman walked out, leaving her ominous words to reverberate in Kate's ears.

6

Monday, September 23

C offee chic?" Molly stared in bewilderment at her news director as he perched on the edge of her desk in the newsroom. "What about it?"

Moments earlier Nick Myers had walked over to welcome her back to the newsroom and to offer his condolences on her loss. His compassion had lasted all of twenty seconds before he'd reverted to form.

"Okay I got a biggie for you today, Heskell. It's coffee chic."

Molly thought she detected a glimmer of amusement in his myopic eyes as she'd echoed his words.

"So, what exactly is the angle, Nick?" She stared blankly at him as her thoughts wandered: Nick had a dark green truck. A Jeep. She wished she'd paid closer attention to the truck, which had been parked on her street the night before. She was sure it had belonged to the intruder because when she'd finally realized that he'd really gone she'd checked out the window and the truck had gone, too.

"Cappuccino bars are the big thing now, you know, Heskell?" Nick Myers was prattling on. She narrowed her eyes and tried to imagine him with a black ski mask over his head. Then she blinked. Dear God, was she going to look at everybody who owned a truck with this sort of suspicion?

"Come on, Heskell. Wake up and smell the coffee. They've become the singles bars of the nineties. I want you to do a roundup of the best and worst in Center City. Get some m-o-s interviews. Get people talking about how it's a better place to meet and so on." He got to his feet. "Oh, I suggest going out early evening, after regular working hours."

Of course, Nick. Then you can watch me rush back and go nuts trying to make the ten o'clock deadline to put together a stupid little puff piece.

Molly watched him pace back across the newsroom, bitterness welling up inside her. It was only just after nine in the morning. Reporters and producers were drifting in and the assignment desk was jumping. Phones were ringing, hold lights were blinking. Things were happening in Philadelphia and she was going to do a puff piece on coffee bars! It wasn't even a new idea.

The only good thing about it was that she'd have time to sit down and talk with Jennifer as soon as the anchorwoman came in for the noon newsbrief. Noisily, she spread the *Inquirer* across her desk and tried to focus on the headline.

"Hi! Welcome back."

Molly looked up and acknowledged Marilyn Spenser, a stunningly attractive general assignment reporter whom Nick Myers had brought with him from the Seattle affiliate.

"Hey, guess who's on the cover of *People* this week." Marilyn perched on Molly's desk in the exact same spot where Nick had perched. She held the cover to her chest.

Molly shrugged. "I haven't a clue."

"Ta-da!" Marilyn flipped the cover in front of her face. "Look! Gabriella Grant."

Molly blinked and forced a smile to her lips. "That's Gabriella, all right."

"She was here at Channel Seven for only a few months before she got that network job, right?"

Molly saw the awe in the girl's eyes—and the glint of ambition—as the young reporter moved around to Molly's side of the desk, peering over her shoulder at the cover line alongside Gabriella's beaming smile:

EXCLUSIVE:

The fastest-rising star in TV news talks about her famous father—at last.

"Hey! Spenser!" The voice of Pete Norcross, the assignment editor, echoed across the newsroom. "Come on up here."

Marilyn started guiltily. "Oops. I'm supposed to be covering the Jogger Murder trial. Gotta run."

Of course. Molly clenched her teeth. Who else would get the lead story of the day if not a rookie reporter who hadn't even been in the city when the murder had occurred?

She stared down at her desk where Marilyn had left the magazine and couldn't suppress the feelings of envy and regret that suddenly bubbled up inside her. She held no ill will towards Gabriella, though. She and Gabriella had been friends, or as friendly, at least, as any two female reporters working in the same newsroom could ever get, and Gabriella had stayed in touch even after her move to New York.

In fact, to her credit, Gabriella was among only a handful of acquaintances who'd had the guts to visit Molly after she'd come home from the hospital. Colleagues had sent cards and flowers but few of them had actually been able to face her, no doubt because they'd not known what to say.

Gabriella, however, had offered advice from the standpoint of one who'd been through a similar experience. "I know having a miscarriage at four months isn't a loss of the same magnitude, but I do have an idea of what you're going through," she'd assured Molly, arriving at the house with flowers, fruit, and a specially edited tape of funny outtakes and bloopers from the new show she was anchoring with Sam.

By the end of the afternoon she'd coaxed Molly out of bed and downstairs to have a glass of Cabernet. "The worst thing you can do to yourself is wallow in bed and stare at the walls," she'd declared firmly. "You have to get back to work as soon as you can. It's what saved me. You just have to get over it."

"I intend to," Molly had agreed, and then hesitantly added, "but I'd like to make a complete break . . . Sam tells me that Jack is planning to launch a couple of other news shows."

"True." Gabriella had nodded. "And I think it would be a perfect move for you. You really don't have any reason to stay in Philly anymore." She had raised her glass of wine in a toast. "Here's to New York. I'll speak to Jack about it. Tell him how you feel. He'll understand."

Molly had noticed the proprietary note in Gabriella's voice but was not surprised. She had long ago suspected that Gabriella Grant had taken her place in New York with Jack Kane—in every way.

She quashed that memory now and quickly turned to the page where the cover story started, letting her eyes roam over the double-page spread. The words ran around four pictures, including the obligatory toddler picture of Gabriella Grant at four years old: a serious little face with mousy straight hair tied back in a big bow.

Idly, Molly wondered which of her baby pictures she would have handed over to *People*, then forced herself to focus on the words:

> There were many times on her way to the top when Gabriella Grant was tempted to use her famous father's name. Ben Grant, the late, beloved star of the long-running nighttime soap *Malibu*, could have opened many doors. But says Gabriella, "I wanted to do it on my own. Now that I'm established, sort of"—*she pauses and*

*laughs—"I can talk about my father without people
accusing me of using his name." For years, Grant kept the
secret of her paternity from everyone but a handful of
friends . . .*

Molly laid the magazine aside, remembering the big
eight-by-ten picture of Ben Grant that had stood on
Gabriella's desk in the newsroom. You only had to ask
Gabriella why she kept a framed picture of an aging
Hollywood has-been on her desk for her to smile that enig-
matic smile of hers. In response to the raised eyebrow she
would laugh. "Now, don't go jumping to conclusions. He's
old enough to be my father."

One afternoon, during a longish lunch at the Dickens
Inn, Gabriella had confided the true story to Molly about
her mother's brief fling with a young, struggling, and then-
unknown actor appearing in a summer stock production.
Molly, her eyes skimming over the print, saw that *People*
had nothing she didn't already know. Gabriella had told the
whole story. It was a master stroke, guaranteed to put her on
the cover, and Molly envied her friend's evident talent for
self-promotion.

She closed the magazine and glanced at the clock. It
would be a couple of hours yet before Jennifer Reed arrived.
Impatiently she got to her feet, slipping into the jacket
she'd tossed carelessly over the back of the chair. She
paused at the assignment desk on her way out. "I'm going
out to do some preliminary research on my big piece for
tonight," she said to Pete Norcross. "Scout out some of the
better coffee dives."

He stared quizzically at her over the top of his glasses.
"You know, Pete, my big investigation into coffee—the
drug of the nineties?"

Then he'd nodded and shrugged, his eyes telling her he
was sympathetic to her plight but could do nothing about it.
She knew that Pete himself felt as if his days were num-
bered.

Jennifer Reed was wrapping up the noon newsbrief when
Molly sauntered back into the newsroom. The monitor

over the assignment desk was tuned to their station. The other two were tuned to a daytime soap and MTV. As the newsbrief ended and went to a commercial break, Molly watched for Jennifer to appear through the elevator doors from the fifth floor studio. She gave the anchorwoman a minute to reach her office and then followed her down the short corridor off the newsroom.

Jennifer was hanging up her jacket, brushing down the lapels, when Molly appeared in her doorway.

"Well, greetings, stranger. Good to see you back!" She grinned at Molly. "Come on in. How are you feeling?"

Molly stepped into the office and slid down onto the couch as Jennifer Reed settled herself behind her desk, picking up a pencil to make a notation in a big fat diary.

"So." She looked up at Molly. "You look good."

"I was getting to feel much better, too—until last night."

Jennifer arched a perfectly waxed eyebrow.

"I had a break-in last night." Molly cleared her throat. "He was waiting for me when I got back from my sister's."

"Oh, shit!" The pencil in Jennifer's hands snapped.

The anchorwoman crossed the room and closed her office door, then returned to her desk and sank into the chair with a loud sigh. "He didn't hurt you." It was a statement not a question.

Molly grimaced. "You know what they say: The *threat* of rain is as much of a damper as a storm. I thought he was going to kill me. Then he mentioned your name. He said you and I should chat and compare notes . . ." Molly paused as her throat tightened. "He said, 'Before you think of going to the cops, talk to Jennifer, she's a smart girl.' "

Jennifer shook her head. "He said the same thing to me except he told me Diane Lamont was the smart girl."

Molly's mouth widened into a silent O. "He videotaped Diane?"

Jennifer nodded. "And she wasn't the first, either. Janey Sumner was—just before she moved to Fox."

Molly threw her head back against the couch, anger and shock rendering her speechless for a moment before propelling her to her feet. "Good God, Jennifer! And none of you said anything? I mean—" She broke off for a moment.

"I thought I understood what had happened. If it had been just you . . . well, that might have been tough to explain. I know how he tried to make it look. But three of you? You don't think the cops are that cynical, do you?"

Jennifer's lips set in a thin firm line.

"Well?" Molly fixed her with an angry look. "If you'd reported it maybe that would have stopped him. And, you would have alerted someone like me to the fact that this wacko was running around."

Jennifer's face reddened. She got out of her chair and went to stand by her window. "I'm sorry, Molly. If I'd had any idea, any clue that you would be his next victim, of course I would have said something. You don't need this grief on top of everything else. But . . ."

"But?" Molly echoed the word as Jennifer shrugged.

"But." Jennifer paced back to her chair. "We discussed it. We came to the conclusion that it would just make things worse if the cops actually caught him."

The anchorwoman sighed. "Think about it, Molly. Think about what would happen down the road . . . think about the trial . . . think about those tapes being presented as evidence—and they would be—probably by the prosecution, certainly by the defense."

"The judge would clear the courtroom."

Jennifer laughed shrilly. "So what? Do you honestly think that as soon as the news broke, all those sleazy tabloid TV shows wouldn't be killing themselves in the scramble to get copies?

"Can't you just imagine one of those *Hard Copy* reporters looking oh-so-concerned, so disgusted but so sympathetic. And he'd stand there talking about the devious, cunning, nasty, modern-day, hi-tech Peeping Tom: 'You may ask yourself, viewers. Why didn't these high-powered, tough career newswomen report this modern-day, hi-tech Peeping Tom? Well, viewers, you judge for yourself. What would you have done if you'd been forced to smile into his camera? We have the exclusive tapes . . .'" Jennifer paused and Molly noticed her hands were trembling. "Do you want to see yourself on TV with a blue dot over your crotch?"

Molly shook off the nightmare scenario that Jennifer had

outlined. "I'd say he was more than just a Peeping Tom," she countered hoarsely.

Jennifer waved off her words. "Bottom line, Molly: He didn't rape us or maim us. Or even touch us."

"He threatened me with a box cutter," Molly said.

"Anyway," Jennifer continued as if Molly hadn't even spoken, "setting aside the whole tortuous process of convincing a jury—who'd probably would think we're all sluts anyway and who'd probably resent the hell out of us for making so much money—even if they convicted him, what do you think he'd get? A slap on the wrist, maybe a couple of years for breaking and entering, maybe possession of a deadly weapon. Maybe. Meanwhile we're finished. You think anyone would treat us seriously again? You think Nick Myers isn't waiting for an excuse to get rid of me, too? Forget it, Molly. I'm not ruining everything I ever worked for just to see some little pervert get sent away for psychiatric treatment."

There was a silence in the office as Jennifer finished her tirade and Molly considered everything the anchorwoman had said. Then, she broke the silence: "A little pervert who's clever enough to find out where we live and break in with the minimum of effort. Ice cool, too. He got into my place in full view of a whole park full of people."

Jennifer nodded. "He sneaked into mine on the day my cleaning lady was there."

"How about Janey and Diane?"

Jennifer grimaced. "Well, Janey was a cinch. She leaves a spare key in one of those really stupid fake-looking gray rocks. And, she never set her alarm when she was out of the house."

"It's someone who knows all about us, isn't it?" Molly echoed the thought aloud. "Probably someone who works right here at Channel Seven." She paused, shivering. "That's what we have in common: We all work or did work, in Janey and Diane's cases, for this station."

"Yeah." Jennifer nodded. "And we're all single, living alone. And . . ." She suddenly grimaced. "We're all blondes."

"Why do you think he's doing it? Aren't you afraid those

tapes are going to turn up in one of those adult video stores on Market Street? *TV Blondes Bare All?*"

"What? And risk having them traced back to him? I wouldn't hesitate telling the cops about what he'd done if that happened."

"What about blackmail?"

Jennifer allowed a smile. "We thought about that, too. But it hasn't happened." She shrugged. "If I had to make a wild guess I'd say he's doing it for himself. He's probably a disturbed, lonely individual who watches a lot of TV and can probably only get off by watching tapes of his dream women. He's just taken it to a higher level than some of those jerks who write to us and tell us what they'd like to do to us."

Molly found herself grimacing in response. "You sound like one of those FBI criminal profile analysts. Have you actually spoken to anyone about it?"

The anchorwoman shook her head. "Nuh. Are you kidding?"

"What about hiring a private investigator?"

"For what? I don't ever want to see him again. Listen, Molly, do what the rest of us are doing. Thank your lucky stars the damage wasn't worse, move to a secure apartment building, and get on with your life."

Molly felt the conversation had run out of steam. But she was unhappy about the outcome. "It bothers me, Jen, that there are other women, colleagues, who might be next. We can't just let him go on."

"What do you suggest? We put a big warning notice up in the ladies' room? Sign our names to it?"

"Not necessarily. Maybe we can warn the next likely victim. If he's sticking to a pattern, which he seems to have done, we know he's targeting blond newswomen who are or were linked to Channel Seven, and who are single or living alone. And . . ." Molly paused as another link occurred to her.

"And what?" Jennifer eyed her suspiciously.

Molly cleared her throat. She'd had suspicions but she had never known exactly what each woman's relationship with Jack Kane had been. She decided to be subtle. "We all posed together for that picture with Jack Kane at his farewell party at the beginning of the year. You know the one that appeared in the *Daily News*?"

Jennifer eyed her pensively. "I didn't even think about that . . ." She paused. "But if that's what set him off, well, then he's gotten to all of us now." She moved back behind her desk. "I promise you if it happens to anyone else then we'll rethink and we'll do something about it. But let's hope it's over."

It wasn't till Molly was back at her desk that she found herself wondering about Jennifer's reaction to her mention of the picture. It had seemed genuine enough, as if she really hadn't made the connection, and Molly could not imagine that if the three other women had seriously thought she was the next victim, they wouldn't have warned her.

Still, the sense of betrayal and their irresponsibility was hard to stomach. Bottom line: They had not cared enough about anyone else, only their own images and their own careers. She sank down in her chair and stared at the telephone on her desk. She wanted out so badly. It was obvious she had no future here, and no friends. And she missed Jack more than ever.

She didn't even need to look up his number. Swiftly, before she could change her mind, she reached for the phone and punched out the digits for his personal, direct line.

"Jack? It's Molly," she announced when he picked up on the second ring.

"Hey, Malone! How the hell are you?"

Malone? She raised her voice a notch. "Jack? It's me, Molly."

"Yeah, yeah. I know. I got your message." His voice sounded so clear and loud she couldn't believe that he still hadn't recognized her voice. "I was going to get back to you this morning but now I've got one foot out the door. My wife's here and we've got appointments to look at real estate, but I'll get back to you later. Promise."

She hung up abruptly, getting his message immediately the word "wife" was out of his mouth.

"Are you okay?" She jumped as a heavy hand dropped on

her shoulder and looked up to see Pete Norcross staring at her with concern. "You look pale."

She forced a half smile to her lips. "No, I'm not okay. But it's nothing a cup of cappuccino won't fix," she answered sarcastically. "Who's my crew on this coffee caper, Pete?"

"You've got the tops, love. Bayliss and Jagger—when they return from the courthouse with Marilyn."

Sure, Pete. Twist the knife while you're at it. She watched him walk away, tapping her fingernails on the desk, her anger stewing inside her.

Unbelievable, she thought, staring at the phone. The first time she tried to get through to Jack, Emma had to be in his office.

Emma Kane seemed determined to thwart her at every turn.

7

Thursday, September 26

He pressed the doorbell twice and waited. The wait always made him angry because he was on the doorstep at the same time, most mornings, to hand Mrs. Jarski her copy of the *New York Post*. He picked up the paper for her at the newsstand at Broad and Locust on his way home from work. He'd been doing it for more than a year and his timing had never been off by more than five minutes either way. So why did she always make him wait?

Today it made him especially irritable because he was anxious to get home and get on with the project. It was all coming together now and finally the end was in sight.

Now that Molly Heskell was in the bag he could relax a little. He had worried about her but the footage had turned out perfectly. Now, he had just one more shoot to go, and he wanted to get home so that he could prepare for it the way he'd prepared for Molly Heskell.

The door flew open—finally. "Louie! How wonderful to see you!"

"You too, Mrs. Jarski." He forced a smile to his lips. Why did she always look so surprised to see him? One day he'd ring her bell wearing his black ski mask. That would really surprise her. He handed her the paper. "Here you go. All the news that's *not* fit to print."

He said the same thing every morning, and every morning she giggled in the same way. And, every morning she thanked him for making a native New Yorker happy.

"You're welcome, Mrs. Jarski." He gave her a little salute and walked back down her path to the sidewalk. Native New Yorker indeed! He never reminded her that she'd told him about being born in Warsaw. He never said any of the things that popped into his head because Mrs. Jarski was also a snoop and a gossip, and in the unlikely event the police ever came around asking questions, he wanted her on his side.

"Louie! You want to know about Louie?" He could hear her talking in that thick Polish accent. "He's the best. Looks after his neighbors, oh, yes . . . when he has such important things to do. He works in TV, you know. At Channel Seven. Makes documentaries, I think."

Yes, she would get enough of it right, he thought. And for that reason he also let her get away with calling him Louie when he had not answered to any name but Lewis since Jessica.

But his pace picked up as he approached his own front door. Coming home always made him feel good. He had the best house on the street. At the end of the row, his was the only house with a garage. The house was always freshly painted on the outside every year and he repapered and painted inside every two years. It was a far cry from the pigsty his mother had left him.

He stepped over the threshold and slid out of his coat,

hanging it on a hanger in the closet by the door. Then he headed straight for the kitchen, glancing only briefly towards the four Chia Pets in his display cabinet in the living room. Usually he stopped to check on how they were doing, but he was in a hurry today. So much of a hurry that he was going to allow himself to eat at his desk.

He poured orange juice and popped an English muffin into the toaster before spreading a paper napkin on his tray. Then, when the muffin was toasted and dripping with butter, he took the tray and carefully walked to the basement door. A few seconds later he was happily ensconced in his little studio.

It had taken him six months of backbreaking work to clean up the basement and construct and equip it with monitors, editing machines, and a computer. He had even managed to acquire a second-hand studio camera, which faced a miniature set. He had built the anchor desk himself and set it against a crudely painted backdrop of the Philadelphia skyline.

He knew how to use every piece of equipment. He had learned well. In every poky, small market where he'd managed to find a job after Kane had fired him and forced him to leave Philadelphia, he had added another important skill. In Green Bay he had learned editing skills; in Des Moines he had operated the studio cameras and gone out with the cameramen. In Wichita he had brought coffee and sandwiches to reporters and then hung out with them, watching as they put together their stories, logged their tapes, wrote scripts, and laid down their audio tracks. Finally, in Duluth, he'd had his shot at the big time, making it all the way to the assignment desk.

He bit into his muffin, cursing as a dollop of melted butter dripped onto his pants. He dabbed at it furiously with his napkin, not wanting to break away to get the Stain Stick. He was all fired up. The memories from Duluth always did that to him.

He'd had it all together in Duluth, planning to use his new position as a launching pad for his return to Philadelphia. Of course, he'd never dreamt that Jack Kane was still out to get him. And he had never imagined in his worst nightmares that Jack Kane would block his move back to the City of Brotherly Love by resurrecting the dreadful lies of the past against him. To wreck a man's life and career once . . . well, that could have been an accident. Kane had been young then, too. He might not have understood his own power back then. But to do it all over again, a second time, that was unforgiveable.

It was a deed that could not go unpunished, Lewis had decided, though it had taken him a while to figure out how he could strike back. Kane, the scumbag, had seemed invincible. But Lewis knew that even Kane had to have a weak spot.

It was only after Kane had moved from Channel Seven to WorldMedia that Lewis had been able to worm his own way in to the TV station to research his subject. He had spent weeks listening to war stories about the great Jack Kane, picking up gossip and tidbits of information here and there until he'd finally zeroed in on Kane's dirty little secret.

After that it had been a painstaking process of making a list of the women's names, researching locations and setting up the shoots with Janey and Diane and Jennifer and Molly. It had taken him almost nine months to put it all together, although two of those weeks had been an utter waste of time.

He'd spent his summer vacation shadowing Kane on the streets of New York in the hope of picking up a clue to the identity of the current floozy. But it had proved a futile mission. Underground parking garages and security-tight buildings had proved to be insurmountable obstacles. The only occasion he'd witnessed Kane with another woman was when he'd seen him helping his new star, Gabriella Grant, into a long white limo outside the WorldMedia offices. But there had been nothing even vaguely incriminating in their conduct: no pat on the butt for the new blonde, not even a chaste air-kiss in the vicinity of her lovely cheeks.

No matter, thought Lewis now. He was on the brink of completing his project. He had just one more shoot to schedule. Abruptly he pushed away from his desk and paced across the small studio to his mahogany filing cabinets. The top three drawers were crammed with his files on Kane. Armed with the one that held clippings and releases about

Kane's most recent achievements at WorldMedia, he returned to his desk.

He turned his attention to the thick manila folder, leafing through the newspaper clippings briskly until he reached the announcement of Jack Kane's appointment at WorldMedia. There was a picture taken at the Four Seasons on the day of the announcement. Kane and Seth Reilly, the chairman of WorldMedia, were in the picture. So were their wives. The caption read:

TOP TV WIVES FIND DOUBLE REASON FOR CELEBRATION:

Emma Kane and Kathy Reilly meeting for the first time, discovered they both celebrated 20th wedding anniversaries last week.

Lewis stared hard at the picture, focusing on Emma Kane. She had a pretty face but her eyes were cold. She looked as if she was made of sterner stuff than the ditzy anchorwomen. She looked as if she might put up a fight . . .

He blinked away the thought. No, he had to get Emma Kane—and he had to do it before he lost his nerve. Quickly, he riffled through the rest of the folder until he found another useful clipping. This one, a three-line item in Gail Shister's TV column in a recent *Inquirer*.

Jack Kane, now a top TV network honcho in the Big Apple, paid a fleeting visit to his old stomping grounds in Center City last week. Talking about the hardships of commuter marriage, he said his lovely wife, Emma, planned on moving to New York by the end of the year.

Perfect, he thought. Emma was still rattling around the Kane homestead on Cherry Lane.

He closed the folder, glanced at his watch, and got to his feet. He would have to wait several more hours for nightfall. But he could make a start now by driving over to the Mobil station. He didn't want to be running out of gas in Emma Kane's driveway tonight.

8

Harry Holmsby was on his third waffle when the call came. He took the first message on his cell phone, then excused himself and went through into the den to use the phone. Kate knew immediately that it was something big. Not only was Harry using a more secure line but he wanted privacy from both her and Maysie.

Kate grinned to herself, zipping up her ankle-length boots so that she'd be ready to roll with him as soon as he was finished on the phone. Action at last, she thought.

It had been four days since Harry had cleared her access to the police department and to her chronicling his work day. He'd been very gracious about it, too, and though Kate suspected Maysie's breakfasts had something to do with it, he even stopped by the house each morning to pick her up. But the exercise so far had been less exciting than she'd hoped it would be, and only the mopping-up on the Anna Mae Whitman case had held any real interest for her.

A detailed autopsy report on the realtor had proved inconclusive as to manner of death. Cause of death had been simple to determine: Epidural hematoma, which translated roughly into instant death by a blow to the head. The realtor's liver had also ruptured. But manner of death required a determination of homicide, suicide, or accident, and that had remained up in the air until Wednesday when a statement from a housekeeper at the Bateman estate had confirmed the existence of a woman client. A follow-up interview with Stan Nixon, the prime suspect, had convinced Harry to close the file on Anna Mae Whitman.

"The guy had no ax to grind," he told Kate. "They were partners for twelve years. No evidence of financial problems, no evidence of marital problems on his side. Whitman's ex was in Cleveland. There was no money or jewelry missing from her person or belongings. I can't see a motive for Nixon—or anyone else."

"So, what about the woman client?" Kate had asked. "You never did find out her name, and she was the last one to see Anna Mae."

Harry had shrugged. "Stan Nixon said they had lunch together before Anna Mae went to Reed's house. Do you really think it's worth going through every client name in Whitman's Rolodex just so that this woman can tell us what Anna Mae drank for lunch?" He paused. "That's what it all keeps coming back to, Kate. I think the moral of this one is: If you have one cocktail too many at lunch, don't go prancing around on circular staircases."

Kate had made notes as they went along and she checked now to see if the notebook was still in her bag. It looked like she'd be needing it again this morning. Then she reached for the navy wool blazer hanging on the back of the kitchen door just as Harry reappeared from the den.

"It's a shooting on Cherry Lane." He ran his hand over his head. "Two victims. Both ten-seven. Thanks for the waffles, Maysie, I gotta run."

Kate moved towards the door with him. Ten-seven was police code for out of service. Harry meant both victims were dead. On Cherry Lane—one of the most desirable streets in the neighborhood.

"Whoa!" Harry stopped her as she followed him out onto the porch. "I don't know about you coming out on this one right away, Kate."

"What!"

He shook his head. "This isn't a good idea. The county investigators are on their way, too. The place is going to be crawling as it is. Why don't you hang back just till—"

"Harry!" She cleared the porch steps in one jump and ran

after him. "Just hold it. I got unlimited access, remember? Where you go, I go."

Harry stopped with his hand on the car door handle as Kate leaned against the door.

"Kilgore okayed it himself. Remember? He didn't say unlimited access *except* to homicides that will also involve the county investigators. This is still going to be your case, isn't it?"

Harry hesitated but only for a moment longer, apparently reassured by the invocation of the police superintendent's name, and Kate moved quickly to the passenger-side door.

Secure in her seat beside Harry, she prodded for more details. "So who are the victims? Do you have names?" she asked as they turned onto the main road.

"One male, one female," Harry replied. "And that's as much as I know right now." He took a deep breath. "Just remember, Kate, you're going to have to stay out of the way while the county investigators are there. And you can't touch anything. I mean not one tiny, blessed thing. You know that, don't you?" He paused again. "I don't want some hot-shot defense attorney down the road cross-examining me about sloppy police work or tainted evidence."

She nodded and Harry seemed to relax, but he didn't speak again until they were waved through the wrought-iron gates of what looked like a small estate. Kate stared with envy at the landscaping and the mature trees, shrubs, and plantings that surrounded the house. "This is like driving through a park."

"Yeh, nice and secluded," Harry commented. "Bet the neighbors never heard a damn thing." He pulled in behind a large van, which Kate recognized as the mobile crime lab.

"Looks like the county guys are here already," she said, following him out of the car and along the driveway to the front doors.

The house, a rambling stone mansion reminiscent of an English manor, was huge, at least three times the size of hers. She figured, at first glance, there was probably ten thousand square feet under the gray slate roof.

A uniformed officer standing by the front door greeted

them and informed Harry that he'd been first on the scene. "A friend of the owners found the bodies and called us. She's inside." He retrieved a notebook and glanced at the open page. "The house belongs to a couple by the name of Kane."

Kate's sudden sharp intake of breath was ignored as the cop continued. "The friend says the male victim isn't Mr. Kane. We found him on the landing. She didn't ID the female. We found her in the master bathroom. The friend didn't get a look." There was a pause. Then: "Oh, and, Sarge, she says she was here to meet Mrs. Kane. They were flying to Arizona this morning. She got no answer so she let herself in through the garage. There's one of those electronic openers on it, you know, where you punch in your code?"

"Okay." Harry nodded and walked into the house, glancing sideways at Kate. "What was the gasp for?"

"Kane," Kate echoed. "That's the one who's president of news at WorldMedia. Remember, his name came up when we were at Jennifer Reed's?"

Harry nodded and glanced up to a second-floor landing where Kate recognized Tom Lansing and Norm Rogers, two detectives whom she'd met in the squad room during the week. They were standing over the body of the male victim. Kate noted the shock of dark, almost black hair against the pale white carpeting. He was lying facedown in a navy-colored bathrobe.

"And, Harry." Kate caught his sleeve as he stepped towards the staircase. "This is one of the houses Anna Mae Whitman showed to that woman client." She raised an eyebrow. "Isn't that weird, or what?"

Harry stopped at the bottom of the staircase and grinned at her. "Noted and filed," he said, tapping his temple with an index finger. "But let's not get too excited, just yet."

He glanced back at the cop by the door. "Hines, get down to the front gates and make sure they're secured. The owner here is some kind of TV big-shot. I'm sure the press will start descending in droves when the word gets out."

"Harry." Kate stopped him again. "Will I be able to go upstairs later? I want to get the feel of the scene . . . see the bodies like you get to see them. See you guys at work, you know, the whole enchilada."

"Yeah, yeah, yeah." Harry nodded impatiently. "You'll get to see everything. But I'm not going to be looking at the bodies right now. You know the first rule: Bodies stay. The crime scene changes. We're going to be looking for evidence first. Tagging it, logging it, taking pictures of it, getting it on videotape, vacuuming, bagging, and so on and so on. We're going to be here for a while. So relax."

Kate nodded. "Okay, okay." She looked towards the back of the house. "I'll wait down here."

"Fine," Harry agreed. "But don't—"

"Touch anything." Kate finished the sentence for him and saw his mouth twitch as he headed upstairs. She watched him stop on the landing, crouch down beside the body for a moment. Then he straightened up and walked through a door on his left, disappearing from her view.

Kate took a deep breath and walked slowly across the tiled foyer, the noise of her footsteps echoing around her. The foyer accessed maybe a half-dozen rooms through open arched doorways. She looked into each in turn, noting the marble fireplaces in the living and dining rooms, a kitchen equipped with a Sub-Zero and a wine refrigerator as well as two dishwashers, a game room with a pool table and wet bar, a music room with grand piano and vaulted ceiling, and a garden room with a cathedral ceiling made entirely of glass. Everything in the house shrieked money from the imported-tile floors to the leather-moulded book-shelving in the music room, where dozens of silver-framed photographs on the grand piano beckoned to Kate. As she walked towards them she counted four pairs of French doors leading out of the room onto a flagstone terrace that stepped down to a swimming pool.

"I'm over here." A woman's voice stopped her halfway towards the grand piano. Kate whirled around, but it was a moment before she saw the woman: a petite redhead dwarfed by the high-backed, overstuffed chair in which she was sitting. Kate changed direction and walked towards her.

The woman held out her hand to Kate, who noticed an improbably slender wrist weighed down by heavy gold. "I'm Betsy Wright, Emma's friend. Is she . . . dead, detective?"

"I'm not a detective." Kate shook her head. "But I'm here

with Detective-Sergeant Holmsby and I believe Mrs. Kane *is* dead. I'm sorry."

Betsy Wright covered her face with both hands, shaking her head.

"Mrs. Wright?" Kate touched her arm gently. "Can I get you a glass of water?"

"No. No thank you." She shook her head. "This is such a shock. Such a shock . . ." Her words drifted into a stunned silence.

Kate noticed that despite expertly applied makeup, Betsy Wright's face had an unhealthy pallor to it. She looked very frail altogether. Kate figured she could not weigh more than one hundred pounds. "Would you like to walk outside?" she asked. "Maybe the fresh air will help."

Betsy got to her feet. "I think I would. I feel as if I'm going to pass out."

Kate followed her across the room, heading towards one set of atrium doors. She wondered if it would be all right to touch the handle. She hesitated at the door and then realized that Betsy Wright had stopped by the piano and was staring at the photographs. Kate retraced her steps to join her.

"That's Emma." Betsy pointed to the most prominent framed picture of a smiling blonde. "That was taken last year." It was a studio portrait and Kate guessed that all laugh lines and wrinkles had been artfully airbrushed out. The face that stared out from the picture was unlined and unharried, the eyes a cool and serene blue, and the jewelry stunning. Emma Kane had worn a diamond choker with long diamond teardrop earrings. Her chin rested on a gently curled fist—all the better to show off the zillion-carat rock on her finger, thought Kate.

Her eyes swept over the whole display. Most were of Emma. Portraits through the decades. She could tell by the change in hairstyles that Emma Kane had been something of a slave to the fashions of the day.

"Oh, and this is Emma with her daughter, Angela." Betsy Wright pointed to a set of mother and daughter pictures. "She was at Villanova, then she transferred to the

University of California." Betsy shook her head and looked away abruptly. "This is going to kill Angela."

Kate made a soothing noise but her attention was caught by another photograph. "I guess this is Mr. Kane," she said, pointing to a tall, broad-shouldered man standing at the helm of what looked like a very sleek, long sailboat.

Betsy nodded. "Yes, that's Jack. On his boat. I think that was taken on the Chesapeake last summer." Kate stared at the strong, handsome face, the wide generous smile, and the dark hair blowing in the wind. He looked like a man who knew how to enjoy life's finer pleasures.

She was still staring at the photograph when Harry walked into the room followed closely by Mike Travis. Evidently Harry had explained her presence already because Mike nodded in her direction, acknowledging her briefly with a smile. Then he turned to Betsy Wright. "We'd like to ask you some questions, Mrs. Wright."

The little group moved towards an arrangement of chairs by a large picture window that overlooked a small brick patio while Kate stayed where she was, perching herself on the piano stool.

Harry asked the first question about Betsy's arrival at the house, confirming that she'd let herself in through the garage after getting no reply to the doorbell.

"There was a code, a set of numbers you had to punch in to open the doors?"

"Yes. Emma hated the damn thing. She changed the code every other week and gave me the numbers in case she forgot them."

"Were you the only one who had the code?"

Betsy shrugged. "Aside from Mr. Kane, yes. Emma was very careful. She was always worrying about burglaries and break-ins."

"So you came in through the garage?"

"That's right." Betsy nodded. "And when I got to the foyer I saw . . . what was on the landing upstairs and I turned and ran straight to my car and called nine-one-one."

"And when the police arrived and brought you back into the house you told them it wasn't Mr. Kane?"

"No, it wasn't. I could see that. Besides Jack lives in New York—that's where he works now."

"Are the Kanes separated? Divorced?" Mike Travis asked.

"Oh, no." Betsy Wright shook her head insistently. "The plan was for Emma to move to New York after the house was sold. It's been on the market since almost the beginning of the year."

"Were you and Mrs. Kane close friends?" Mike jumped in again.

"Very." Betsy nodded firmly. "I knew Emma for fifteen years. Our daughters went to school together."

"Would you say the Kanes had a good marriage?"

"I would say it was very good, considering." She nodded her head vigorously.

"Considering what?" Harry prodded.

"Considering Jack Kane is very wrapped up in his work and Emma has . . . I mean *had* her own interests. That's why she wasn't very happy about moving to New York. She didn't really want to leave here." Betsy Wright looked anxiously at Harry as if wondering if she'd said the wrong thing.

Too late. Mike was right on it. "Did they fight about that?"

"Fight?" Betsy smiled nervously. "No. But they had discussed it." She paused. Then quickly added: "Jack wasn't around much; he was hardly home at all . . . so Emma had gotten used to doing her own thing."

"So it would appear," Harry weighed in dryly.

There was a brief silence and Betsy picked nervously at the charms on her heavy gold bracelet. Then Harry leaned forward, his hands planted firmly on his knees. "Mrs. Wright, can you tell us anything about the male victim?"

Betsy Wright shook her head insistently. "No. I don't know anything about him." Her voice had dropped to a half whisper and she turned away momentarily to stare out of the picture window.

"Do you know his name?"

Another shake of the head. "I didn't really look at him that closely."

"Mrs. Wright." Harry leaned forward a little more. "You're not helping your friend if you're keeping any information from us. Could you maybe narrow it down to one name or two? He looks to be in his early thirties. How many young male friends did Mrs. Kane have?"

Betsy suddenly straightened up in her chair. "If you're trying to imply that Emma was . . . was doing something she shouldn't be, well, let me tell you, you've got it wrong." She took a long, deep, audible breath before continuing. "Emma went to church every Sunday. She used to read at the Mass and she sometimes sang in the choir. She had a lovely voice, too. She was in TV herself before she got married, you know." Betsy's voice cracked and Kate saw tears start to roll down her cheeks. "I don't know what you want me to tell you."

Kate saw Harry and Mike exchange glances. Then Mike stood up. "We're sorry if we're upsetting you, Mrs. Wright, but we're looking at conflicting evidence here. That young man was upstairs right outside Mrs. Kane's bedroom, wearing a bathrobe. We thought you might be able to tell us something more."

"Well, I can't," Betsy Wright suddenly interrupted. "All I know is that Emma sometimes had a young man over here to fix things around the house. That's all I know."

Kate saw another exchange of glances between Mike and Harry, with the detective-sergeant rolling his eyes exaggeratedly. It was obvious that they didn't believe Betsy Wright was telling them the whole story. But evidently they also realized they'd gain nothing by pressuring her any further. Harry got to his feet. "Okay, Mrs. Wright, just one more question. When did you last speak with Mrs. Kane?"

"Last night, just after eight. We were on the phone several times during the day and evening, you know, because of our trip . . ."

"So you spoke to her around eight?"

A curt nod. "I tried to call her again, later, around ten, maybe just after ten, but I didn't get through——" Betsy Wright suddenly seemed to choke on her words, her hand moving to her mouth. "I left a message for her. I thought maybe she was in the shower . . . but . . . she must have been . . . was she already . . . ?"

Harry shook his head. "We haven't ascertained the time

of death, yet." He crouched down beside Betsy's chair and patted the chair arm. "Will you be all right to drive home? Or would you like one of our police officers to accompany you?"

Betsy slumped back in the chair, her hand still covering her mouth. "No, thank you. I'll be okay. I just need a couple of minutes."

When Harry and Mike Travis left the room, Kate followed and stayed right behind them as they headed upstairs again. There was a man on the landing—a technician, Kate guessed, noticing a clear plastic Baggie in his hands.

Harry paused briefly on the landing, pointing to a sophisticated-looking intercom on the wall just above the body. "Larry, get Ken to take the prints off that intercom when he comes by here."

Kate peered at the intercom. "You can open the front door from up here," she observed. Then she glanced down at the body by her feet. "Do you think he let the killer in?"

"Possibly." Harry nodded, a pensive look in his eyes. "There are no signs of any forced entry and all the doors and windows were locked. But then he'd have to have waited up here for the killer to come right up to him. See that entrance wound at the base of the skull?"

She nodded, staring at the jagged, torn flesh.

"See the star shape around it? That looks like a contact entrance wound. Like the perp held the gun to his head."

Kate nodded again. "You're saying if he let the killer get that close, it must have been someone he or Emma Kane knew?" She stared at the brownish splotch that had seeped into the white rug under the head.

Harry shrugged. "Unless the killer was already in the house and Johnny Doe heard something, came out to investigate, and ran smack bang into him."

"You're thinking it could be Jack Kane?"

The detective-sergeant smiled at Kate. "I'm not jumping to any conclusions at this stage."

"Johnny Doe," Kate echoed. "Haven't you found any ID for him? Where's his wallet?"

"In his pants, I imagine." Harry laughed. "It's a big house, Kate. We're looking, okay?" He beckoned her to follow him into the master bedroom, which was not so much a room as a sumptuous suite with a sitting area around a big tiled fireplace and a little office area next to it. An antique mahogany desk sitting under a huge lead-paned window seemed more decorative than functional but was large enough to hold a computer and a fax machine. Heavy, expensive drapes framed the window and puddled chicly on the thick carpet.

At the opposite end of the room a king-size four-poster that would have dominated any regular-sized bedroom looked small in the space. Kate noticed an open, half-packed suitcase standing on an ornately carved wooden storage chest at the foot of the bed. A half-dozen outfits lay one on top of the other on the neatly made bed.

There were at least a dozen people working in the room, and Kate saw they included crime lab technicians and detectives from both the Lower Merion police department and from Montgomery County. She spotted Mike Travis in the center of a group that had gathered on one side of the room at the entrance to a long narrow hallway. He looked up as she approached the group.

"I've never seen so many people at a crime scene," she remarked. "What would you do in a smaller house?"

"We'd all get real close and intimate." Mike eyed her with an amused look that swept from her face to her feet. Then abruptly his expression became serious. "If you're going to be poking around here you're going to have to wear something over your shoes." He reached into his pocket. "Here, put these on."

He handed her a pair of paper bootees, and while she crouched to slip them on, he added, "This is where Emma Kane was standing when the first shot hit her. The first slug went into the doorjamb. We're attempting to retrieve it right now."

Kate noticed blood spatters on the wall and on the rug. "Where is she?"

Mike pointed down the hallway that had doors on either side. "Past all those closets there. In the bathroom. It's the one on the left."

Kate raised an eyebrow.

Mike nodded. "There's two, side by side. His and hers. At least we know they never argued over who showers first."

Kate smiled. "Can I go down there now?"

Mike blocked the entrance to the hallway. "Do you really want to? It's bad, Kate."

She thrust her shoulders forward. "I'm a big girl, Mike. I've covered homicides before."

He shrugged and stepped aside. "Be my guest then." Kate was aware of her heart thudding as she walked down the hallway, the voices and mutterings receding behind her. It suddenly seemed very quiet and still in this part of the house. It felt like death but didn't smell like it. Instead, the odor seemed to be a mixture of sweet, heavy, pungent aromas as if someone had gone berserk at the cosmetics counter in Strawbridge's.

"What is that smell?" she asked, turning to Mike who was a step behind her. He motioned for her to walk through the open doorway to her left, and she found herself in a small dressing room. A smooth white Corian countertop ran the length of a mirrored wall, which was framed by some two-dozen theater dressing room–type lightbulbs.

On the countertop sat one solitary lipstick. Everything else had been swept off the counter onto the floor. Kate stared at the mess of broken glass and the congealing contents of the myriad bottles and containers of lotions, creams, nail polish, and perfume.

"My God, she must have put up some kind of fight."

"No, I don't think so." Mike shook his head. "These look like they were all knocked off in one clean sweep. You can see, it's like someone just reached out and—poof—cleared everything off the countertop." He paused. "Ready?" He motioned Kate across the green-and-gold marble floor towards the main bathroom area. She sidestepped the mess on the floor, and as she approached the arched doorway, her eyes were drawn immediately to the center of the floor, to the double-size Jacuzzi tub filled with water. Emma Kane's body was slumped against the tub. She appeared to be half sitting, half sprawling on the marble floor, her head cocked to one side. She was wearing a short, thin terrycloth robe, which had once had a pretty floral design to it but was now soaked with blood.

There was blood everywhere. It had spattered over the gleaming tile around the tub and all over the green-and-gold marble floor. It was on Emma Kane's legs and on her arms. A big splotch surrounded an ugly gash on her upper thigh. Blood had also oozed onto her chest from a gaping opening in her neck. Kate stepped to the side and inclined her head to match the angle of Emma Kane's head as it rested on the edge of the tub. It was then she saw that the right side of Emma Kane's face was gone. There was nothing left but a mess of raw flesh and bone.

Kate felt herself gagging, her stomach heaving in an effort to empty itself. She looked away.

"Closed casket for Mrs. Kane, I think." Mike's voice echoed in the bathroom as Kate focussed on the sight of three graceful tree branches framed by an octagonal window above the Jacuzzi tub. She crossed her hands over her belly and took a long deep breath, the strange, pungent odor suddenly assaulting her nostrils like smelling salts. The last thing in the world she wanted was to throw up in front of Mike Travis.

She backed out of the bathroom and felt his hand cupping her elbow, helping her across the dressing room.

"Take another deep breath," he suggested kindly. "This is a particularly bad one. Whoever did this really disliked Emma Kane. All those shots in the face . . ." He paused and made a tutting noise with his tongue.

"He trapped her, cornered her in the bathroom. She must have been terrified." Kate shivered. "Do you think Jack Kane could have done this?"

Mike's mouth twitched into a half smile. "The husband's always a good starting point when a wife and her lover get shot in the act." He patted her arm. "Are you okay, now?"

She nodded and smiled back at him. "Thanks for your help."

"No problem. Harry told me about your new book." He paused. "This could be interesting."

Kate wasn't immediately sure whether he meant the case itself—or the fact that she was going to be around. But before either of them could say anything else, Harry appeared at the other end of the hallway.

"Yo, Travis," Harry called out. "Hines tells me a camera crew just arrived outside the gates. We're going to have to locate hubby and call him—like right now."

"Coming." Mike strode down the hallway where Harry thrust something into his hand. "Here, take a look at what we found in the desk drawers while I get a bug on the phone. We'll need to record this conversation."

Kate sidled up to Mike to see that he was holding a newspaper clipping and an envelope. His eyes skimmed quickly over both before handing them to Kate.

She glanced at the envelope. It was addressed to Emma Kane and had a Philadelphia postmark. Then she looked at the clipping. It was from the gossip column of a New York paper. The item referred to a party Jack Kane had thrown at 21 to celebrate the phenomenal ratings success of *We Expose*, the first show he'd launched at WorldMedia. *"Kane attributed much of the show's success to his favorite anchorwoman, Gabriella Grant. The couple later drove off together, apparently to continue their celebration in private."*

She folded the clipping and put it back in the envelope. "Well," she said, handing it back to Mike. "It seems to me that neither of the Kanes was too interested in the Spouse of the Year Award."

9

Friday morning. New York

Gabriella Grant took it easy on Fridays. It was the day she and Sam Packer taped *We Expose*, and she believed it was more important for her to look rested and vibrant than to attend the morning news meeting.

So it was almost ten o'clock when she left her apartment and took the elevator down to the lobby.

"It's okay, Jose, I'll walk today," she told the doorman who held the front door open for her, ready to precede her into the street to hail a cab. Now that the heat and humidity of summer was behind them, Gabriella looked forward to walking the crosstown blocks between Central Park West and the WorldMedia offices on Tenth, less for the exercise, more for the satisfaction of having passersby recognize her.

She didn't make it too difficult for them. Today, she wore her favorite Chanel suit, a bright orange, fitted jacket over a short-short black skirt. Her hair was tucked into a matching orange fringed scarf, with only her blond bangs peeking out, and her eyes were masked behind a pair of Marilyn Monroe–style dark glasses.

Most New Yorkers acted blasé about celebrities and would not approach her in the street, but she was aware of those who passed and gave her a double take over their shoulders as they hurried by.

WorldMedia had poured a lot of money into buying recognition for her and the show. Jack Kane had launched the show just after Memorial Day to take advantage of viewers' boredom with the usual reruns offered during the summer months.

In June and July her face and Sam Packer's had appeared on the sides of buses and at busstops. The fledgling WorldMedia network had run nonstop commercials for *We Expose* and had spent megabucks on advertising in the New York papers.

Jack had also brought in a publicity whiz kid who'd worked tirelessly with Sam and her to arrange interviews for them in top entertainment magazines like *People* and *Entertainment Weekly* and to get their names into all the major gossip columns.

Gabriella and Sam's grooming had been a carefully orchestrated exercise at WorldMedia to prepare for the launch of the twenty-four-hour cable news channel. It was exciting—and nerve-wracking. Every major network was getting in on the act. NBC had signed a deal with Microsoft and launched a joint effort; Fox TV had been next but had gotten bogged down at the start with their failure to find a cable channel in the city. WorldMedia had arrived on the scene a while later and Jack Kane had succeeded in securing a channel on the city's cable system, but it had been a tough fight and Gabriella knew he'd made enemies in the process. Personally, she had wondered if it was all worth it, if it wasn't all too much of a good thing. Who the hell was going to watch all this unedited, blanket-coverage news, anyway?

She had been more interested in her own role at WorldMedia and Jack Kane's insistence that if they were going to take on CNN, they had to beat the frontrunner in its main area of weakness: recognizable on-air personalities. As he'd pointed out, CNN's legal correspondent, Greta Van Susteren, had more recognition than any of the female or male anchors.

Gabriella had been happy to do her bit, even submitting to a tortuous half hour with Don Imus that had degenerated within minutes when the outrageous radio talk show host had started quizzing her about her Victoria's Secret underwear. Her appearance on the cover of *People* magazine earlier in the week had been her moment of glory, however. It had brought a beaming Jack Kane to the newsroom, where he'd actually hugged her in full view of all the staffers.

Her mother was the only one who'd dampened her big moment. "My God, Gabriella, what have you done? I didn't know you were going to name Ben Grant."

Gabriella had withstood the tirade, which had been punctuated on the other end of the line by the sound of ice chinking in a glass. There was no point in explaining to her mother that this was showbiz. You had to use every advantage.

The story of an innocent Gloria Rossiter kissing a young struggling actor good-bye and letting him go to find fame in Hollywood, not knowing that she was pregnant, was romantic and poignant—and great copy.

Gabriella knew she'd done the right thing because her story had brought a tear to the eyes of the hard-bitten magazine reporter as Gabriella had explained how her mother had lost touch with Ben Grant, how Gloria had gone to pieces some thirteen years later when the first episode of *Family Ways* (Ben Grant's first big break on TV) had aired, and how Gabriella had caught her looking through a box of mementoes a few weeks later. "It was a little treasure box with a playbill from the summer stock production, a dried single rose, and a signed picture from Ben Grant to my mom—all tied with a pink ribbon. I checked the date of the playbill and that's when everything clicked," she'd explained to the *People* reporter.

"Did you ask your mother about it then?" the reporter had asked.

"Of course," Gabriella replied. "I came straight out with it and said, 'Ben Grant is my father, isn't he?'"

"And?"

Gabriella had smiled wanly. "She was shocked that I'd pieced it all together. She was even more shocked when I eventually changed my name to his. She said, 'Gabriella, you shouldn't go around telling people that Ben Grant is your father. They'll just laugh at you.'"

Well, no one's laughing now, Mother, she thought, grinning to herself as she turned left onto Tenth Avenue and hurried into the cool lobby of WorldMedia, where the security guard at the desk blocked her path as she headed for the elevators, her heels clicking on marble tile.

"I need to see your pass, miss."

"What?" Gabriella stopped in midstride. The guard was new, obviously.

"Your building pass," he repeated.

She smiled and pointed over his shoulder. The walls of the lobby were lined with giant studio portraits of WorldMedia's on-air talent. Her own face was sandwiched between Sam Packer, her co-anchor, and Sally Nightingale, anchor of the local newscast, *News at Eleven*.

"Will that do?" she asked, not bothering to disguise the sarcasm in her voice. "That's me, over there. See?"

He turned around but barely glanced at the portrait. "I'm sorry, miss, I need to see ID. That's the new rules." He stood his ground, feet firmly planted in front of her.

Gabriella took a deep breath, unzipped her purse, and

rummaged around for the security pass. Then she removed her dark glasses. "Take a good look at this face," she told the security guard in a calm voice. "You'll be seeing it every day. Don't ask me for ID again—or there'll be trouble. I'll see to it."

He studied the pass and stepped aside. "You have a good day, Miz Grant."

Gabriella kept her thoughts to herself as she stepped onto the elevator and stabbed the button for the fifth floor, but her cheeks were flushed with anger and inside she was seething. In the old days she would have just let fly but she was aware that anything she said or did now could become instant fodder for the gossip columns, and she didn't want to get a reputation as a prima donna. That wouldn't please Jack at all.

So she swallowed her anger as best she could and strode through the newsroom to her office where, slamming the door firmly behind her, she realized she wasn't alone. Alison Haley, one of the show's production assistants was waiting for her.

"Good morning." Alison stared at her with a concerned expression. "Are you okay?"

"Not really." Gabriella smiled at the young PA. Alison was one of the brighter and more enthusiastic production assistants. Eager to learn and to please, she constantly hovered around Gabriella's office, watching the anchorwoman at work, asking questions, and never objecting to running personal errands.

Gabriella took off her jacket and hung it up. "The bozo security guard downstairs gave me a hard time."

"Give a man a uniform and you've got yourself a general." Alison nodded sympathetically. "Can I get you some coffee?"

"Maybe tea this morning," Gabriella replied. "I need something to settle my stomach."

Alison arched an eyebrow and Gabriella laughed. "No. No reason for alarm this week. Just bad Chinese last night, I think—" She broke off as the door opened and Sam Packer looked in.

"Got a moment?" her co-anchor asked.

"Of course." Gabriella nodded as he walked in unsmiling, and waited for Alison to leave the room. Then he closed the door behind the production assistant.

Gabriella stared quizzically at him. "What's up? You look as if you just got the word that our show was canceled."

"It's worse than that," he said simply. "Emma Kane is dead."

Gabriella sat down abruptly. "Emma Kane is dead? You're kidding." She took a deep breath. "No, of course you're not. What a stupid thing to say." She leaned forward across her desk. "How? A car accident?"

"No. She was shot."

"By accident?" Gabriella mouthed the words, staring at Sam, her eyes mirroring the stunned look in his.

"No. Not by accident. She was murdered. She was shot at home. In their home. Jack just got a call from the local police. I was in his office when he got it. He's got to drive down there."

Gabriella jumped to her feet. "Don't you think one of us should go with him? My God, he shouldn't be alone."

Sam held up one hand. "I offered but he didn't want it. He wants the show taped this afternoon as normal."

Gabriella immediately sank back into her chair. "Oh, God. Poor Jack. I hope he's going to be all right."

"I'm sure Jack will be fine," Sam said, not sounding totally convinced. "So long as he's got an airtight alibi."

"What are you talking about?"

Sam cleared his throat. "There were two fatalities. Emma—and some young guy."

"Emma was screwing around?" An involuntary giggle escaped Gabriella's lips but died almost instantly. "Come on!"

Sam shrugged. "I don't know the details. But if she was, it won't look good for Jack. You know a jealous husband is going to be a prime suspect."

Gabriella laughed derisively. "Jack jealous? I don't think so!"

"Not the point, Gabriella. It doesn't matter what we think . . ."

"Well." Gabriella shrugged. "I'm sure Jack is covered. He

was probably here when it happened. He's always here." She stared coldly at Sam, challenging him to disagree. She didn't like his negative attitude. She had no intention of dwelling on the possibility of Jack Kane embroiled in some tedious police investigation. Without Jack, everything they had worked for would go down the tubes. She wished she had been the one in Jack's office when he'd taken the call from the cops. She wished she'd had a chance to discuss it with him.

She slumped back in her deep leather chair. "How did he take it? Was he in shock?"

Sam shook his head, as if in disbelief. "He was stunned. Totally stunned."

Of course, Gabriella nodded. It would be devastating for him. For a while and maybe longer. And there would be feelings of guilt, too. She was sure of that. Not that Gabriella thought that he'd treated Emma poorly. On the contrary, she'd always thought Jack had treated Emma too well: letting her swan around on the Main Line when what he really needed was a wife who could be a real partner and mate—someone who understood and shared his passion for TV news. She had never understood why Emma hadn't realized that if she wasn't around to fill that role, Jack was bound to find someone who did.

Gabriella took a deep breath as Sam walked to the door and focussed on the one fact she had no trouble grasping: Emma was dead. Finally, out of the picture.

10

I n the Channel Seven newsroom Pete Norcross grabbed at a ringing phone but kept his eyes on the newsroom doors. Molly Heskell was due in any moment and he wanted to grab her before she heard the news from anyone else.

It was just after ten when she finally walked through the doors. He watched her stop at the coffee machine before making her way to her desk and then he picked up his phone and dialed her extension. "Morning. Meet me in the conference room, will ya?"

He saw her quizzical look across the newsroom but she dropped her bag on the floor, picked up her coffee cup and cigarettes, and threaded her way through the desks to the back of the room.

Following her into the conference room, he closed the door behind him.

"What's up, Pete?" There was a wary look in her eyes.

He decided to come straight to the point. "Emma Kane bought the farm last night."

"Emma Kane bought the farm?" Her eyes searched his face as if she was not sure she'd heard correctly. "How?" She took a step back and leaned against the conference table.

"We haven't got all the details yet. Only just got this in our TIPS hotline. Some guy with a police scanner out on the Main Line called it in about twenty minutes ago."

Molly took the little pink message slip on which Pete had scrawled the words himself: *Police responding to a call at 17 Cherry Lane. Apparent fatal shooting.*

Molly exhaled loudly. "She was shot? By accident?"

Norcross shook his head. "I don't think so. I had Barry call one of his contacts. It was a double. There are two victims. Emma Kane and a young male whom they haven't identified so far."

Molly made a strange sound, midway between a giggle and a gasp. "Emma was screwing around?" Her eyes reflected amusement tinged with disbelief.

"I know as much as you do."

Molly reached for a cigarette from her pack and lit up. "Poor Jack," she said quietly, shaking her head and picking up her coffee cup. "I guess I'd better get moving then. Who's my crew?"

Pete held up one hand and cleared his throat nervously. "I'm sorry, you're not covering this one, Molly. Lonnie's already on her way."

"What!" She banged the cup down on the desk so that hot coffee flew out, spattering a stack of memos beside it.

"Hey, Molly. Calm down. Come on." He looked anxiously towards the closed door. "Nick Myers thinks you're too close to the story."

"Too close? What the hell does that mean? How can you be too close to a story?" She angrily stubbed out the freshly lit cigarette.

Pete watched her pace across the room. "Molly, don't make a big stink about it . . . I'm advising you as a friend." He paused. He had not been surprised by Nick's decision. It was one of the rare times he'd agreed with Nick Myers. "Nick seems to feel that the reporter covering the deaths should have at least some empathy for the victims." He fixed Molly with a pointed stare.

"Bullshit!" she exploded. "He's saying I can't report objectively on a murder investigation because I hated Emma's guts. That's just bullshit."

"Hold it, Molly." Pete watched her pause with her hand on the door handle. "I'm telling you, this is one you're definitely going to lose with Myers. Come on, fair's fair. He's not the best news director around, but even I would hesitate on this assignment."

Molly shook her head and Pete realized she was itching for a fight.

"I want to hear it from him, Pete." She glared at him. "This is my story—and I'm not going to stand by and watch it assigned to a newcomer like Lonnie."

She flung the door open and stormed out, charging across the newsroom towards Nick Myers' office. Taking a deep breath, Pete followed, arriving in the news director's office just as Molly was about to slam the door closed. He slid in behind her, undaunted by Nick Myers' icy stare. Pete had never seen Molly so angry, but Nick Myers seized control of the situation immediately.

"Close the door and sit down." He beckoned to Molly. "I can see you're not happy about today's assignment, am I right?"

"Damn right!" Molly shot back. She ignored the invitation to sit and Pete could see her back was rigid with anger. "Just tell me, how can a reporter be too close to the story?"

Nick got to his feet and pushed his chair in behind his desk. Then he took off his thick-rimmed glasses and rubbed his eyes. "I don't have to give any explanation, Molly, but since you're so upset I'll give you my thoughts on it."

Pete suddenly wished he had not followed Molly into the director's office. He could see it coming now. The only reason that Nick was discussing the issue with her at all was to let her have it with both barrels.

Nick sighed as if the conversation was causing him real distress. "I'm going to have to be blunt, though—and we all know what I'm getting at here. The problem is that we have no idea where this investigation is heading, but I think it's likely that the cops will be looking at Jack Kane somewhere along the line—"

"Baloney!" Molly erupted. "Jack Kane had nothing to do with it. If Jack Kane ever thought of killing anyone, it would be a reporter who misses a scoop—"

"And since you and Jack Kane were involved in some sort of personal relationship," Nick Myers continued as if Molly hadn't spoken, "I believe that your coverage would have to be somewhat biased."

Pete watched as the news director paced back and forth across his office. "Of course the more worrisome aspect," Myers continued, "and please don't take this the wrong way, but looking at it from the cops' point of view, I think they could well decide to ask some questions around here."

"What exactly does that mean?" Pete heard the catch in Molly's voice.

"I have to spell it out for you?" Nick rolled his eyes. "Listen, even I've heard about your run-in with Emma Kane at La Buca's, and I wasn't even there. Isn't it common knowledge around here that if it wasn't for Emma Kane you'd be a hotshot TV star in New York?" He paused, Pete suspected, for dramatic effect. "Bottom line, Molly, I can't put a reporter on the assignment if that reporter is likely to become part of the investigation."

It was an obvious call, thought Pete, though he felt that Nick Myers was enjoying the moment more than he should have.

"Let me get this straight." Molly's voice sounded dangerously clipped. "You're saying you think I could be a suspect?"

"Not me." Myers smiled slyly. "But I'm saying the cops might see it that way."

Molly wheeled around and headed for the door where she paused for an instant. "Fuck you, Nick," she said quietly and walked out.

As Pete followed her, he was aware that the buzz in the newsroom had softened to a quiet hum. He was aware of the raised heads and eyes looking in their direction. He knew the word of Emma Kane's murder was out. He knew that everyone in the newsroom had an idea of what had gone down in Myers' office. He suddenly felt sorry for Molly.

She headed straight for the ladies' room, ignoring the stares of her colleagues as she made her way past their desks. No one tried to stop her or engage her in conversation. They're all thinking the same thing, she thought. Like Nick Myers.

In the bathroom she threw cold water on her face, and let it run in little rivers down her hot cheeks as she stared into the bathroom mirror. Then she leaned over the sink and pressed her cheeks to the cold porcelain.

She was furious with herself. She had handed herself on a platter to Nick Myers—and he had enjoyed every moment of the encounter.

Of course. He'd held all the cards. If the cops started asking questions about Jack Kane they would eventually show up on her doorstep, for sure. Naturally, she would never ever admit that there had been many days, way back, when she'd actually fantasized about walking into the newsroom and getting the very news Pete had delivered today about Emma Kane. But they would find out about everything else probably right down to her most recent phone calls to Jack Kane in New York.

"So tell us, Ms. Heskell, what was Mr. Kane's reaction when you asked him for a job at WorldMedia?"

"He said he'd call me back."

"Why was that?"

"Because his wife happened to be in the office when I called."

"Was that a problem?"

"He seemed to think so."

"Did he get back to you?"

"Yes."

"And?"

"He said he was delighted I wanted to work with him again. He just needed time to work out some personal stuff with Emma."

"What was that?"

"He didn't go into details. He just said we shouldn't rock the boat."

"Your coming to New York would have rocked the boat?"

"Probably not, Jack said. But he wasn't going to take any chances because you could never tell what was going on in Emma's featherbrain, and she'd always had it in for me."

"And where were you on the night of the murder?"

"At home . . . with my feel-good pills and a bottle of wine."

Molly stared at her reflection in the bathroom mirror and shivered, suddenly feeling cold. How was she going to account for her time to the cops when all she could remember was pouring the last of the wine, then waking in the morning, still dressed, on the living room couch?

Then she shook her head. There was no way she was going to let it get that far. No way she was going to wait for the cops to come after her. There was, after all, a better direction in which to steer them.

She wiped her face with a brown paper towel and smoothed her hair back. Then she stepped out into the newsroom and headed straight for Jennifer Reed's office. The anchorwoman was taking off her jacket when Molly looked in.

"Jennifer?"

"Yes?"

Molly closed the door. "I don't know exactly how we're going to go about this, how we're going to explain ourselves, but we've got to tell the cops everything now."

"Like what?" Jennifer settled herself into her chair and swiveled around to look into the big magnifying mirror that she brought out of her bottom drawer.

"Like what?" Molly echoed, staring bemused at the anchorwoman. "Didn't Pete Norcross call you in to do a newsbrief on Emma Kane's murder?"

"Yes." Jennifer's brow furrowed. "So?"

Molly sat down in the chair across the desk from Jennifer Reed. Was Jennifer on Valium or what? She peered at the anchorwoman over the top of the magnifying mirror.

"Hey, Jen, wake up. Diane, Janey, you, me—and now Emma. We can't keep quiet any longer."

"You think the wacko shot Emma?" Jennifer pushed aside the mirror and reached across the desk for the wire copy that Pete Norcross had delivered to her earlier. She scanned the wire copy, her eyes blinking. "I don't see anything here . . . I mean, Emma doesn't have any connection with us."

"Except she was Jack's wife." Molly retorted, determinedly pursuing the point.

The anchorwoman shrugged. "It's not the first thought that came into my mind. Look, this is a murder, a *shooting*, and there was another person in the house with Emma Kane.

She wasn't *alone* like we were." Jennifer laid aside the wire copy and shook her head. "I don't know, Molly. It doesn't sound right. Guys like this wacko, this Peeping Tom who didn't lay a finger on us, don't usually start shooting people."

"Maybe he shot Emma because there were two of them, and he wasn't expecting two people in the house."

Jennifer paled under her makeup.

"We should go to the cops, Jen."

The anchorwoman reached for the mirror again and then, taking a deep breath, said: "Listen, I've got to go on with the newsbrief in a few minutes, and I'm not stalling because you may have a point, but let's not get involved until we have more information. Let's see what the cops say later today. If they point the finger at some unknown intruder then I'm with you."

A sudden sharp rap at the door made Molly jump as Pete Norcross poked his head into Jennifer's office. "On in five." He pointed at Jennifer. Then he noticed Molly. "There you are. I've got you a piece of the action, girl. We've just had word they've ID'd the second victim." He paused to look at his wrist, where he'd scribbled something in dark ink. "The name's Tony Salerno. In his late twenties. Apparently a student at Villanova law school. He was shot in the head. Get to it, Heskell." He grinned at her as if he'd just announced that she was a lottery winner and disappeared, slamming the door closed again.

Across the desk, Jennifer appeared to be grinning. "See what I mean? There's a whole heap of shit here that just doesn't fit in with our wacko, Molly." She took an eyebrow pencil out of her makeup purse and stared again into her mirror. "Look at it this way: Look at the other victim. Salerno, right? A lawyer, name ends in a vowel . . . he's shot in the head. Could be a Mob thing."

Molly rose wearily from the chair. "I think you're deluding yourself, Jennifer. The cops should have all the facts, and you're just putting off what you know has to be done. It's not our job to say what's relevant and what isn't."

"I'm not saying it is," Jennifer countered firmly. "But the cops don't need to know all the facts today, and I'm certainly not going to stir up any trouble for myself until I know more." She put away her magnifying mirror and closed her desk drawer with a slam that sounded as final as the tone of her voice.

Then she got to her feet, staring at Molly, and added: "As for Emma Kane, I bet the police have a whole list of suspects with more motive than our wacko for wanting to see her dead."

Molly watched as Jennifer swept out of her office, struggling to quell the wave of panic that threatened to engulf her. The anchorwoman's parting words had been less damning than the news director's. But there was little doubt in Molly's mind as to what Jennifer had meant. Everyone knew Molly had hated Emma Kane. So how long would it take for the cops to find out?

11

Lewis woke late and knew it was going to be a bad day. The sun forcing its way into his bedroom through the thin, unlined drapes told him it had to be close to noon. He eased his head off the pillow to look at his alarm clock and felt the room spinning. He lay back and groaned in pain. His head felt heavy and his eyes were itching.

His allergies had kicked in the day before and he knew he was going to go through a couple weeks of hell. He knew already, by the way the day had started, that he would have to call in sick again tonight.

He reached for a Kleenex from the box on his nightstand and dabbed at his eyes and nose, cursing softly under his breath. Going to Emma Kane's home the previous night had been a mistake. He had felt as sick as a dog all evening but just before eight, fortified by a megadose of antihistamines, he had suddenly felt clearheaded enough to drive to the Main Line.

He had pulled into the service driveway of the Kane house, killing the truck lights as he followed the dimly lit road to the back of the house where he had found a cluster of trees for cover. From his seat he'd had a perfect view through a huge bay window into what appeared to be some kind of breakfast room, just off the kitchen. It was here he'd first spotted Emma in a short, pretty little bathrobe, moving around, preparing some late-night snack. He'd watched her open the refrigerator and had felt his first moment of unease when he saw her place two glasses on a tray. She had poured some juice into both. Moments later he'd seen the man walk into the kitchen. A big guy with a shock of longish, dark hair, also wearing a bathrobe.

First had come the severe jolt of disappointment. Then, as he'd watched them sit down at the kitchen table, another thought had entered his mind. He'd reached for his camcorder and set it up, wedging it gingerly into place so that it rested on the dashboard and gear shift of the truck. Always thinking, he'd muttered to himself, grinning at the thought of how useful a videotape of Emma Kane with another man could prove when he finally got to Emma.

He forced himself to sit up in bed as his head began to throb with a dull ache and he glanced over to his nightstand, wondering where he'd put his medication. He'd taken too much of it last night, that was for sure. It was the antihistamines that had made him feel so drowsy, sitting in the car seat, watching Emma and her lover boy. Not that there'd been much hanky-panky going on in the kitchen. Watching Emma holding out a plate of crackers to her lover was the last thing he remembered seeing . . . until the thump on the roof of the truck had jolted his eyes open again.

Lewis snatched at another Kleenex, dabbing at his eyes as his body temperature rose several degrees. He threw off his blankets.

The thump had made him wet his pants. He remembered that okay. That, and the fact that everything had suddenly seemed so bright. As if a dozen klieg lights had suddenly been switched on. He remembered pulling the camcorder off the dashboard and flinging it onto the seat beside him. The dampness of his seat had been little discomfort compared to the heart-pounding terror he'd felt thinking that the faces of a half-dozen cops would appear surrounding his truck and ordering him out with his hands in the air.

He'd started wheezing, his chest constricting with pain, and then, just as suddenly, he was sitting in the dark again and everything around him was still and quiet. He'd sat wet and terror-stricken for at least five minutes, staring into the darkness, noting that the kitchen and den were dark. No sign of Emma or lover boy, anywhere. Had he imagined the flash of light and the thump on his car roof?

He didn't think so. On the furious ride back to the city, he'd figured that maybe a cat or some raccoon-type animal had jumped out of the branches onto the truck. But now he wasn't so sure. The thump had sounded heavier and sharper than any animal landing on its paws.

He slid out of his bed and stood up, holding onto his nightstand, afraid that he was going to fall facedown onto the floor. Then he reached for the plaid bathrobe lying at the foot of the bed.

The damn thing had sounded heavy. It had probably put a dent in his roof.

He made his way downstairs and paused in the kitchen to fill the kettle with water. In the pantry he looked for some of his favorite herbal tea. Then, placing the sachet in a big heavy mug, he opened the kitchen door into the garage. Shivering slightly in the cooler air he stared at the roof, allowing his eyes to get accustomed to the dim light.

But even from the kitchen doorway he could see something caught in his roof rack, sticking out like a branch or a piece of tubing. A pipe of some kind.

He took a couple of paces to the truck and reached up for the object, struggling for a few seconds to free it from the rack. His fingers grasped something cold and metallic and he pulled at it, recognizing what it was just a split second before his hand tightened around the handle of a short-barreled revolver.

12

Kate had just settled into the corner of a deep couch with her notebook and pen when a flash of movement outside the living room windows caught her eye.

She glanced up to see a sleek dark green Jaguar glide to a stop outside the Kane mansion, and she immediately jumped to her feet. It had to be Jack Kane. Who else?

Before she got to the window, Kane was already at the front door, taking the steps in two easy strides, nodding curtly to the uniformed cop who stood aside without a word.

From where she stood, Kate only had to turn her head for a clear view through the arched doorway as Jack Kane entered the foyer. At the same time she saw Harry coming down the stairs to meet him.

She edged closer to the doorway and took the opportunity to size up the victim's husband. From the framed pictures she'd seen on the piano she'd been prepared for a tall, handsome man in his late forties, but she saw now that the picture had not accurately conveyed either his good looks or his size. Jack Kane was a big man, just over six feet tall, she figured, and powerfully built, with broad shoulders and a strong, handsome face that looked wind-bronzed and healthy. He towered over Harry as the detective-sergeant introduced himself. "You got here fast, Mr. Kane," Harry added.

"I made it a point to do so, detective." Kane's tone was clipped and Kate caught the flash of a heavy gold link bracelet as he glanced at his watch. Twenty thousand dollars' worth of solid gold Rolex, Kate figured, her eyes skipping to onyx and gold cuff links, which peeked from below the sleeves of an impeccably tailored light gray suit. Impeccable was the word, all right, she thought. Right down to the hand-painted silk tie, which was curiously, she thought, still knotted at his collar. What kind of a man made this kind of trip without loosening his tie, for heaven's sake?

She hovered in the doorway, her attention momentarily distracted as Mike walked down the stairs followed by the deputy coroner and two aides carrying one of the black body bags atop a stretcher.

Harry cleared his throat. "Mr. Kane, I'm sorry to have to ask you this, but we'd appreciate you making a positive identification of your wife—if you can do it now."

As Jack Kane nodded, his face a grim and immobile mask, Kate reflected that Harry's tone was somewhat deferential considering the remarks he'd made after speaking to the TV executive earlier on the phone. "He'll answer all our questions when he gets here," Harry had mimicked Jack Kane's response, then had added his own interpretation. "When he's had an hour or two to figure out the best story."

She had been a little surprised at how swiftly both Harry and Mike had zeroed in on Jack Kane. He appeared high on the list, if for no other reason than because of the lack of evidence of a forcible entry. Kate had wanted to ask Harry about his list of suspects, but there had been little time. He'd been preoccupied with the crime scene and the arrival of the deputy coroner. There had been a moment of excitement when Tom Lansing found a wallet in the kitchen and ascertained it belonged to the male victim, finally identified as Tony Salerno. The wallet had contained a student library card for Villanova University library and a driver's license giving Salerno's age as twenty-nine and a home address in South Philly.

Moments later one of the fingerprint technicians had summoned Harry to the kitchen, where he had pointed out that the handles on the doors leading from kitchen to mud room and from mud room into the garage were clean.

"No partials, no smudges, no prints of any kind," he'd remarked. "That's pretty strange. These would be the most-used doors in the house. You'd expect, at least, the owner's prints on these but it looks like these were wiped clean deliberately."

"Unless the maid was in yesterday," Harry had suggested.

"Well, if she was, she missed every other door handle and knob in this kitchen. There's prints all over those," the technician had retorted drily.

Gradually the house had emptied. The crime lab technicians had left with the collected evidence: dozens of plastic Baggies containing dirt that had been tracked in, and hairs and fibers and blood samples that had been found in Emma Kane's bedroom.

The Baggies would be delivered to the state crime lab near Allentown. The rest of the evidence, the dozens of pictures that had been taken of the crime scene, would be handed to Harry. Every stain and splotch and spatter of blood had been photographed and videotaped. Ditto for the bodies and the salient areas of the bedroom and master bathroom. Now, only a handful of technicians remained on the grounds.

Harry gestured to the body bag and motioned for Jack Kane to approach the stretcher. The noise of the zipper echoed gruesomely in the foyer.

Jack Kane's eyes widened, and Kate noticed that his lips clamped together tightly as he stared into the bag. Then he nodded. "Yes, that's Emma."

Harry gave him a moment before walking him over to the second body bag that had been brought down after Emma's. This time Jack Kane shook his head. "That's my bathrobe, but I'm afraid I can't help you with an ID."

He looked, as Kate would later recall, totally stricken as he stared at the two black body bags on the floor of his elegant foyer. Then abruptly he turned towards Harry. "Can you tell me what happened? You said she was shot but . . . my God . . . you didn't say anything about her face."

Harry took a deep breath. "I'm sorry about that, Mr. Kane." He paused. "And I'm afraid we can't tell you very much more at the moment. But maybe you can help us."

"Of course." Kane nodded, glancing from one to the other before his eyes came to rest on Kate in the doorway. Harry followed his gaze and identified Kate. "She's here with me. Mrs. McCusker is an author—"

Jack Kane stepped towards her, and the grim look in his eyes softened momentarily. "I know who she is," he interrupted. "*Root of All Evil*, right?" He extended his hand to her and Kate covered her surprise by responding to his firm, cool grip. "We covered the Basinger case at Channel Seven when I was there." He nodded as if the memory was a good one. "Your book was a helluva good read, Mrs. McCusker." He paused and she saw his eyes glancing down at the wedding band on her left hand before he added: "You jumped on this one, very fast."

Kate couldn't tell immediately if the comment was one of approval or censure but then Harry interrupted their exchange and said, "Actually, Mrs. McCusker was already working on a new project about Main Line crime. Do you have any objections if she stays?"

Bless you, Harry, she thought as Jack Kane shook his head and said, "Let's talk in here." He indicated with an outstretched hand that they move from the foyer into what Kate recognized as the game room, and as Mike led the way to a sitting area between the pool table and a magnificent stone fireplace, Jack Kane waited till last like a gracious host.

Then, he paced across to a mahogany wet bar. "Excuse me, but I'm going to have a drink."

Kate sat down beside the fireplace, and while Jack Kane filled his glass, took the opportunity to look at him more closely. She found it interesting that he made no excuses or apologies, like most people would, for pouring himself a drink so early in the day. Not even a passing reference to the shock over his wife's death. She had the feeling that Jack Kane wasn't in the habit of explaining himself to people.

When he'd filled his glass he walked to a chair across from where Kate sat. "I'm going to be very honest with you, detective," he started, directing himself to Harry as he sat down. "More honest than any attorney would allow me to be, I'm sure. But I'm going to give you all the facts so that you can eliminate me as quickly as possible and get on with finding the person who did kill my wife—"

"So, maybe you can answer our first question," Mike interrupted and Kate heard the note of impatience in his voice. "It's the one Sergeant Holmsby asked you on the phone: When did you last see or speak to your wife?"

Watch out, thought Kate as Jack Kane leaned forward with his hands circling his heavy crystal glass. The movement seemed designed to shut out Mike. Kane didn't even glance at the younger investigator. He stared directly at Harry and said: "Yesterday. I saw her yesterday afternoon. I drove home yesterday."

Harry nodded without expressing surprise at the admission. "That was unusual, wasn't it? Driving home from New York on a Thursday afternoon?"

"Yes, it was. Very. I haven't been home much in the last several months." He hesitated and cleared his throat. "But Emma and I were talking on the phone . . . arguing really, and I decided to drive down to resolve things face-to-face."

There was a moment's silence and Kate could sense Harry was grappling with this bombshell of information. Jack Kane sensed it, too. He glanced fleetingly at Kate as he sipped his drink, and the look in his eye told her he knew he'd thrown them a hot potato.

"Okay." Mike was first to break the silence. "You decided to drive down. You hung up on your wife and jumped into your car and drove a hundred miles to finish your argument. You must have been pretty steamed to do that."

"That's not exactly what I said." He smiled briefly and coldly at Mike, then turned his attention back to Harry. "Trust me, detective, neither of you have to put words in my mouth because I'm probably going to hang myself without your help. But I wasn't steamed. I was frustrated."

"Over what?"

Kate studied Jack Kane's calm demeanor as he placed his glass on the table in front of him. He was seated less than six feet away from her, close enough for her to catch the sudden familiar scent of the dark gold liquor in the glass. It was Chivas—Steve's favorite.

"Over what?" Kane repeated. "Specifically, because

Emma was stalling over signing off on a contract of sale on the house. It was a good offer. You don't get many on a house like this and she'd had the contract since the weekend."

He paused and excused himself to leave the room. When he returned a few minutes later, he was holding the document in his hand. He handed it to Harry. "She was sitting on this. So, I was annoyed because she was dithering. Emma had been making excuses for the last eight months."

"Excuses for what?"

"For not selling the house, for not moving to New York."

Kate recalled Betsy Wright's comment about Emma's reluctance to leave the Main Line as Harry, glancing around the room, asked: "Can you blame her for wanting to stay put?"

"Of course not. She had a life here and I give her credit for that. I wasn't around much even when I worked at Channel Seven, but Emma was good about doing things on her own with her own friends, and she had plenty of them." Jack Kane paused and picked up his glass again. "But instead of telling me what was on her mind, she kept dithering."

"Dithering?" Harry repeated. "Can you explain that?"

"Yes I can." Jack Kane nodded. "Take this week, for example. On Monday she was very excited about the offer we'd got on this house and she drove up to New York to look at properties. She actually liked one townhouse in particular." He smiled. "She started talking about redecorating and renovating before we even finished looking at the place. But yesterday one of the realtors here called me and told me Emma had not returned the signed contract. I called her to find out what was going on and she then tells me she's really not so sure about the New York townhouse and she thinks it's the wrong time of the year to move." Kane paused and shrugged. "It's tough dealing with that sort of reasoning, or lack of reasoning, I should say."

"So, you decided to deal with it face to face?" Mike got to his feet and walked to a spot behind Harry's chair presumably, thought Kate, so that Jack Kane would answer this one to his face. "It sounds like you'd pretty much had it with her dithering. Is that what you're trying to tell us?"

"Not trying, detective." Jack Kane smiled, apparently aware of what Mike was implying. "I'm saying that was the case. I wanted to get things resolved. I'm tired of living in a shoebox in New York and there was absolutely no reason for Emma to stall now. I'd tried to convince her to sell this house even before my move to New York. I suggested it after our daughter left for college. I mean, for heaven's sake, look around you, it was really way too big for just the two of us."

But such a perfect size for three, Kate thought, struggling with a sudden urge to laugh.

"So, Mr. Kane," Harry continued, "what happened after that?" He paused. "What time did you arrive?"

"About four." Kane took a deep breath and a sip of Scotch. "Yes, about four. Emma was upstairs packing . . . She was going to a spa in Arizona with her friend, Betsy, so I followed her around while she got her packing done. But I couldn't get her to sit down and discuss anything sensibly. Finally, I told her that the contract had to be signed and the house was going to be sold."

"Just like that?" Mike raised an eyebrow.

"No, not just like that." Kane shook his head. "I told her she still had plenty of time to decide about New York. We didn't have to buy the townhouse. In fact, I said if she really wanted to stay here on the Main Line we could split the assets and buy separate homes."

"Sounds like you were suggesting divorce, Mr. Kane," Mike persisted.

"It was Emma's choice to make."

"Did you want a divorce?"

"I wasn't going to commute on weekends."

"Did you want a divorce, Mr. Kane?"

"Look," he said finally. "It's not something I really thought about. There was no need for a divorce. The truth is Emma and I had already been going our separate ways for a long time. I didn't interfere with her spending and she gave me a long leash. If you start digging around in my personal affairs, which I'm sure you will, you'll find all sorts of marital misdemeanors: flings, dalliances, affairs." He paused to loosen his tie and undo the top button of his shirt. At last, thought Kate, wondering if it was a nervous gesture, but even as she stared at him she realized he was staring right back, his eyes meeting hers in a cool, unflinching glance. "I meet a lot of smart, beautiful women in my business." He turned his attention back to Harry. "And I happen to enjoy their company. Sometimes, at the end of a long day, it's hard to resist temptation. Emma understood." He paused and shrugged. "Or at least seemed to, most of the time. It was an arrangement that worked quite well for both of us."

Kate crossed her legs and leaned back in her chair, staring with even greater interest at Kane. She didn't know many men who would have admitted openly to philandering without at least trying to excuse or explain their behavior by blaming a bad marriage or an indifferent wife.

"For both of you?" Mike prodded. "You mean your wife had her flings, too?"

"God, no!" Jack Kane laughed suddenly, sounding genuinely amused. "I didn't mean that. I meant she was fairly open-minded about my—"

"The young man who was shot with your wife was found upstairs." Harry interjected wearily.

"In the bedroom?" Kane looked surprised and shocked. "When I arrived he was outside fixing something in the backyard . . . the sprinklers, I think."

"You said you couldn't ID him." Mike was right in there again. "Your wife didn't introduce you?"

Jack Kane looked at him with an amused glance. "No, she didn't. But she did point him out and she told me that she was going to offer him room and board in exchange for doing work around the house."

"Room and board?" Mike weighed in again. "What did you take that to mean?"

Kane's mouth twisted into a half-grimace. "I took that to mean, Fuck you, Jack."

"I beg your pardon?" Mike leaned forward, resting his arm on the back of Harry's chair.

"It was Emma's way of saying that even though I'd made her fire the couple who took care of the house, she could find a way around that."

Mike raised an eyebrow. "Was this something else you argued about?"

"Not really." Jack shook his head. "I told her about six months ago that it was a waste of money maintaining a house of this size for just one person. The bills were enormous. So I told her to get rid of the housekeepers and I told her no more redecorating. Emma didn't like that much. She loved spending money and I had never put her on a budget before."

No kidding, thought Kate, the image of Emma Kane's bulging closets flashing into her mind. She'd taken a peek earlier at the three oversized closets, had noted the designer outfits hung by alphabetical order from Adolfo to Yves St. Laurent. Had started to count the sweaters and tops in dozens of different shades but had stopped when she reached fifty-two in the first closet . . . and had stared open-mouthed at the racks of shoes, pumps, sandals, and evening slippers that hung on tidy shoe trees on the closet floors.

"So you accepted her explanation about the young guy in your backyard?"

"Yes."

"He was wearing your bathrobe."

Jack Kane shrugged. "I saw."

Mike shifted his weight from one foot to the other. "What about you, Mr. Kane? Are you involved with anyone at the moment?"

Jack Kane glanced briefly at Kate. "No. Unless you count Seth Reilly, the owner of WorldMedia." He cracked a small smile, returning his attention to Harry. "Launching a new news network doesn't leave much time for romance."

"What about Gabriella Grant?"

Kane looked puzzled, then amused. "Why are you asking about Gabriella?"

"Why not?" Mike said quietly. "You and she have been linked, haven't you?"

Kate thought Mike's question was clever. He was assuming, no doubt, that there had been more gossip items about the couple than just the one they'd seen upstairs.

But Kane's eyes narrowed immediately. "Come on, detective. You're talking about one *gossip* item." He shook his head. "The one about us leaving a party together, right? Well, there was nothing to that. Miss Grant asked me for a ride home, that's all."

"Let's get back to yesterday afternoon," Mike said quickly. "Did you get angry with your wife?"

"Yes."

"Did it get physical?"

"No. We never got physically violent." Jack Kane stared at Mike.

"You never got angry enough to throw things around?"

Kate thought about the mess of broken glass on the dressing room floor and knew where Mike was heading. Jack Kane seemed to know, too.

"If you're asking about the broken glass in the bathroom, that's a bottle of lotion. Emma asked me to unscrew the top for her. It was very tight and it slipped out of my hands."

"Just the one?" Mike persisted.

Jack Kane's brow creased into a puzzled frown. "Yes. Just the one."

Mike looked down at the contract, which Harry still held in his hands. "But in the end, after all of this arguing, your wife didn't sign the contract?"

"She said she would."

"But she didn't."

"She said she'd drop it off at the realtor's on her way to the airport."

"But you weren't certain she would, were you?"

Jack Kane shrugged. "I think she realized there was no point in stalling any longer but it just wouldn't have been Emma's style to sign there and then. That would look as if she was caving in too easily." He leaned back in his chair.

"So, what time did you leave?" Mike's voice was hard now.

"I guess it was a little before six."

"And you drove straight to New York?"

"No. I stopped in a bar for something to eat. I guess it was about eight when I got on the road again."

"You had a few drinks?"

"A couple."

Harry leaned forward in his chair. "Look, Mr. Kane, we've got some idea . . . We understand how frustrating it must have been for you. You seem to have been patient for a very long time but everyone has a breaking point—"

"Forget it, detective," Jack Kane cut in abruptly. "If that's how you understand it then you're way off course. Like I said, I believed Emma and I had agreed on the contract. I stopped for a drink, a bite to eat, and then I got on the road. I was home in time to watch Fox News at ten."

"That's not much of an alibi."

Jack Kane shook his head. "I guess not, but I didn't know I'd be needing one."

"Do you own a gun, Mr. Kane?" Harry asked.

"No. Never have."

"Did your wife have one?"

"Certainly not." There was a brief silence before he spoke again, looking at Harry: "I didn't kill my wife, detective. I know you're good at what you do and I know you're going to discover that for yourself. I'm just afraid you're going to waste a lot of valuable time looking in the wrong place."

Harry nodded absently. "And do you have any ideas about the *right* place, Mr. Kane? Did your wife have a lot of enemies?"

Jack Kane sighed. "I don't think so. She annoyed a few shoe salesmen and interior decorators in her time but . . ." He paused. "I made enough enemies for the both of us."

"Oh?" Mike raised an eyebrow.

Kane's jaw clenched. "I'm in a very competitive business, detective. And, these are cutthroat times. I've had a few successes recently that have, let's say, displeased some of our competitors."

"Are you saying that someone may have killed your wife to get even with you?"

Jack Kane shook his head. "I'm saying I can't imagine anyone hating Emma enough to kill her. I'm just struggling with the same questions you are, detective." He got to his feet as if to signal that their conversation was over, and Kate found herself thinking about the way he had kept control of the interview from the start. It had seemed to come naturally to him, and she suspected that's how it was in most situations involving Jack Kane.

"Okay, Mr. Kane." Harry stood, too. "We're going to need one more thing right now. I'm going to have to ask you to come with us to Bryn Mawr hospital so that we can take blood and hair and tissue samples."

"Fine." Kane nodded. "But I'll drive myself."

"Excuse me?" Mike looked shocked for the first time that afternoon.

"I said I'd like to drive there myself."

"We'd prefer you didn't. We're going to have a search warrant here to impound your car within the next hour. It's the green Jaguar out front, right?"

Kane nodded curtly. Then he said, "I'll take Emma's car. And you don't need to go for a search warrant. I'll give my consent to any search you want to make, either here or in New York, wherever. I want you to get on with this case." He ran his fingers through his hair and stared at Harry. "But I don't want to ride out of here escorted by two detectives. There's a crowd of TV and newspaper people outside the gates. There's going to be enough innuendo and rumors in their reports as it is. I don't want to fuel them up anymore, and I think we can avoid it. Unless, that is, you are planning to take me into custody."

Kate was temporarily floored, recognizing his words as a challenge. Either Jack Kane was a very knowledgeable newsman who, having been on the other side of situations like this, knew exactly what his rights and limits were. Or he was being extraordinarily arrogant. Surely he realized he'd said enough to justify being taken into custody for twenty-four hours, at least.

It seemed that in the next moment the same thought occurred to him because his tone softened as he added, "I'll do whatever you need me to do, detective. I'll help you in any way I can but I would like to go and pick up my daughter at the airport. Her plane is due in at seven this evening." He hesitated. "Please, detective, I'd like to be there for her."

Harry stared at Jack Kane. "Are you going to bring her back here?"

"Of course, if that's all right. I have to make funeral arrangements, too. I plan to be around for a few days."

Harry nodded abruptly. "Very well. We'll meet you at the hospital. I'll let you know when we're ready to leave."

With a final nod, Harry followed Mike and Kate outside to the flagstone patio overlooking the backyard.

The younger detective waited till they had walked to the back of the house, where a couple of uniformed officers and three technicians were still checking out the grounds. Then he turned on Harry: "I can't believe you let him get away with that. You're going to let him waltz off to the airport?"

Harry snorted. "What did you want me to do? Slap handcuffs on him and read him his rights? Right now it's to our advantage that we can deal with him without the interference of some big-shot attorney, so let's just take it step by step."

"I would have liked to see him at the police station in an interrogation room instead of sipping an expensive Scotch while he answered our questions." Mike paused and shook his head in disbelief. "He gave us the whole story, the whole damn story. The only thing he left out was the bit where he threw the cap into both of them."

"Yeah." Harry laughed. "Exactly. And right now we don't have a single item of evidence that even suggests he made that leap. We've a ways to go here, partner—" Harry broke off as a shout from across the backyard interrupted his reply.

"Hey, sarge! Want to come and look over here?" A uniformed officer beckoned at Harry, pointing to a cluster of trees beside the service driveway.

"What is it?" Harry yelled back.

"Tire tracks." The officer walked towards them. "The vehicle was parked there for a while. Looks like somebody was watching the house, sarge."

13

The early evening brought a chill to the air, but still it was warmer outside than it had been in the morgue. Carrying a small Styrofoam cup of coffee from the hospital cafeteria, Kate made her way to a bench outside the main doors of Bryn Mawr hospital, and ignoring the cigarette butts that lay strewn all around the bench, she took several long deep gulps of air before reaching into her purse for her notebook.

She had not gagged in the morgue but she had felt faint and light-headed. Annoyed with herself because she'd always thought she was made of stronger stuff, she had dismissed the sensation of nausea as hunger pangs. She had not, after all, eaten since breakfast. So she had stayed with Harry while Art Johnson had worked on Tony Salerno. She had remained in the room, her eyes roaming over the ceiling and walls, while she focussed on the snatches of conversation between the two men as they attempted to reconstruct the moment of death.

At the house, Art had given Harry the roughest of estimates. Death had occurred ten to twelve hours before Betsy Wright's discovery of the bodies that morning. Harry had put this together with Betsy's information about her phone calls, estimating the time as somewhere between eight in the evening and around ten, when Betsy had received no answer either to her call or the message she'd left on the machine. Neither method was accurate or foolproof but it would have to do for now, Harry had said, moving around the table to neatly block her view of Salerno.

Tony Salerno had been six feet two inches tall, one hundred and eighty pounds—all muscle. "Difficult to imagine that he wouldn't have put up some kind of struggle," Harry remarked.

"Especially with someone smaller and shorter," Art agreed. The .38 caliber bullet, which he handed Harry, and which had embedded itself in Tony Salerno's skull, shattering the bone, had entered at a slightly upward angle. Nor had Art found any significant evidence under Salerno's fingernails: no skin tissue or fibers to indicate that Salerno had even touched his killer, even though the gun had been held to his head. Harry had surmised that the killer had possibly taken Salerno by surprise.

Kate had hovered in the doorway, ready to bolt, as Art had then removed various internal organs and weighed them like some demonic butcher. Salerno's stomach had contained partially digested cheese and crackers, which Art estimated had been consumed no more than an hour or so before death. Even Kate knew that wasn't very helpful and didn't take them much further than the rough estimates unless they could pinpoint the time Salerno had consumed the cheese and crackers.

By the time Art turned his attention to Emma Kane, the little cotton balls soaked in Kate's expensive White Linen perfume and inserted in her nostrils—a little trick Harry had shown her—were beginning to lose some of their magic. And when Kate saw Emma brought out of the freezer, her bloodied body laid out on the slab, she finally admitted she'd had more than her fill of the sight and smell of death.

She left abruptly when Art had started poking around with something sharp and long and gleaming in what he had described as a ventral wound in the abdomen. She'd gleaned sufficient atmosphere and information from Artie Johnson for one day. If she needed more detail for the book, she could get it from Art over a drink in more cheerful surroundings.

She sipped her coffee and flipped to a fresh page in the notebook even as she heard footsteps on the path behind her.

"Kate McCusker?"

The voice startled her and she glanced up to find herself staring at Jack Kane, his jacket slung over his shoulder and his shirtsleeves rolled up. She glanced around for Mike. He had met up with Kane at the hospital lab while she had driven with Harry. But he was nowhere in sight now, and she assumed that he'd gone to join the duo in the morgue.

She turned her attention back to Jack Kane, staring at the Band-Aid on the inside of his left arm.

He followed her glance and smiled wearily. "I'm not sure I've done the right thing. I guess I should have called my attorney."

Kate didn't answer immediately. She suspected Kane was about to pump her for some information. For sure he'd want to know how Harry and Mike had reacted to his statements. But the question didn't come.

Kate cleared her throat. "So, why didn't you?" she asked.

He shrugged. "I suppose because I still believe that if you're innocent and have nothing to hide there's no reason to scream for an attorney." He smiled wanly. "Not very smart of me, perhaps."

Kate shrugged, recalling that he had seemed smart enough back at the house. She stared at him as he rolled down his shirtsleeves. Up close, his face looked more lived in but not in a haggard way. More as if the lines and wrinkles around his eyes were the result of years of ready laughter and smiles rather than age.

Then she lowered her eyes and stared at his hands as his fingers worked to fasten the cuff links. From where she sat she could now see letters etched in the gold circling the onyx. They spelled out Bulgari. Another fifteen hundred, she thought absently. The man's wrists were worth more than a family car.

He slipped into his jacket and brushed down the lapels. "It's a strange thing," he said, his words breaking into her thoughts. "I've spent my life in the news business covering crashes, fires, homicides, major accidents, and you imagine you know everything there is to know about human tragedy, yet when it touches your own life, you realize there's just nothing that could have prepared you for the shock of it."

"I know exactly what you mean," Kate agreed.

He stared at her quizzically, and then a sudden flicker of realization registered in his eyes. "Of course," he said softly. "I remember now. I remember the story about your husband. That was just before I left Philadelphia."

"Yes." She nodded. "A year ago . . . A drunk plowed into him on the Schuylkill."

He nodded, his eyes searching her face as if looking for the emotion that had been lacking in her voice. Then, he said, "But life does go on, right, Kate? It must get better. There can't be anywhere to go but up from something like this."

She studied his face for a moment, reflecting that this was the closest he'd come to showing any distress all day. And as understated as it was, it struck her as genuine. She laid a hand on his arm.

"Of course. Like they say, time heals . . ." She smiled awkwardly as his eyes lingered on her for a moment longer. Then he held out his hand to her. "I have to head out to the airport now. I expect I'll be seeing you again, though." He squeezed her fingers lightly.

"I expect you will," she agreed.

"I hope so," he said simply but in a tone of voice that left her wondering what it would be like to meet him under different circumstances.

She watched him walk to the main road and tried to picture Jack Kane standing in his wife's bathroom, his finger on the trigger of a .38 as he pumped bullets into her face.

But somehow the picture wouldn't gel. Not then, and not later, when, seated in a booth at O'Malley's, she listened to Harry and Mike Travis attempting to place Jack Kane at the crime scene.

Mike tapped the table with his index finger. "So, here's how it went down: He left the house after arguing with Emma, stopped at a bar like he said, had a couple of Scotches, and then decided he wasn't going to drive back empty-handed. See, that's the first thing that doesn't jibe.

He doesn't strike me as the kind of guy who'd let a woman call the shots."

He paused as the waitress set three plates in front of them. Kate stared at the giant hamburger on her plate with longing. On the way to O'Malley's she'd wondered if she'd be able to eat a thing despite her hunger. But the moment she'd slid into the booth and taken her first sip of Chardonnay all her appetite had surprisingly returned. She'd ordered the All-American, a burger with everything on it. All she had to do was smother her French fries with ketchup.

Mike stared at her as she lifted the giant concoction to her mouth. Then he continued. "So, he drives back to the house and walks upstairs, and that's when he discovers the real reason why Emma has been dithering. Suddenly it hits him: She doesn't want to move to New York because she's got a new man here. And, to add insult to injury, lover boy is wearing his bathrobe. That's when he lost it."

Kate wiped her mouth with a napkin and put her burger down on the plate, her exterior calmness masking the sudden surge of annoyance inside her. She doubted that Mike or Harry had ever quizzed a suspect as direct and forthright as Jack Kane. She could not recollect one question that had fazed him or made him stumble or stutter . . . or look away guiltily. Yet none of this apparently counted in his favor. All Mike and Harry seemed interested in was tailoring a scenario that would allow them to nail Kane as the killer.

She took a deep breath. "So, you're saying he got upstairs, caught them in the act, lost it, and reached into his inside pocket for the handy-dandy revolver he keeps there for just such an occasion.

"And then when he realized what he'd done, he ran downstairs and was so panicked he forgot to consider that with all the doors and windows secured the finger of suspicion would point at the only other person with access to the house, but was not so panicked by the time he got to the kitchen because then he remembered to wipe off his prints from all the door handles leading to the garage."

Mike's eyes narrowed in the silence that followed her words. He looked taken aback for a moment but then abruptly and dismissively he turned his attention to Harry. "Like I said, I think he came down here to resolve things. I don't think he had any intention of driving back to New York without the signed contract. That's how I think it went down. He was here. In the area, in the house. He was steamed enough as it was, and then to catch his wife in the act—"

Harry took a gulp of his beer and belched. "But he didn't catch them in the act. There was no evidence of semen, no indication that intercourse had taken place."

Mike rolled his eyes. "The Jacuzzi was filled, maybe even bubbling away; Emma and Tony were in their bathrobes. I'd say they were getting ready for some serious foreplay."

Harry took another bite of his cheeseburger. "Which begs the question: If they were getting ready for this serious foreplay, what brought Salerno out of the bedroom?"

Kate noticed that Mike hadn't even started on his cheeseburger. He looked tense and preoccupied. "Maybe he heard the garage door opening. Maybe Emma heard something and sent him out to check—and he ran right into Kane."

"Okay." Harry nodded, reaching into his pocket for a pen. He slid his cocktail napkin into the center of the table and drew a square on it. "Okay, this is the upstairs landing and here's the door of the bedroom." He made a check mark on one of the sides of the square. "Over here, a distance of about six feet, I'd say, is where we found Salerno. By the intercom." Harry marked the spot with an X. "So, why's Salerno by the intercom if Kane was about to walk through the bedroom door?"

Harry pushed the napkin towards Mike. "That's what puzzles me."

"Okay." Mike threw up both hands in the air in a sign of surrender. "What's the alternative? Salerno's standing at the intercom because someone rang the doorbell. In which case it's got to be someone he feels comfortable about because he lets them in and lets them walk upstairs and right up towards him, and he probably doesn't even see the gun till it's too late, till it's sticking into his head." Mike laughed. "And that certainly rules out Kane, doesn't it?"

"I would say." Harry nodded. "No lover boy is going to stand there waiting for an irate husband—with or without a gun—to walk right up to him."

"Especially not when he's wearing the irate husband's bathrobe." Kate laughed, sensing that the tide had turned a little. "And how would the tire tracks in the backyard fit in with Kane, anyway? Somehow I don't think he's the type to lurk outside his own windows."

Harry shrugged. "They may not fit in at all. The lab will check out the lifted tire prints but it could be they were left by a landscaping truck, someone trimming the trees . . . The point is, if Salerno let in the killer, it opens up a whole array of possibilities, from a malevolent pizza delivery boy to a scorned girlfriend."

"But Emma Kane was the target," Mike reminded him quietly.

"Yeah." Harry grunted. "That's why I'm still leaning towards Kane. I think he's a clever prick and I think he thinks so, too. Put it this way: If we arrested him tonight and went to trial tomorrow, he could tell a jury the same story he told us and probably walk. Every bit of evidence linking him to the crime scene could be explained by that story. Every hair, fiber, even blood that leads to him is covered by the story of his earlier visit. Which leaves us to come up with the one bit of evidence that places him in that bathroom holding the gun in Emma's face."

Mike nodded. "We need the gun. You know what they say: A no-gun case is a lost case." He paused and glanced at his watch. "I say we get an early start tomorrow and check out his crib in New York."

Kate finished off her Chardonnay. "You don't honestly think he'd be stupid enough to leave the murder weapon lying around. If he did it," she added quickly.

Mike looked as if he was going to ignore her again. But then suddenly he smiled coldly at her. "The good thing about smart fuckers like Kane is that sometimes they outsmart themselves. You heard him: You don't need a search warrant, guys, I'll give my consent. Why? Because it makes him sound as if he has nothing to hide, and so he's betting we're going to say, Well what's the point of going all the way to New York when he's obviously got nothing to hide? Okay?"

Kate said nothing as Mike eyed her with a challenging look. She thought his tone had been unnecessarily cutting and harsh. She felt his attitude towards her had shifted noticeably since the morning, when he'd been so helpful at the crime scene. Only a few hours before she had even found herself looking forward to seeing more of him as he worked the case with Harry. Now she just felt foolish.

Harry must have sensed her discomfort because suddenly he was patting her hand. "We have to check it out. Want to come?"

Kate nodded. "Of course. Where you go, I go," she retorted flatly. Out of the corner of her eye she thought she saw Mike roll his eyes again. Screw him, she thought. She didn't need to make nice with him.

It was a pleasing thought that lasted only till she got into Harry's car, where he laid his hand on hers and shook his head. "A piece of advice, Kate: You want to stay on the inside of this investigation, don't beat up on Mike Travis—"

"Beat up on him! Did I beat up on him?"

"Yeah, you heard." Harry switched on the engine. "You had a point to make and that was okay. But the way you went for Mike was uncalled for. We were bouncing ideas around, that's all. It shouldn't become personal."

Kate shrugged. "Well, he was so . . . so aggressive."

"He's from New York." Harry grinned. Then immediately got serious again. "And right now he's with the District Attorney's office, and if he decides you're an obstreperous broad he can see to it that you're cut out of the loop. Understand?"

"Okay, okay." Kate nodded and gritted her teeth. "What's his problem anyway? Didn't he have to resign from the New York P.D. because of some woman? I guess she was obstreperous, too."

Harry glanced sharply at her. "Where did you hear that?"

"At the party. The way I heard it there was some off-duty incident over a woman he was involved with. He was a bad boy, is what I heard."

Harry shook his head. "Montgomery County doesn't hire bad boys, Kate. You should know better than to listen to gossip."

"So? What's the real story?"

Harry shrugged. "You'll have to ask him for the full story. So far as I know, the incident involved an attempted rape, and his girlfriend was the victim. He arrived in time to stop the assault . . ."

"By shooting the perp?"

Harry nodded. "Something like that."

"Did he kill him?"

"No," Harry replied.

"So, why did he have to resign?"

"I told you I don't know the full story, Kate." Harry sighed then lapsed into a pensive silence for the rest of the ride. Kate didn't speak either, until Harry pulled up outside her front door. Then she said, "You guys have pretty much set your hearts on Kane, haven't you?"

Harry laughed. "Jeez, Kate, you make it sound so emotional." He turned in his seat to face her. "But it's really not that complicated. Picture any regular Joe in that position: He's angry, he steams home from the construction site during his lunch hour and finds his wife in bed with another man. Next thing you know the wife is dead. Who would be top of your list there?" He paused and shook his head. "Why should it be different in Jack Kane's case? You know there's no such thing as too rich or too good-looking—or too famous—when it comes to murder."

"Oh, come on, give me some credit, Harry." Kate laughed aloud. "I'm just curious why you're discounting any other suspects. I mean there could be another spouse in the picture. You don't even know if there is a Mrs. Salerno."

"Yes, we do, and there is. Only she's seventy years old and doesn't speak English." Harry grinned and shook his head. "It's Salerno's mother. Lansing and Rogers were with her just about an hour ago. They were waiting for a daughter to translate and fill them in on young Tony. Who knows? Maybe he had Mob connections."

"Well now, there you go, Harry. That might even explain those tire tracks in the backyard."

Harry shook his head as Kate got out of the car. "But that's all speculation, Kate. What we need is the murder weapon—and Jack Kane's apartment is as good a place as any to start looking."

He rolled down his window and stuck his head out as she headed for the porch steps. "You don't have a problem with that, do you, Kate?"

She paused beside her two porch dummies, and deciding to ignore Harry's teasing question, blew him a goodnight kiss before turning to adjust Ma's hat to a more jaunty angle.

14

He felt better after dark. Not quite well enough to make it in to work but well enough to think about preparing a little light supper. Waiting for his soup to heat up, Lewis tried not to think about the gun. He'd thought about it enough already and there was just no way he could figure how it had landed on his roof. Nothing made sense: Guns did not just fall out of the sky, and if Emma Kane or the man had spotted him and wanted to scare him off they would have fired it at him, not thrown it at the truck. Better still, they would surely have summoned the cops.

He lifted the pot off the stove and poured the steaming chicken noodle soup into a white bowl, staring for a moment at the thin broth with disgust. Chicken *noodle* soup? What a joke. He counted eight noodles in the bowl. His mother had made great chicken noodle soup with thick long egg noodles, but she'd used every pot in the kitchen to do it—and had then left them to stand in the sink for days afterwards. One day he'd come home from school to find maggots in the sink. He shuddered at the memory and switched on the faucet, holding the pot under steaming water before squirting in some Dove and scouring it with a stiff brush. Then he wiped it dry with a paper towel and replaced it on its shelf in the cabinet. Giving the countertop a quick wipedown, he glanced at the clock. It was almost ten. Time for the news.

He placed his bowl of soup on a tray and started upstairs, carrying the tray carefully and watching his step so that by the time he was back in bed and settled with the tray on his lap, the ten o'clock news was already underway. Jennifer Reed's talking head bobbed in silence for a moment until he adjusted the volume to catch the tail end of her lede: "Full details of the shocking double slaying on the Main Line. Molly Heskell is on the campus of Villanova Law School. Our Lonnie Johnson is at the crime scene." Her close-up dissolved to the reporter standing outside a big dark house, and Lewis caught the name Emma Kane but barely heard the rest as he stared at the screen in horror.

Suddenly the live shot dissolved to a tape obviously produced earlier in the day. It started with an aerial shot over the Kane estate. "Police say the victims, Mrs. Emma Kane and Villanova student Tony Salerno, were shot inside this grand Main Line mansion, apparently some time late yesterday evening . . ." Jumbled images flashed before his eyes as the camera panned the estate then zoomed in on uniformed cops searching the grounds.

Lewis stared open-mouthed as he saw them cross the service driveway and head for the very same cluster of trees where he'd parked his truck. Somewhere in the distance, he heard a strange sound: a tinny, rapping noise, which he suddenly realized was his spoon clattering on the rim of his soup bowl. He looked down to see his hand shaking uncontrollably.

"The gruesome discovery of the bodies was made early this morning by a friend of Mrs. Kane's." He turned down the volume, struggling to catch his breath as his chest tightened. The cops would find his tire tracks. The soup slopped out of the bowl. He ignored it and forced his thoughts back to the moment when he'd heard the thud of the gun on the roof of his truck.

He knew now what had happened: No one had *thrown* the gun at him or his truck. Emma Kane's killer had tossed it into the dark trees. He had the murder weapon downstairs.

He pushed his tray aside and closed his eyes, summoning up the rest of the memory. The bright light had almost blinded him. Otherwise, maybe he'd have caught a glimpse of the killer running from the house . . .

Or the garage. He remembered the garage to the left of the bay window. He remembered the big sensor lights over the garage doors. He'd been careful enough to keep a distance between himself and those sensor lights. But obviously the killer hadn't. That's where the sudden bright light had come from. It had been activated by the killer running out of the garage door.

The killer had dumped the gun and run. Now Lewis had the gun and he had left his tire tracks on the property. A loud wheezing noise suddenly escaped his lips as he thought about the cops tracing him through his tires, descending on him, surrounding his little house . . .

He clutched his chest and forced himself to take long deep breaths and as his breathing calmed another thought suddenly struck him: He remembered his camcorder wedged on the dashboard and pointing at the house. He had turned it on just before nodding off. He had thrown it onto the seat just before pulling out of the driveway. The camcorder had been running the entire time.

He moved so abruptly and quickly out of bed, he didn't realize his foot was caught in the sheet until he felt it dragging behind him in a tangle with his top quilt. He stopped and groaned at the sight of the upturned bowl and tray—and the big, wet, greasy stain spreading across his coverlet.

Damn. Damn. Damn. If he let the soup soak in and dry, the stain would never wash out. He bent down, grabbed the quilt off the floor, and carried it across the tiny hallway to his bathroom.

15

The roar of a motorcycle speeding down the driveway cut Kate off in midsentence as she sat with Tommy at the breakfast table. "I'll go and see who it is." Tommy jumped up from the table.

"No." Kate got to her feet, looking quizzically at Maysie. "You stay here. I'll go and see."

"Don't look at me." Maysie laughed, stirring up some fresh batter by the stove. "I'm not expecting the Biker Club for breakfast this morning."

Kate hurried to the door with Tommy right behind her.

"Wow! Totally awesome, Mom. Check it out," he gasped as she opened the door to be greeted by the sight of Mike Travis alighting from a polished, gleaming chrome monster bike.

"Good morning." He waved at them as he came up the porch steps, taking off his sunglasses and helmet.

Seeing the bright, cheerful look on his face, Kate decided to write off the previous evening to frayed tempers at the end of a long day. "That's some machine." She nodded in the direction of the bike as Tommy ran right past him to take a closer look.

"Isn't she?" Mike acknowledged, grinning as he unzipped his brown leather jacket and followed her down the hall into the kitchen.

"Did you eat?" she asked politely.

"No. Harry told me if I got here on time, I'd get the best breakfast in Pennsylvania." He looked across at Maysie.

"You must be the world-famous Maysie." He walked across the kitchen and shook her hand. "I'm Mike Travis."

"Nice to meet you, Mike; do sit down," Maysie greeted him warmly. "I'll have these ready any minute. Is Harry on his way?"

Mike took a seat at the table. "Harry sends his apologies. He got diverted this morning." He looked at Kate. "So, it's just the two of us, and the techies."

"I see." Kate picked up her coffee mug and sipped, wondering if this was Harry's way of giving the two of them a chance to mend some fences. Or did he, despite what he'd said about the need to check out Kane's apartment, realize they were going on a fool's errand? She sighed. "And are you suggesting I ride with you to New York on that machine?"

Mike laughed. "That would be a trip." His eyes met hers. "But I don't imagine you'd feel comfortable going that far the first time." He paused for a beat, as if expecting some snappy response to his obvious double meaning, and when none was forthcoming, added: "Of course, we can always ride up separately, if you prefer."

Ball in your court, McCusker.

She shrugged, finished her coffee, and watched Maysie set down a half-dozen pancakes in front of him. He attacked them hungrily, glancing around the kitchen as he ate. "This is quite a place, Kate. Very striking." He nodded towards the cabinets.

Kate nodded. "Thank you." Guests always remarked on the kitchen. The cabinets had been painted red and sanded after painting for a deliberately distressed look that softened the starkness of the color. She had been dubious about the idea when Steve had first suggested it, but together with the Mexican tiled floor and the white-and-navy-tiled countertops, the effect had turned out bold but warm. "It was Steve's idea to go with red." She pushed away from the table, abruptly. "I'll go get my purse and jacket while you finish up."

When she returned he was rinsing off his plate in the sink, with Tommy hovering next to him as he stared at a framed photograph that hung over the sink. It was a photo that had been taken on the set of *Root of All Evil* of Steve standing with his arms around her and Sharon Stone.

"She was in the movie?" Mike asked. "I never saw it but I can't recall any character in the book that she'd want to play."

Kate's chest tightened suddenly as a long-distant memory forced its way into her head. A vivid image of Steve standing, dripping wet and naked in the bathroom when she'd run in to tell him that *Root of All Evil* had been cast for a feature movie.

"You and Harry are going to be immortalized on the big screen," she'd announced. "That's the good news.

"Anthony Hopkins is going to play Harry's role." She'd started to giggle. "That's good news, too."

"You bet, baby." He'd swung her up in his arms. "That's a big-money star. So, who gets my part? Mel Gibson? No, Kevin Costner. No second bananas, right?"

"It's a very big star. A blonde."

"That'll work, too. Who is it? Michael Douglas?"

"No, I mean a blond blonde, as in Sharon Stone."

The sight of Steve, her tall, broad-shouldered, muscular, and stark naked husband, walking around the bathroom, looking at his reflection in the bathroom mirrors, and plaintively repeating "Sharon Stone is going to play me?" had sent her into convulsive fits of laughter. It was an image that sometimes still brought a smile to her face. But not today.

She shrugged it off quickly. "Oh, you know how it is in Hollywood. They like to change things around, all the time." She paused. "So you read the book?"

"Of course." He nodded. "I bought a copy the day after we met."

He turned his attention quickly back to the other framed photographs and articles that hung on the kitchen wall. "I didn't know you were so famous."

Kate shrugged again. "I'm not. It was my fifteen minutes."

"Did you enjoy it?"

She gave him a quick half smile. "Mostly it was hard work. You have to travel around the country to promote the book and you get to appear on dozens of TV shows and you always have to look your best, and it's really tough being interviewed when you're the one used to asking the questions."

He laughed. "There's got to be an upside."

Kate laughed, too. "Oh yes, there is. It's great to hear people say they loved your book. And you can always get a reservation in tony restaurants, and you get to visit the movie set and meet really glamorous people, and then just when you're starting to enjoy it, it's over and they put you back in your box."

"Until the next time, right?" Mike paused. "You'll get a bestseller out of this case, I bet."

"Maybe," she agreed, walking to the door where Tommy was hopping from foot to foot.

"Mom, I have a great idea." He turned on his most charming smile for her. "Why don't I ride on the bike with Mike and you can follow in the car. Okay?"

Kate laughed and bent down to kiss him. He dodged her. "Is that okay, Mom? Can I go to New York with you? Please?"

She shook her head. "We went through this last night, sweetie. You can't come on this trip."

"Oh fine, Mom." He turned away pouting. "That's just great." He turned to Mike. "Two Moms. One's going to New York, the other's gone to the shore—and none of them want me around."

"Tommy!" Kate stared as he pushed his way out of the back door. She followed him out and caught up with him as he ran down the porch steps. "Sweetheart, come on. You know I have to go. Brendan's mom will pick you up at lunchtime and I'll try to be back early, and then I'll ask Mike to take you for a spin. Deal?" She held out her hand.

Her son hesitated for a second then sighed and limply offered his own. "Okay, deal," he agreed, finally.

Kate walked around the back of the house to the garage, where Mike was already waiting, admiring the Porsche. Deliberately ignoring his interest in the car she walked to her Jeep Cherokee.

"You don't like driving a stick shift?"

She paused with her hand on the door handle of the Jeep and shrugged. "That was Steve's car. I'm going to sell it."

There was a mischievous look in Mike's eyes. "Come on. We'll make the trip in half the time." He flashed his badge. "After all, we're on police business."

She hesitated, suppressing a laugh as she remembered the same look on Steve's face—and the many occasions when he had flashed his badge at troopers who stopped him speeding on the highway. She slammed the door of the Jeep closed and walked to the Porsche. "If we take the Porsche, you take Tommy for a spin on your bike when we get back. Okay?"

"You got it." He slid into the seat beside her, stretching his jeaned legs out in front of him. "But we'll need to pick up a helmet for him."

Mike waited till she was out of the driveway before picking up the conversation again but only to make small talk about the area. He seemed to be just enjoying the ride and it wasn't till they were on the turnpike that he attempted to venture into more personal territory, asking her about Steve.

"I've heard quite a bit about him," he said. "He sounds like one of the good guys."

"He was." Kate nodded. "And I suppose I'm lucky that we had four terrific years together." She paused. "They were four of the best years of my life. I thank God for every day we had . . ."

"That's a lot of good memories."

"Maybe more than some people have from a lifetime." She nodded. Then before he could pry further, she posed her own question. "Were you ever married?"

"No."

She glanced sideways at him, but he appeared to be engrossed in the passing scenery. *On the New Jersey Turnpike?* "Ever come close?" she prodded.

"Once."

"How close?"

He leaned back in his seat. "I was a week away from tying the knot."

"So, who got the cold feet? You or her?"

He laughed. "It was a little more dramatic than getting cold feet." He paused. "I caught her with another man."

"Oh." The answer caught her off guard. She had thought he was talking about the same woman that Harry had mentioned but that surely couldn't be. Who would characterize an attempted rape as catching your fiancée with another man?

She noticed she'd hit ninety and eased her foot off the gas. She also noticed that Mike wasn't volunteering any more information. "You're not going to leave me in suspense, are you?" she said, attempting to steer the conversation back to him.

"For the moment," he replied, glancing at his watch as they approached the entrance into the Lincoln Tunnel, and she knew his mind was back on the case as he added: "We made good time."

Yes, just under two hours, thought Kate. But in a Porsche.

"I bet you can make this trip in just about two hours in a Jag, too," Mike echoed, as if reading her thoughts. "That could put Kane at the crime scene with plenty of time to make it back for Fox News at ten."

"Mmmm." Kate paid the toll into the tunnel. "Assuming traffic was light and assuming he was prepared to get stopped for speeding . . . always a dodgy thing, I find, when you're driving in blood-spattered clothes with a murder weapon in your glove compartment." They plunged into the fluorescent-lit tunnel. "Do you really think you're going to find the gun in Jack Kane's apartment?"

She sensed rather than saw him shrug. "You never know."

Emerging from the tunnel she turned left. Kate was not overly familiar with Manhattan but one didn't have to be, she figured. She could stay on Tenth till she got up into the sixties. Then, she'd swing right.

It seemed to be a busy Saturday morning in the city, and there was plenty of traffic traveling uptown. Growing more confident as she dodged and weaved through it, she maneuvered through side streets to bring them right outside Jack Kane's building across the street from the park.

Mike told her it was okay to park near the fire hydrant, and in the lobby he flashed his badge at the doorman. "We need access to Mr. Kane's apartment," he said. "And keep your eye on that car out there, okay?"

"Very well, sir." The doorman nodded. "There are two more gentlemen waiting to go up there. I'll get the super for you now."

Indeed, the two crime lab technicians, Joel Fisher and his partner, were waiting for them by the elevators. Together the little group followed the superintendent to the fifteenth floor. Kate noted that there were only four apartments to each floor. The building had an air of muted, comfortable grandeur about it.

"Well." Mike gave a low whistle as the super let them into the apartment. "I guess Kane's idea of a shoebox differs slightly from mine."

Kate could only nod. The passageway from the door led into a big living room with high ceilings and French doors that opened up onto a bricked terrace. "Not too shabby." There were a half-dozen potted plants and ferns on the terrace and a little wooden bench. The view overlooked Central Park. "Not too shabby at all."

She heard Mike talking to Joel, giving the technician instructions to check sink traps in the bathroom and kitchen, and to use the vacuum in all the rooms. "Are you coming?" Mike beckoned to Kate. "Let's go find some bloody socks."

Kate rolled her eyes but followed him across the living room and down another short hallway. They found the master bedroom on the left. Its windows also overlooked the park, and Kate noted there was a big wood-burning fireplace opposite the bed. She also noted that Jack Kane had obviously not considered the apartment home. Unlike his house on the Main Line there were few pictures on the walls and no mementoes of family or home in evidence on tables or nightstands.

She watched Mike opening closets and drawers. Then she heard him whistle under his breath again. "Take a look at this." He was staring into a walk-in closet where Jack Kane's suits in varying shades of navy and gray and tan hung along the length of one wall. "How many suits does a TV executive need?"

Kate wasn't sure whether Mike's tone was one of disgust or awe. On the opposite wall a tie rack held at least four dozen ties. All silk, Kate noted. About three dozen shirts hung next to them.

The apartment seemed very neat and tidy. Almost too

neat and tidy. The bed had been made. There were no clothes strewn on the floor nor magazines or newspapers on the various little tables. No dirty coffee cups or glasses.

Off the bedroom was the master bathroom. A claw-footed tub dominated the small space. Mirrors and light gray marble had been used to make it appear larger. Kate was right behind Mike as he started opening cabinet doors.

The shelves were mainly empty. A bottle of Lauren after-shave and cologne stood on a shelf in the center cabinet. Two slim bars of soap were stacked on the top shelf next to an old-fashioned razor. Mike picked it up and stared at the blade. Then he reached into his pocket for a Ziploc bag and dropped the razor into it, together with the packet of blades that lay beside it, and continued his inspection.

A box of Trojan condoms stood on the bottom shelf. Mike picked up the box and turned to look at Kate. "Just in case Seth Reilly drops in, do you think?"

She laughed. "He didn't say he'd taken a vow of celibacy, for God's sake." A pause. "How many are missing?"

Mike put the box back on the shelf. "None. It's still shrinkwrapped." He crouched down to open the cabinets under the sink. "Where the hell is his laundry hamper?"

Joel Fisher and his partner appeared in the bathroom doorway. "We're done in the kitchen. Can we get in here?"

Mike nodded. "Yeah. I guess. I'm finished."

Kate backed out into the bedroom and glanced around for the missing hamper. "It's probably in the closet. Look for plastic bags. He probably has a maid service that picks up his dry cleaning and laundry."

Mike stepped back into the walk-in and Kate heard the clatter of hangers as Mike riffled through the suits and opened and closed drawers of the built-in chests, cursing to himself. He emerged from the closet, frowning. "Nothing."

Kate was sure now that someone had been in to clean the apartment. She walked into the kitchen to look for a bulletin board or something with handy phone numbers on it. Then she picked up the intercom and buzzed the doorman, handing the phone to Mike immediately. "The doorman will know about maid service."

A couple of moments later, Mike was grinning as he hung

up the phone. "Bingo. He uses an agency, West Side Housekeepers."

It took about an hour to track down the maid who'd cleaned Jack Kane's apartment the day before. By that time Joel and Dave had finished their work and had left to head back for Pennsylvania. Kate walked through the rooms opening the blinds that Joel and Dave had drawn for a Luminol test on two initially suspicious-looking stains. Then she returned to the kitchen and listened to Mike on the phone. She heard varying degrees of persuasion and coercion in Mike's voice as he attempted to locate the maid through the agency.

Finally, after threatening to walk over to the agency with a warrant, he had the woman's home phone number. And some twenty minutes later Maria Torres returned his call at the apartment.

Yes, she cleaned Mr. Kane's apartment every Friday. Yes, she deposited his suits and shirts at the dry cleaners on Sixty-ninth Street. No, she couldn't remember the name but it was just around the corner. She did the laundry herself downstairs in the building's laundry room. She had put back all his clean underwear and socks in his drawers.

And no, she had not seen any evidence of blood anywhere in the apartment on Friday morning.

"Sonuvabitch." Mike banged the phone down in its cradle and went back into the closet, flinging open drawers and emptying socks and underwear into a black plastic bag that Joel had left for him. "It's okay with me if he wants to play hardball. He can wear the same pair of shorts all week."

Kate stifled a laugh at the thought of Jack Kane making do with one pair of shorts and socks. As if he wouldn't send out for new. She walked back to the kitchen and opened the refrigerator door and studied the contents of the refrigerator. Not much to study there, either. An unopened six-pack of beer lay on the bottom shelf. Above it a packet of Carr's water crackers nestled next to an unopened slab of what looked like cheddar cheese. She also noted a bottle of tonic water and a bottle of club soda.

"It certainly doesn't look like he spends any time here— except maybe to sleep, shower, and change," she remarked.

Mike grunted and stared into the refrigerator himself. "And maybe not even sleep. No milk, no cereal, not even orange juice." He shrugged. "Come on, let's wrap it up and go pick up the suits from the cleaners."

Kate sensed his dejection as they returned to the car with the four suits and a pair of tan slacks that the Korean dry cleaner had handed over without any protest. She suggested they stop for a cup of coffee, maybe a sandwich, before driving back. There was a café next door to the building. A solitary couple sat at one of the outside tables and Kate suggested they do the same.

"Sure." Mike nodded.

Kate waited till the waiter brought their coffee before she asked him about the suits they'd picked up from the dry cleaners. Were they covered by the search warrant? Would they be admissible evidence?

"It's academic." He laughed. "I really didn't expect to find a bloody suit. Gun, maybe, that's a valuable item. It's tough to destroy and it's traceable. But I'm sure that anyone who owns thirty or forty suits wouldn't think twice about dumping one of them somewhere on the road between here and Gladwyne or burning it in the building incinerator."

Kate nodded, and was about to ask another question when a passerby on the sidewalk caught her eye. The striking canary yellow color of the pants suit caught her attention first, but when she looked at the face she thought she recognized the woman. She turned to watch her walk along the sidewalk before the woman turned into Jack Kane's apartment building.

Suddenly Kate realized who she was. She turned to Mike. "That was Gabriella Grant who just walked into Jack Kane's apartment building."

Mike sat up straight on his chair. Then he signaled for the waiter to bring their check. He kept his eyes on the doors of the apartment building. But Gabriella Grant did not reemerge through them.

When they arrived in the lobby she was not there either. Mike walked to the front desk.

"Was that Gabriella Grant who just walked in here?"

The doorman hesitated a second.

"You couldn't have missed her," Kate chimed in. "She was wearing yellow. Bright yellow."

The doorman nodded. "Yes, Miss Grant. I saw her."

"Is she on her way up?"

"I guess so." The doorman made a big show of looking around the lobby. "Unless she's back there picking up her mail."

"Her mail?"

"The mailboxes are round the back."

"She gets mail here?"

The doorman looked at Mike quizzically. "I'm sure she does. She lives here."

16

Mike strode purposefully towards the elevator with Kate alongside him. "Okay, so she's three floors below Kane's apartment. I still say it's a damn cozy arrangement." He punched the button for the twelfth floor and stared at Kate over the tops of his shades. "When he said all he did was give her a ride home, I suppose it just slipped his mind that her home is under the same roof as his. Maybe he forgot about eating breakfast there, too."

He stabbed at the button again just as the elevator doors opened, and Kate got on without making any comment.

Gabriella Grant's apartment was at the end of the hallway on the opposite side of the building to Jack Kane's. There would be no view of the park for Gabriella, thought Kate as they waited for the TV newswoman to come to the door. But it took a second ring of the doorbell before she opened the door.

Mike had his badge ready. "Miss Grant? I'm Detective Travis with the Montgomery County District Attorney's office. I'm investigating the deaths of Mrs. Emma Kane and Tony Salerno. Could I have a word with you?"

"About what?" Gabriella Grant made no move to open the door any wider or to invite them in. Kate noticed that the TV newswoman was barefoot and she had unbuttoned her elegant jacket to reveal a clingy, low-cut silk top underneath. Her question was met with a brief silence on Mike's part, and before he could say anything Gabriella shook her head. "I'm sorry, I've really got nothing to say. I didn't know Mrs. Kane."

"You know Jack Kane. You live under the same roof."

"So does the executive producer of the show." She paused. "I think he's on the third floor, and the VP of news rents an apartment on the fifth." She surveyed both Mike and Kate with calm, guileless blue eyes. Then she smiled. "We get a break on the rent. I think one of Seth Reilly's companies has a piece of the action here. And it's very convenient for the office, all right?"

"I see." Mike stared right back at her. "We'd still like to ask you a few questions about Mr. Kane." He paused, waiting for Gabriella Grant to invite them into the apartment but she stood her ground.

"Like what?"

Mike took off his sunglasses. "Did Jack Kane ever discuss his personal life with you? Did he ever talk about his wife?"

Gabriella seemed to consider the question. Then she shook her head again, a half smile playing on her generous mouth. "Listen, detective, I don't know how much you understand about our business but when you're launching new shows and trying to set up a new network it doesn't leave much time to discuss extraneous areas of your life."

"Marriage isn't what I'd call an extraneous area."

Gabriella gave a short laugh. "Well, maybe not. But then again you're not running the news division of the biggest media conglomerate in the world, are you, detective?"

"So you're saying that Mr. Kane's marriage was not a priority for him?" Mike paused.

Gabriella's half smile blossomed into the real thing as she tutted. "Really, detective, how could I possibly answer that?" She looked as if she was going to close the door in their faces, and Kate saw Mike slide his foot towards the opening.

"You don't discuss anything except business with him?" Mike paused, but obviously not for an answer. He then added, "We spoke to Mr. Kane yesterday. He told us how it is in the TV business. He told us about some of his extraneous activities, or should I say, extracurricular activities. He was refreshingly honest, as a matter of fact . . . about his affairs and dalliances."

Nice one, Mike. A bit sly but worth the try, thought Kate as she noticed a little color creep into the newswoman's face. But the moment was short-lived.

"You're fishing, detective." She seemed to draw herself up. She was tall, Kate noted. Even without shoes she stood an inch or so taller than Kate. "I'm sure Mr. Kane did not name me as one of his dalliances." She put a heavy emphasis on the last word, as if a dalliance was the last thing in the world she would ever consider.

"He brought you to New York from Philadelphia with him. Isn't that correct?" Mike cut in abruptly.

"So?" The large blue eyes blinked at Mike. "I wasn't his first choice, you know."

"Who was?"

Gabriella seemed to hesitate. Then she shrugged. "Well that's no big secret, I suppose. It was a reporter by the name of Molly Heskell."

"Is she at WorldMedia, too?"

"Oh, no. No." Gabriella shook her head emphatically. "And that's because she *was* one of Jack's dalliances. That's no big secret either, detective."

"Meaning?"

"Meaning that Jack left her in Philadelphia after Emma Kane found out about their relationship and went nutso." Mike glanced across at Kate with a look that seemed to say, So much for Emma turning a blind eye. But Gabriella didn't seem to notice. She was still talking. "Personally, I thought there was a lesson to be learned from that, detective."

"So, you aren't involved with Jack Kane in any way?"

Gabriella laughed out loud. "Of course I'm involved with him. We work together—and that accounts for a major part of both our lives. It means I've probably spent more time with him than his wife has over the last few months, and, yes, of course I adore him. He's brilliant and talented and he's made my career." She paused and her eyes bore angrily into the both of them. "But please don't twist our relationship into something it isn't. Trust me, I certainly wouldn't jeopardize my career for a one-night stand."

There was a brief silence. Then Mike asked: "Did you see Mr. Kane at all on Thursday night?"

"Night?"

"Evening, late evening?"

Gabriella looked as if she was thinking hard. "I'm not sure. I'm sorry but after a while when you're working eighteen-hour days, every day seems very much like another."

"Can you remember where you were on Thursday night?"

The big blue eyes widened a fraction. "I was here or I was at WorldMedia. It's either here or there. But I was probably home by around seven."

"Alone?"

"Yes, alone." Gabriella blinked.

"And, you stayed in all evening? You didn't leave this apartment all evening? You didn't go knock on Jack Kane's door to borrow a cup of sugar, perhaps?"

Kate heard the sarcasm in Mike's voice and noticed it wasn't lost on Gabriella Grant either.

"No, and I didn't invite him down for dinner either." Her eyes flashed and her tone was clipped and cold when she added: "Although I should have, of course."

"Why, are you a good cook?"

Kate bit the inside of her lip to stifle a laugh at Mike's touch of humor because, of course, Gabriella Grant's meaning was crystal clear: If she had invited Jack Kane for dinner she would have been his alibi, and the cops wouldn't be pestering her with questions about him now.

"I don't cook at all, detective." She came right back at him. "You don't have to in New York. I order in. The best Chinese restaurant in the city is right around the corner."

She glanced at her watch as if to indicate that they'd had their time, and Mike seemed to take the hint. No doubt, Kate surmised, because he realized he was not going to get anything more useful from Gabriella Grant.

He thanked her even as she was already closing the door on them.

"That's one cool cookie," Kate remarked as they walked down the hallway.

"Cookie is not the word I'd use." Mike adjusted his sunglasses. "I wish we'd known she lived in the same building. We should have gotten a search warrant for her apartment, too." He paused as they reached the elevators and he stabbed at the down button.

"You think she was lying about Jack Kane?"

"Of course. If Jack Kane isn't jumping her bones then he isn't half the swordsman he thinks he is."

"So you think she's that desirable?"

He stared at her, his eyes reflecting a tinge of amusement. "I was looking at her from Kane's point of view, not my own."

"Really? A sort of objective assessment, huh?" Kate prodded, attempting to match the teasing note in his voice. "Are you saying she's not your type?"

Mike's mouth curved into a half smile as he put his sunglasses on. "Is that a serious question, McCusker?"

She hesitated. She really didn't know if it was a serious question. She wasn't even sure why she'd asked him about Gabriella. She decided to shrug it off. "More like idle curiosity. Just making small talk, detective."

"Pity," he laughed softly, surveying Kate over the tops of his shades. "For a moment there, I thought you cared."

17

"Of course they're lying," Mike said softly and emphatically. It was the first time he'd spoken since pulling away from Jack Kane's apartment building more than a half hour before.

Kate had offered to let him drive and he'd taken the wheel, maneuvering the Porsche expertly through the Saturday afternoon traffic. But he had done it in a pensive silence and Kate had guessed he needed time to think.

She had spent the time constructively, too, setting up her laptop computer on her knees. If Mike was going to mull things over, she could make notes on her own observations. She liked to think of herself as a methodical writer and she kept her notes and research updated in neat files in her computer. Like reporting for a newspaper, writing true crime required accurate facts and an eye for detail—and the ability to capture first impressions as they came.

Ignoring the tourists and shoppers scurrying along, she had stared at the blank screen, playing with words in her head as she stole the occasional glance at the detective in the driver's seat. Mike Travis would have to be in the book, of course, and if in the end it turned out that Jack Kane had indeed killed his wife, she would give him credit for being on top of it from the start. She put her fingers on the keyboard and started to type:

Detective Mike Travis believed Jack Kane was guilty from day one. Travis, at 37, had a solid if not stellar reputation.

*A cop for more than fifteen years he had left the NYPD
under a cloud (?), which wrecked not only his career but
also his personal life. (Fill) ?????*

Kate had paused. She would certainly have to get Mike to
open up about his past. Somewhere along the line she'd
need the correct facts for the book, though she could get by
without them now. Her first drafts often started out this
way: dotted with innumerable question marks and (fill)s to
remind her where to insert further information. As they
emerged from the Lincoln Tunnel, she started tapping the
keys again:

*The double murder of Emma Kane and 29-year-old Tony
Salerno was Travis' first big case for the Montgomery
County District Attorney's office. Travis brought a New
York urgency and pace to the investigation. And when he
was on the job, his cool charm took a backseat to his
tough, relentless pursuit of the truth. Tall and lean,
Travis had a clean-cut, sensual appeal about him. Off
duty he rode a Harley Davidson Road King, but anyone
not knowing what he did for a living could be forgiven for
mistaking him for a male model. Indeed, Travis had been
a model as a college student, working his way through
John Jay Criminal College, posing for the bodice-ripper
covers of romantic novels. On the day following the discovery of the bodies of Emma Kane and Tony Salerno,
however, there was no glamour boy charm in his
demeanor. Mike Travis was out for blood . . . literally
and figuratively.*

Kate scanned what she'd written, aware that she'd made
Mike sound like a character from one of the romance novels. But what the hell? Readers of true crime needed a hero
to root for, too.

"Both of them are lying through their teeth." Mike
voiced the thought again, and sensing that he was ready to
talk, Kate looked up from her laptop.

"Are you throwing that out for discussion or have you
made up your mind on it?"

Mike laughed drily. "I just get this feeling that we're being given the finger. That Jack Kane and Gabriella Grant are playing games with us."

Kate logged off and closed the laptop. "Playing games?" she echoed.

Mike glanced in the rearview mirror as he changed lanes. "Yeah. On the one hand you've got Kane who admits to everything—driving to the scene, arguing with his wife, getting steamed with her—but no, he didn't kill her. On the other hand you have the bodacious Miss Grant living in the same building, admitting she adores Kane, admitting that they spend all their time together and that she owes him big time for making her a star—but no, she's never even sucked his dick."

He stopped abruptly and looked at Kate. "So, what do you think?"

I think your vocabulary needs cleaning up. She tapped her laptop with a fingernail. "I think that's one way of looking at it. On the other hand, it could be the truth."

Mike made a noise that sounded like a snort of disgust. "I'm sorry, but the more I think about it, the less likely that seems. Look at Kane and the way he seemed to bend over backwards yesterday to help our investigation. So agreeable, he hands over his car keys and signs the consent to search form—only he never tells us that his cleaning service comes in on Friday mornings. How many other things has he not mentioned?"

Kate nodded. Mike had a point. "But why lie about an affair with Gabriella Grant? He didn't exactly try to paint himself as a model, faithful husband."

"Exactly." Mike broke in. "Why lie about something so seemingly inconsequential? Unless of course it's not inconsequential but actually a motive for murder."

"An affair?" Kate shook her head. "I don't think that would drive someone like Jack Kane to kill—and so brutally. It would be much simpler to get a divorce. It sounded as if that's the way things were heading, anyway."

"Yeah." Mike laughed. "Except he couldn't even get Emma to agree to the sale of the house."

"But he was backing her into a corner on it. Forcing her to fire the housekeepers, cutting her allowance . . . That seems much more his style. I think he'd be more comfortable manipulating than shooting someone in the face."

They slowed down for the turnpike tolls and Mike waited till he'd retrieved the ticket. "Depends on how much time he thought he had. Maybe Gabriella Grant was putting the pressure on him. Maybe she didn't want to be the Other Woman anymore."

Kate shook her head. "I really think you're reading this wrong, Mike. Do you see Jack Kane as the kind of guy who'd give in to that sort of pressure? Because I don't. I don't think you get to where he is by giving in to any kind of pressure." She paused and weighed her next words carefully. "If you want my opinion, I think they're telling the truth about it. Both of them were very adamant. There wasn't a hint of hesitation on Jack Kane's part, yesterday. Just straight-out denial. Same with Gabriella. I don't think both of them could lie about something like that so forcefully."

"Really?"

Kate glanced anxiously at Mike. She wondered how it was possible to inject so much sarcasm and skepticism into one word. She also wondered if she was stepping over the line. Was this what Harry had meant by beating up on him? She was about to soften her argument by saying that what rang the truest about Gabriella was her point about not wanting to risk her career for a fling with Jack Kane but Mike cut her off.

"I don't go along with it—but it's almost a better motive."

"What is?"

"Gabriella Grant holding out on him. Refusing his advances until he can make an honest woman out of her. Putting on that kind of pressure could make a man crazy, too." He laughed. "Whichever way you look at it there are plenty enough motives for Kane."

"Well, I'm sorry." Kate shook her head. "But I'm just not hearing the one that would get him convicted by a jury of his peers."

"That's because you don't like the idea."

"What idea?"

"Take your pick. The idea of Kane with Gabriella Grant. The idea of Kane killing his wife for Gabriella. Either or both, he seems to have gotten to you, Kate."

"What's that supposed to mean?"

"Oh come on." The skepticism returned with full force.

Kate stared at her fingernails and noticed the polish was starting to peel off her left thumbnail. She suspected the conversation was about to take a sharp downhill turn and she considered just ignoring his comment. But Mike wasn't ready to let it go.

"I'm talking about yesterday. I wish I had a videotape so you could see it for yourself: the body language, the looks—"

"What!"

Mike laughed brusquely. "Sure, tell me you don't know what I'm talking about. C'mon, you must have noticed . . . first thing he did was check out your wedding band."

Kate stared at him, trying to mask her surprise. "My, we are observant," she said, somewhat lamely.

Mike smiled, evidently amused by her surprise. "It's part of the job. I was watching every move he made, listening to every word he said."

"And what is it, exactly, that you read into his moves and body language?"

"He was playing to you, Kate. From the moment he was introduced to you. 'Oh, I know who she is.'" Mike mimicked Kane. "When he loosened his tie, he was looking straight at you. When he was talking about how much he enjoyed being with smart, beautiful women, he was looking at you, eyeing you, playing to you."

She laughed nervously. Mike hadn't missed much, she thought. But she suspected he was reading more into the fleeting moment than was warranted. "So, okay," she said finally. "He was looking at me. Is that a crime? I'm more attractive than you or Harry, you know."

Her attempt at levity was met with a stony stare. "The vibes seemed to go both ways."

Kate felt a surge of annoyance. "Really?"

"Yeah, really." Mike speeded up to make a lane change

and Kate noticed the speedometer touching ninety. "You hardly took your eyes off him."

"Well forgive me! But he was the subject of the interrogation—"

"And your eyes are very expressive, Kate," he added, as if she hadn't spoken. "It's a little distracting when someone who's got access to a police investigation is batting her eyelashes at the prime suspect."

"Oh come on, Mike." Kate laughed out loud, then lapsed into a momentary silence, suspecting that his words were prompted by more than just objective observation. The idea that he was using his position to make her uncomfortable about her reaction to Jack Kane annoyed her. But she knew it was wiser not to pursue that particular avenue much further.

"Okay." She nodded, breaking the silence. "You've got it. No more batting eyelashes at Jack Kane." She paused. "I'm curious about him, that's all. Men like Jack Kane are a pretty rare breed."

"Idle curiosity again, McCusker?"

"Professional rather than idle," she corrected him.

"But you wouldn't turn down a dinner date with him?"

She hesitated. He was clearly baiting her about Jack Kane and she wasn't quite sure how to handle it. She decided to check her annoyance and play it safe. "There's nothing unprofessional about a dinner date," she said primly. "Relaxing over a good meal is a good way to get to know people."

Mike laughed suddenly. "But not Kane. The way he was talking yesterday, it didn't sound as if he wasted much time on wining and dining 'em."

She turned to stare at him in open disbelief as her anger finally bubbled. Did he think he was so much better than Jack Kane? "Well, isn't that a shame for me." She flung the words out before she could stop herself. "I just can't seem to get away from you hit-and-run types."

He glanced at her sharply, and she saw the anger in his own eyes. For a moment he looked as if he was going to call her on it. Then quietly he said, "Maybe that's because you don't really want to, Kate. I don't remember hearing any complaints from your side of the road last week."

The memory of how she'd eased into his arms came flashing into her mind, and her anger surged again. How dare he use a moment's weakness against her? "Then you weren't listening," she shot back. "And, you don't have the first clue about what I want—"

"Really?" he cut in abruptly. "Then I must have gotten my signals mixed up because I could have sworn that last week you were looking for something more than just a bit of belly-rubbing on the dance floor."

Kate's reaction was swift. Instant, really. Her open palm lashed out and caught him squarely on the jaw. "Pull over," she said.

He said nothing but glanced in the rearview mirror and then switched lanes, maneuvering onto the hard shoulder just past a sign for Exit 6. Nor did he say anything when Kate told him to get out of the car.

Not until she came around to the driver's side of the Porsche did he say anything—and then only to say that he could not let her drive away with the bagged evidence.

"I have to preserve the chain of custody," he pointed out tersely.

She slid into the driver's seat and popped the trunk open. Then, keeping her eye on the side mirror for a break in the traffic, she made sure Mike Travis was clear of the car before gunning the accelerator. Her heart was still pounding angrily when she lost sight of him in the rearview mirror.

It wasn't till she was exiting the Pennsylvania Turnpike, headed for the Blue Route, that the stupidity of what she'd done hit her.

Smooth move, McCusker, she admonished herself, wondering why she had allowed herself to get so riled. Why had she allowed herself to get drawn in when Mike had started rambling about Jack Kane? How the hell had it all gotten so out of hand?

She would appeal to Harry, of course, tell him what had happened, but somehow she wasn't sure it would do much good. She thought about Harry's warning. If you want to stay in the loop, don't beat up on Travis, he'd said.

Well, she'd gone a little ways beyond that: She'd left Mike Travis, an on-duty detective with the Montgomery County District Attorney's office, stranded on the turnpike.

18

He paced back and forth across the small basement studio, chewing his nails and cursing under his breath. Every now and then he stopped to stare at the shot that he'd freeze-framed on his monitor but that only made things worse.

Almost twenty-four hours had passed since he'd first raced down to the basement to retrieve the videotape from his camcorder and to run it through his playback machine. He'd been beside himself with anxiety as he'd punched the Play button. If he had Emma Kane's killer on the tape then he had nothing to worry about. If the police came knocking at his door . . . If things started looking really bad for him then at least he could produce it in a last-ditch attempt to stave off disaster.

He had no clue as to how he was going to explain his presence—with a video camera—on Jack Kane's property but that sort of embarrassment was minor compared to facing charges in a double homicide.

He had forced himself to watch every minute of the tape the first time around. From the moment the lens had zoomed in on Emma Kane in her kitchen, his eyes had been glued to the screen. He had watched her moving between the refrigerator and the kitchen table by the window, had watched her set the two glasses on the table and fill them with juice, had watched her prepare a lovely plate of crackers and cheese.

Then the man had walked in and Emma Kane had sat

down opposite him, holding out the plate of crackers to him. They had talked; they had refilled their glasses with juice and they had consumed the entire plate of crackers. It was a boring sequence of events that lasted for almost twenty minutes but he'd been pleased to note that Emma Kane was as clean and tidy in her kitchen as he was in his. When the toyboy in the bathrobe had finally walked out of the kitchen, Emma Kane had stayed to rinse off the plates and glasses and she'd even wiped down the table-top. Then she too had left the kitchen, switching off the light and plunging the back of the house into almost total darkness. Only the patio lights on either side of the big bay kitchen window had been left to cast an eerie illumi-nation over the flagstones and flowerbeds.

For the next twenty minutes that's all he'd seen on the tape. Nothing had moved in Emma Kane's backyard or across her flagstone patio until the light had exploded and flooded into the lens a split second before the audio had registered the *thwump* sound, which Lewis recognized as the sound that had woken him, the sound that he now realized was the gun landing on the roof of his truck. Staring more intently at the tape, he had seen a shadow move across the screen from the garage on his left towards the kitchen patio on his right. The shadow had become a grainy silhouette as it moved from the arc of brightness thrown out by the garage sensor lights into the grayer area illuminated by the patio lights. And then it was gone, past the bay window and out of the camera's range.

He had replayed that portion of the tape at least a dozen times, freeze-framing and enhancing the sequence shot by shot, until he'd zeroed in on one shot where the shadowy, fuzzy silhouette had half turned towards him—and the camera.

It was something. It was, at least, a shot they could work with. If worst came to worst and the cops came knocking . . . hell, he could even point them to the videoprocessor in the Channel Seven newsroom. That machine worked magic. It made pictures sharper and brighter. It turned shit into art. And, it would surely get him off the hook . . .

He punched the Eject button and momentarily entertained the thought of fiddling with the videoprocessor himself. But no, he thought, aware that his palms had broken out in a cold sweat. That was asking for trouble. That was asking to get caught red-handed.

He snatched up the tape and placed it in his bottom drawer. Enough messing around, he told himself. It was time to get back to his project. Nothing else should divert him, now that it was so close to completion.

He reached for his master tape from the shelf above the editing machines and inserted the tape into the editing machine. It had taken him months to gather all the footage and video. His own shoots had been a piece of cake compared to the painstaking job of gathering the background material from recorded portions of news broadcasts and still photos. He had written the script and laid down the audio track weeks ago. He'd started editing the footage, last week. Now, at each working session he replayed his work-in-progress from the top.

He waited for the title to scroll up: JACK KANE: PRESIDENT OR PIMP? Then stared at the monitor as his voice filled the small, soundproof studio. "This man is Jack Kane. Today he is president of WorldMedia News network. But does he deserve to run the news division of the largest media conglomerate in the world?"

Lewis nodded in silent approval at his choice of footage to cover the lede-in: Kane exiting Channel Seven in Philly, dissolve to shot of the WorldMedia offices on Tenth Avenue in Manhattan. Music up. Fade. Voiceover.

"In the next hour, we're going to examine the life and career of this man whom some call a starmaker but whom others know as just a star-fucker. A man who has elevated brainless bimbos to new heights in TV news—in return for sordid sexual favors . . ."

Lewis smiled to himself, mesmerized by the masterful way he'd covered this portion of the voiceover with a series of tight shots dissolving from Jennifer Reed signing off at the Channel Seven anchor desk to a still photo of Jack Kane with his arm around her shoulders to the shots from his own video of Jennifer Reed lying on her bed, her bare legs splayed open, naked from the waist down.

He punched at the freeze-frame button on the editing machine and exhaled loudly. He always gave himself a couple of minutes to deliberate the effect this introductory series of images would have on Jack Kane when he received his copy, together with the note that informed him that copies had been sent to the gossip columnists of all the major tabloids in New York and Los Angeles and of course, to Seth Reilly, his chairman. A man who, according to Lewis' files, had supported Pat Buchanan in the 1996 primaries and was the first TV network boss to ban Calvin Klein commercials.

There was always the danger that Reilly would rip the tape from his VCR and throw it in the trash. There was the certainty that Kane would try to lie his way out of all the allegations, but once the tabloids got their hands on it there would be no going back.

The more aggressive newshounds would start digging, pestering the WorldMedia publicity department and doorstepping "anonymous sources" at Channel Seven, where there were enough insiders who knew the real Jack Kane.

For sure there would be enough of a scandal to prompt Seth Reilly to take a good close look at his top executive. And after that, Lewis did not imagine Jack Kane would have much of a career left.

Nor would Lewis. Not at Channel Seven, anyway. He'd have to be long gone out of there before he sent out the tape and before the Philly cops started looking for the stalker who'd terrorized four of the city's newswomen.

Most of the time he tried not to dwell on that thought. After all, his trail would be long cold, fingerprints and footprints long obliterated . . . but the cops were very much on his mind, today.

Distracted, he picked up his remote to switch on the TV and flick through the channels searching for a news update on the murder investigation. He almost missed the Fox newsbrief but a picture of the WorldMedia high-rise caught his eye.

He turned up the volume in time to hear a male reporter informing viewers that detectives from Pennsylvania had traveled to New York earlier in the day to search the Manhattan pied-à-terre of Jack Kane.

He stared at the monitor in disbelief, his heart suddenly leaping crazily in his chest as the reporter concluded that the president of WorldMedia News had not, as of that moment, been eliminated as a suspect in his wife's homicide.

Feverishly Lewis started clicking through the channels looking for another news station to confirm the story about Jack Kane. Then, throwing the remote aside impatiently, he rolled his chair towards the desk drawers and grabbed for the videotape, throwing it into the playback machine, stabbing at the buttons in a frenzy until he found the shot.

He felt almost giddy as he stared at the fuzzy picture. Could it be Kane? It had to be Kane. The cops were pursuing Kane, not Lewis. Jack Kane was the prime suspect in his wife's murder, not Lewis. There had been no mention of tire tracks found at the back of the house, no mention of trucks parked suspiciously on the grounds, only the story of cops searching Kane's apartment.

He laid his head down on his desk as a sudden wave of dizziness washed over him. It was eye strain, he told himself. He was making himself sick with the effort to superimpose Kane's hateful face on the blurry image. But it would do him no good to strain his eyes any further here.

Risky or not, he was just going to have to find a way to get to the videoprocessor in the newsroom. This, after all, was a whole new ballgame.

19

Every time the phone rang out in her den, Kate held her breath as she picked up, anticipating the sound of Harry's voice at the other end. She'd had a handful of calls during the evening since returning from the seven o'clock Mass but none, so far, had heralded Harry's angry tones demanding to know why she had left a detective—and a bag of evidence—on the New Jersey Turnpike.

She knew he had spoken to Maysie earlier that morning. He had called before she was even out of bed to say he'd be taking a rain check on brunch. He was supervising another search for the murder weapon on the grounds of the Kane mansion.

But it was way too late to be searching for anything now, thought Kate, staring out of the window above her desk. Maybe Harry felt that he didn't need to spell it out for her. Maybe his silence was intended as confirmation that she was no longer welcome on the investigation.

She let out a long sigh and forced her attention back to the words on her computer screen. She had downloaded a couple of feature articles about WorldMedia from the *New York Times* and a cover story about Gabriella Grant from the current issue of *People* magazine. She had already copied the more interesting and relevant details into her own files. Now, she needed to review the news stories that had appeared in the papers over the weekend.

Tommy appeared in the doorway as she picked up an article she'd clipped from the morning's *Inquirer*. "Hey, sweetheart." She swiveled around on her chair and saw that he was already in his pajamas, his face still glowing and healthy from the playdate she'd set up for him with his friend Joey. She'd enjoyed the crisp fall afternoon, too, sipping mimosas on the patio with Joey's mother, basking in the scent of late-blooming honeysuckle as they'd watched the boys knocking balls around the Nevins' tennis court.

"All ready for school tomorrow?" she asked, holding her arms open and beckoning him.

He walked towards her, one hand behind his back. "I've got a note for you from Sister Kathleen." He thrust a white envelope at her. "I forgot to give it to you on Friday."

She opened it and read the note from the school principal, aware that her son was staring at her with a frown on his face. "I'm in trouble, aren't I?"

"Goodness, no." She laughed. "Sister Kathleen just wants me to come in and have a chat with her."

"About me, I bet."

"Of course about you, you silly goose." She laid the note aside and rumpled his hair. "Why else would she want to see me?"

"I'm in trouble, I bet." The frown deepened.

"Oh I don't think so. And anyway, if it was really serious trouble I'm sure she'd have called me. She wouldn't let something like that stew over a whole weekend."

"She gave me the note on Thursday. I forgot to give it to you. So, I'm in trouble already."

"Oh . . ." Kate paused and stared hard at her son. He looked so worried. She took his hand in hers. "Well I wouldn't worry about it now. I'll deal with it tomorrow. Okay?"

"Really?"

"Really, truly," she assured him.

The frown disappeared and was replaced by a wide grin. "Hey, Mom, I got a question for you."

"Shoot."

"Okay. Why did the doctor take the doorbell off his door?"

"Hmmm . . ." Kate pretended to think about it, then shook her head. "I don't know. Why did the doctor take his doorbell off the door?"

Tommy giggled. "Because he wanted to win the Nobel prize, of course. Get it, Mom? The *No Bell* prize?"

"I get it." She laughed loudly and threw her arms around him. "Now, off to bed, silly goose."

"Mom." He struggled out of her grip. "I never did get a ride on the motorbike, and you promised . . ."

"Ah, well, it was really late by the time Detective Travis got back here." She got to her feet quickly and took his hand. "Come on, I'll tuck you in."

"Yeah, that's okay." Tommy nodded. "I thought it was something like that 'cause I heard the bike in the middle of the night."

Not quite the middle of the night, thought Kate, returning to her desk. But it had been late. The Road King was still parked in her driveway when she'd retired to bed and she'd been on the verge of sleep when the sound of the engine revving up had shattered the quiet.

Reassured that he'd made it back safely, she'd then turned over and slept. Maybe he'd simply decided to overlook the whole sorry incident, she thought now. Maybe he hadn't even told Harry. It really had been more of a personal disagreement in which Mike Travis was not totally without blame.

She turned to her keyboard and flipped through the subdirectory in her hard drive. She'd already created files for all the main characters: Emma Kane, Jack, and Tony Salerno. She had a file on the investigation and had already typed in notes detailing everything from her arrival at the Kane mansion with Harry Holmsby, including a note about Anna Mae Whitman and the realtor's visit to the Kane mansion on the morning of her own death.

In Emma Kane's file, she had jotted down the observations she'd made about the decor and furnishings of the house and the clothes in Emma's closets. And a little pen picture based on what she'd gleaned from the woman's best friend and from what Jack Kane himself had said about his wife.

Loving wife and mother, Kate added, recalling the homily from Mass. The pastor of her church had attempted to put the local tragedy into some sort of spiritual when-bad-things-happen-to-good-people perspective. In this case, he'd said, to a sweet, loving wife and mother. She wondered if the pastor had read about Tony Salerno, and she changed the period to a question mark after the word mother, then turned her attention back to Tony Salerno.

The morning papers had given his elderly mother's address in South Philly and had noted he was a Villanova graduate who had apparently dropped out of law school in his second year. He had returned to complete the law course, six months previously.

All the newspapers had speculated about Emma and Salerno's relationship. Much had been made of the fact that Jack Kane had moved to New York nine months before, and that the couple were virtually estranged. Pat Norris in the *News* had quoted a police spokesman describing Salerno as a part-time handyman at the Kane household, thereby casting Emma into a Lady Chatterley–type role.

Kate hoped she would be able to portray Emma as a sympathetic victim: a wife and mother who had done all the right things and then found herself in the throes of a passionate affair, a last-ditch attempt to find some fulfillment.

She wondered if Tony Salerno had a history of relationships with older women. The address on his driver's license was his mother's address. Did he live with his mother?

What she needed were some solid answers. She had to know the life stories of all the main characters. She would have to trace the paths of both victims—almost from birth to the point where fate had brought them together. How had Emma and Salerno met? A pickup in the street? In the mall? She started jotting down a list of possible starting points: *Salerno's mother/South Philly, Friends, fellow classmates, professors/Villanova law school, Ex-girlfriends . . .*

Then she exited the file and created a new one where she planned to keep track of the crime lab findings. She had visions of the file remaining empty—unless Harry softened and slipped her the information under Maysie's kitchen table.

The ringing of the phone made her fingers jump on the keyboard. This time it had to be Harry, she thought, grabbing the receiver and holding it hesitantly to her ear.

But it wasn't. A deep male voice on the other end identified himself as Lester Franks. "You may remember me," he added. "We met a couple of years ago on the set of your movie."

Your movie? *Nice touch, Lester.* She smiled to herself. She recalled him immediately. A seasoned veteran reporter for a supermarket tabloid, he'd wormed his way onto the movie set to dig up the dirt on a TV actress who'd been cast in a supporting role.

"So, what can I do for you, Lester?" she asked amiably. She had no quarrel with Franks or the job he'd done. The actress had been an awful prima donna and Lester's copy had been good publicity for the movie—and her book.

Now she listened as Lester explained he needed information on the Main Line murders, how he understood that she had an in with the cops, and how the *Enquirer* would make it worth her while if she merely confirmed a tip he'd picked up at the scene.

"Like what?" she asked.

"A tip that Emma Kane and this Salerno dude were shot in the middle of the act, so to speak."

"A tip?" She tutted. "Your editor's already written the headline, hasn't he? What is it? Slaughter of TV Exec's Wife Stops Night of Lust and Passion Dead?" She paused. "No deal, Lester."

"Well, the thing is, we've got quite a good little piece on Mrs. Kane and the Italian Stallion. You know, when and how they met, that sort of thing. I'd just like to nail down this one, teeny little fact."

"You've got a story on how and when they met?" Kate's interest perked.

"Yeah, it's in the issue that's closing tomorrow night. It'll be out on the stand next week."

"So, where and when did they meet?"

There was a pause at the other end and Kate cursed herself for jumping on it too quickly.

"Tit for tat, Kate."

"I can wait, Lester. I've got plenty of time." She could, of course, but her curiosity was piqued now.

"Come on," he wheedled. "Were they doing it? Were they in bed?"

Kate paused to consider what exactly she would be giving away. "When did they meet?"

"Mrs. Kane's birthday. In June. Your turn, Kate."

"You already have the answer, Lester. The police gave a statement on Friday saying that she hadn't been sexually assaulted."

"That's not the question I'm asking."

"*Where* did they meet?" Kate prodded.

"Now, that's the really interesting part." He was stringing her along, she suspected. "We're going with it on the cover. Pictures and all."

Kate knew she'd have to tell Lester what he wanted to know—but in a way that couldn't be traced back to her. She thought quickly.

"Okay, let me help you figure this out, Lester. The police said there was no evidence of sexual assault. That was Friday and way too soon to analyze *any* bodily fluids—or eliminate anyone." She paused. "Are you with me?" Another pause while Lester Franks grunted into the phone. "So that would suggest, if I were working this story, at least, that there weren't any traces of semen to analyze, which would indicate—"

"Any used condoms in sight?"

"Lester . . . where did they meet?"

"Condoms or no?"

"This had better be good, Lester."

"You won't be disappointed." He sounded sincere.

"Okay. No."

"No?" His own disappointment was clear at the other end.

"Well?" She waited for what seemed like a while.

"They met through an outfit called Midnite Men."

"On the Main Line?" It was more of an exclamation than a question.

"Center City."

"Midnite Men?" Kate repeated the name. "An escort service?"

Lester Franks laughed. "Not quite. Toodle-oo, Kate."

And he hung up.

20

K ate was happy that she had her own lead to pursue as the new week dawned. As soon as Tommy left on the school bus, she headed for the shower and was dressed and ready to roll by nine. If Mike was waiting for a showdown with her in Harry's office then he'd have a long wait, she thought as she sped towards Center City.

She had found an entry for Midnite Men in the Philadelphia telephone directory after Lester's phone call. She had called the number and heard a recorded message: a young male voice suggesting huskily that she call back during business hours. Despite Lester's denial, she had looked for the name under Escort Services in the *Yellow Pages* anyway. Also on a real long shot she'd checked it out under the entry for Caterers. She'd finally given up but had made a note of the address listed in the phone book. Midnite Men was located on Ninth Street, somewhere close to Market, she judged.

The office turned out to be on the corner of Ninth and Market—up one steep flight of uncarpeted stairs above an adult bookstore. It was located at one end of a long, dingy corridor. Black lettering on the frosted glass pane simply read MIDNITE MEN. At the other end a bright neon light flashed a welcome to NUDIE PEEPSHOWS—24 HOURS. Like two pornographic book ends, thought Kate, anticipating the worst as she pushed open the door.

The smell of Johnson's Country Fresh deodorizer hit her as soon as she walked in. It was mixed in with a lingering scent of Lemon Endust. Clean but sparsely furnished, the office was dominated by a large desk on which sat a telephone with four buttons indicating four lines. Three high filing cabinets stood against one wall. Behind the desk sat a young woman who had perfected the Big Hair look. She was thumbing through a copy of the *Enquirer* but put it down as Kate walked towards her. She looked surprised, as if customers rarely ventured onto the premises. Probably they didn't, thought Kate. It was, no doubt, some sort of service that was usually ordered by phone.

"Can I help you?"

"I'm sure you can." Kate smiled cheerfully at her. "I'm looking for some information. I'm writing a book."

The girl perked up. "About strippergrams?"

Strippergrams. The naughty version of singing telegrams. Bingo. Kate grinned, making the obvious connection: Tony Salerno, a student working his way through college, had delivered a strippergram to Emma Kane on her forty-sixth birthday.

She shook her head as the girl stared at her through thickly mascaraed eyelashes. "As a matter of fact, it's about the Main Line murders. I believe Tony Salerno used to work here."

The girl's face immediately took on an appropriately somber expression. "Oh, poor Tony. That was so, so terrible. He was such a sweetie, too. And you're right, he did work for us for a while."

She held up the *Enquirer*. "As a matter of fact, there was a reporter from this paper here the other day, asking the same question. I gave him a picture of Tony. I'm really sorry but I don't have any left."

"That's okay, I don't need one right now. I'd just like to know a little bit more about Tony and when he met Emma Kane, the woman who was—"

"Birthday," the girl replied without waiting to hear the rest. "Tony was booked for her birthday party."

"What kind of a strippergram?"

The girl thought for a moment then walked across the room to one of the filing cabinets and took out a manila folder. "It was back in June. He went as a cop." She nodded.

"That's right. That's the one where he informs the birthday girl that a car"—she glanced down at the folder—"in this case a green Jaguar, registered to her address has been identified by a witness as the getaway car in a bank robbery in Center City. Then when she protests, of course, he whips out the cuffs, puts them on her, and proceeds to take off his uniform."

"Neat," Kate observed drily. "Half your customers probably don't see another birthday."

The girl looked at her quizzically.

Kate smiled. "I mean the shock could . . . Oh, never mind, it was just a joke. Who booked the telegram for Mrs. Kane?"

The girl consulted the folder again as Kate prodded: "Not Mr. Kane, by any chance, was it?"

The girl shook her head. "No, it was a friend of Mrs. Kane's. It was paid for by a Betsy Wright."

Well that was interesting, thought Kate. Betsy Wright had denied knowing Tony Salerno or anything about him. But she had surely been at the party. Or had she? Maybe it had been a private party—just Emma and the stripper?

"Are you also an escort service?"

The girl looked offended. "Certainly not. Whatever Tony was doing at Mrs. Kane's last week, he was doing it on his own time. Maybe she took a fancy to him when he performed at her birthday party. That's the only thing I can think of. Tony was a hunk, you know. We often had women calling here for his home phone number."

"Did Mrs. Kane call for his number?"

The girl shook her head. "Not that I recall. Maybe she asked him for it at the party."

Maybe.

"Anyway, Tony stopped working for us during the summer," the girl added.

"Why?"

"He didn't really want to quit because the money and the tips are so good, but he was getting a lot of flak from his S.O."

"S.O.?"

"You know, significant other, as in girlfriend. I don't

think she was very happy about him doing this sort of thing. I got the feeling she was a bit snooty."

"Did you ever meet her?"

The girl shook her head.

"What makes you think she was snooty?"

"Oh just the way she answered the phone when we called for Tony."

"Do you know who she is? Where she lives?"

"They lived together."

"Is that so?"

"Mmmm." The girl nodded. "Hold on a sec. I've got the address here. That's where we sent his checks. Here it is. Wallace Street."

"The Art Museum area, right?" Kate asked but didn't really need confirmation from the girl. She knew the city well.

The Art Museum area was a mixture of rundown blocks with the sort of street corners where crack dealers might lurk. It was peppered with empty lots, which were used as trash dumps, but there were pockets where old brownstones were being renovated and turned into large, airy apartments and were, no doubt, being snapped up by young professionals. She found the house where Tony Salerno had lived on an up-and-coming block. A big brownstone with a glossy, painted red door. There were three nameplates and an intercom alongside. None of the names was Salerno. There was a Maxwell, a Greenstreet, and a Tibbetts/Kasey.

Kate pressed the top one, and when she got no answer proceeded to the next. No answer there either. Tibbetts/Kasey finally produced a response from a young, graceful-looking male who came to the front door wearing a silk smoking jacket.

"Yes? Can I help you?"

"I'm looking for . . ." Kate hesitated. "For Tony Salerno's girlfriend."

"Are you a reporter?"

"No." Kate shook her head and extended her hand. "I'm Kate McCusker. I'm a writer. I've been working with the detectives investigating the murders for a book on the case."

Kate sensed the young man's sudden interest. "Did you know Tony?"

The young man made a noise that sounded like a cross between sniffing and choking. "Better than I wanted to." Then he held the door open wide. "Oh, you may as well come in."

Kate followed him down a passageway to a front door on the first floor and then into a cavernous living room with ceilings that she estimated were at least eighteen feet high. The big bay window looked out onto the street. The apartment was exquisitely decorated and furnished. A polished, shiny wood floor provided a surround for the heavy Oriental rugs. Huge potted plants stood by the window. Bright, modern art decorated the lilac walls. She recognized the music from *Swan Lake* playing softly, and through an arched doorway, glimpsed a reflection in what appeared to be a mirrored wall. Another young man was at the barre that ran along one wall, practicing pliés.

"I'm Hugh Kasey, by the way." The man in the smoking jacket motioned for her to sit down on one of the oversized couches in the room. "You said you were working with the detectives. Tell me everything."

Kate detected more than just a glimmer of curiosity in Hugh Kasey's eyes. "I hope the little shit suffered."

Immediately his hand flew to his mouth. "Oops, please don't write that in your book. I didn't mean for that to slip out. It's just that Jill is so much better off without him."

"You knew them both?" Kate prodded. It was obvious that Hugh had not only known both but had known them well enough to develop some strong feelings towards Tony Salerno.

"We, myself and Brian"—he waved his hand toward the ballet dancer—"we've been friends of Jill and Caroline's for ages, ever since we all moved in to this building. Brian and I were the first to move in. Then a couple of weeks later Jill and Caroline moved in on the top floor. We're really more like family."

"Caroline?" Kate echoed. Hugh and Brian. Jill and Caroline. She wondered where Tony Salerno had fit in?

As if understanding her confusion, Hugh quickly added: "Caroline is an absolute little sweetheart. We've known her since she was four. Jill was doing a magnificent job till that putz came back."

Kate nodded. "Caroline is Jill's daughter?"

Hugh nodded in response. "Exactly so. Can I get you a cup of tea, by the way? We have a delicious herbal brew we just found in Reading Terminal."

Kate shook her head quickly, not wanting Hugh to interrupt himself. "You were saying Caroline is Jill's daughter . . ."

"Yes." Hugh got up off the couch and walked into the back room. He was gone a few moments before returning with a sketch pad. "That's Caroline, the sweetie. I drew that a couple of weeks ago." He offered the sketch pad to Kate, open to a page with a pencil sketch of a little girl with dark curls and a dimple in her left cheek. "You can see the resemblance." He sniffed again.

Kate raised an eyebrow as realization dawned. "Salerno was Caroline's father?" As Hugh nodded, she said, "You said something about Salerno coming back. From where?"

Hugh rolled his eyes. "Who knows. The man was a loser. He couldn't stick with anything. For a while he was on the West Coast. Took off for Hollywood, thought he was going to be the next Richard Gere or something. He could have graduated law school like Jill. But no. I guess the idea of supporting a family was too overwhelming for him."

"They met at Villanova?"

"Oh, so you know. I don't have to tell you—"

"No, I don't know the whole story. I just know he was registered at the law school this semester."

"Yes, that's a laugh, too. He promised Jill all kinds of things, like for one, he was going to graduate and get a job."

Kate reflected that Hugh was only too happy to spill his neighbors' secrets, and he had obviously been privy to many of Jill's.

"They were both at Villanova when Jill got pregnant. But then he dropped out. Jill graduated five months after Caroline was born and got a job immediately."

"Where does she work?"

"She's with Swain and Carruthers now. They have offices at One Liberty Plaza."

Kate made a note of the name. She wasn't familiar with the law firm.

"Anyway," Hugh continued, "Jill did it all on her own and then Salerno comes creeping back about a year ago. A total failure, of course. So he worms his way back into her life, making all kinds of promises."

"Maybe he intended to make good on the promises?"

Hugh sputtered. "He was using her. He knew he was onto a good thing. He had a nice place to live and Jill paid some of his tuition. He said he was going to pay her back and pay his way but all he ever got was piddling little jobs."

"Like the one at Midnite Men? Jill apparently didn't want him working there."

"Well, would you? She's working for a big-time law firm and her live-in is a stripper! Come on. She was willing to put up with a lot of bullshit but even Jill drew the line somewhere."

"Why did she take him back?"

"Good question." Hugh paused. "I suppose mainly for Caroline's sake. She wanted Caroline to have a father." Hugh shrugged as if the idea was too difficult to comprehend.

"Did you ever hear about Emma Kane before last Thursday?"

"No, but I remember saying to Brian that I wasn't surprised. You know, when we read about Salerno doing it with a woman old enough to be his mother. I'm sure he was making her pay for it because she sure as hell wasn't paying him to fix things around the house like one of the TV reports said last night." Hugh laughed out loud. "Tony was not someone who fixed things around the house. He's the type who had to call an electrician to change the setting on the thermostat."

"You didn't think very highly of him, did you, Hugh?" Kate remarked drily.

Her tone was not lost on Hugh Kasey. "Listen, I'm trying very hard not to be bitchy," he countered. "But you said you were writing a book and I don't think you should make the mistake of eulogizing Salerno as some sort of clean-cut American Golden Boy whose only dream was to get a good job so that he could provide for his family."

Kate smiled and got to her feet. "Well, thank you, Hugh; I think I've certainly got a more balanced picture now."

She let herself out, and walking down the steps to the sidewalk, glimpsed a TV satellite news van turning the corner and heading towards her. She crossed the street to her Jeep quickly and sat in the car watching the news van.

She noted the Channel Seven logo on the side of the van, and as it pulled to a stop she saw a slim blonde jump out and run up the steps to Jill Maxwell's brownstone. A couple of moments later Hugh came to the door again. She saw him beckoning the blonde into the house.

Evidently Hugh was determined that no one was going to eulogize Tony Salerno. Kate picked up her car phone and dialed the number of the Lower Merion P.D. "Harry Holmsby, please." It was only right to let him know about Jill Maxwell. It would be all over the evening news tonight.

"Katey!" His voice boomed on the line. "I was wondering what happened to you. You didn't call."

Kate took a deep breath. It didn't sound as if Mike had said anything to Harry, yet. "As a matter of fact I was following up on a lead of my own. Did you know Salerno had a seven-year-old daughter? He was living with her and the child's mother, a Jill Maxwell, on Wallace Street?"

She heard Harry chuckle. "We're on it, McCusker. Lansing and Travis are interviewing Ms. Maxwell even as we speak."

"Have you spoken to Mike Travis?"

"Not about the interview. He should be back soon, though."

"Anything else happening?"

"We had a couple of B-and-Es overnight in Bryn Mawr."

"You know what I mean. On the investigation. Did you find the gun, yet?"

"Negative." Harry sounded resigned. "No gun, and none of the neighbors heard or saw squat."

"What about the stuff we brought back from Jack Kane's apartment?"

"Not processed yet. Crime lab guys are backed up as usual."

"Hmmm. Can I call you later, Harry? See what your guys

turn up on Ms. Maxwell. I spoke to a neighbor. It sounds like an interesting situation."

There was a pause on the other end. Uh-oh, thought Kate. Now he was going to tell her she was out of the loop. "Harry?"

"Yeah, why not? They should have a report typed for me later this afternoon."

"Any chance I can get my hands on a copy?"

"I'll see. If it's ready, I'll bring it along when I stop by to pick up Maysie. But I doubt they'll have it done by then. Oh, remind her to be ready around six. It's the P.B.A. annual dinner dance. I don't want to miss cocktails."

"I don't blame you." She laughed and hung up, relieved that Mike had evidently decided against mentioning Saturday's debacle to Harry. She hoped it was a permanent reprieve, even though she knew it was going to be awkward seeing him again. But she'd just have to deal with that when it happened, she decided, dismissing the thought.

Across the street, the news van was still parked outside the house. The door was closed. She'd definitely have to tune in to Channel Seven news tonight. They'd probably have something on the six o'clock edition. Maybe she could catch the story between making dinner for Tommy and checking his homework.

The thought of her son suddenly reminded her that she had forgotten to call his principal and she groaned. She looked at her watch and realized that school was just about wrapped for the day. It was five past three. She grabbed her phone again and dialed the number.

Mrs. Masters, the school secretary, answered and Kate identified herself. "I was supposed to call Sister Kathleen and arrange to come in and see her. But I've been on the run all day. Could I reschedule for tomorrow, perhaps?"

There was a little pause at the other end. "Oh, dear, I wish you had let us know earlier." Mrs. Masters sounded concerned. "I'm afraid there was some confusion over whether he had delivered the note to you. Would you hold for a moment, please?"

Seconds later, Sister Kathleen herself was on the phone. "It's not a serious problem, Mrs. McCusker," she said in her quiet, reassuring tones. "But I felt you should know that Mrs. Basualdo came in to see me last week. We should discuss it."

Kate blinked. Belinda was checking out Tommy's school and she hadn't even mentioned it to Kate. What the hell was going on?

She's worming her way in . . . pushing for more. Her mother-in-law's words suddenly came hammering back at her.

"I'll be in first thing tomorrow, Sister," she said, her head starting to throb as she hung up.

21

There was hell to pay when she got home. And the guilt stayed with her all evening. If anything, it was even worse after Tommy was finally in bed that night. Curled up on the couch in her study, Kate felt more remorse than when she'd first pulled up to the house to face Tommy, who was sitting waiting for her on the porch, his face dark and sad. She was hardly out of the car before he'd let fly. "You were supposed to be at school, Mom. I gave you the note. You said you were going to be there."

"I'm so sorry, honey."

"Sorry? Sorry!" Tommy's face had creased into an angry frown. "That's not good enough, Mom. I had to go to the principal's office and she asked me why I didn't give you the note. She made it sound like it was all my fault."

Kate put her arms around him but he shrugged her off. "I got into trouble, Mom, and it was all your fault."

Her chest tightened. "Tommy, I'm seeing Sister Kathleen tomorrow. I'll explain everything. I promise, sweetheart. You're right; it was all my fault. I just got so wrapped up in running around today, by the time I remembered about the note you were already out of school."

She had spent the rest of the evening trying to make him feel better. Hovering attentively beside him as he did his homework, she'd even given him all the answers to his math problems without making him work them out for himself. She'd been so preoccupied with the effort that she'd forgotten all about the six o'clock news—and she had burned the casserole stew that Maysie had left in the refrigerator to heat up for their dinner.

In a way the whole evening had served to drive home her failures, she reflected as she slumped on her couch, sipping a small Scotch. She'd lit a fire and chosen a soothing Harry Connick CD. But her spirits were taking a long time to lift. She was a lousy cook, she told herself; she was okay on math but knew nothing about Spanish verbs, and she broke promises. She was a poor substitute for a mother.

Fleetingly, she surmised that Belinda would have done no better but almost immediately she banished the thought. Comparing herself favorably to a mother who had abandoned her son was small comfort. Why was she always making these silly comparisons, anyway? Every time she thought about Belinda it was almost as if Kate was preparing herself for some dramatic battle in court.

"And, a further point, your Honor," Belinda's lawyer would accuse. "Mrs. McCusker, the child's guardian, neglected to keep an important school appointment with the principal simply because she was doing some minor research for her book."

"But your Honor," her own counsel would say, "the child's natural mother neglected to keep any school appointments or birthdays or playdates for the entire first half of her son's life."

"Mom!" Tommy's voice interrupted the courtroom duel and she looked up to see him standing in the doorway in his pajamas. "There's someone at the door. I think it's that detective. I heard his bike."

I don't think so. "You're hearing that bike in your dreams,

Tommy. Now go back to bed." She laughed. But even as she shook her head, the doorbell chimed again.

She ran down the stairs into the kitchen and through the foyer to open the door. She saw the gleaming Road King first, parked in the driveway, and then her eyes focussed on Mike Travis, leaning against the doorjamb. Her hand went to her hair, which she'd unpinned before settling down with her drink. She felt half dressed with her hair hanging loosely around her shoulders. But Mike Travis didn't seem to notice her discomfort.

"Hi." He attempted a smile. "I was wondering if you had five minutes."

"For what?"

"To talk." He paused, and she opened the door a little wider. "I wanted to apologize."

Apologize? It was not what she'd expected from him.

"I'm sorry for what I said. I was way out of line."

Kate stared at him unflinching.

"I brought you something." The smile flashed at full wattage this time.

"That wasn't necessary." She couldn't see anything in his hands.

"No, it wasn't necessary." He paused. "But I know you're going to appreciate the gesture."

He put his hand inside his jacket and brought out a cassette. An audiotape.

"What is it?" She grinned suddenly. "Not the Jill Maxwell interview, by any chance?"

"No." He shook his head. "We don't have a tape of that. This is Betsy Wright. I figured she had some explaining to do since she's the one who arranged Salerno's appearance at Emma's birthday party. I think you'll find this more interesting than what Jill Maxwell had to say."

The way he said it prompted Kate to hold the door open. "Why don't you come in?"

She led the way back through the kitchen and up the stairs to her study and invited him to sit down. Connick was in mellow mode and she heard herself offering Mike a drink.

She handed him a Scotch, then walked over to her stereo system, silenced Connick, slipped the cassette tape into the tape deck, and pushed the Start button. Mike's voice echoed through the speakers, picking up midway through his opening salvo.

". . . Just need some straight answers, Mrs. Wright. I know last time we talked you were probably upset and confused."

"You're being kind, detective," Betsy Wright's voice was soft and hesitant, and Kate turned up the volume. "I'm sorry I wasn't very truthful with you, but I didn't know what to say. I was so shocked to see that young boy upstairs in Mr. Kane's bathrobe."

"You didn't know Mrs. Kane was seeing him?"

"She wasn't seeing him." Betsy sounded adamant. "That's not how it was at all." Betsy cleared her throat. "When he was at her house, for the birthday party, I mean, she found out that he was attending Villanova Law School. She told him there were less demeaning ways of working his way through school—"

"Like?" Mike interrupted.

"Like doing work around the house for her. She needed someone after Jack told her to get rid of the housekeepers. Tony wasn't that good but I think she felt sorry for him. He was supposed to drive us to the airport that morning."

"I see. And you think that's why he was spending the night?" Mike sounded skeptical and there was a short pause on the tape. Then he spoke again. "Did Emma tell you that she'd offered Salerno room and board in exchange for taking care of those little odd jobs around the house?"

"No!" Betsy sounded shocked.

"She told her husband that she had. Did you know Salerno was at the house on Thursday afternoon when Mr. Kane arrived?"

There was a much longer pause on the tape before Betsy Wright cleared her throat again. "No. Emma didn't mention it." Then Kate heard a curious sound, like a short, throaty laugh before Betsy spoke again. "But it sounds like the sort of thing Emma would say and do just to rile Jack."

"You mean you think she was deliberately flaunting Salerno in front of her husband?"

"It's possible. Emma was quite capable of playing her own little games, especially when she was angry with Jack."

"And she was angry with him on that Thursday, right?"

There was a long silence. So long that Kate thought the tape was switching sides. Then, Betsy said, "Yes. I guess she was."

"She called you?"

"After Jack had gone, yes." Betsy's voice was no more than an unhappy whisper.

"What did she say, Mrs. Wright?"

"She was upset. She said she thought Jack was pushing her into a divorce."

"How so?" Mike's voice sounded deceptively soft on the tape.

"She said he'd told her that the house had to be sold and after that she could do what she wanted. They could split the proceeds and she could stay here on the Main Line."

"That doesn't sound very pushy." Mike sounded disappointed. "If he really wanted a divorce, wouldn't Jack Kane have been a little more direct?"

Betsy seemed to think a long time about the question. "Well, Emma thought he was being careful because he didn't want to appear to be the bad guy. He didn't want it to look as if the divorce was his idea."

Kate raised an eyebrow in Mike's direction but he merely shook his head and pointed at the tape deck, as if to say, All will be revealed. She noticed his glass was almost empty and thought about offering him another Scotch but then Betsy Wright said: "I think he felt he had to be careful, working at WorldMedia."

"Why?"

"Well because of Seth Reilly. Apparently he's something of a straight arrow."

"Yeah, I think I've read that about him." Mike sounded as if he was grinning. "But he couldn't expect all his employees to be as puritan as he is."

Betsy's laugh pealed out in Kate's study. "That would be tough, I suppose. On the other hand I don't think he's the kind of boss who'd turn a blind eye to his top executive ditching a wife of twenty years." There was a pause. Then Betsy added: "Emma told me she and the Reillys really hit it off when they first met, and she thought the fact that she and Jack had been married so long gave Jack an edge in getting the job. I mean she didn't make a big point about it but then I suppose all other things being equal, Seth Reilly was probably more inclined to choose someone who seemed as conservative and stable as he is."

Mike jumped to his feet and crossed the room to pause the tape, then looked at Kate, grinning. "Interesting, don't you think?"

Kate had to agree. "I suppose it would also explain why he'd be so secretive about an affair. I guess that's why he backed off taking that other reporter to New York, the one that Gabriella Grant mentioned. The one Emma freaked over. I guess even a Jack Kane has to be careful about pissing off the big boss." She rose from the couch and poured Mike another drink. A smaller one this time.

"My thoughts exactly." Mike took the glass from her hand. "And, I'm sure that goes doubly so for Ms. Grant."

Kate nodded, recalling the article she'd downloaded from *People* magazine about the anchorwoman. "She's married, too. Apparently there's a husband in the Pittsburgh area somewhere, although the article I read implied that they're estranged."

Mike grinned. "It sounds like it might be worth checking out, though." He sipped his Scotch. "I'm convinced that everything hinges on that pair."

Kate ran her finger around the rim of her glass, understanding that he was referring to Kane and Gabriella Grant. "So, I guess you ruled out Jill Maxwell then?"

Mike's puzzled expression confirmed that he'd evidently not given the woman a second thought since his visit with Betsy Wright. Then he shook his head. "She said she didn't know about Emma Kane, and it sounded to me like she couldn't have cared less." He reached into his back pocket for a notebook, and flipped it open. "Her exact words were, 'If I was going to worry about Tony with other women, there were dozens of others, younger and prettier, I could have wasted my time on—' "

"Yeah, but Emma Kane was the one he was fooling

around with," Kate interrupted as he closed the notebook.
"Don't you think Maxwell sounds just a bit too laid-back for
someone who was paying his rent and tuition?"

Mike shrugged. "She was very adamant that her daughter
was her priority. So long as Salerno was playing the good
daddy, she seemed to think everything was cool."

Kate sipped her drink, reflecting that Jill Maxwell's
neighbor Hugh had said more or less the same thing.

"Anyway," Mike continued, "Jack Kane's the one who
had everything to gain." He paced across to the tape deck
and punched the Fast Forward button. "You haven't heard
the punch line, yet. Listen to this." He punched the Play
button, listened for a second, then hit the buttons again
before letting the tape pick up the tail end of a question.

Then Betsy Wright's sigh came through the speakers,
loud and clear. "No, she wasn't happy about anything. She
didn't want to move to New York, but she didn't like the
idea of separate homes, either. She said she told Jack that if
she decided to stay on the Main Line, she wanted more
than half the money from the sale of the house. She told
him she wanted the same percentage that she'd put into the
house when they bought it."

"Meaning?" Mike sounded puzzled.

"All of it." Betsy laughed nervously. "They bought the
house with money Emma inherited from her parents. Of
course it was Jack's money that they poured into it, over the
years, to turn it into the mansion it is now. But that was
Emma." Betsy paused. "Look, don't get me wrong, Emma was
my dearest friend but she could be a real you-know-what if
you got on the wrong side of her. I think she was letting Jack
know that she wasn't just going to step aside quietly."

Mike stopped the tape in midsentence and paced towards
the fireplace, a satisfied look on his face. "Now, that doesn't
sound quite as laid-back as Kane made it all sound, does it?"
He shook his head. "I think you were right about him wanting to manipulate Emma out of the house, and out of the
marriage. But she was obviously a tougher cookie than we
thought. She makes it clear it's going to be a messy, not to
say very costly process. I would think that a shortcut must
have looked very tempting to Kane that Thursday night."

Kate wasn't sure she could find much to disagree with in Mike's terse summary. Except, as she pointed out, staring absently at the leaping flames in the fireplace, Betsy's account was secondhand and relied heavily on Emma Kane's interpretation of her husband's suggestion about separate homes. "Maybe she read more into that than he intended."

"Whatever she read into it doesn't matter," Mike said. "I think what's more relevant is that Emma apparently had a special talent for acting like a prize bitch. The question is, in this instance did she go too far? Did she actually push Kane to a breaking point? And I think she possibly might have done."

Kate looked up as Mike placed his empty glass on the coffee table and reached for his leather jacket from the back of her swivel chair. Then he hesitated, as if waiting for her to offer him another drink, before slipping into the jacket.

Kate hesitated, too, not wanting him to leave just yet. She was enjoying their discussion, but she knew she couldn't let him ride home if he had another Scotch. Instead she led the way to the top of the kitchen stairs where she thanked him for bringing the tape. "And thanks for not snitching on me to Harry," she added quickly.

"You mean about stranding me on the turnpike?" He laughed softly. "Now why would I do that?" He paused and his expression grew serious. "It was my fault, Kate. I behaved like a jerk. What I said had nothing to do with the investigation. The truth is . . ." He paused again, as if he was searching for the right words, then shrugged. "Let's just say I let my personal feelings get the better of me."

His eyes lingered on her face and Kate didn't look away. Few men, she reflected, would have had the guts to be so honest, especially when his outburst had been prompted in part by her own scathing—and somewhat less than truthful—putdown. She found herself reconsidering the idea of offering him another drink even as he reached out to brush back a strand of hair behind her ear.

But before she could say anything he'd stepped back and turned towards the stairs. "Thanks for the drinks, Kate," he said. "I'll see myself out."

For a while after he'd gone, she sat on her couch flicking idly through the channels on TV as she allowed her thoughts to drift. She wondered how it would have been if she'd asked him to stay. She had few doubts that he would have been more than happy had she given him the slightest encouragement, and she was not surprised that this thought prompted a series of mildly erotic images to suddenly pop unbidden into her head. Nor was she shocked by the equally sudden arousal that accompanied them. After a year of widowhood she had to admit that while Mike's turn of phrase about her eagerness to succumb to his charms had lacked a certain finesse, his observation had struck closer to the truth than he knew.

She stared at the flickering TV screen and regretted that she'd been so hesitant with him, then almost immediately told herself it was just as well. Mike Travis had reignited the spark, but was he the man to fan the flames? She laughed softly to herself, amused by her own turn of phrase, and she might have dwelt further on the thought but just then a familiar-looking face on the TV screen caught her attention.

She found herself staring at the reporter she'd seen outside Jill Maxwell's house earlier in the day but who was now reporting live from the police station in Lower Merion.

Her breathless voice announced: "A major turning point in the Kane murder investigation as police today quizzed Jill Maxwell, the live-in girlfriend of victim Tony Salerno."

Kate stared at the note at the bottom of the screen, which gave the reporter's name as Molly Heskell. "Earlier I spoke to friends and neighbors about the couple's very stormy relationship," Molly said, her words leading into a video package, obviously taped earlier in the day. It depicted Molly Heskell and Hugh Kasey in conversation outside the house but the audio was a voiceover and the report really contained no more solid information than what Hugh Kasey had imparted to Kate. But the way Molly Heskell had dressed it up with a lot of hyperbole, it sounded as if Tony Salerno and Jill Maxwell had come to blows on more than one occasion over his fickle lifestyle.

Maybe Hugh had exaggerated his story for TV. Maybe this was just typical TV hype, thought Kate as the scene switched again to Molly live in Lower Merion, but her eyes widened anew as she heard the reporter state: "A police source tonight would not confirm when—or whether—Jill Maxwell will be charged in the brutal double homicide."

What the hell is she talking about? Kate sat up straight on the couch as she suddenly realized that this was the reporter he'd left behind, the one Gabriella Grant had named as Jack Kane's former mistress.

She stared, mesmerized by the screen as the camera suddenly zoomed out to a two-shot of Jennifer Reed sitting at the anchor desk, the live scene now at her left elbow as she half turned to ad-lib with Molly Heskell. "So there could be a speedy conclusion to this awful tragedy."

Molly Heskell nodded. "And if there is, that would be very welcome news for Emma Kane's husband, who, as some viewers may know . . ."

Suddenly the live screen faded to black and Jennifer Reed found herself covering swiftly by blaming a technical problem before going to a commercial break.

More like a personal problem, thought Kate, jumping to her feet and pacing to her desk. She wanted to make a note about the report while the words were still fresh in her head. It had looked to her as if the producer had deliberately pulled the plug on Molly Heskell, and long after Jennifer Reed reappeared with another news story, Kate found herself reassessing what she had seen. The more she thought about it, the more convinced she was that Molly Heskell had actually skewed her story to portray Jill Maxwell as a jealous girlfriend with a motive to kill.

Talk about loyalty, thought Kate. For sure, Molly Heskell would find herself without a job in the morning, and it seemed outrageous to Kate that the young reporter had put her career on the line for a former boss and lover. The woman had to be nuts.

22

Molly knew there'd be trouble when she returned to the newsroom. Pete Norcross had given her some warning as she drove back to Center City with the camera crew. Even so, no one could have really prepared her for the extent of Nick Myers' wrath—nor the fact that he chose to embarrass her in front of the whole newsroom.

"Who the fuck elected you district attorney, Heskell?" he yelled as she stepped off the elevator. "What was all that bullshit about charging Maxwell? What the hell was going on in your head? She's a fucking lawyer in case it escaped your notice. Are you deliberately trying to get us involved in a damn lawsuit—or shall I just write Maxwell a big fat check now?"

Molly withstood the tirade in silence. Then when it seemed that Myers was finished she said, "I did my job, that's all. I asked the question. I've got it on tape."

"Yeah, what was the question, Heskell?"

"The usual one," she stared back at him. "I asked Holmsby himself if they were going to charge her."

"Yeah? Yeah and what did he say? Let me guess. No comment, right? But you turned the whole effing thing around."

Molly wanted to say that this was hardly the first time that a Channel Seven reporter had interpreted a police spokesman's "No Comment" to give it a more dramatic twist. Instead, she said, "The cops spent three hours with Maxwell today, Nick. They escorted her to Bryn Mawr Hospital.

They weren't taking her to dinner in the goddamn hospital cafeteria."

Nick Myers came striding across the newsroom, his face red with anger. "Don't be a smartass, Heskell. You can't talk about a speedy conclusion to the investigation and Jill Maxwell's propensity towards violent arguments with her boyfriend in the same breath. That little tidbit certainly didn't come from the cops." He paused, eyeing her with a malevolent glint. "I know this development suits you, but if you pull a stunt like that again, you're fired. Understood?"

She tried to tell herself she didn't care. Fire me, you prick, she thought. But not tonight. She needed to stay on top of the story. She needed time to do some investigating of her own.

Jennifer Reed had adamantly refused to reconsider talking to the cops about the assaults. Only that morning she'd beckoned Molly into her office and thrust a piece of wire copy into her hands. "Look at this. See? It says that according to a source close to the investigation, the cops think Salerno let in the killer himself."

"So?"

"Well, that means they think the killer came to the front door, rang the doorbell. That's not our wacko, Molly. He didn't ring any doorbells so far as I recall."

Molly hadn't bothered arguing any further. It was obvious that Jennifer had dug in her heels. But that didn't mean Molly couldn't do some digging around on her own. If the cops came looking for her she wanted to be ready with a name or two. Even if it turned out that the pervert had nothing to do with Emma Kane's murder, the memory of what he had done to her rankled. She wanted something done about it. But she knew she was on her own.

She had already spoken to Diane and Janey and questioned them about the assaults. She had come away from the conversations convinced of two things: that they were as adamant as Jennifer about maintaining the conspiracy of silence, and that whoever had broken into their homes had been someone with inside knowledge of their comings and goings.

In her book, that meant it had to be someone connected

with Channel Seven—and someone who most likely drove a dark-colored truck. It was the only lead she had and one she felt she should pursue before Nick Myers threw her out of the office.

She waited till Myers withdrew into his office, then gathered up her things and left the newsroom. Instead of exiting on the ground floor however, she took the elevator right down to the basement garage. She had no clear idea of how she was going to get the information she needed until she was within a half-dozen feet of the garage attendant. He looked at her quizzically as she approached, no doubt because she never parked her car in the station garage.

"Hi!" She smiled at him as he jumped to his feet. "I'm Molly Heskell; I work in the newsroom upstairs."

"Sure, Miss Heskell, I just saw you on TV." He grinned back at her.

"The thing is . . ." She paused and peered at the name tag he wore on his jacket. "The thing is, Jake, we were having a bet upstairs about cars. And I bet that more than twenty percent of the staff here are now driving utility vehicles. You know, counting Jeeps and Blazers and Explorers?"

"Hmmm, that's an interesting one." He looked as if he was thinking hard. "I don't know that you're going to win this one, Miss Heskell." He turned abruptly and reached into his booth. "I've got a list of all the cars that are authorized to park in here. Let me see . . . of course, they may own a truck that they don't drive to work."

"Well." Molly relaxed into the quizzing. "Let's start with the ones you actually see in here."

He winked at her. "Well, there's your boss for starters, Mr. Myers."

"That's a forest green Jeep, right?"

"Correct." He nodded. "Then Pat Sellers, the programming VP, he drives a white Explorer."

Molly mentally crossed Pat's name off her list.

"Then Manzo drives a black Explorer—"

"Manzo?" She didn't recognize the name.

"Manzowski. He works late shifts."

"Doing what?"

Jake's eyes narrowed. "You should know better than me. I

only park his car. But I've seen him up in the newsroom when I go upstairs to steal a cup of coffee when everyone's gone."

"Doing what?"

"He's usually sitting, staring at one of the TV screens with headphones on."

"Oh." Molly smiled. "He transcribes and logs tapes."

Jake frowned and shrugged and Molly didn't bother explaining the job of preparing transcripts of tapes for reporters who were working on series or investigative reports. It was a menial task that required watching each tape and typing out all the soundbites alongside a timecode.

"Okay." She smiled again at Jake. "Anyone else?"

"Let's see." He ran his finger down a list that was attached to a clipboard. "June Ratner in sales drives a Jeep, Lenny Simpson has an Blazer . . ."

Molly nodded, discounting June Ratner. Lenny was a new cameraman who'd been hired by Nick Myers some six months before.

". . . and Terrenzio. He has a Blazer, too."

"Terrenzio?" she echoed. It was another name she wasn't familiar with.

"That's Terry." Jake paused. "I believe he's another one of those late shift guys who lugs tapes."

Molly grinned. "Logs, Jake. The word is logs. What color are the Blazers by the way?"

Jake consulted the clipboard. "Simpson's is black and Terry's is a dark green. Then, you've also got Vasco. She's in programming. That's a cherry red Explorer and . . ." He paused again. "That's it. So, let's see. That'll be seven trucks out of about forty-two cars that are parked here on a regular basis." He looked up at her, shrugging.

She patted Jake on the arm. "That's okay, Jake. It's close enough. Thanks for your help."

"Any time, Miss Heskell."

She headed back towards the elevator, repeating three names to herself: Simpson, Manzowski, and Terrenzio. As much as she hated his guts, she did not think that Nick Myers was a serious suspect. He didn't need to creep around or break in. He got his kicks by humiliating her in public.

The other three were more promising prospects. She had not worked with Lenny Simpson but she'd seen him around. A tall, quiet guy who sat at the back of the newsroom reading *Popular Electronics* when he wasn't out on a job. The other two she'd have to take a look at: She was always gone by the time the transcribers arrived. So was everyone else, she thought. Which left either of them plenty of time and space to nose around and look through desk drawers and files.

She glanced at her watch. It was almost eleven-thirty. The newsroom emptied rapidly after the show finished, and the loggers arrived anytime between then and midnight. No one paid attention to their schedules so long as they got the work done. She wondered if either Manzowski or Terrenzio had already arrived. She needed to get a look at them at least. Maybe get them talking.

But what if one of them was indeed the pervert? What if he realized she was checking him out? What if she found herself face to face with the sicko, alone in the empty newsroom? What excuse could she engineer for returning to the newsroom and engaging him in conversation?

What the hell, she thought suddenly, shrugging off the little shiver that ran up her arms. She didn't need to explain herself to loggers. She got on the elevator and punched the button for the newsroom.

23

Lewis stared at the small screen in front of him, then at the big newsroom clock. Then he got up from his desk and sauntered towards the men's room. The hallway led past the editing bays, and he had already located the videoprocessor in the last bay on the right, next to the bathrooms. He had even tested the door earlier to make sure it didn't get locked for the night and had nosed around for a couple more minutes to reassure himself that it was the same model he'd worked on in Duluth.

Just as well that he'd spent those extra moments nosing around, because returning down the hallway he'd suddenly heard the elevator doors open and seen Molly Heskell step into the newsroom.

She had not seen him disappearing quickly into the nearest editing room or watching her through the peephole window, his pulse racing as she walked over to the desks where they worked. He had seen her talk to his colleague, exchanging a few words, then glancing around the newsroom—as if looking for him. His heart had pounded dangerously. Why was she looking for him? He had not seen any of her tapes in his workload. In the next moment though he told himself that he was just acting like a nervous Nellie as she walked away and stepped back on the elevator. She had probably just been exchanging pleasantries.

Now he told himself to forget about her. There was no way she could be onto him. No way. That was past and gone, and it was just a waste of time thinking about it. He had to focus his thoughts on the more pressing matter of getting to the videoprocessor.

He turned and glanced quickly at the desk behind him, attempting to estimate how much work his colleague still had to get through.

Lewis had hoped to be alone in the newsroom. Sometimes Monday nights were light and only one of them had to show up. He always had first dibs at the graveyard shift because he'd been at the station longer. But tonight he saw that both of them would be occupied till well into the early morning. He chewed on his thumbnail. He couldn't risk anyone catching him at the videoprocessor.

He swiveled around again in his chair. "Big workload tonight," he said loudly, pointing to the stack of tapes. "Think you'll get through it?"

The other man nodded. "Got to. I don't want to be in tomorrow; it's my mom's birthday."

Okay! Lewis turned back to his own monitor, a fresh excitement coursing through him. So, tomorrow he'd be alone. Tomorrow he'd get his shot. Tomorrow could be the best day of his life. If he had Jack Kane on his tape, well that would just about accomplish everything he'd set out to do in the first place. And more. If he could nail the bastard but good, how sweet it would be. This would be more than just humiliation for Kane. This would be better than any downfall Lewis could orchestrate. Jack Kane could never slink back after this. This would mean an arrest, a conviction, and a career ended forever with the slamming of a cell door. He doubted that Kane would be able to survive jail.

Lewis blinked, picturing Kane as the cell doors clanged shut. He knew exactly what that would feel like. The memory of his own stint in the slammer was fresh enough: He could still hear the noises and smell the smells and feel his skin crawling. Thirty-two months had seemed like a lifetime in that godforsaken hole outside Duluth. Not that he had ever once blamed Stefanie. She had not wanted to press charges. She had understood. She was the one who'd tried to help him. She was the one who'd come closest to making him feel like a man again. So she had understood his frustrations and why, in the end, he had just lost control. But she'd been forced into turning against him by the lies they'd told her. You've got to stop him, they'd said. He's done it before, they'd told her, repeating all the lies Kane had told them. The scumbag.

Lewis stared down at his keyboard, his fists clenching over the keys. Well, Kane was going to get his, finally. If Kane was on that videotape, then he was history. All Lewis had to do then was figure out the logistics of getting the tape to the cops.

Could he send it FedEx? UPS? Or just walk into the police station and leave it on the desk? For sure, they didn't need him to authenticate it. He might type a short note to include in the package but the tape would speak for itself. There was a date and a time on it, and the Kane mansion was easily identified. It was not an insurmountable problem. What would the cops care, anyway, about how he'd gotten the tape? If necessary, he could follow up with an anonymous phone call. But right there was his quandary.

He didn't want the cops quizzing him about the night— but he didn't want to remain anonymous, either. For sure, he wanted Jack Kane to be in no doubt that it was Lewis who had provided the damning evidence against him.

He drummed his fingers on the desk. It was something to think about. Something he could work on and figure out with his usual care, down to the last detail before coming into work tomorrow. He'd have it all worked out by then.

24

Tuesday, October 1

Mike reached the outskirts of Pittsburgh before noon. He had set out early, figuring to give himself at least four hours to cover the three hundred miles between Ardmore and the quiet hamlet of Bellmore. It had not been difficult finding an address for Gabriella Grant's husband. The *People* magazine story had indeed mentioned him—or rather had dismissed him in about two sentences, one of which had described him as part owner of a construction company in Pittsburgh. One phone call had led him to Kevin Walker's home address just outside the city.

He pulled up in front of the small ranch house as the sky darkened, and for a moment he sat on his bike, letting the wind whip around him. It looked like the kind of day that would be perfect for staying in and lounging in front of a log fire. He pictured the fireplace in Kate McCusker's den. He got off his bike before Kate herself became part of the picture again.

He had woken thinking about her. Judging by his erection he figured he'd probably dreamt about her, too. He wasn't surprised. She'd been on his mind when he'd returned home the previous night, her delicate scent still lingering in his nostrils.

He had wanted to stay with her. Had she taken just one small step towards him, given him one miniscule opening, he'd have taken it from there. He'd wanted her the first time he'd seen her, and nothing he'd seen since had dampened any of the desire. If anything, he'd seen enough to know that she wasn't the sort of woman he'd want to walk away from in the morning. It was the first time he'd felt this way since Cheryl.

He'd tussled with the thought, standing under the cold spray of the shower that morning, wondering if he was ready to make that sort of effort again. By the time he'd switched off the faucet, he hadn't reached any dramatic conclusion but he'd picked up the phone to call her, only to learn that she was on her way out and headed for New York.

She had writer things to do, she'd said: lunch with her agent and a publisher, and then she planned to visit the WorldMedia offices. For research, she'd added. Maybe to talk to some employees so that she could get a better feel for her subject. He'd read that to mean Jack Kane and had found himself wondering about the chances of her bumping into Kane somewhere in the WorldMedia building? But it had not been a very comfortable thought. He knew that she did not see Kane the way he did. Evidently, in her eyes, men like Kane were above the pressures afflicting lesser mortals. As if Jack Kane didn't put his pants on one leg at a time.

Why did she find it so difficult to picture a philanderer like Kane cracking under the pressure of being trapped between two women? Especially the two in this case, Mike thought as he strode up the path to the ranch house. He already had a good idea of what Emma Kane had been like. Now, with any luck, he'd confirm his impression of Gabriella Grant as a ball-buster of equal magnitude.

His finger on the doorbell produced an instant response—the shrill cries of a baby—and he double-checked the number on the door of the ranch house against the note he'd made. The numbers were the same. So, he pressed the doorbell again. It took a couple of minutes before it finally opened.

"Yes?"

The woman who stood in the doorway with a baby cradled against her chest looked young. A pretty face, Mike thought, but straggly red hair that would benefit from shampoo.

Mike took his badge out. "I'm looking for Kevin Walker."

The woman didn't blink but opened the door a little wider and beckoned Mike in. "He's out back chopping wood."

Mike stepped into the hallway, almost tripping over a drop cloth and can of paint. He realized that there was some redecorating going on—in the hallway, in the kitchen that he passed through, and in the living room, which he caught a glimpse of on his way to the back porch.

He grinned awkwardly at the woman. "I'm sure you can't wait for your renovations to get finished."

She shrugged. "If I can't then it's tough luck for me. It's been like this for the last six months."

Mike let himself out the back door and crossed the yard to where Kevin Walker was about to swing down onto a massive tree trunk with an ax.

"Mr. Walker?"

"That would be me," the man answered without looking up. He brought the ax down with a sharp swing. Then he straightened up and looked at Mike.

"Detective Mike Travis. I'm with the Montgomery County DA's office," he added as Walker continued to stare at him blankly.

Mike judged him to be in his early forties. Walker had a strong face, as strong as the rest of his muscular body, but his hair was tinged with gray and there were dark shadows under his eyes. The eyes themselves surveyed Mike with a cold blue stare. He was evidently a man of few words. And even less curiosity.

"What can I do for you?"

"I'm investigating a double homicide. One of the victims was a woman by the name of Emma Kane."

Walker continued to stare, the name obviously not registering at all.

"She was the wife of Jack Kane—your wife's boss."

Walker shook his head. "I don't think so, detective. My wife doesn't have a boss"—he motioned back towards the house, and his lips seemed to curve into the makings of a smile—"unless you call that fifteen-pound cherub in there her boss."

Mike stepped back a pace. "I'm sorry, I was talking about . . .

I was under the impression you were married to Gabriella Grant, the TV newswoman."

The lips tightened and Kevin Walker turned away, picked up another log. "I was," he muttered dismissively.

"But you're not anymore?"

"I am. But that's on paper. That's the real thing back there. Okay, detective?"

Mike stepped in front of him. "No, not okay, Mr. Walker. I need some clarification here. I'm investigating two murders. I need to know what your marital status is."

Walker sat down on the tree trunk and let a bead of sweat roll down his cheek without brushing it away. "What's it got to do with your investigation? Are you investigating Gabriella?"

"I'm investigating anyone connected to Jack Kane."

"That could be Gabriella." Walker nodded more to himself. "You said he was her boss?"

"Yes."

"That sounds about right then."

Mike sat down beside Walker. "Could you be a little bit more . . ." He paused.

". . . helpful?" Walker finished the sentence for him.

"Exactly."

"Yeah, I suppose. What is it you want to know, detective?"

"Are you still legally married to Gabriella Grant?"

"Yes, I am."

Mike decided that despite Walker's best intentions, he was in for a long haul.

"But you've been separated for a while?"

"Yes, almost two years."

"You didn't get a divorce?" Mike rolled his eyes backwards towards the house. "I presume that's your girlfriend, your child."

He saw the jaw and fists tighten at the same time. "Yes. You're right about that. My girlfriend and my child. No mistake about that."

"Okay, so why no divorce, Mr. Walker?"

"She wouldn't agree to the settlement I wanted."

"That *you* wanted?"

"Yes. I was asking for four hundred thousand dollars."

"Four hundred thousand. That's a lot of settlement."

"Hundred thousand for every month of our marriage."

Mike felt the conversation slipping away from him again. Kevin Walker obviously found it difficult to volunteer information. Mike would have to elicit it by painful Q and A. But he was having a hard time choosing the right questions.

"How did you arrive at that figure? Even Ms. Grant can't be making that much money."

"That wasn't just equitable distribution of assets, detective. That amount included compensation for the breakdown I had because of her—"

"Breakdown?" Mike echoed.

"Yes. She was cheating on me from the start—with her boss, by the way."

Mike nodded. "Would you care to tell me about it?"

Kevin Walker got to his feet abruptly. "I damn well wouldn't. But I suppose that's what you're here for."

Mike nodded again and Walker sat down. "Okay, in simple words: I met her when she hired me to build her a house. We fell in love, or at least I thought we were in love. I asked her to marry me and she said yes. We got married, she got pregnant. We were very happy . . . I thought."

He paused for an intake of breath. "Then in about her fourth month, on the day I went out to get building materials to finish the nursery, she told me that I shouldn't get so excited about the baby. It wasn't mine and she was leaving me to go off with the guy who'd gotten her pregnant. They were moving to Philadelphia."

Walker paused and Mike wanted to prod him to get on with the story. But the man was obviously still having a hard time with the memory.

Finally, he seemed to regain some control. "Anyway, bottom line is she did leave me, although she never had the baby. She said she had a miscarriage. I had my doubts. I think she just got rid of it."

"Why's that?"

"Because the guy she was running around with decided not to leave his wife. He came to see me after she was gone, after Gabriella moved to Philadelphia. He said his wife had tried to slash her wrists. I think he wanted to explain himself, apologize maybe, I don't know, but I wasn't in any mood to listen. I had my own problems, being in the nuthouse at the time."

"The *nuthouse?*"

"I went to pieces, detective. That's what I meant by a breakdown. I guess I didn't handle Gabriella's confession too well. I don't know, maybe it's different for TV people but I just couldn't take it in. Anyway, the four hundred thousand, it was really to make her aware that's what it cost me, losing most of my business while I got treated in the psychiatric hospital. I didn't really think I had much chance of getting it, but I threw the figure out there and said I'd stall the divorce until she made some counteroffer. I was banking on the fact that she wouldn't want it to go to court and become public."

"What was her reaction?"

He laughed brusquely. "She kept the thing bouncing between lawyers, dragging things out especially after she found out about Viv and the baby. She wasn't going to let me off the hook and pay for it."

"So, she didn't seem at all anxious to get a divorce?"

"Not back then . . ."

Mike felt an anticipatory tingle on his forearms. "But eventually?"

Kevin Walker nodded. "Yeah, eventually. She said she was willing to talk terms. Said she'd settle at two hundred thousand, spread over four years."

It still seemed like a lot of money. An overly large amount. But then again perhaps not if you were anticipating the merger of *two* megabuck paychecks. Mike leaned forward. "And when did this happen?"

Walker's forehead creased into furrows. "Just recently."

"Can you be a little more specific?"

"Let me see . . ." The furrows deepened. "Viv took her call. And she wasn't very pleasant about it—Gabriella, I mean. She said something to Viv about how Viv could now make her little bastard legitimate."

"The call, Mr. Walker. When did Gabriella make the call?"

"Saturday. It was Saturday, because I get home early Saturdays and I remember calling her back to tell her she had a deal."

"You mean this last Saturday? Just three days ago, right?"

Walker gave him a strange look, as if Mike hadn't been paying attention. "Last Saturday. That's what I said, didn't I?"

Mike cautioned himself to stay patient. "So, she wasn't in any great big hurry until last Saturday? Did she sound anxious on Saturday? Did she appear anxious to get on with it?"

"Hell, I don't know, detective. You say appear. She could appear to be anything she wanted. She fooled me for our entire marriage. So, I don't know if she was anxious, and I don't care. Now, if you've gotten what you came for . . ." Kevin Walker extended his hand in a farewell gesture.

Mike shook it, thanking the man for his time and his help, though as he trekked around the side of the house to the road, he felt oddly ambivalent. In a way he had gotten much more than he'd come for: After stringing her husband out for two years, Gabriella Grant had suddenly agreed to a large settlement. It was surely no coincidence that her agreement had come less than forty-eight hours after Emma Kane had bought the farm. And yet the blatancy of it surprised him. Had Grant not considered that the timing would raise suspicion? Or had she just simply and wrongly figured that it would not come to light during the investigation?

25

Gabriella huddled inside her tan cashmere jacket as she pushed through the revolving doors of the WorldMedia building. The day had been pleasant and warm, but as soon as the sun went down the warmth had disappeared right along with it. She raised her collar to shield against the discernible chill out on the street and quickened her step.

She had no particular destination in mind, but she made it a point to take a break and get out of the stuffy newsroom at around this time each day. Today, she especially needed to clear her head.

She had seen Jack Kane return to the newsroom and had recognized the tall blond woman with him as the one who'd appeared with the detective on her doorstep during the weekend. Through her open office door, Gabriella had heard Jack introduce her to the show producer as Kate McCusker. She'd wanted to warn Jack that this McCusker woman had been in his apartment last weekend, together with the cop who'd searched it. But then she heard him fobbing her off onto Jim: "I bumped into Mrs. McCusker downstairs," Jack had said. "Show her around, Jim. She's a writer and she's curious about what we do at WorldMedia."

She'd sat back in her chair, reassured. Of course Jack was too smart to get drawn unsuspectingly into any conversations with a police snitch. Or the cops themselves, for that matter. What on earth had they been thinking, coming to search his apartment, anyway?

She shook her head in disbelief even as her thoughts about Jack prompted her to turn the corner onto Seventy-first and into a small, classy lingerie boutique two doors down the block.

She spent a few moments glancing idly through the racks, flicking through the hangers until a lace-trimmed rose teddy caught her eye. Then, at the end of the rack, she spotted a skimpy silk chemise in a bold jade color. She took both garments over to a long mirror on the wall, holding first one then the other against herself. It was hard to tell which would look sexier on naked flesh.

She stared into the mirror, suddenly catching a glimpse of a man's face in the reflection. She thought she'd seen him come into the store and head for the display of long nightgowns. But now he was staring in her direction. As she held the jade chemise against her body, he smiled and nodded as if to say, That's the one.

She grinned right back and carried the chemise to the cash register. Moments later she was out in the street again.

"A good choice," she heard a voice behind her say, and she knew it was the man from the store following her down the street. She picked up her pace and heard his footsteps quicken behind her, too.

He caught up with her on the corner. "It's Gabriella Grant, right?"

She turned then, and flashed him a wide smile. "Yes," she acknowledged. "And, thank you for your help in the store. Now, if you'll excuse me—"

"I have to admit I followed you into the store, Miss Grant." The man blocked her path and Gabriella sighed. She was more annoyed than afraid. There were plenty of people on the street. But then his next words made her stomach sink. "I'm Lester Franks. I work for the *Enquirer*."

She recovered quickly. "Congratulations, Mr. Franks. You seem to have yourself a scoop: Gabriella Grant purchases nightwear on Seventy-first Street. I hope your editor—"

He cut her off in midsentence. "I just read the *People* article about you, and I was wondering if—"

"I'm sorry, Lester," Gabriella didn't let him finish either.

"I don't have anything more to add to that. I said it all in *People*." She took a step away from him.

"Oh, but wait, Miss Grant. I'm not asking for you to say any more. We're more interested in your mother's story. It is really her story, I mean about her affair with Ben Grant."

Gabriella stopped walking, suddenly wary. Unless the stodgy *Inquirer* had changed dramatically since she'd left Philadelphia, there was no way they'd be picking up on a decades-old affair. "Did you say you were from the *Philadelphia Inquirer?*"

Lester Franks cleared his throat. "No, not the *Philadelphia Inquirer . . .*"

Her voice was ice-cool as she asked: "Then, which *Inquirer?*"

"*The National Enquirer.*"

Gabriella laughed. "Well, good luck, Lester."

"Wait. At least hear me out." He fell into step beside her. "All I want to do is make your mother an offer for her story about Ben Grant."

"My mother won't talk."

"Not for ten thousand dollars?"

She laughed. "My mother doesn't need the money."

"Why not let her make the decision? Could you at least pass the offer on to her?"

Lester Franks had obviously failed to locate Gloria. That's why he was bugging her. Gabriella smiled to herself. "I'm sorry, Mr. Franks. There's really no point."

His hand shot out and came to rest on her arm. "Miss Grant, you're not going to stop me you know; you're only slowing me down. I'll find your mother and put the offer to her myself."

Try it, she wanted to say. Her mother was not listed anywhere on the tax rolls. Gabriella owned the house. Gloria didn't even own a car. So she would not be that easy to find. But sleazeballs like Lester Franks used all kinds of dirty little tricks, and she didn't want it to sound like a challenge.

She brushed his hand off her arm. "Okay, Mr. Franks," she finally replied. "I'll ask her and I'll call you back."

He looked as if he suspected she was going to stall him.

"I'll give you a couple of days, then," he said, reaching into his pocket for a business card. "Here are my phone numbers. I'll be waiting."

Gabriella snatched the card from him and turned away, putting the card in her pocket and wiping the palms of her hands on her jacket as she started to run towards the offices. Her fingers felt sweaty. The thought of Lester Franks ambushing her like that made her feel ill. The thought of him finding her mother was even worse. A slimebucket like Franks would be able to worm anything out of Gloria, especially in her current aggrieved state. Gloria might even enjoy "correcting" all the little facts she'd accused Gabriella of getting wrong in the story.

Like the part where the reporter had asked Gabriella why her mother had never contacted Ben Grant in Hollywood to tell him he had a daughter. Gabriella had said something about her mother's pride, her mother's belief that if he'd really cared he would have come back for her, that he would have made an effort to find her.

Her mother had really freaked out over that quote. "You've made a liar out of me, Gabriella," she'd yelled down the phone. "You know damn well why I never contacted Ben Grant."

Gabriella had shrugged it off. "Well, so long as you keep that part of it to yourself, everything will be just fine."

Now she grimaced at the thought. The image of Gloria sitting across her kitchen table from Franks, a bottle of Cutty Sark planted firmly in the middle of the table, a check for ten thousand dollars staring her in the face popped into Gabriella's head.

A chill ran through her. It could not happen. She'd give it a day or two and call Franks back with her mother's refusal. No, better still, she would get her mother to write to Lester Franks herself. The last thing she needed right now was the threat of this kind of disaster hanging over her.

26

She was getting the star treatment. No doubt about it. When Jack Kane had suggested dinner "in a little place around the corner," Kate had imagined some journalists' dive. Le Ciel de Paris was very obviously more than that. Elegant, intimate, and probably horrendously expensive, she thought but had no way of knowing because the menu that the maître d' handed her had no prices on it. Jack hadn't taken a menu. Nor had the waiter asked what he wanted to drink but had brought a Chivas on the rocks for him along with a bottle of white wine for Kate, which he'd served from an elegant ice bucket at the table.

She waited for Jack Kane to ask about the investigation, suspecting that's why he'd looked so delighted to see her in the WorldMedia lobby, and why he'd whisked her straight past the security guard who'd been halfway through his Checkpoint Charlie routine. But he had not quizzed her in the office nor on the short walk to the restaurant.

Now he looked as if he was just content to be relaxing after a long, tough day. She hoped she'd be able to get him to talk about himself. Whatever his motive for the invitation to dinner, she hadn't even thought twice about accepting. The opportunity to spend some time with the man at the center of the investigation was too good to pass up.

She laid aside her menu. "I'll just have what you're having. I'm sure it will be excellent." She smiled and picked up her wineglass. "This is really a very pleasant end to a rather disappointing day."

"A wasted trip to the Big Apple?" Kane shook his head. "I'm sorry to hear that. Tell me what happened."

The setbacks had actually started before her drive to New York but Kate didn't think he'd want to hear about her meeting with Tommy's principal—or that Belinda had asked for copies of Tommy's school reports and requested to attend parent-teacher conferences.

Sister Kathleen had been understanding. "Of course, we're only obliged to send one copy of the reports," she'd said, "and that's to you. You're his legal guardian."

Kate had considered the problem. She felt Belinda should have mentioned it to her first. Going to the school behind Kate's back was the biggest step yet that Belinda had taken to gain a firmer foothold in Tommy's life. The specter of a courtroom battle had loomed before Kate's eyes, but she had determined that she would not prompt it by a confrontation over reports. What kind of a monster would she look like, anyway, if she denied a mother her son's school reports? "Let her have the copies, Sister, if it's no trouble for you," she'd finally agreed.

She realized Jack Kane was staring at her, waiting for an answer to his question. "So?" he said. "What were you up to in the city, anyway?"

"I came in for lunch." She smiled. "With my agent and a publisher. To discuss my new book."

"The one you were working on about Main Line crime?"

She decided to be honest but not brutally. "No. That's been superseded by events." There was no need for her to elaborate; his nod indicated that he knew exactly what she was talking about.

"Of course. I'm sure there'll be plenty of others following in your footsteps, too."

She did not take his words as criticism but said, "I'm sure it doesn't come as a surprise to you. You're in the business yourself. If this had happened to your counterpart at CBS, you'd be all over—"

He held his hand up. "You don't have to explain it to me." A hint of a smile glimmered in his eyes. Then disappeared. "But this isn't a remake of the Simpson murders. When the police conclude their investigation and I'm not the one they arrest, the interest will fade pretty fast. I'm sure it's going to be a disappointment for a lot of people."

"Yes," Kate agreed, quietly adding, "Howard Mason, for one."

The name got a bigger reaction from Kane than she'd expected. "The publisher at Marley House? You had lunch with him? He's a bit of a hard nut, isn't he?"

Kate nodded, recalling how specific and direct Mason had been. "I want to be the first one out with a book on the Kane murders. As soon as they charge Kane, I want to have it in the bag, with all the dirt you can dig up on him and his womanizing."

Kate had been appalled. She'd never worked with this publishing company and it was evident they didn't really know much about her work, either. The book Mason was talking about would be better suited to a hack writer, not someone like herself who'd been compared with the likes of Joe McGuinniss and Shana Alexander.

"The cops aren't that close to nailing Jack Kane," she'd stalled, even as Mason had started talking money. He'd offered fifty thousand dollars. Twenty on signing the contract and the balance on delivery of the manuscript within thirty days. "Everyone knows Kane did it," Mason had concluded. "No point in pussyfooting around."

Barbara, her agent, had calmed her as they'd walked uptown together after the lunch. "Just think about it. You've got nothing to lose. If Kane is innocent, Mason will have to shelve the book but you'll still be fifty grand ahead. If you do the work, he can't ask you to return the money."

So Kate had thought about it, continuing her walk uptown towards the WorldMedia offices. Fifty grand was a comfortable amount to stash in the bank, and it would be more than enough to retain a good attorney should she need to go to court over Tommy.

Kane broke the silence now, clinking her glass with his to get her attention. "Let me guess, Mason wants a book about me. That's why you turned up on my doorstep, right?"

Kate's face flushed with color. It was as if he'd read her thoughts. "Well, not exactly . . ."

He leaned forward, and not waiting for her to finish said:

"You must be aware, Kate, that Marley House is an imprint of Meyer Books?"

She nodded.

"So then you also know that Meyer Books is part of the same conglomerate as Fuller Broadcasting, right?"

"Of course—" She broke off as the meaning of his words suddenly hit her. WorldMedia had fought Fuller Broadcasting in court for access to the city's cable channels.

Kane's eyes bore into her. "There's a lot of people out there who want to see me out of this business." He brought his palm down on the tabletop. "That's what the cops should be checking into. Who has a motive for removing me from the scene? For framing me? Why was Emma murdered on the very day that I happened to be the last person to see her alive?"

Well now, thought Kate, almost sputtering into her wineglass. Talk about a novel spin on *that* question. She was relieved that the waiter brought out their food in that moment and she didn't have to answer. Not that Jack Kane was waiting for an answer. But his face was still grim as he picked up his fork.

His usual turned out to be a lobster salad in some kind of rich heavy sauce. It was delicious and Kate attacked hers enthusiastically. They ate for a few moments in silence and when Jack spoke again, the grim look in his eyes had softened.

"You know you're not going to get a blockbuster book out of this case, don't you, Kate?"

She wiped her mouth with the napkin. "Are you trying to discourage me, Mr. Kane?"

"I don't think I have to make that big an effort. I don't think you truly believe I'm guilty." He paused. Then without waiting for her reply, he said, "I know what makes good TV news, Kate, and I believe I know what people are interested in. I may be the only person right now to know that in this case the husband didn't do it. And without me, there won't be much of a book—"

"Unless of course your theory that you were set up by someone working for a rival conglomerate turns out to be true," she interrupted pointedly.

Jack Kane nodded and smiled. "In which case I'll be thrilled to work with you to give you all the background information. But that'll be different from your digging around into my life and Emma's and looking for a story of passion, greed, lust, or revenge—all those buzzwords that sell books."

"You forgot betrayal."

He stared at her and she saw a flicker of amusement in his eyes.

"There was no betrayal, Kate. Emma wasn't fooling around with anyone, especially not Salerno."

"You sound very sure of that, considering the evidence."

Jack Kane smoothed a crease in the neatly pressed white linen tablecloth. "Let me tell you, if Emma asked Salerno to stay I could give you one hundred reasons off the top of my head that would make more sense than her wanting to sleep with him."

"For one?"

"For one to help with her suitcases, maybe." He waved off the question. "The point is, the cops think Emma was fooling around with Salerno because he was found outside my bedroom wearing my bathrobe."

"That's right."

"So he went from messing around with the sprinkler system to the landing at the top of the stairs."

"That's how it appeared."

Jack Kane laughed. "Except that he stopped in the mudroom first, and because his clothes were probably soaked from the sprinklers, he took them off, popped them in the dryer, and Emma handed him my bathrobe to wear while his clothes dried. Angela found them in the drier this morning."

"Oh." Kate sipped her wine slowly, giving herself a moment to digest this new bit of information. It was interesting and fit in with Betsy Wright's denials of any relationship between Emma and the young hunk, but it didn't matter for the moment because Jack Kane had misunderstood her words. She ran a hand over her hair, smoothing it back. "When I said betrayal, I wasn't referring to your wife's."

There was a silence between them and she saw the grimace on Jack Kane's face, which turned into a half smile. "If you're talking about me . . ." He cupped his glass between two hands. "I think betrayal is too strong a word, Kate."

Emboldened by his relaxed demeanor, Kate said, "It works for me."

"For you and for every other reporter who's digging into my life, I suppose." Jack Kane sighed. "I guess by the time this is over the world will know about every woman I ever smiled at." He signaled the waiter to bring him another drink.

"You told Harry Holmsby that if he started digging around he'd find out about your flings and affairs. You told him your wife knew about them. You couldn't have been very discreet."

"I didn't know my life was going to get splashed across the front page someday." Jack Kane leaned back in his chair, his face somber again. "Emma and I had gone our separate ways for a long time. She had her own life and wasn't very interested in mine. You have some idea what this business is like, Kate. You worked in it. You know that when your day is finished most other people are already in bed. You're ready to unwind and they're asleep. So, who do you end up with at the end of the day? The people you work with."

He paused as the waiter cleared their plates. "And I've always worked with beautiful women. I've enjoyed helping them professionally and I've enjoyed their company. They weren't interested in long-term commitments any more than I was. It worked for both sides."

"Keep it light. No one gets hurt. Everyone moves on. Is that it?" Kate was aware of the censorious tone of her voice. But Jack Kane didn't seem to notice.

"Mostly." He nodded, cradling his glass. Kate sensed that the mood at the table had shifted. Jack Kane seemed to be talking to her, not as someone who might write a book exposing all his secrets but more as if he was talking to a friend. "There was only one woman in my life who might have meant more. She was the only one who made me come close to thinking about leaving Emma, and I suppose in the end we were both hurt."

"Someone in Philly?" Kate's interest leaped.

Jack Kane nodded. "It was a while ago."

"She's still in Philly?"

Jack Kane smiled wanly. "Are you making notes in your head, Kate? You want a name so that you can follow up?"

"I think I know the name. You're talking about Molly Heskell, aren't you?"

He looked surprised. "Have you spoken to Molly?" he asked.

"No. I saw her on TV last night. She produced a somewhat one-sided report on Salerno's girlfriend, all but convicting her of the murders."

Kane's eyes narrowed. "That doesn't sound like Molly." He sipped his drink. "She's an excellent reporter. I wanted her to come to WorldMedia with me."

"Why didn't she?" Kate prodded, choosing not to admit that she'd heard this already from Gabriella Grant.

"It's a long story." He shrugged.

Kate studied his face. She got the impression that Jack Kane's feelings for Molly Heskell had gone deep.

"Do you still see her? Talk to her?"

"She called me a couple of weeks back. Out of the blue. It was the first time we'd talked in months." He shrugged. "She wanted to talk about a job at WorldMedia. She was very unhappy in Philly. Unfortunately my wife was in the office when she called." He paused and sipped. "Some timing. She's the one woman Emma always had a bee in her bonnet about."

"What did you tell her?"

"I said I'd get back to her. I said I was trying to sort things out with Emma. Trying to get her to make up her mind about moving or not moving or whatever the hell she was going to decide. I didn't want to rock the boat."

"Your wife still had a bee in her bonnet about Molly Heskell?"

Jack shrugged. "Who knows? I never knew what was going on in Emma's head. But I didn't want to take the chance."

Of what? Kate was going to ask but Jack Kane leaned back in his seat and said, "She was the best reporter I ever had."

Kate let his words hang as her mouth twitched into a half smile at the Freudian slip.

Jack Kane caught on quickly. "Had working for me, I meant."

Kate allowed a moment's silence between them, pondering Jack Kane's openness. She realized she might not get another opportunity like this one. "What about Gabriella Grant?" Kate asked in what she hoped was a casual manner as she took a mouthful from her plate. "You brought her from Philadelphia, instead."

"She's an excellent reporter. A natural on air."

"But not the best you ever had?" She kept her tone light.

"I never had Gabriella." She heard the definitive note in his voice. "I think I already said that."

Kate waited for the waiter to refill her glass, recalling how Gabriella had suddenly materialized earlier as Kate and Jack were leaving the newsroom. "Are you leaving for the night, Jack?" the anchorwoman had asked with an anxious look on her face. "Aren't you coming back?"

"I could," Kane had replied, "if I'm needed." Kate had wondered then if there had been a double meaning in his words to Gabriella, assuring her that of course he would return especially if *she* needed him. On the other hand the exchange had been somewhat cool on Jack's side.

"Tell me why Gabriella's name keeps coming up." Jack picked up the conversation again. "Not because of that one stupid gossip item, I hope. There have been gossip items about me and Katie Couric, too."

"Katie Couric doesn't live in your apartment building, does she?"

"I wouldn't know." Jack Kane shrugged, looking as if he didn't care either. He stared across the restaurant, a distant look in his eye as if he was deliberating with himself. Then he turned back to Kate. "I hope the police aren't making something big of the fact that Gabriella lives in the same apartment building. There's nothing to it, you know."

"Nothing?"

"Nothing." Kane leaned forward and looked as if he was going to say something important but then seemed to change his mind. As the waiter cleared their plates, he grinned. "Believe me, she's not the frivolous fling type."

"What type is that exactly?"

"Not someone who's married, that's for sure. That's the sort of complication I don't need."

"I thought she was separated, estranged."

There was a pause in the conversation, then Jack nodded. "But her divorce seems to be a messy deal. God knows why. She was married for less than a year."

Kate wondered if she'd imagined the hint of impatience and irritation in his voice, and the thought struck her that maybe Gabriella had refused to get a divorce until Jack himself did. But it was gone in the next moment as he leaned forward in his chair. "I'm being honest, Kate—and I was the other day when I told the cops I wasn't involved with anyone right now. Not frivolous or otherwise."

Kate realized that the conversation had just taken another major shift.

Jack Kane circled his fingers around his glass and leaned further across the small table so that their glasses—and fingers—touched. "Forget about the book, Kate. Come and work for me. I could build a show around you. An hour-long crime show. You could produce it, write it, hell, hire a team of writers to help you, even. We'd look at one real-life crime a week. Like a minidrama. I thought about it while you were wandering around the office. It's the best idea I've had today."

Kate stared at him quizzically as he continued. "You could anchor the show, too. You're a very beautiful woman." He stopped, eyeing her through narrowed eyes. "I could make it happen for you, Kate. I'd be there to help you. Show you the fun side of it, too."

"Bestseller or TV stardom." Kate laughed softly. "I don't know, Jack, it's a tough choice to make."

"Will you think about it?"

She toyed with her glass. *Think about taking the job? Or letting you show me the fun side? Think about what?*

"I'm flattered," she said finally. "Maybe I will think about it but . . ."

"Not till you're sure I'm going to be around to make good on my offer." Kane jumped in, grinning. "I will be, you know, Kate. And very soon we're going to have dinner again—when everything is wrapped." He pushed away from the table. "Come on, let's have a nightcap at the bar."

Kate shook her head. "I'd better not. I have a long drive ahead."

He came around to her chair and took her hand to help her from the table. "Do you have to rush home tonight?"

She didn't answer immediately because the question— and the slight pressure of his fingers around hers—caught her off guard. Jack Kane certainly didn't waste time playing games. When he wanted something, he just went for it, she thought. Tonight, it seemed, he wanted her.

Kate found this a dangerously sensual thought: One of the most powerful media executives in New York was wooing her professionally and personally. Had the circumstances been different she would have, for sure, accepted the invitation for a nightcap.

But it was not an option tonight. She freed her hand from his and made a move towards the doors. "I really must go, Jack," she said. "I was expected home hours ago."

As they parted outside the restaurant, Kate told herself she'd made the right decision. As things stood, it was wiser not to get any more involved with Jack Kane. She still could not see him the way Mike had painted him—as a man who under pressure had taken a shortcut by murdering his wife. But if anything, the dinner date had raised more questions than it answered. Why had he planted the suggestion of some conspiratorial business motive for Emma's murder? Was it paranoia on his part? Did he really believe it could have happened that way? Or more important, was he banking on the assumption that she would pass it all on to her police pals?

Why had he offered her a job? To divert her from the book? Or because he wanted to pursue a relationship with her? Or was it because he'd simply thought it was a great idea for a TV show? Then again, maybe there was no one simple answer to any of the questions about Jack Kane. He was a complex man who obviously pursued every situation for every advantage.

By the time she was in her car, having taken a cab to the parking garage downtown, Kate decided that at least one issue had been settled for her: She could not sign a contract with Marley House. Maybe Jack Kane's suspicion about a publisher like Howard Mason being out to ruin him was far-fetched but then again, maybe it was naive of her to think that it wasn't a possibility. Either way the deal was tainted for her and she wasn't that upset. She would write her book the way she wanted, and Barbara would just have to place it elsewhere.

The Lincoln Tunnel was several miles behind her when Kate's thoughts turned to Molly Heskell. After what Jack Kane had said about her, Kate knew that Molly had to play some major role in the book. Her view of the Kane marriage would alone be worth an interview.

She glanced at the car clock before reaching for her cell phone. It was ten-thirty. There was a chance that the reporter was still in the Channel Seven newsroom. She redialed after getting the number from information and asked for Molly Heskell as soon as she was through to the newsdesk.

"She's not here anymore," a bored male voice informed her.

"Then I'd like to leave a—" Kate interrupted herself. Yeah, like this guy would make the effort to pass on a message. "I mean, could you tell me what time she's due in tomorrow?"

"I meant she's not at Seven anymore," the man announced impatiently.

"She was fired." It was a statement not a question and Kate was surprised to hear the man correcting her.

"No, not fired. Heskell quit this morning."

Kate hung up and stared at the road ahead of her. Sure, she thought, it made sense now. Molly's news report last night had been a last hurrah. Not loyalty to a former boss but a favor to her new boss. A chance to slant things in Jack's favor before she quit and moved on to WorldMedia now that Emma wasn't around to rock the boat anymore.

She felt strangely disappointed that Jack Kane had failed to mention this important detail about Molly over dinner.

27

Tuesday night, Philadelphia

Lewis stared at the screen but missed the sound bite. Usually, logging tapes was a snap. He didn't even have to think about what he was doing. The words in his headphones automatically rushed through his fingers and into the keyboard. But tonight his fingers felt wooden and his mind numb. He could not focus on his work. All he could think about was his videotape. It was lying at the bottom of his black bag. Every now and then he slid his foot deep under the desk to nudge the bag with his toes, to reassure himself that it was still there. That was plain silly of him, of course. Like what did he think? That it could walk away on its own and disappear? Still, the sooner he could get into the editing bay with the videoprocessor, the happier he would be.

He decided to give it another fifteen minutes. Usually around eleven-thirty, Jake, the garage attendant, wandered up to make himself a thermos of coffee. He wanted to be sitting at his desk as normal when Jake came up. It wouldn't do for Jake to come sniffing around, looking for him all over the place. He didn't want word getting back to any of the higher-ups that he was messing around with the videoprocessor.

Out of the corner of his eye he saw the newsroom doors open. Sure enough Jake had arrived with his little thermos. Lewis ignored him. On a couple of rare occasions Jake had wandered over to engage him in idle chitchat but Lewis had learned to keep his headphones on at all times, even when he was taking a snack break. That way no one ever bothered him.

Come on, he egged Jake on silently through clenched teeth. Come on, fill up your stupid little thermos and get out. He noticed his hands were beginning to sweat. But he kept his eyes glued to the screen in front of him until he sensed the swish of the newsroom doors closing behind Jake. Then he reached under the desk for his black bag and walked across the newsroom to the editing bay.

Inside the bay he locked the door and pulled the little shade down over the peephole window before taking his videotape out of the bag and inserting it into the processor. Thanks to a short stint working for a video production company in Appleton, Wisconsin, and then the TV station in Duluth, he knew what he needed to do to enhance the images and pull the grain out. It could be a tedious process cranking up the video level, and he expected it to take a while as he acquainted himself with the machine.

He was surprised, though, when he next glanced at his watch and realized he'd been in the editing bay for almost ninety minutes. He stared at the monitor, disheartened. He had pulled a lot of the grain out, but the features of the face eluded him. It looked like the killer had worn some kind of hooded sweat top, and the hood had covered all the hair and thrown a nasty shadow over the most salient features of the face. But he'd done the best he could. Only the FBI with their computers could improve on what he was looking at now.

The worst of it was that as the fuzzy silhouette had grown sharper and clearer from the neck down he had realized, with a severe jolt of disappointment, that the slender black-clad form was either a woman or a very gracefully built man.

But not, dammit, Jack Kane.

28

Wednesday, October 2

The shot went wild at the fifteen-yard line and straight into the sand bank at the far end of the range. The range officer had instructed them to fire six rounds, kneeling, and Kate had dropped to one knee reluctantly. She was wearing suede hip huggers. They were new and she was worrying about grass stains when her target swiveled sideways and she missed. "I wouldn't care about my pants if this were the real thing." She laughed, standing back as Mike dropped to a prone position on the ground and fired off six rounds, hitting his target right in the center mass.

She'd done well enough, she thought, considering she hadn't been at the range for more than a year. But what Steve had taught her had stayed with her. At least she'd hit eight of the ten targets from the ten-yard line, aiming for the center. She could tell by the look on Mike's face that he was impressed anyway.

She watched as he completed the course, and wondered how Harry was faring at the doctor's. He'd been on his way out of the squad room when she'd arrived earlier that morning. He suspected an ulcer. Kate suspected he was right: Stress was clearly visible on his face these days.

"You can hang out here and wait for me," he told her. "Or you can go link up with Travis at the range. He'll fill you in on what you missed while you were gallivanting in the Big Apple yesterday."

From the tone of his voice she didn't expect she'd missed much but she made the short drive to Belmont Hills anyway. She was curious about Mike's reaction to the information she assumed Jack Kane intended her to pass on.

By the time he was done, Mike had dropped only two points. It was an excellent score but he asked the range officer to set up the targets one more time. There were ten of them: paper cutouts fixed to plywood torsos that swiveled on mobile stands. Normal practice, she knew, required police officers to take aim from varying positions of between three and fifteen yards.

But this time from a standing position he took aim with both hands and fired off a round that peppered the first target on the left shoulder.

He muttered something to himself and fired again, hitting an area around the target's left hand. He dropped the empty cartridge and reloaded.

Then she heard him say something that sounded like "balls." He grinned at her and then fired, his shot discharging directly into the groin area.

Kate stared at him quizzically as he walked towards her. "What was all that about?"

Mike shrugged. "Just testing myself. Making sure I haven't lost my touch."

"If you intended to turn that last one into a soprano then I'd say you haven't lost your touch." She paused. "Is it a form of therapy?"

He threw her a puzzled look.

"I mean, do you think about the guy you caught with your fiancée when you do that?"

"No, I don't have to fantasize about that. I dealt with him at the time." Mike grimaced. "That's why I had to resign."

"What did you do?"

He laughed abruptly. "I shot him. Not in the balls, but close enough."

Kate stared at him wide-eyed. Obviously someone had gotten their stories mixed up somewhere. She cleared her throat. "Harry said you resigned after shooting a rapist who was assaulting your girlfriend. I presume this wasn't the same woman?"

"Yes it was." Mike gave her a half smile. "And Harry was right. Same fiancée. Same incident."

"Oh, I see," Kate said, not quite sure that she did. "So you were just playing with words when you told me you'd caught her with another man?"

Mike shrugged. It was obvious he didn't really want to talk about it, but then he said, "I happened to stop by our apartment one morning in the middle of my shift, and walked in on it. Cheryl was screaming and he was on top of her. It was an automatic reaction, I suppose. I went for my gun."

Kate let out a long sigh. "So what was wrong with that? What were you supposed to have done? They made you resign for that? Where did you hit him?"

Mike laughed as her questions came tumbling out. "I grazed him, but he didn't take it very well. He claimed Cheryl had invited him up after they'd been jogging together."

Mike laughed again. "Cheryl's story was that he'd asked to come up for a drink of water, and then came onto her and forced her."

"Oh." Kate hesitated. "So, it was more like date rape, you mean."

"No." Mike shook his head. "It was more like a date, period, exactly the way the guy claimed. It was Cheryl who was lying. She *had* invited him up. She'd been going jogging with him for a while, had probably brought him back to the apartment on more than one occasion before that, too."

"She admitted it, eventually?"

"No." Mike shook his head. "I figured it out for myself. I know when I opened that apartment door that's what I wanted to believe. That it was a crime in progress. But I also knew I'd gone there in the first place because I'd suspected for a while that she was fooling around with other men." He shrugged. "When I went over the whole scene again in my head, when it clicked that she'd started screaming only after I pushed open the bedroom door, I knew she was lying. In the end, the fact that Cheryl wouldn't press charges against the guy kind of nailed it."

"Were you asked to resign?"

"It was suggested, yes. But I would have done it, anyway. I knew I'd crossed some thin line and I knew I should get out of there."

"That's some story." Kate sighed. "I'm sorry—"

"Don't be," he cut in abruptly. "It's all over. Anyway . . ." He paused and grinned at her, and Kate knew he was about to change the subject. "You did pretty well out there yourself."

"Pretty well?" Kate raised an eyebrow.

"Okay, very well." He paused. "As a matter of fact, amazingly well for a beginner." He stared at her. "But you're not a beginner, are you? You've been here before."

A smile played on her lips. "Once or twice. With Steve." She paused. "There were guns around the house. I told him either I learn how to use them, or get them out of our home."

"That's smart thinking."

"I thought so." She fell into step beside him as they walked back towards the parking lot. Then she said: "Harry tells me I missed some exciting developments yesterday."

Mike shrugged. "Kane's car and clothes came back clean. And we got a make back on the prints from the intercom on the landing outside Emma's bedroom. They were all Salerno's, with a big clear beauty from the button that opens the front door."

"Okay." She nodded, deciding not to verbalize the obvious. There seemed to be more to come. "So, you're saying . . . ?"

"So, I'm saying we also got a lab report matching a hair from the scene to a sample we took from Jill Maxwell."

"Okay," Kate repeated. "Everything seems to be pointing to Jill Maxwell here, but the look on your face tells me there's no punch line coming."

"That about sums it up." He nodded. "We went back to talk to Maxwell and said we'd found some evidence placing her at the scene."

"And?"

"We couldn't shake her. She wouldn't budge from her story. She said she'd never heard of Emma Kane before Friday morning, and she'd certainly never been to her house."

"But she's lying, right?"

Mike shrugged. "We got one hair, Kate. You ever watch that little trial out in L.A.? The one where they had all that blood in the Bronco, and all those hairs in a ski cap left at the murder scene? Hair is difficult. Salerno could have brought one of her hairs in on the sole of his shoe or even on his clothes."

"Point taken."

"The point was made by Miss Maxwell. She didn't even ask what the evidence was. Just pointed out that it had better be unimpeachable if we were going to charge her." He shrugged again. "The lady's a lawyer. She knows what she's talking about."

Kate leaned back against the hood of her car. "Well, maybe she's got a clear conscience, but isn't it possible that her hair was brought into the house by someone other than Salerno? I mean, did you ever talk to Maxwell's neighbors? The two guys who live downstairs? They seemed very protective of her, and very hostile towards Salerno. The one I spoke to, anyway, was very scathing about their relationship."

Mike stared into the distance and appeared to be thinking about her question, but Kate could tell he wasn't much interested in Jill Maxwell's neighbors. Finally, he said, "Maybe I'll come back to them, but only when we've exhausted all the other more promising leads."

"Like what?" Kate came right back at him. "It sounds to me like you've got to rule out Jack Kane. If you've got a scenario where Salerno answers the intercom and opens the door, it's unlikely he opened it for Kane. You said so yourself. He wouldn't do that from the landing outside the bedroom, much less stand there in Kane's bathrobe, waiting for him to walk up the stairs."

"True," Mike agreed. "It doesn't seem likely it could have happened that way. But I'm not sure that entirely eliminates him from the picture."

Kate brushed a dried mud stain off her suede pants. "I talked to him yesterday."

"Kane?" Mike's left eyebrow rose.

"I bumped into him in the WorldMedia lobby." Kate proceeded to fill Mike in on her lunch date with the publisher of Marley House and Jack Kane's theory about being set up.

Mike laughed out loud before she finished. "So he's suggesting he was framed by someone who's pissed off that he got his twenty-four-hour cable news onto the cable system in New York? That's pretty bizarre, Kate."

"I thought so too when I first heard it. But it is a multi-million dollar business, Mike. Just think how vicious things got with Fox and Time-Warner. Don't you remember? Ted Turner himself said he wanted to kill Murdoch at one point? Then, Fuller Broadcasting and WorldMedia crowded into the picture."

Mike shook his head, his eyes still flickering with amusement. "So who are the suspects, Kate? Rupert Murdoch? Ted Turner? Jeremy Fuller? I don't think so. I think it's someone with a more personal motive. I think we're looking for someone who Salerno wouldn't think twice about letting into the house. Someone nonthreatening, like a woman. And, I think it all comes back to Jack Kane. I think it's the woman Jack Kane called right after his argument with Emma."

Kate paced between her car and Mike's Road King. "You're not back to Gabriella Grant, are you?"

He nodded curtly. "I spoke to her husband yesterday. He said they've been dickering around with a divorce settlement for almost two years. He wants money; she won't pay up. Then, lo and behold, two days after Emma buys the farm, Gabriella agrees to his demands. There's something there, Kate."

She lapsed into a momentary silence. Then she grinned. "Okay, well how about this? Molly Heskell, the reporter Kane wanted to take to New York till Emma went ballistic, calls him looking for a job a couple of weeks ago. Kane told me this himself, over dinner. He said he had to stall her because Emma was actually in the office when Heskell called. He gave the impression that Emma would have gone ballistic all over again if he'd hired Molly. So, would it interest you to know that yesterday Heskell quit her job at Seven to move to WorldMedia?"

Mike grinned right back. "One all, McCusker. Except for the fact that Heskell isn't the one who's spent the last nine or ten months with Kane, and she's not the one living under the same roof."

Kate shook her head. "I don't know, Mike. The way he was talking about Grant last night . . . well, he just seemed to be telling the truth. He was very adamant."

"You talked about Gabriella Grant? What kind of a conversation were you having?"

"We were talking about my book mostly, and he seemed to want to explain his infidelities."

Mike nodded, his jaw tightening visibly. "Like, 'I'm not really a bad guy. I just happen to screw anything that walks.' "

"Oh c'mon, Mike. He was trying to convince me that he's not a good subject for a book. He doesn't want me to write the book. He offered me a job at WorldMedia instead."

"Where did you go for dinner? The Four Seasons? Twenty-one?"

"A small restaurant around the corner from the newsroom."

"So what did he say about Gabriella?"

"That she was an excellent reporter but not the frivolous fling type."

Mike laughed so loudly that several uniformed cops who were crossing the car park towards their cruiser turned around to look at him.

"Kind of proves my point, doesn't it? Not the frivolous fling type. No, you'd better believe it. She's the sort that goes for keeps."

He kicked at a loose stone on the blacktop. "My money's on Gabriella. I think Kane called her after his visit with Emma and told her Emma was hanging tough."

"And she jumped in her car and drove down to take care of things?"

"I think she's got the balls to do that, yes. And, she's got a better motive. Kane gets to keep all his assets, and she gets to pay off her husband so she can get a divorce and marry Kane. I think that's a better motive than a job at WorldMedia."

"Unless Molly Heskell was after more than a job. Maybe she planned to pick up with Kane again."

Mike shrugged and started towards his motorbike. "Well, we'll see, but I'm going to deal with Grant first."

"If you're right, she'll be at the funeral tomorrow."

"No." Mike grinned, zipping up his jacket. "If I'm right she won't go anywhere near it. The last thing she'll want to do is to be seen with Jack Kane at his wife's funeral."

She opened the car door and got in, with Mike watching as she switched on the ignition. Then he motioned for her to roll down the window. "By the way, did you say you'd take the job in New York?"

"I didn't say anything. I thought it was a premature offer."

He nodded and got astride his bike.

29

Thursday, October 3

Big dark gray clouds threatened rain, and the bone-numbing chill in the early morning air had sent people scurrying into the backs of their closets for warmer coats. Perfect funeral weather, thought Kate.

Outside the small church, TV vans, news crews, and photographers had gathered in a large crowd. Inside, the small church was filled with family, friends, and possibly just the curious.

Kate and Harry found a spot in a side aisle and watched Jack Kane arrive with a young mousy blond woman whom Kate recognized as his daughter, Angela. Betsy Wright sat in the pew behind them. Kate also recognized Molly Heskell, sandwiched between Angela on her left and a tall, dark, good-looking man on her right, whom she identified as Sam Packer, Molly's recently estranged husband.

Well, there it was, thought Kate. Point to Mike. Gabriella was a no-show, staying out of the spotlight, like he'd predicted, and Molly Heskell was sitting right alongside the family. Bold as brass, and therefore innocent.

But only according to Mike's logic. It could well be, thought Kate, that Molly Heskell was guilty as sin but determined to tough it out. She had been blatant enough in her TV report. She also had Sam Packer as a beard here.

As the funeral Mass proceeded, Kate kept her eyes on the front pew. At one point she saw Molly put her arm around Angela's shoulder as the girl started sobbing into a tissue.

From where she and Harry stood, it was difficult to see the faces and Kate would have liked to see Molly Heskell's face. She'd given Molly a lot of thought, and had returned home the previous afternoon from the pistol range to study all the newspaper clippings she'd been able to find about her. She had brought them in for Harry to scan before leaving for the funeral.

"Heskell had a baby that was stillborn about a month ago. Her husband moved out of their home a couple of weeks later." She pointed Harry to an *Inquirer* item on the top of the pile. "Then right after that, she calls Jack Kane looking for a job at WorldMedia, only he can't talk to her because Emma's around." She paused. "Well, guess what? Last night Heskell quit her job at Channel Seven."

Harry had listened and studied the clippings. "That's interesting, Kate," he'd said in a tone of voice that implied exactly the opposite. Now Kate poked him in the ribs and motioned for him to follow her outside.

"So, what do you think?" she said as soon as they were outside.

"About what?" Harry winced and clutched his stomach. Then he belched.

"I'm sorry about your ulcer, Harry"—Kate threw him a sympathetic look—"but do you think it's significant that Heskell's right there with Jack Kane and his daughter?"

Harry grunted, lit a cigarette, and crouched down to sit on the top step. Kate sat down next to him. She felt his dejection. She knew he was getting some flak from the brass. She didn't have the heart to lecture him about the smoke.

Harry shook his head. "I don't know anymore, Kate. Maybe we're looking in all the wrong places. The more I think about it, the more I think about the way it went down, the way the killer breezed in, blew away two people, and calmly walked out, not leaving any trace of him or herself, the more I think that maybe the killer was a hired gun."

Harry paused and took a long drag on his cigarette. "Salerno could have opened the door to a delivery person. It's been done before."

"Hired by whom?"

"Kane, maybe . . . probably." Harry shrugged. "He may not be the type to get his own hands dirty but he's certainly got enough money to pay someone."

"To blow his wife away on the very day he drove down to argue with her? That's either incredibly fast work or bad planning or both." Kate stared at a snag in her tights.

Harry stared across the street at the camera crews, most of whom were idling. Kate saw a Channel Three reporter doing a stand-up. Any moment now, she figured someone would recognize Harry and come bearing down on him. She suggested they walk around to the side door.

She continued with her train of thought there. "What about the mess in Emma's bathroom? Why would a hired killer stop to smash all her makeup? Why pump all those bullets into her face? Mike Travis said that was something personal, done by someone who felt a lot of anger."

"Good point," Harry agreed. "But anger isn't an emotion I've detected in any of our suspects so far. They're all so damn cool, it makes you wonder—"

"What about Molly Heskell?" Kate cut in.

Harry didn't say anything for a moment. Then he dropped his cigarette and stubbed it out with his toe. "Yeah, maybe." He paused and his eyes narrowed as if he was working something out in his head. "Let's see. Kane left Philadelphia around the beginning of the year. He wanted to take Heskell with him but Emma Kane blew her stack. So what happened then? Next thing, she's married to Sam Packer and pregnant. Is it possible the baby was Kane's?"

"I don't know." Kate shook her head. "But whatever she had going with Jack Kane it went deep for both of them— and Emma didn't like it."

Out of the corner of her eye, Kate saw a ripple of movement among the camera crews and reporters across the street. "They must be starting to leave the church," she told Harry and they both started slowly back to the street. The two of them stood to the side as Emma Kane's sleek, polished mahogany coffin was loaded into the hearse. She tried to catch a glimpse of Jack Kane but he was lost in the crowd milling outside the church. It took her a few moments longer to spot Molly Heskell—and then only to see the reporter slide into the first limo behind the hearse. Jack's daughter got in next to her and seconds later Kate finally saw Jack, just as he disappeared into the same limo as his daughter and Molly Heskell.

"Did you see that?" Kate stared at Harry.

"I did." Harry nodded. "Now, *that's* interesting. Where's the estranged husband?"

He glanced around and it took him a couple of moments to locate the anchorman. Sam Packer was standing by the curb, lighting up a cigarette.

"Okay, let's go and find out what's going on," Harry said and seemed to brighten a little as they approached Molly Heskell's husband. "Mr. Packer?"

"You got him." Sam Packer stared at Harry and Kate with a quizzical look.

Harry introduced himself. "I'm investigating Mrs. Kane's murder."

Sam Packer smiled, although the smile didn't quite reach his eyes. "I thought only detectives in movies went to the funeral of a victim expecting the killer to show."

Harry ignored the comment. "We wanted to have a word with your wife."

"With Molly?" The look of surprise on Sam Packer's face was genuine.

"Why did she leave with Mr. Kane and his daughter?"

Sam Packer grinned. "She's throwing Channel Seven a final finger, detective."

"I don't follow."

Packer shrugged. "Her way of saying Screw you, look at the story you could have had." He stared at Harry. "She quit yesterday because the news director refused to let her cover this funeral—even though he knows she's got the inside track with Jack."

"Yes." Harry nodded, jumping right in. "That's what we wanted to talk to her about, her relationship with Jack Kane."

Packer shrugged again and looked from Harry to Kate, as if he was about to ask Kate a question, then his gaze rested on Harry again. "You mean her affair with Jack? That was a long time ago, detective. Before Molly and I married."

"You're separated now, though?"

"That's correct."

"But you know she's moving to WorldMedia?"

Sam Packer's lips curved into a half smile. "I haven't heard the official announcement but I assume she'll be joining us. Where else would she go?"

"Did you know that your wife called Mr. Kane a couple of weeks back to ask him for the job?"

"I know she was unhappy at Seven. I know she always wanted to move to New York. Jack wanted her to come with him when he first got the job."

"But Emma Kane put a stop to that, right?"

"Right."

"So she stayed here and married you instead. She sounds like an easy-going lady. If option A doesn't work, move to option B."

Sam Packer grinned. "Not quite, detective. We started going out together because Molly was still pursuing option A, if you will. She thought Emma would back off if she thought Molly was involved with someone else."

"But that didn't work out, did it?"

"No, because our relationship got more serious."

"For you?"

"And for Molly." Sam Packer nodded. "It was Molly's idea to stay in Philly after she got pregnant. Her priorities changed, even though there was little Emma Kane could have done at that point. She could hardly object to Molly moving to New York to be with me."

Sam looked around. People had drifted away and the TV news crews were wrapping up with standups in front of the church. He turned his attention back to Harry. "Everything would have been just fine between us if our daughter had lived, detective. Who knows, maybe it will work itself out . . . one day. When she gets over . . . well, when she gets better." Sam Packer shrugged, and looked as if he wanted the conversation to be over.

"She took it very badly?"

"Very." Packer nodded. "Everything came crashing down around her. Her situation with her boss at Channel Seven didn't help either. I guess she felt everything in her life was wrong and that included me."

"So, you just got the hell out of there?"

"It's what Molly wanted." Packer sighed loudly. "I don't know what experience you have with cases like this, detective, but it seems to me you don't argue with someone who is in that sort of fragile mental state. I moved out but I kept in touch."

"You were concerned about her mental state?"

"Of course. She was supposed to be on medication, but she was very much against taking any kind of feel-good pills, so that didn't help either."

"How bad was her depression?" Kate heard the softness in Harry's voice but the direction in which he was heading was not misunderstood by Sam Packer.

"Not bad enough for her to go crazy and kill Emma Kane, if that's what you're getting at."

"How do you know?"

"Because I talked to her almost every day on the phone. She was upset, depressed, miserable. Her anger was over the loss of the baby. Emma Kane had nothing to do with that. If she blamed anyone it was me."

"Did she tell you she'd called Jack Kane recently?"

"No."

"She never mentioned that Jack Kane had stalled her so that he could sort out the situation with his wife?"

"He did?" Sam Packer stared down the street in the direction the limo had taken when it had pulled away from the curb.

Harry glanced at Kate and raised an eyebrow. Then he cleared his throat. "Do you own a gun, Mr. Packer?"

Packer laughed. "Yeah, or at least I did, detective, but we got rid of it when we found out the baby was on the way."

"What was it?"

"I believe it was a Smith and Wesson. A thirty-eight."

"How did you get rid of it, Mr. Packer?"

"Molly got rid of it. I don't know exactly how."

"How can you be sure of that?"

"That's one thing I can be sure about. I know it wasn't in our house when I moved out. Considering Molly's fragile state of mind, I wasn't going to leave her with a gun in the house." He paused, as if wondering if he'd said something wrong. As if acknowledging that if he was afraid that Molly might harm herself then surely the idea of her harming someone else was not so ridiculous. Then he sighed. "I looked for it from top to bottom and couldn't find it and since we'd talked about getting rid of it, I assumed that's what Molly had done."

"But you didn't ask her."

Sam Packer looked shaken for a moment. "No, I didn't ask her. I didn't want to bring up any mention of guns or deadly weapons. I didn't want to put any thoughts into her head about my fears." He hesitated again, sighed wearily this time—as if he wanted to be out of there, out of the situation. "I think you're scraping the bottom of the barrel, detective. I'm sure when you talk to Molly she'll be able to answer all your questions."

"I hope so, Mr. Packer," Harry, retorted as the anchorman stepped off the curb. Kate watched him cross the street and get into a dark blue Lincoln Continental. Then she turned to Harry. "So, what do you think?"

Harry shook his head. "I think you could be one hell of a detective, McCusker."

Kate sighed. "Come on, Harry, be serious."

He stared at her pointedly. "What have you got against Molly Heskell, anyway?"

Kate stared at him wide-eyed. Then shook her head. "Look all I know is that when Jack Kane mentioned Molly Heskell's phone call I wondered how I'd have felt in Molly's place. You know, you want to get your life together but there's always this obstacle standing in your way. Throw in her fragile mental state, and you've got a little walking time bomb. A very angry little time bomb . . ."

"Angry little walking time bombs don't usually make such clean and efficient killers," Harry cut in. "But fine, I'm not totally disagreeing with you."

"When are you going to talk to her?"

"Tomorrow."

"Tomorrow! Suppose Sam Packer tells her you were asking questions. Tips her off."

"You mean gives her time to concoct a story?" Harry smiled, reaching into his coat pocket for his cell phone. "Don't you think she's had plenty of time to concoct a story already?"

"No, I mean supposing she splits?"

Harry shook his head. "That would be a resounding admission of guilt, don't you think?" He paused. "But just so's you don't lose sleep over it, I'll get Wayne to keep an eye on her." He punched in a number on his cell phone, and then a beeper number, adding, "I want to discuss it with Travis. See what he comes up with in New York. Let's take it one step at a time."

Kate got the message. There was no point in looking at Molly Heskell because Mike was going to deliver the goods on Gabriella.

30

Thursday, New York

Gabriella stared at the rundown lying on her desk. Alison had brought her the lineup of stories for the noon news show just a few minutes before, distracting her attention from a CNN special news broadcast on Emma Kane's funeral. She gritted her teeth. She should have been with Jack today, she told herself. She should have been at his side to help him through the ordeal. She knew that and he knew that. He had obviously given the matter some thought though, because he'd refused to have any kind of discussion about it.

"I appreciate the thought," he'd told her, his eyes making it clear that he wished it could be different. "But you'll be of much more help to me here. I want you to anchor the noon news show and the ten o'clock news. Make sure that our coverage of the funeral is tasteful, okay?" Then he'd given her that look which she knew meant, I've thought about this carefully. There's nothing further to say.

She knew he had a point. She knew what he meant by tasteful, too. How tasteful would it look if Gabriella appeared at his side at the funeral Mass?

She stared at the rundown. She was much more use to him here. And after all, that's what it was about. Her use to him. His to her. They were a team. They complemented one another.

The phone in her office rang out shrilly and she grabbed for it.

"Gabriella?" Her mother's scratchy voice echoed down the line. "Gabriella? I've been trying to get through to you for hours."

Gabriella frowned. Probably her mother meant minutes. She resisted the temptation to point out to her mother that if she'd only stop drinking long enough to sober up occasionally, then her fingers would stand more chance of hitting the right digits. Instead, she said, "I don't know why you have a problem, Mom. I'm here most of the time and I answer the phone myself."

"Don't get smart with me, Gabriella." The voice suddenly sounded stronger and harder. "You're the one who's gotten me into this mess, and I expect you to get me out of it."

"What mess is that, Mom?" Gabriella tried to keep her own tone pleasant and even.

"You said I didn't have to worry but they're here."

Gabriella took a deep breath. "Who's there?"

"The reporter from the *Enquirer*. He's been on my doorstep for the last twenty-four hours. His photographer jumped out at me from the bushes this morning and I'm telling you I wasn't looking my best."

Gabriella stared into the receiver, her heart suddenly pounding painfully. "The reporter from the *National Enquirer* is on your doorstep?"

"Didn't I just say that? With a photographer who jumped out of—"

"Shut up, Mother!" Gabriella snapped suddenly and closed her eyes, trying to think. What the hell was going on? Franks had said he'd give her a couple of days to talk to her mother, but he must have tracked her down himself.

She took a deep breath. "Okay, Mom, listen to me. I'm going to take care of it. I'm probably going to have to come down there to deal with it. If they're still around tomorrow, maybe tomorrow night I'll drive down, or Saturday. But remember you must not, under any circumstances, open the door to them. Don't talk to them and don't for God's sake try to *correct* those little mistakes you think I made in the other interview. Because you know what will happen? They'll get you talking and then they'll put words in your mouth. Do you understand, Mom?"

"I think so." Her mother sounded uncertain.

"I mean it, Mom. You may think you're telling them nothing but you just don't know these people. All it takes is one little slip of the tongue. Stay away from them. Ignore them. If you say anything to them, you could ruin everything I've ever worked for."

"Okay, I understand," Gloria said, but sounded even less certain now.

"And, Mom, you might think about staying off the sauce for a night or so. Just till I get there."

Her mother didn't reply and finally Gabriella slammed the phone down in disgust. She straightened out the fingers that had gripped the phone and noticed they were trembling. She took another deep breath just as Alison Haley poked her head round the doorway. "I got Paolo for you. He can fit you in for a trim in about fifteen minutes, okay?"

Gabriella smiled at the girl. Showtime. "That'll be just peachy keen, Alison. Thank you." She got to her feet and walked over to the coat stand for her umbrella. Then she changed her mind. Instead she stuck her head out of the door and yelled for Alison to return. "Crank up a limo for me, would you, Ali?" She smiled again. "It's pouring out there."

31

It had just started to rain as Mike exited the Lincoln Tunnel. The West Side was familiar territory and he grinned to himself as the memory of a six-month stint on a houseboat, docked at the Seventy-ninth Street Basin, came flooding back to him. Those had been good days. Just before he'd met Cheryl. She'd said she loved the water but had made him give up the boat after the first couple of times on board. He still didn't understand where he'd gone wrong with her, but at least the thought didn't hurt anymore. Funny he could barely conjure up the image of her face, these days. It had gone, just as had the good memories of the city.

The rain was really beating down by the time he got to the WorldMedia office building. He showed his badge to the security guard, who peered at it for several moments. "Who are you here to see?" He reached for a phone on his desk.

"I'll find the person I'm here to see, thank you very much." He walked past the desk and to the elevator. "Which floor is the newsroom on?"

"Fifth." The answer was barely out of the guard's mouth when the elevator doors opened and Mike was taken aback to see Gabriella Grant herself get off.

"Ms. Grant?"

She was startled, too, he realized as she jumped at the sound of her name. "It's Detective Travis. You recall we spoke at your apartment building."

She smiled then, but briefly. "Are you here to see me?"

"Among others . . ." He let the words hang. "Do you have a moment?"

"Not really." She looked impatiently at her watch. "I have a hair appointment in five minutes and I have to be back here in about a half hour to do a promo, and then . . ."

"I can wait till you're done," he said agreeably, but hoped she'd get the message that he did not intend to leave until she'd spoken to him. For a moment she stared at him as if wondering if he'd have that sort of tenacity. He stared right back, noticing the flamboyant short red dress she wore. It stopped at midthigh, barely longer than the matching, tailored jacket she wore over it.

She sighed and beckoned him across the lobby and sat down on one of the banquettes against the mirrored wall, smoothing down the skirt as if trying to make it stretch over her knees. "What is it you want to know, detective?"

"I'm still curious about your relationship with Jack Kane."

She rolled her eyes. "I told you all about it last Saturday. He's my boss. I work for him."

"You've done very well under his guidance."

"Yes, I have." She stared directly at Mike. "Do you find that curious? Do you think the only women who do well in TV are the ones who sleep with their bosses?"

"Didn't Jack Kane want to sleep with you?"

The question caught her off guard. He could see the momentary confusion but then suddenly she laughed.

"Detective, if I fucked every man who wanted to sleep with me, I'd never have time to anchor the news."

She delivered the laugh and the answer with such a hard edge to her voice, Mike did a double take, reflecting that maybe he'd overestimated her desirability.

"I see, pressure of time." Mike nodded. "Is that why your marriage failed?"

"My marriage has nothing to do with you." She got to her feet.

"I'm not sure about that. I spoke to your husband yesterday."

Gabriella sat down again. "You spoke to Kevin?"

"I did. He told me you'd finally agreed to a settlement. He

said you called him, oh . . ." He paused and reached into his back pocket as if to retrieve his notebook.

"I called him on Saturday. So?"

"After stalling him for almost two years, isn't that a little coincidental?"

"To what?"

Mike leaned back against the banquette and sighed. "Emma Kane's murder. It was just two days after Emma Kane was murdered."

Gabriella got to her feet again and she was smiling broadly. "I could understand your question, detective, if I'd agreed to the settlement, say two days *before* Emma Kane was murdered. Even I would find that slightly suspicious, but I really don't see what you're driving at here." She glanced at her watch. "I really have to be going. I'm so late."

Mike rose, too. "Just one more question, Ms. Grant. Can you tell me exactly where you were between eight and ten on that Thursday evening when Emma Kane was murdered?"

She tapped her foot on the marble floor. "I think I told you. I was at home. I don't have an alibi, if that's what you're looking for. I was alone. Oh, except for the two minutes or so when the delivery boy brought up my meal."

"At what time?"

She appeared to be thinking. "I usually eat later on Thursdays because I stay late in the office. I'd say around ten. But why don't you check with Alison, my assistant? She usually orders for me before I leave the office. Or you can check with the restaurant."

"Which one?" Mike asked.

She smiled at him. "The Szechuan Palace on Seventy-second," she said. "Now, can I run?"

Mike nodded, watching her stride away on tortuously high-heeled pumps. He found himself wondering about Kate's legs as he walked to the elevator. Whenever he was with Kate, she always wore pants.

He had imagined the newsroom would be busier, noisier. In his time in New York he'd had occasion to visit a couple of local TV newsrooms. They had always seemed like bustling ant-type places with producers and reporters screaming at each other. Here, the mood seemed more muted, until he realized that there was a group standing around a TV monitor. They were watching a CNN broadcast on Emma Kane's funeral.

He walked over to a horseshoe-shaped desk in the center of the large open-plan office and flashed his badge at the lone male manning the phones. The man had phones held to both ears but hung up both when he saw the badge.

"I'm looking for Alison, Ms. Grant's assistant," Mike told him.

"Sure." The man looked around the room. "Let's see, Alison is over there." He pointed across the floor. "The red-headed woman with the clipboard."

The woman turned around as if catching the sound of her name and Mike nodded towards her. "Detective Mike Travis." He flashed his badge again. "Is there somewhere private we could talk?"

Her forehead furrowed momentarily. "Will it take long? I have a piece to edit for tonight's news. I'm—"

"It won't take too long," Mike assured her.

She nodded and beckoned him to follow her. "Here, we can talk here," she said. "I'm going to edit in here anyway as soon as Larry's off his break."

It was a small soundproof room with editing machines taking up most of the workspace. One chair was pulled up to the workspace and another positioned behind it. Alison sat down and invited him to do likewise.

"Ms. Grant said you'd be able to help me," he said, getting right down to it. "I need to verify the time that a Chinese meal was delivered to her apartment a week ago, last Thursday."

Alison's eyes narrowed. "I'm not sure I can . . ."

"Miz Grant said you usually place the order before she leaves the office."

"Yes." Alison nodded but still looked unhappy. "Let me think. Last Thursday, I did order for her but . . ." She paused and shook her head. "I really can't remember what time, detective." Another pause. "Did you say you spoke to Ms. Grant?"

"Yes, I bumped into her in the lobby. I must say I was surprised to see her here. I thought she'd be with Mr. Kane at the funeral." A small lie. He wasn't surprised at all.

Alison's eyes narrowed again. "Why would she go? She didn't know Mrs. Kane."

"But she came with Mr. Kane from Philadelphia?"

"Yes, she worked with him at Channel Seven. But I don't think she was a close family friend."

"She and Mr. Kane weren't friends?"

"Well, yes, I suppose." Alison paused to give the question some more thought. "She admired Mr. Kane tremendously. She was beside herself on the morning we found out about the murders."

"Beside herself?"

"Well." Alison paused and her face flushed. "I . . . I guess it was a stupid thing to say on my part, but after I heard about it, I just casually happened to mention something like I hoped this wasn't going to turn out like the Simpson case, and Gabriella heard and came down on me, saying there was no way Jack Kane could ever do such a thing."

Mike nodded. "I guess she knows him better than anyone else here."

"Well, she worked with him before."

"Did you ever get the feeling that it was more than just working with him?"

Alison stared at a spot on the wall, above Mike's head.

"I didn't really have any feelings about it, detective. It's not what I think about nights."

Mike leaned forward in his chair. "Listen, Alison, I won't waste your time, but don't waste mine, either. I'm investigating a double homicide. Mr. Kane's wife was one of the victims. Mr. Kane, as you quite rightly surmised, could be viewed as a suspect. Until he's eliminated, however, it's my job to find out anything I can about his relationship with his wife and/or any other woman in his life. I'm asking for your help."

Alison took a deep breath. "You're asking me if Jack Kane was fooling around with Gabriella Grant and I'm telling you that neither he nor she confided in me."

Mike leaned back in his chair. "Okay, Alison, let me ask you this: Did you ever see them working late together? Leaving the building together? Leaving for lunch together?"

She seemed to ponder the question. "Well, not that exactly but I suppose they were together when they traveled, when they were visiting affiliates. But that's kind of normal. Those TV stations out in the boonies get a big kick when the network star comes to visit."

"Okay." Mike nodded, feeling he was getting somewhere finally but then Alison added: "But I have no idea what happened between them on those trips. All I know is that here in the newsroom it was all very professional. Mr. Kane was very polite to her but he never spent any time looking at her or making especially nice to her, if that's what you're asking me. And he never called her Gabby like some of us do."

Mike rubbed his eyes. "Do you know anything at all about Ms. Grant's personal life?"

Alison shrugged. "Not much. I know she was separated, and I assumed there was a man in her life."

"Why?"

Alison giggled. "Well, I assumed that's where the long-stemmed roses came from. They'd hardly come from her mother, would they?"

"How often did she get roses?"

"Oh, maybe a handful of times since I've been here." She paused. Then quickly added: "And no, I don't remember which florist sent them."

"They could have been sent by a fan, couldn't they? What made you think it was a boyfriend?"

Alison's lips puckered together and she shook her head. "Oh, God, don't make me do this. I shouldn't be telling you any of this."

"You're doing the right thing, Alison," Mike said quietly. "And don't worry. Our conversation stays right here."

"Okay." She sighed. "I just figured there was someone because of the roses and because . . ." She took a deep breath and looked up at the ceiling. "Well, because she recently asked me to pick up one of those home pregnancy testing kits from the drugstore on the corner."

It took some effort to keep his expression impassive. "You're sure it was for herself?"

She nodded. "Absolutely. It was only a week or so ago.

DELUSION 227

She said she felt nauseous and dizzy. In fact it was the Friday before last."

"You mean one week before Mrs. Kane was murdered?"

"Yes."

"Are you sure?"

"I'm positive now because last Friday was the day she complained about feeling nauseous again. That was the second time because then she said she'd finally figured out that it was the Chinese takeout. She thought they were putting MSG in the food. I heard her complaining on the phone to them, and that was just after we all heard the news about Mrs. Kane."

"You're absolutely sure, Alison?"

"Of course, because I remember thinking: How could she even think about complaining about a stomachache when Mr. Kane's wife was dead." Alison shrugged. "It was just a thought that popped into my mind."

He stopped at a deli for a cup of coffee on his way to the Szechuan Palace, allowing himself a break to savor the moment. It looked like Alison had handed him the last piece of the puzzle.

If Gabriella suspected she was pregnant, it explained almost everything: why Jack Kane had driven down to the Main Line to resolve things with his wife, why he had tried to back Emma Kane into a corner over a divorce. Hell, it certainly explained why he needed one. But he had come away empty-handed, and no doubt when he'd called her with the news, it was Gabriella who'd felt herself painted into a corner.

He had a feeling that the Szechuan Palace would confirm that Gabriella Grant had called to cancel her delivery that night. If, that is, anyone had any recollection or records.

He found himself crossing his fingers as he walked into the restaurant some ten minutes later.

"No problem," the manager assured him. "We have computer now."

Mike stared at the screen as the manager's fingers pecked at the keyboard. "Yes." The man's face broke into a broad smile. "Yes. Delivery to Ms. Grant at ten o'clock. Good, huh?"

No. Not good. Mike grimaced but wasn't ready to give up. "May I speak to the delivery boy?"

It took another half hour before the boy returned from making his lunch rounds only to confirm what the computer had shown.

"She has delivery every Thursday night," he assured Mike.

"But I'm talking about last Thursday. Are you sure about it?"

"Yes, then too."

"So she was in the apartment when you delivered the food?"

"Yes." Another nod.

"You know what she looks like, right? You recognized Ms. Grant? You definitely saw her in the apartment?"

He said something that sounded like *col snot*, which Mike interpreted to mean of course not. His pulse quickened. "Did you see Ms. Grant, or not?"

"Did not see her." He shook his head. "Not possible. Ms. Grant . . . in the shower? She said to leave dinner on table, take money, and close door behind me."

Mike took a deep breath. "You're saying she was in the shower but she called out to you, right? Did you recognize her voice? You know what she sounds like?"

"Not me. Not speaking to me. To her doorman. He calls apartment. She tell him. He tell me."

"I see." Mike nodded. "So, you didn't see or talk to Ms. Grant at all. Correct?"

The boy looked at him as if Mike had suggested something obscene. "In shower? Of course not."

Mike thanked him and the manager, knowing there was no point in pressing for more. There was no way the boy could know who the doorman had spoken to. He wondered how long it would take to track down the doorman. He glanced at his watch and prepared himself for a wait.

32

olly Heskell directed the cab to drop her off outside the TV station. She didn't imagine there'd be a problem getting inside. After all, she hadn't been fired, she'd quit. Nick Myers had no reason to warn security to keep her out at all costs. With just a quick backwards glance to make sure that the blue Chevy was nowhere in sight, she hurried into the building.

She was not stupid. She'd spotted the Chevy behind them, returning from the cemetery with Sam. She had seen it slide into a vacant spot halfway down their block, just minutes after Sam had pulled into a space outside their house. They were cops, she knew that much. It had not taken a genius to figure it out, especially after Sam had repeated his conversation with Det.-Sgt. Holmsby to her.

All the way back from Gladwyne he had kept up the insistent questions about the gun. "The cops will want to know what you did with it. This is serious, Molly. They know about you and Jack. They're going to be asking you questions."

She had told him she hadn't touched the gun. She'd forgotten all about getting rid of it. So far as she knew it was still in the nightstand. He had gone speeding up the stairs ahead of her, thrown open his nightstand drawer first, then hers.

"It's not here, Molly."

His eyes focussed on her with dark unspoken accusation, while her heart pounded against her ribcage.

"Then it must have been stolen. I had a break-in a couple of weeks ago."

"Oh, Molly." Sam had sighed wearily. "Are you sure?"

"It wasn't another hallucination, if that's what you're thinking."

Sam shook his head. "Did you report it to the cops?"

"No." A pause and she had looked away. "Nothing valuable seemed to be gone. I didn't think to check for the gun. I forgot . . ."

He sat down on the bed and patted the spot beside him. "Come on, Molly. Sit down with me. Let's talk this over, see if we can make some sense out of it."

She had stared into his eyes and seen dark, sad pools. Sam doesn't believe a word of it, she had thought. He thinks I killed Emma. And if Sam was harboring that kind of suspicion, then what could she expect from the cops? She realized the only way she was going to get out of this was to force Jennifer to speak up.

So she'd ignored his invitation to sit and instead had pulled off her navy sheath dress. Tossing it on the floor she reached for a pair of black leggings and a thick, oversized sweatshirt and her small jogging purse before running downstairs.

Sam had followed her, offering her a drink as he poured one for himself. "No," she'd said. "I've got to get out of here. I've got to get some air." He'd suggested coming with her but she'd rejected that offer, too, telling him she'd probably head for her sister's house. "And don't be calling Vickie and worrying her with all this bullshit, Sam. Okay?"

At the mention of her sister's name he'd seemed to relax. "Okay, but call me if you want me to come and pick you up," he'd said as she let herself out of the kitchen sliding doors and across the courtyard to the gate. The alley had taken her to Fourth Street, and not glancing backwards she had run towards South, flagging down a cab just as she reached the corner of Pine.

Now, her heart hammering, she took the elevator to the third floor. It was almost eleven and the newsroom was already half-deserted. Everyone who was still working was either in the control room or on the set. Only Tom Shanley, the sports anchor, was still at his desk, getting the late scores on the sportsline. And a couple of interns were manning the phones for late-breaking tips. They didn't question her appearance in the newsroom. Maybe they didn't even know yet that she'd quit.

"Hey Molly," one of the interns called out to her. "You and Jack Kane made the news on all the stations—except ours. You're lucky Myers isn't still around. He was in a snit like you've never seen."

"Screw him." Molly laughed, heading for her old desk. "He should have put me on the story. We could have had a great exclusive."

She glanced at the monitor in the newsroom and saw that Gary Dupree was anchoring the show.

"Where's Jennifer?" she called out to the intern who'd addressed her.

"She's off tonight. She called in with laryngitis."

Damn. She slumped down on the chair at her desk and thought about calling Jennifer at home, maybe even going to see her, but then again, did she really need Jennifer's cooperation?

If the cops asked Molly about the gun she was going to tell them about the assaults. Jennifer—and the other two— would just have to bite the bullet and back her up on it. If Jennifer didn't back her, if the others refused to back her, the cops would look at her the same way that Sam had.

"But why didn't you report the break-in, Ms. Haskell? Why are you telling us about it now? Why are you making up this convenient story to explain the missing gun?"

A little hysterical bubble of laughter sprang to her lips. The idea that Jennifer and the others would insist on keeping quiet now was preposterous, of course. This was serious business. They could not lie to the cops.

She didn't care about Jennifer's precious little theory that the sicko could not be the killer because the police were looking for someone who'd rung the front doorbell and the sicko didn't ring doorbells, blah, blah, blah.

Her own theory right now was that the pervert had taken

Sam's .38. Whether he'd used it to kill Emma was another matter entirely. No one had declared Sam's .38 as the murder weapon, but obviously it had to be found.

She stared at her blank computer screen and forced herself to rethink the scenario. But no, she had to be right about this. After all there were only two options. Either the sicko had stolen Sam's .38 or he had not. And if he had not, then where was it?

She brushed her damp palms on her leggings and she was aware of suddenly feeling hot and sticky even though the temperature in the newsroom was always several degrees below comfortable. Was it possible that the pervert had not stolen the gun? That she herself had taken the gun and used it on Emma Kane? And then blanked everything out?

She'd been very sure about seeing the woman in the park. Maybe her mind worked both ways—and this was something her mind was refusing to remember. People suffered hallucinations. That was a medical fact. People suffered from selective amnesia, too—especially after being involved in something horrendous.

The thought struck her hard. She had never pretended anything but to despise Emma. She had even wished her dead. She closed her eyes, trying desperately to conjure up some image of the events that might have sent her steaming to Emma Kane's house. And what had she done with the gun? She just did not remember holding it in her hands. She had no memory at all of facing Emma Kane . . . or shooting her.

"Missing us already, huh?"

The voice made her jump and she opened her eyes to find herself looking at Tom Shanley. She smiled. "Actually, I just came in to pick up the rest of my stuff." A small lie. She'd cleared out everything she really needed.

Tom nodded. "You look very pale."

"Probably hunger pangs," she heard herself say. "I didn't eat today."

"Then let me buy you a big plate of bangers and mash at the Dickens Inn. I'm headed that way with Doreen and Ron."

Molly shook her head. "Bangers and mash aren't my thing, but thanks anyway, Tom."

"Okay." He grinned at her, then looked across the newsroom as the elevator doors opened. "Ah, the graveyard shift has arrived. It must be getting late."

The graveyard shift. The transcribers, thought Molly with a sudden jolt. She'd not had another chance to check out Manzowski and Terrenzio since Monday. But now she was here and they were here and the thought suddenly lifted her mood a little. She felt as if she was being forced back on track. Whatever the truth about Emma Kane's murder, there was one thing she had neither blanked out nor hallucinated. The assault had been real enough and one of those two, she was certain, had assaulted her and her three colleagues. He had also stolen Sam's gun. She was sure of it. The alternative was just too bizarre to think about.

She glanced over the top of her computer screen across the newsroom to where they sat at two of the reporters' desks. Both wore headphones over their ears, their eyes glued to the monitors that stood on trolleys by the desks. Their fingers tapped away as if they had a life of their own. Staring at them, she realized she had no idea which one was Manzowski and which one Terrenzio. They were both big and dark-haired. Both of them looked engrossed in their work.

She thought about going down to the garage to check out their trucks. The garage attendant would have their keys, and if it was the same one she'd spoken to the previous night, he might even let her snoop around.

Yeah, just in case one or the other has left the porn videos—or the gun—on the back seat. She chewed on the inside of her lip nervously. No, not on the back seat but the videos would be at home, for sure. Probably along with the gun.

She glanced again over the top of her computer screen and then logged on. She held her breath as she punched in her password, but Myers evidently hadn't thought to block her access to the newsroom files either. Quickly she opened up the staff directory. Someone had had the bright idea of inputting staff names and addresses in a departmental order rather than alphabetically so she scrolled down to T for transcribers but saw no entry for it. She scrolled up again more slowly and caught the entry under G for graveyard shift. Someone with a sense of humor, she thought, stopping at the two names that drew her attention. And obviously someone who hadn't bothered to make the acquaintance of any of the transcribers. There were four names listed. Manzowski appeared as Manzo and Terrenzio appeared as Terry. The other two likewise had been abbreviated to Snicks and Jody. It didn't matter: The addresses and phone numbers were listed in full.

She jotted them both down. Manzowski lived in Port Richmond. With a name like that, where else? She smiled. The neighborhood was heavily Polish. Terrenzio, she noted, her smile disappearing, lived in the area around the Italian Market. She hoped that didn't mean they lived with their families.

Excuse me, I work with Terry. He asked me to pick up a video for him . . .

She got to her feet, then sat down again suddenly and reached for a sheet of paper and her pen. Quickly she scribbled out a note for Jennifer Reed: *I'm doing what we should have done a long time ago. I'm checking two names at their addresses.* Then she scribbled both names and addresses down and signed the note. If something happened to her, Jennifer would figure it out. She sealed the envelope and left it on her desk, tucking a corner of it under her phone. If something happened to her, the cops would come looking for clues any place she'd been recently.

She logged off the computer and glanced across one more time at the two men. They didn't seem to be aware that she was in the newsroom. It was as if they were tethered to the monitors. In their own little worlds—where they would stay till their shift finished at six.

Eeny, meeny, miny, mo. Which to tackle first?

It was an easy call. Terrenzio first, she decided. It was closer and the cab ride would be cheaper.

She hurried out of the main newsroom doors, not even glancing in their direction. It was only when she slid into the back seat of the cab, outside the station doors, that she realized she was planning to break into a house without the faintest idea of how to go about it. Maybe she was a little crazy, after all. But all she really knew was that she had to find Sam's gun. She had to track it down. Only then would she be able to prove that she had not killed Emma Kane.

He watched Molly Heskell hurry out of the newsroom but pretended not to notice. His fingers stayed tapping at the keyboard as he followed the sound bite through his headphones. He was back on form tonight and it looked like a very light shift. The two of them had six tapes apiece. He was already on his second. It would be a breeze.

He wondered what Molly Heskell was doing back in the newsroom, back at her desk. Hadn't she quit the day before? He had caught her glancing over towards their corner. He had thought she looked nervous. Not quite so composed and self-assured as she'd looked on the six o'clock news.

The funeral had been the lead story on all the news shows in Philly, but Seven had avoided showing any footage of Molly.

Lewis had turned to Channel Three for the full scoop, and he'd been a little startled to see Molly Heskell getting into the first limo with Jack Kane.

That image had stayed with him all evening along with the thought that nagged at him now: Molly, who had always been Jack Kane's favorite, was back in the picture again. Did that mean something? Anything?

Before leaving for work he had inserted his edited tape into the playback machine, running it through until he reached the grainy silhouette. He'd freeze-framed the shot, staring at it with a new eye as he tried to superimpose Molly Heskell's face onto the grayish, fuzzy features. But there was still no way he could identify any distinctive characteristics.

A violent fit of sneezing behind him interrupted his thoughts. He grimaced to himself. All those germs flying around made him feel nervous. He turned sideways and beckoned for his colleague to take off his headphones.

"Why don't you go home to bed and take something for that cold?" he suggested as kindly as he could. "It's a light night; I can probably finish off for you."

"Are you sure?" The other man looked relieved. "I was going to call in sick but, you know . . ." He waved at the cassettes arrayed on the trolley.

"No problem." Lewis shook his head. And, if they don't get done, no big deal, either, he thought.

He turned back to his own work, and a few moments later he heard the sound of footsteps walking towards the newsroom doors.

He waited two or three minutes and then got up from his chair. Alone, working without company, he felt more relaxed and comfortable. Alone, he was free to wander around and snoop a little, if he wanted. He paced across the newsroom but his thoughts stayed with Molly Heskell.

Was it possible that Molly was the woman in his video? Was it possible that Molly had killed Emma Kane? And if she had, did Jack Kane know or suspect?

What would Lewis' video be worth to Jack Kane if he knew that Molly's face would emerge from an enhancement?

Would he be grateful that his wife's killer had been found? Or would he want to bury the tape to avoid the scandal that would erupt when the cops determined that his mistress had killed his wife?

He narrowed his eyes and tried to recall the images from the six o'clock news. Kane and Molly together. In the church. In the limo. On the news. For all the world to see that Molly had stepped right into Emma Kane's shoes.

He hesitated beside Molly's desk and glanced around just to make sure he was completely alone. He reached out and casually flicked back the pages of a small square desk diary where she'd noted her assignments and appointments. There was no point in letting his suspicions run away with him if Molly could account for her time on that Thursday night by pointing to an interview or an assignment she'd covered for work. He flipped the pages back and stared at the blank white space. Okay, he thought. Now, to be really thorough he'd go and get the aircheck for that night's show, too, just in case she had done a live stand-up for the ten o'clock.

The name Jennifer Reed scrawled across a long white envelope caught his attention in midthought. A corner of it was tucked under the telephone. Curious, he thought. If Molly wanted Jennifer to get the note, why hadn't she put it on the anchorwoman's desk? And why was Molly Heskell writing notes to Jennifer Reed anyway?

He picked it up and hesitated for a second more before ripping it open. He stared at the two-line message, his brow furrowing as he recognized his own address.

He put the note back in the envelope and tucked it into his pocket, then paced back across the newsroom. He wished he hadn't told the other guy to leave. If he walked off the job, too, there'd be a shitload of explaining to do in the morning.

But it couldn't be helped. Molly Heskell was headed for his house. Without even turning off his monitor, he picked up his bag and ran towards the newsroom doors.

33

M olly asked the cab driver to drop her off at the corner of Tenth and Washington. Terrenzio lived three blocks off the main market thoroughfare. She didn't mind walking, and she figured she needed the time to psych herself for what she was about to do. The streets were quiet at this time of night, although during the day vendors and shoppers and appetizing smells filled the street. She had shopped at the market occasionally when Sam had been around. His stint in Rome had given him an appreciation for good Italian food, and in the beginning she'd made the effort to follow the various recipes he'd jotted down.

She also knew that the area around the market was a modest one of neat little rowhouses that had been immortalized in the first of the Sly Stallone *Rocky* movies. Not the sort of neighborhood that usually attracted burglars.

She turned off the main thoroughfare and onto Gaskill Lane, noting that the houses here had little front yards rather than steps, which led directly from the front door onto the sidewalk. She checked off the house numbers as she walked and wondered again if she could really pull off breaking into someone else's house.

She imagined her first step would have to be a check in case Terrenzio had a wife or a girlfriend whom he had left tucked up in bed. So, when she reached number twenty-four, she walked right up to the front door and rang the bell. She left her finger on the buzzer for at least thirty seconds and she heard it echo through the dark house. It didn't seem as if there was anyone inside, but she pressed it a second time just in case.

No one came to the door. Nor did any face appear at the upstairs window.

Okay. She took a deep breath and tried the door handle. That would have been too easy, she laughed silently to herself. So, now what?

For a moment she hesitated. It was not a good neighborhood for a break-in. She wondered if someone in a neighboring house was watching even as she stood there planning her next move. What would she do if the cops suddenly swooped down the street? She blinked to erase the thought. She had come this far, she had to press on. Good Lord, she couldn't lose her nerve now. She had another address to check out if she turned up nothing here.

She glanced at the downstairs window and noted that it was the old-fashioned type with spring locks. Which would have been easy to open, she thought, had she had the foresight to bring some useful tool with her.

Go home, Molly, she told herself. You're not cut out for this.

She backed out of the front yard and stood staring up at the house, knowing that she could not quit so easily. She could at least check out the back of the house, since she was already here. She walked to the end of the street and turned the corner, and halfway down the next block she saw the

entrance into an alleyway that predictably led to all the
backyards. She walked slowly into the alley and then
stopped at the first gate, staring through the cheap chicken
wire in disbelief at the raised open window on the first floor.
She took a step back but knew there was no chance that she
was at the wrong house. Terrenzio's rowhouse was an end
unit and this was the last backyard on the alley.

Her heart beating furiously, she snaked her hand over the
top of the gate and released the latch. As the gate swung
open and she crept forward she wondered if she was going
to get caught in a sudden flash of blinding sensor lights. But
she was still in darkness when she reached the window.

It was raised about eighteen inches and she pushed up
with her hand to open it wider. It didn't budge. Terrenzio was
evidently not quite so trusting as it appeared. But then neither was she as big as the average intruder. There was an
advantage to being skinny after all. She slid her head into
the open space and wedged in her shoulders, pushing up off
the ground onto the sill. A couple of seconds later she was
inside the house.

It took a few seconds longer for her eyes to become accustomed to the dark interior, but at least an outside lamp in
the alleyway shed some light into what was obviously
Terrenzio's kitchen. Next time bring a flashlight, too, she
admonished herself, giggling suddenly and nervously, as she
realized it was too dark to conduct any sort of useful search.

Well here goes, she thought, taking a deep breath as she
stepped back to the window and boldly swung the drapes
across it. Crossing the kitchen she entered the living room
and did the same there. Then she switched on the lights.

One glance told her there wasn't much to search. The
rooms were tiny. In the living room little knickknacks stood
on the shelves of three free-standing display units, and magazines lay on two end tables at either end of a bright plaid-
patterned couch. There was no TV or VCR either in the
living room or kitchen. She threw open the drawers of the
kitchen cabinets one by one but saw they were filled with
kitchen utensils. One door in the kitchen revealed a pantry
and another led into a garage that was empty. On her way
up she flung open a door at the bottom of the stairs and

found herself looking into a coat closet where a shelf held only telephone directories.

Upstairs in the front bedroom she finally found a TV. It was a small nineteen-inch model standing on a big oak dresser that faced the bed. She opened the drawers of the dresser one by one as she'd done in the kitchen. In the back bedroom she found nothing except a bed and a nightstand. There was nothing on the nightstand or in the nightstand or in the walk-in closet.

No VCRs, no camcorders, and no cassettes or tapes. And definitely no gun. She hurried downstairs and glanced around again, trying to stifle her disappointment. There were no more doors to open. Nothing leading to a basement or any sort of crawl space. She had checked everything, she was sure of that. She had imagined that the pervert who'd videotaped her would have at least a VCR somewhere in the house, but Terrenzio obviously didn't even have one of those.

She switched off the light in the kitchen and stepped towards the lamp standing on the end table by the couch. But as she reached to kill the light her hand suddenly froze in midair and she stopped to listen for the sound that had disturbed the silence in the room.

Then she heard it again—a scraping sound at the front door. Very much like a key being inserted into the lock. A moment later the door swung open and she found herself staring at Terrenzio stepping across the threshold into his living room.

They stood for a moment facing each other like two figures in a waxwork tableau. Then Terrenzio finally exhaled loudly and long. "Whoa! Molly Heskell. This is some surprise." He dropped his bag to the floor by the open door and stepped towards her. "What the hell are you doing here?"

She could not very well ask him the same thing, although that's what she felt like saying. She could not, in fact, say anything. "I—I—" she stammered, unable to get any words out. She wondered if the shock of being caught by Terrenzio had turned her literally speechless not to mention a bright beet red. Her whole body was bathed in a clammy sweat.

She opened her mouth to take a gulp of air and a curious-sounding rattle emerged from her throat.

"Hey." Terrenzio took another step toward her. "It's okay. I'm sure you've got an excellent explanation. Just don't pass out on me, okay? Here, sit down a moment."

She didn't need a second invitation but sank down onto the ghastly patterned couch. He picked up one of the magazines from the end table and waved it in front of her face. "Here, take another deep breath." He crouched down beside her. "Do you want to go outside? Shall I leave the door open?"

Did she want to go outside? Of course she wanted to go outside. And then she wanted to run like the blazes and get the hell out of here. She would have laughed had she not been so embarrassed. Instead she shook her head.

"I'm sorry." She finally got the words out. "I'm really sorry. I don't know what to say."

Terrenzio gave her a half smile and sat down beside her. "Well, you could start by explaining what brought you here. Were you looking for me?"

"No, I made a terrible mistake." She took another deep breath, grateful for the cool air sweeping in through the open door. "I thought I was going to find something here."

"Like what?" He sounded genuinely puzzled.

Molly sighed. She'd have to give him some sort of explanation. Of course she would. But she couldn't admit to the whole story. "I was looking for a gun," she said simply. "I had a break-in a while ago and that's one of the things that was taken."

"And you thought I had it?" Both of his eyebrows threatened to disappear into the shock of his dark hair.

She swallowed, trying to ease the tightness in her throat. "I thought the break-in was an inside job. I mean I figured out, because of a number of things, that it was someone who worked at Channel Seven and drove a dark-colored truck. Those were the only leads I had and you fit. But you weren't the only one on the list—" She broke off and attempted a smile, to which Terrenzio fortunately responded.

"Well, okay, that'll do for openers." He paused. "Are you thinking of breaking into any other homes tonight?"

She shook her head quickly. "No, this was a bad idea, obviously. I mean, I was going to . . ." She stared down at her hands and noticed they were shaking.

Terrenzio noticed, too. "You're cold," he said, getting to his feet. "Why don't I close the door and make you a good hot cup of tea?"

"No, really don't trouble yourself." She made a move to get up. She wanted out of there. "I should call my husband. He'll come and pick me up. Unless you're thinking of calling the police, that is . . ." She gave him a half smile, hoping he took the suggestion in the light-hearted way she'd intended it.

"Oh, I think I can let it pass," he said calmly. "So long as I'm off that list." He paused. "I am, aren't I?"

"Yes. Of course." She laughed nervously, wondering if she'd imagined the sudden change of tone in his voice. Was it just her imagination that made it suddenly sound familiar?

It had to be, she assured herself as he said: "Well, good. If that's settled, just relax. I'll put the kettle on, anyway. He stared at her for a moment. "Maybe you can tell me the whole story before your husband gets here."

34

Friday, October 4

Mike Travis was sitting at Harry's desk when Kate arrived in the unit just before eight.

"Morning." He smiled cheerily at her as she placed a big Dunkin' Donuts bag on the desk. One of the cups had leaked and the bag was soggy on the bottom. She took the cups out, throwing out the one that had leaked, and then handed one to Mike. "Black, right?"

"Yep." His smile broadened as he took a sip. "That's more like it."

"So?" She removed the top from her cup. "How did it go in New York with Miss Grant yesterday?"

He shrugged. "Better than I expected, not as good as I hoped. I was just giving Harry the scoop but Grimes called him in." Mike inclined his head towards the lieutenant's office. "And that was forty minutes ago." Kate saw that the door was closed.

"Trouble?" she asked.

"I don't think so. Just the usual BS."

Kate pulled up a chair on the other side of the desk just as Harry emerged from the lieutenant's office with a bundle of manila folders under his arm. He dropped them on his desk with a sigh, nodded at Kate, and sat down on the chair that Mike vacated.

"So?" He picked up one of the coffee cups. "Let's get back to the big one."

Kate glanced at the stack of manila folders and guessed that the lieutenant had asked Harry for an update of all his pending cases. She wondered how he managed to keep track of anything but the murder investigation. She thought he looked more tired and pale than ever and the day was only just beginning.

"Okay." He leaned back in his chair, picking up one of the extra Styrofoam cups from the desk. "We're going to spread the net wide on this one now. Wayne is going to be knocking on Ms. Heskell's door any moment. If she can't produce her husband's thirty-eight and doesn't come up with a reasonable explanation of where it is, he'll let us know. In the meantime, Mike, let's get back to Ms. Grant and her alibi. Did it check out?"

Kate got the impression that she was coming in at the tail end of the conversation. "Did you speak to Gabriella?" she asked as Mike pulled up another chair. "How did she explain agreeing to a settlement two days after the murder?"

"She didn't," Mike replied. "She didn't think it was significant. She's a real tough nut, the type that won't crack until we can hit her with hard facts."

"Did you get anything on her and Jack Kane?"

She caught the glance between Mike and Harry and wondered what was coming as Mike perched on the desk.

"Only from her assistant," he said. "Grant sent her out for one of those home pregnancy test kits the week before Emma was murdered."

Kate felt as if someone had punched her in the stomach. Unbidden, the image of the unopened box of condoms in Jack Kane's bathroom cabinet suddenly jumped into Kate's head. Sure. Why open the box when the horse had already bolted?

She jumped in her seat as Harry's ringing phone startled her out of her thoughts.

"Okay, okay," she heard Harry say. "Give them fifteen minutes and go back in." He hung up and glanced at Kate. "That was Wayne at Heskell's house. Packer answered the door in his pajamas." He paused. "Anyway, where were we?"

"Well, we're at two-zip, aren't we, Kate?" Mike grinned. "I believe I'm two points ahead now."

She bristled. "So, did Gabriella actually tell this assistant that Kane might be the daddy?"

Mike shook his head. "No, the assistant didn't know anything about Kane."

Kate chewed on the inside of her lip. "Isn't that something of a giant leap, then?"

"Not exactly giant, Kate." Harry weighed in. "Not when you put it together with everything else." Then he nodded at Mike. "Bottom line: Does she have an alibi or not?"

Mike reached into his pocket and brought out a notebook and said nothing as he flipped through the pages. Then he looked up at Harry. "It seems she does." He glanced down at his notebook. "But I don't know. There's just something that seems off about it. You tell me. She had a Chinese meal delivered to her apartment just before ten. I spoke to the delivery boy and he said Gabriella was in the shower and he was told to put the bag on the kitchen table, take the money, and close the door behind him—"

"You're right," Harry interrupted. "That's not much of an alibi at all. He didn't see her in the shower, did he?"

"Of course not." Mike grinned. Then the grin disappeared and he shook his head. "He didn't talk to her either. But then I checked with Rafael, the doorman, who said he was the one who gave the delivery boy the instructions after buzzing up to Gabriella's apartment. He says he talked to her when the delivery boy arrived in the building."

Harry sat up straight. "He couldn't swear that it was Gabriella Grant, could he?"

Mike looked down at his notebook. "Well, listen to this. Question: Are you sure you were talking to Miss Grant? Answer: Yes. Question: You recognized her voice? Answer: Of course. Question: There are about three hundred residents in this building . . . are you telling me you recognize them all by their voices? Answer: No. Not all but I know Ms. Grant. For sure. She always calls me Jose. She calls all of us Jose."

Mike paused, shaking his head. Then continued reading. "Question: So she was in her apartment and she said she'd just stepped into the shower? You're quite sure about that? Answer: Yes. I remember because she was a long time answering, and also the phone is ringing several times before she answers." Mike looked up from the notebook.

"Mmmm." Harry took off his bifocals and rubbed his eyes. "I see what you mean. It's not cast iron but it's close. She's home before ten and we know Emma Kane was still alive just after eight. That would be cutting it extremely close—"

"Unless," Mike interrupted, "we're wrong about the time of death and Gabriella ate her Chinese meal then drove down and popped them around midnight—"

"I thought you determined time of death between eight and ten," Kate broke in.

"Well, nothing's etched in stone," Mike said, shaking his head as he flicked back the pages of his notebook. "I know there's something I'm missing here. Something that that doorman said doesn't sound right."

Kate leaned across to peer at the notebook just as Harry's phone rang out. "Well, none of it sounds grammatically correct, if that's what you mean." She smiled. "I'm betting he wasn't an English major."

Mike grimaced as if to indicate that wasn't what he meant, and looked as if he was about to say something more but was distracted by Harry leaping to his feet.

"What are you telling me, Wayne?" Harry yelled into the

phone. "Hold on, hold it just a second." He punched a button on his phone set. "Okay, go ahead now, you're on the speaker phone. Tell us what happened."

Wayne sounded annoyed. "Heskell's not here, Harry. When I came back to the house, Packer said she went out last night to see her sister. I didn't see her leave, by the way."

"Yeah, so?"

"So, she's not at her sister's, either. Packer just checked, and she wasn't there at all last night."

"Are you in the house, now?"

"Yep."

"If Packer's there, put him on."

There was a short silence before Sam Packer's voice echoed across Harry's desk. "I'm sorry, detective. I had no idea that she was going to——"

"You're not helping her, Mr. Packer," Harry cut in coldly, and Kate noticed that the conversation had drawn a couple of detectives to their side of the room. "Did you tell her about our talk yesterday?"

There was a pause on the other end of the line before Packer answered: "Yes, of course. I had to ask her about the gun. I was anxious about it myself."

"Is that right?" Harry glanced at Mike and shook his head, as if in disbelief. "And were you able to dispel your anxiety?"

"No," Sam Packer replied simply.

"She wouldn't tell you what she did with it?"

"She said she hadn't done anything with it. She said we'd had a break-in, and she thought it must have been stolen."

Harry smacked his forehead with the palm of his hand, and then depressed the speaker button, abruptly cutting off Sam Packer.

One of the detectives standing beside Kate suddenly laughed out loud. "She says the gun was stolen? How original! I'm sure I've never heard that one before."

Harry shot Kate a warning look. "Don't say it. It's my fault. Dammit." He brought his fist down on the desk. "I should have brought her in. When Packer mentioned she was depressed and on medication, I should have seen the little red flag."

"Hindsight's always twenty-twenty, Harry," Mike offered from his side of the desk.

"I suppose," Harry agreed. Then he shook his head. "Her husband tells her we want to talk to her—and she bolts. Is that a resounding admission of guilt?"

"Maybe a little too resounding," Mike commented tersely.

Harry's face creased into a frown. "We'll need a warrant for Heskell's house," he said, reaching for his jacket.

As he got to his feet, Kate nudged Mike in the ribs. "A touchdown for my team, detective," she said quietly so that Harry couldn't hear. "I believe that now puts me four points ahead."

35

Harry was quiet on the drive into Center City and Kate suspected he was berating himself over Molly Heskell. It was Mike's doing, she thought, because he'd been so single-minded about going after Gabriella Grant. But then neither of them had been at the dinner with her and Jack Kane to hear the story about Molly calling Jack on the very day Emma Kane was in his office.

Kate could empathize even though she had never experienced the sort of frustration she believed Molly Heskell must have felt. Mike had dismissed her motive as insignificant but he hadn't looked at the whole picture. Emma Kane must have seemed like an immovable obstacle to the reporter. Already in a fragile mental state over the death of her baby, it had probably not taken much for Molly Heskell to become unraveled.

Kate thought about the TV report Molly had produced pointing the finger at Jill Maxwell, and she thought about the newsclipping they'd found in Emma Kane's bedroom about Gabriella Grant. It had been mailed in Philadelphia. Kate wondered if perhaps Molly Heskell had sent it to provoke Emma and cause trouble for Gabriella. She wondered if it was worth reminding Harry about the woman client who'd looked over the Kane home with Anna Mae Whitman on the morning of the realtor's death. Was it possible that Molly Heskell had looked over the house, scoping it out before she busted in on Emma?

But just then they turned onto Delancey Street and Harry interrupted her train of thought with an angry exclamation as he surveyed the scene in front of him.

Kate stared in equal surprise. The little park outside Molly Heskell's house was a mob scene. TV news vans were parked on the sidewalk opposite the house. News reporters and cameramen were huddled in groups around the sculpture of the three bears. Kate surmised they'd been waiting a while: Someone had strung a garland of empty Styrofoam cups around Mother Bear's neck.

Harry slowed down. "Dammit! How did they get here? I'd like to know who leaked this?"

Kate shook her head. "No one necessarily, Harry. You had Wayne asking questions at the TV station, right? I'm sure it wasn't difficult for them to figure things out. They look as if they've been here a while."

Kate looked out of the window and saw Pat Norris from the *News* and behind him, Lester Franks. As soon as Harry pulled up, double-parked outside the house, and stepped out, the crowd moved towards him.

"Are you here to arrest Molly Heskell?" a voice yelled out.

"Do you have a warrant?" another one echoed.

Kate slid out of her seat, ducking her head, and kept right behind Harry, who ignored the questions and said nothing as he banged on Molly Heskell's front door.

The door opened immediately and Sam Packer stood in the hallway. "Are there any more of you coming?" he asked. "A Detective Travis arrived a few minutes ago with a search warrant." Ashen-faced, he beckoned them into the living room, where Kate was surprised to see Jack Kane standing by the fireplace. Mike was standing by the window surveying the scene in the park.

"That's a bad scene out there, detective," Jack Kane commented. "What are you going to tell them?"

"We don't have to tell them squat," Mike replied brusquely. "Why are you here, anyway, Mr. Kane?"

Jack Kane accepted Mike's open hostility calmly. "Sam called me. This is a very difficult situation for both of us, detective. I want to do whatever I can to help find Ms. Heskell."

Mike looked as if he wanted to say something cutting but held back and instead let Harry direct his attention to Sam Packer.

"Have you got a list of her family and friends in the area? Phone numbers?"

Sam Packer handed Harry a sheet of yellow lined paper. "But I've called most of them and she's not there."

"Do you have any idea where she might have gone? Do you have another home?"

Sam shook his head. "Only my apartment in New York. And she definitely didn't turn up there." He paused. "She didn't take her passport or credit cards. I don't know about cash."

Mike turned to Harry. "She was seen in the Channel Seven newsroom some time last night, Wayne says." He glanced at Sam Packer. "Is there anyone at Seven she was particularly close to?"

"She was friends with a lot of her colleagues," he answered. "But I've no idea who she'd turn to in a situation like this."

Harry sighed. "Okay, Mr. Packer, tell me exactly what happened between you and your wife yesterday."

The anchorman nodded. "I asked her about the gun."

Harry nodded. "And?"

"She wouldn't give me a straight answer. At first she said that she hadn't done anything with it and that it was in the nightstand where we'd always kept it. I knew that was a lie because like I told you yesterday I searched the house for it before I left and it definitely wasn't there. So I made her go upstairs . . ."

Sam paused, his brow creasing. "Of course, it wasn't there. Then she said that it must have been stolen. She said there'd been a break-in."

He shook his head and his hand went to his eyes as if he wanted to erase the image in his head. When he looked back at Harry, Kate was shocked to see his eyes moist. "I guess I made it clear I didn't believe her about the break-in. Maybe I was too hard on her."

"You called her a liar?"

Sam shook his head. "I was more cutting than that. I suggested the break-in sounded like one of her hallucinations."

Harry stared at the anchorman, puzzled. "I don't follow."

Sam Packer paced across to his living room window. Then turned around abruptly. "Molly went through a couple of weeks where she was seeing things, imagining things, making them up." He shrugged. "I don't know what to call it really but for example one night she saw a woman with a baby in that park across the street . . . in the middle of the night. Then a few days later she said she'd seen the woman again, and she'd seen the baby fall out of the swing."

"And, these were hallucinations?"

"A woman in a park at the dead of night lets a baby fall from a swing? Look I'm not a shrink but Molly had just lost our baby. It seemed like she was projecting her loss onto this faceless woman." He paused and shrugged. "Anyway, Molly told me that when she went running out to help, there wasn't anyone in the park. It shook her up, you know."

"So, you assumed that the break-in was another hallucination? A figment of her imagination?"

"No. But I did press home the point and asked her if she'd reported it to the police. Of course, she hadn't."

Mike and Harry looked across the room at each other. Then Mike asked: "Did you ask her why she hadn't?"

Sam Packer shrugged. "She was very dismissive about it. She said it looked like nothing was taken. She never thought about checking on the gun. Anyway, the whole thing sounded so outrageous. Christ! We had a plastic trash can stolen out of the backyard once, so to have someone break in and take nothing . . . well, that was plainly ridiculous."

He walked across the room again, and stared out into the street. Kate found herself glancing around the room distractedly, wondering why Sam's words sounded strangely familiar. But before she could dwell on the thought, Sam said, "Look at that mob. What are you going to tell them, detective?"

"It depends what we find, Mr. Packer." Harry beckoned at Mike to hand him the search warrant. "I'm sorry but we're going to have to search the house."

Sam nodded again, with a look in his eyes that seemed to ask: How the hell did I get into this mess? Then he walked to the doorway. "I'll show you upstairs," he said.

Kate was about to follow Harry out of the living room when she saw Jack Kane signaling for her to stay. She suspected that Mike saw it, too, because he stopped in the hallway as if to wait for her. "Are you coming with us, Kate?"

"I'll be right there," Kate called back.

"Protective, isn't he?" Jack Kane laughed. "And he doesn't like me at all."

Kate let it go and said nothing.

Kane's smile vanished. "What the hell is going on, Kate? The cops can't seriously be looking at Molly."

"Oh, I think they are, Jack. You heard Sam. He asked her about the gun, she couldn't explain why it was missing, and then after learning that the police wanted to talk to her, she takes a hike. There's a lot of muddy water swirling around Molly."

Jack shook his head. "It doesn't make any sense to me. I saw her yesterday. She wasn't unhinged or hallucinating or acting weird. The way I hear people talking about her is just not the woman I know."

He stared pointedly at Kate and she felt a sudden strange little stab of envy at the way Jack Kane had jumped right in to defend the woman he'd loved.

"Well, apparently she wasn't in the best of health," Kate said cautiously, glad that he couldn't read her thoughts. What was this bond between them anyway? And why was Jack Kane being so protective of her? Or was there something more to it—like guilt? Was it because he knew that Molly was innocent, because he knew who'd really killed his wife?

Stop it, she told herself. Molly's the one who's bolted. Not Gabriella. For a moment she stared absently at the flashbulbs popping outside the window. Then she took a deep breath. "You care for her very much, don't you?" she said, finally.

Jack Kane paced across the room to join her at the window. "I care what happens to her. I told you the other night, she was very important to me at one time."

"But you didn't tell me the other night that she'd quit her job and was coming to work for you at WorldMedia."

Jack shook his head. "I didn't know that the other night, Kate. She didn't tell me about it till yesterday at the funeral. About quitting, I mean. Her coming to WorldMedia was always in the cards. I told you that." He hesitated. "You sound angry, Kate. Did you think I wasn't being honest with you?"

"The thought crossed my mind." She softened the admission with a half smile, then quickly turned away, feigning interest in the scene outside.

"Kate, look at me," he said, his index finger prodding gently under her chin, forcing her to face him. Outside a flashbulb popped again as Kate found herself staring into his eyes.

They bore into her with intensity. "I'd never be anything but honest with you," he said. "I don't like liars. I think lying is a sign of weakness. I don't lie, Kate. Not in business. Not in my personal life. You'll discover that for yourself, when you get to know me better, when you accept that job offer." He eyed her with a meaningful look.

Kate sighed. "I don't know about the job, Jack. I can't really just up and move to New York. I can't uproot my son and . . ." She hesitated. She could only imagine what Belinda's reaction might be if Kate told her she was moving Tommy out of state. There was no way she could consider a move.

But Jack was shaking his head at her. "You don't have to move, Kate. We live in an age of computers. You could work from home. Hell, you could even tape the show at our Philly affiliate. But I'd insist on you coming in to WorldMedia at least once a month, just out of personal preference," he added. "I'd like to see you once in a while." He cracked a smile, lightening the mood.

Kate found herself smiling back at him. It was hard to resist Jack Kane's charm and forcefulness for very long. She found herself wondering how long she would be able to resist *him* if he showered her with that sort of charm on a daily basis. It was a fleeting thought interrupted by the clatter of footsteps on the stairs.

She stepped into the hallway and saw that Harry was holding a large plastic bag in his hand. "You found something?"

Harry shrugged. "A pair of Heskell's slacks with what looks like bloodstains on them. They were tossed into the back of a closet. Packer thinks she wore them when he rushed her to the hospital. We'll see." He glanced to the top of the stairs at Mike. "I'm going to send in Wayne and Lansing to finish up here in the house. We need to get a BOLO out on Ms. Heskell."

He waited for Sam Packer to join them in the hall. "I'm going to give the press a statement now," he told the anchorman. "I'm going to tell them that your wife is missing and we're looking for her in connection with our murder investigation. I have to tell you privately, though, that if she doesn't turn up in the next twenty-four hours I'll be seeking a fugitive warrant for her arrest."

Sam Packer nodded and said nothing as Harry and Mike trooped towards the front door, but Jack Kane stopped them as they were about to leave, addressing himself to Mike. "Detective, don't you think there's something suspect about Molly's story of the break-in? Don't you think if she . . ." He looked as if he was searching for the right word. "If she, in fact, used the gun she'd have some better story prepared? She could have come up with a dozen better explanations than something that sounds so phony right off the bat. Doesn't that bother you at all?"

"Everything about this case bothers me," Mike retorted curtly before following Harry outside.

Kate hung back for a moment as the reporters swarmed around the two of them, and pondering Jack Kane's question, suddenly remembered why Sam Packer's words had had such a ring of familiarity. Sure, she had heard them before. Jennifer Reed had said the same thing about her break-in. Nothing was taken, the anchorwoman had said, and Jennifer had not reported her incident to the police either.

She waited till Harry and Mike had finished talking to the reporters. Then she reminded Harry about her conversation with Jennifer.

"Yeah." He nodded. "I thought about it myself when Packer was talking. But . . ." He shrugged.

"But what?" Kate interrupted. "Do you think there's something to it? Do you think it happened to Heskell, too?"

Harry hesitated for a moment longer then shook his head. "Right now, I'm more inclined to suspect that Heskell probably heard Reed's story around the newsroom, and when Packer questioned her about the gun, it seemed like a good one to pass off as her own."

"Like it was the first answer that popped into her head?"

"Yeah, something like that." Harry shrugged, and then obviously losing interest in the question, asked: "So are you coming with me or going with Travis?"

Kate looked at Mike as he strapped on his helmet and got astride the bike. "Come on," he beckoned her. "I brought an extra helmet."

Kate hesitated but only because she was still puzzling over the two newswomen and their break-ins. She wasn't sure why it bothered her—except that Molly Heskell had had a week to concoct a good story. Unless her depression and/or medication had totally addled her brain, Kate felt, like Kane obviously did, that she could have come up with something so much more convincing.

36

L ewis spread the morning papers on the counter in front of him and tried to focus on the words of the lead story.

"Another cup of coffee?" The waitress behind the counter interrupted him. He nodded. More coffee wasn't going to do his nerves any good but he couldn't sit staring into an empty cup.

His eyes strayed back to the *Inquirer* headline:

CHANNEL SEVEN EX-REPORTER SOUGHT IN MURDER INQUIRY.

Police last night said they were looking for Molly Heskell, a former reporter for Channel Seven news. Although Det.-Sgt. Harry Holmsby refused to confirm they have a warrant for Ms. Heskell's arrest, he said detectives want to question her about the night of the murders.

Ms. Heskell disappeared from her Society Hill home after attending the funeral of murder victim Emma Kane. The 46-year-old wife of TV news executive Jack Kane was found slain last Thursday at her Main Line home.

Police who went to the home Ms. Heskell shared until recently with her husband, TV newsman Sam Packer, left the house with a bag of evidence.

Lewis took a gulp of coffee that made his eyes water. The hot liquid scalded the roof of his mouth. But immediately the pain was forgotten. He thought instead about the buzz in the newsroom. When he'd arrived last night there had still been people around, talking about Molly in low whispered voices: Could she really have done it? Do you think she really did it?

He had sat down at his corner desk feeling pleased with himself. For once in his life he was ahead of them. He had all the answers. Yes it's true, he'd wanted to shout across the newsroom, Molly Heskell killed Emma Kane. And I got her to confess to it.

It had turned into such a satisfying evening after he'd brought her the tea and told her she couldn't call her husband until she'd searched his entire house. He didn't want her to leave until she was absolutely satisfied, he'd said.

Her face had been a picture when he added: "You didn't search my basement, I bet."

She'd giggled in a silly nervous way. "But you don't have a basement."

"Oh, but I do," he'd said, swiftly removing the hot cup of tea from her reach.

She'd gotten the message when he slid home the bolt on the front door and told her to open the coat closet. "The basement door is behind the coats, Molly."

Of course she had not wanted to go down the steps but he'd forced her, blocked her way out of the house, and made her walk into his studio. He'd let her look around and she had immediately spotted the cassettes. There was no way she could have missed reading the spines of the boxes: Janey, Diane, Jennifer, and Molly. It had been difficult to read her face, though. Her expression had remained sober and resigned and had changed only when she'd spotted the .38 revolver lying on top of his in-tray.

"Is that the gun you stole from me? Is that mine?"

"I don't know. It could be. I didn't steal it, but it's the gun that killed Emma Kane."

Her body had sagged a little but her jaw had jutted out with more determination—as if she had resolved to keep her dignity, no matter what. He admired her for that.

"You stole that gun from me and you killed Emma Kane with it."

"No. I didn't steal it and I didn't kill Emma. But I was there that night. Do you want to know what happened?" He'd pushed the swivel chair at her. "Sit down."

Then he'd played his Emma tape for her, rewinding and replaying the portion that started with the thwump sound on his roof and continued with the shadowy silhouette moving till he had the enhanced shot of the sleek black-clad female. "That was the gun landing on the roof of my truck," he'd said softly, letting the tape roll until he'd freeze-framed his best shot.

He had not watched the tape himself. He had watched Molly Heskell. Had seen her face turn a peculiar grayish shade. He had seen the beads of perspiration erupt on her upper lip. And then he had watched in horror as she'd thrown up violently all over his chair and floor.

Later when he'd cleaned her up and when she'd stopped sobbing, he'd had a nice conversation with her. She had begged him to let her turn herself in. She'd said the cops should have the tape. They would be able to do something more with it. She really wanted to see a clearer picture because she had no recollection of what she'd done. She was on antidepressant medication, she'd told him, and everyone knew that stuff could have weird effects on people.

"What are you going to do?" she'd asked.

"I'll try to work something out," he'd said.

But did she think he was stupid? He gulped another mouthful of coffee. Did she really think he'd let her walk out of his house and go to the cops? How dumb would that be?

He'd end up in the slammer again, for sure. So would Molly Heskell. But Jack Kane would be off, scot-free. He'd thought about this for most of the night at work. He'd tuned into a couple of late-night news shows and he knew the cops were already onto Molly.

He thought it was so unfair. Jack Kane would walk free when it was obvious to Lewis that Molly had done it for him. The more he'd thought about it, the more he'd stewed—until the idea had come to him. He'd put it down on paper immediately, his adrenaline pumping as he scribbled out the quick script.

He reached into his inside pocket now and took out the two pages of yellow legal pad paper. He'd originally thought about videotaping her in his studio—but the cops would ask too many questions about a confession like that. An audio cassette would achieve the same effect.

He stared at his scribbles, addressing Molly's confession to the Channel Seven assignment editor.

Pete, I'm sending this tape to you because we've been friends for a long time, and you'll be able to authenticate my voice and some of the facts herein. I know the cops are looking for me, and will arrest me for Emma Kane's murder. But I couldn't let them do it because I feel that once they've got me in custody their investigation will end and that wouldn't be fair. I'm not the only one involved in this terrible tragedy.

As you know Jack Kane and I were lovers for a long time. He promised me so much but then Emma got in the way. Emma was always getting in the way, Jack always said. He said there was only one way to get her out of the way. We talked about her death many times. At first it was just wishful thinking, then when I was at home after losing the baby, Jack called me and said now was the time for me to move, to be with him again. But Emma had to be gotten rid of. He said if I did it, I would get away with it because a good defense attorney would plead temporary insanity, postpartum depression, whatever. He said I might not even serve any time at all.

The paper shook a little in his hands as he thought about the audacity of this plan. Molly was going to convict Kane from beyond the grave. He would send it to Pete Norcross at Channel Seven, but TV stations all around the country would go berserk trying to steal portions of the audio. They would claim justifiable use of news footage. They would buy, borrow, steal the best parts and it would be seen across the country as a voiceover covering the footage of Molly's body being recovered by the cops . . . in some location many miles from his house.

Well, he had no choice in that. He could not let her go.

But he wondered how he was actually going to bring himself to do the deed. The thought of blood spattering all over the place made him feel sick. Then again, taking her out of the house while she was still alive was even riskier. He wondered whether he knew enough to make it look like suicide.

He chewed nervously on his thumbnail.

"If you're really hungry, the cheese danish is excellent this morning." The dumpy little waitress interrupted his thoughts, and he saw that she was smiling shyly at him. She was new in the diner. Pounds overweight. Where the hell did she get the nerve to think he'd be interested in someone like her?

He stared at her without answering so that she was forced to shrug and move down to another customer at the end of the counter.

Then he looked down at the newspaper and pretended to read. In a moment he'd leave. There was no point in thinking things over for much longer. It was time to get back to Molly. He just hoped the smell of the vomit had cleared by now.

37

Molly woke with a sour, stale taste in her mouth. Her muscles ached, her neck felt stiff and painful. She saw that the digital clock on the playback machine said 8:29. But was that night or day? And what day of the week was it?

She had arrived at Terrenzio's house on Thursday night. . . . Late on Thursday night when Terrenzio was supposed to have been at work. What a fool. What a damn stupid fool she'd been.

Why had she not run? Why had she not fought him? Why had she allowed herself to get trapped? But then, she had been so terrified she'd almost wet herself, seeing him crouched by the door sliding the bolt home. She'd known then that she had found the right house.

After that it had become a nightmare: the basement studio, the tape cassettes lined up on the shelf and labeled with their names, the gun lying in his in-tray. But it was the video of Emma Kane's house on the night of the killings that had caused her to become unglued.

He had freeze-framed the shadowy figure backlit by a bright sensor light and she had found herself staring in horror at the hooded top. The hood had covered the head and shadowed the face, but she saw enough to recognize the sweat top. It had looked exactly like the one she sometimes wore when she went for early morning walks.

That's when she had thrown up.

Terrenzio had been angry about that and had cursed her out as he brought a bowl of warm water and a washcloth to clean her up. He'd cursed and scrubbed at the carpeting and then sprayed everything with strong Lysol deodorizer, leaving her to sit there in her soiled sweatshirt and leggings.

"There now," he'd said when he was finished. "That's better. Can I get you something warm to drink?"

But she had not been able to stop shaking as the enormity of it hit her: She had come to find Sam's gun to prove her innocence, and she had stepped into a horror tale. Her mind had raced from one thought to another. She had gone from protesting that the shadowy figure was not her, that she had no memory of being at Emma's house to pleading with Terrenzio to turn her and the tape into the cops.

"They'll hang you," he'd told her calmly.

"No," she'd said, believing for a moment that he was concerned. "They'll have to understand I was sick. I was on medication. I think it just made me worse."

He'd waited till she was finished before making her take off the soiled leggings and sweatshirt. He had promised to wash them out and had handed her an old, worn chenille robe. A little while later he'd brought her hot oatmeal, a glass of milk, and a sleeping pill, which she had immediately popped into her mouth.

When he came the next time he told her it was late evening and he was going to work. He had brought dinner for her: a piece of tough steak, a baked potato, a glass of orange juice, and another little sleeping pill. Then he'd left, locking the steel door behind him.

She looked again at the digital clock and figured it had to be Saturday morning. She felt as if she had slept a long time, and she knew the rest had done her good. She already felt mentally and physically stronger, strong enough, at least, to think about the videotape again.

Now that her mind was clearer she wanted to see the freeze-framed shot again. She tried to replay it in her head, remembering that along with the moment of recognition something else had struck her. But it had been a detail so tiny that it had been instantly dismissed as she'd stared at the hooded sweat top in horror.

She was focusing so hard on the image in her head that she was only barely aware of the sound of a bolt sliding back on the other side of the studio door. Her heart thudded as Terrenzio came into the room holding a bundle of newspapers under one arm and her clothes in the other.

He placed the clothes on the desk and glanced at her with what she thought was a kindly eye. But she forced the idea out of her head immediately. No, she thought, she wasn't going to allow herself to fall into that hostage syndrome thing.

"They're going to come looking for me, you know," she said in a voice that she hoped sounded strong and firm.

"They're already looking for you, Molly," he retorted, evidently unimpressed with her tone as he flung the newspapers at her feet. "The police think you've gone on the lam."

She bit on the inside of her lip, attempting to mask the wave of anxiety that suddenly washed over her. "They're going to find me," she said. "I let someone know where I was going."

He grinned at her. "I know. I found the note you left for Jennifer Reed."

A sound that was half shriek and half sigh escaped her lips.

Terrenzio was at her side immediately, crouching down beside her. "I'm going to help you, Molly," he said. "I've read all the newspaper stories. Your husband said you weren't well, that you were depressed and supposed to be on medication. He's appealing for you to come home and get help. Don't you want to go home to him?"

She tried to blink back a tear but felt it already rolling down her cheek. "Why don't you just turn me in to the cops?"

He straightened up and pulled over a chair, sitting directly opposite her. "Because I know you didn't do this all by yourself. You were put up to it by someone who took advantage of your depression."

"What are you talking about?"

"I've got a way out for you, Molly." She saw him reach into the inside pocket of his jacket. "I'm going to help you send a message to the police, so that you don't get all the blame." He handed her two yellow lined sheets of paper and then got up and opened a desk drawer. She glanced across to see what he was doing and noticed the little tape recorder in his hand . . .

"I've written a little script for you, Molly. You can change words or phrasing you're not comfortable with, we can work on it together, but"—he grinned at her—"not the substance or the facts."

She glanced down at the childish scribble that filled the two pages and started to read it to herself.

Her eyes focussed on the nonsensical words about her and Jack Kane plotting Emma's murder and all she could think was that Terrenzio was totally unhinged. More unhinged than she'd ever been. She looked up at him. "Why are you doing this?"

He laughed. "For the same reason I came after you the other day. It's Kane's fault. All of this. I have nothing against you, but Jack Kane has to pay."

"For what? Tell me, for God's sake."

He shook his head. "It's too long a story, Molly, but it started here in Philadelphia. I can tell you that much. I was with Jessica then." He paused and crouched down beside her again. "He's a bad person. He ruined my life and he's ruined yours, so this will help you and it will help me."

"But it's not true. Jack never called me."

"Do you want to face the rap all by yourself?"

She ignored the question. She didn't understand his rambling about Jessica or anything else but it was obvious that he was totally off his rocker. What's more, she knew he didn't give a rat's ass about helping her. If she went through with taping the message he would simply kill her. He could not afford to let her go, to correct her story or to spill the truth about him.

He picked up the tape recorder off the desk. "Ready when you are."

"No, I can't do it," she said suddenly.

He sighed. "You're making a mistake. I'm offering you an out."

He spoke in a maddening little singsong voice that made her shiver. "I need something to drink. My throat feels dry, and . . ." She paused. "I'd like to clean up. I can't think straight like this. Look at me." She ran her hand over her hair. "I've never looked so awful and felt so awful." She let out a big gulping sob.

Terrenzio paced to the door and back. She thought he looked agitated. She let the sobbing get louder.

"What is it you want?"

"I want to clean up. I'd like to shower, get dressed in my own clothes. If you really are helping me, please let me at least do that."

He stared at her for a moment longer. She sized him up at the same time. Could she overpower him? Could she kick him, disable him?

"No problem, Molly," he said finally. "You can shower, do your hair, pretty yourself up. Sure, we've got plenty of time." She tried to ignore the sudden change of tone and she hoped she had not put any ideas in his head. But he turned away from her and opened the top desk drawer where he had locked away the revolver. He held it in the air. "No funny stuff, though. Or I'll use this."

He held the gun to the small of her back as he nudged her

up the stairs and out of the basement. On the first floor, she blinked in the bright sunlight streaming through the sheer curtains.

"Come on up the stairs. The bathroom's up there." She felt a sharper nudge, and she felt herself stumbling on the bottom step. He grabbed her arm. Roughly she elbowed her way out of his grasp and hurried up the stairs. The bathroom was on the landing between two bedrooms. It was small, with light coming in only from a skylight some ten or twelve feet above.

"Okay, go ahead." Terrenzio motioned towards the faucet. "But be careful, the water can scald."

She turned to her left to switch on the faucet in the tub. Lewis sat down next to the sink, on the lid of the toilet seat to her right.

She tested the water till it seemed cool enough. Then she turned to him. "You don't have to sit there, do you? There's no way I can get out through that." She pointed to the skylight. "Why don't you wait right outside?"

He smirked. "Why so shy, Molly? I've seen it all before, remember?" Then his lips set in a firm line. "Just get on with it, okay?"

She gritted her teeth and removed the ghastly pink chenille robe, letting it fall on the floor before she removed her bra and panties, turning her back on him as she did so. At least the shower curtain afforded her some privacy, so she stood under the needles of water, letting them cascade over her as she glanced around her. Nothing much in the tub to use against him. She noted that the rod on which the shower curtain hung was one of those adjustable spring rods. It would be unwieldy, though, with the curtain hanging from it. The shower caddy held soap and shampoo. She reached for the shampoo and slowly lathered her hair. Then the soap . . .

She dragged it out for as long as she could. Then she switched off the faucet. "Could I have a towel, please?" She held out her hand.

The shower curtain was pulled back roughly. Terrenzio was on his feet, holding out a rough-looking but clean green towel. She grabbed it and wrapped it around herself, stepping out deliberately onto the chenille robe and not the bath mat. She turned to look in the mirror above the sink, cleaning off the steam with her hand. She was aware that Terrenzio was watching her every move, leaning back against the bathroom door. As surreptitiously as she could, she glanced over the shelves under the mirror. A bottle of Polo aftershave and cologne. A big jar of Vaseline, deodorant in aerosol spray, a toothbrush, and Crest toothpaste.

"Do you have a spare toothbrush?"

"No, you can use mine."

She felt herself gagging and deliberately spread the toothpaste on her finger and put it in her mouth. As she leaned over the sink to rinse, she suddenly felt him leaning into her, pushing against her.

She looked up, her heart pounding, and saw his reflection in the mirror. His face was on her shoulder.

"You know who you look like, don't you?" he said hoarsely. "Especially with your hair smoothed down like that, the way you used to have it. You shouldn't have frizzed it up."

She tensed as he pressed into her, moving against her. But her eyes remained on her own reflection. What had he just said about her hair? Smoothed down, frizzed up.

Suddenly the image of the hooded sweat top in the videotape leaped into her head. What was it about the image that hadn't seemed right?

"You must have heard it from other people." Terrenzio's voice suddenly intruded into her head and she realized he was grabbing at her towel, his hands snaking around her and roughly cupping her breasts. "You must know you look like Jessica's twin." She heard his heavy breathing, then one hand snaked behind her again. He was fiddling with his belt, undoing it, and she felt his pants brush against her naked legs as he let them fall to the floor. He pressed into her, trapping her between his bulk and the edge of the sink.

She let out a scream of anger, fury welling up in her. "No! No!" she screamed. No, she was not going to stand for this. She was not going to be assaulted by this pervert again. She had to get out. Get the tape to the cops, to the FBI. They had to get a clearer picture.

She pushed back from the sink with all the strength her

fury had summoned, grabbing for the aerosol can. Twisting out of his grasp, she flicked off the top and hit the spray button, aiming directly for his eyes.

His howl was angrier and shriller than her scream, his hands dabbing furiously at his eyes.

Molly sprang at him, knocking him backwards into the tub as he struggled, his knees swinging over the edge. She yanked at the curtain rod, pulling it out of the wall, bringing it down on his head, driving it into his face as hard as she could.

His hands flailed trying to cover himself even as Molly grabbed for the faucet and turned it on full blast. Then she swept the robe off the floor and ran, banging the door closed behind her to drown out his cries as the steaming water hit him.

She ran blindly down the stairs, throwing the robe around herself as she ran to the front door and yanked on the handle. It wouldn't move. She remembered Terrenzio crouching down to slide the bolt home. She sank down herself, her fingers tugging at the stiff bolt. It slipped out of her wet fingers.

"Take your fingers off that bolt!"

She froze, not even daring to look to the top of the stairs. But she knew he was standing there, dripping onto the lino in the landing. Then she heard the footsteps slowly coming down. She straightened up and backed up against the door, staring in horror as he walked down with his jeans clinging wetly, still unzipped. A red stain on his hand showed where the hot water had hit him. His face was a mask of shock and anger.

Molly pressed up against the door, pressing herself into it, as if she could pass through it by osmosis. He was still coming towards her, crossing the little foyer.

Any moment his hand would clap down on her shoulder and he'd hustle her right back into the basement.

She screamed again, stared at the gun in his hand and then blindly, without another thought she flung herself right at him.

She was not going quietly. She pounded on his face and shoulders, one hand grappling to get the gun out of his grasp. She held it by the barrel, tugging it towards her, the fingers of her other hand digging into his knuckles to force him to let go. She pushed him back against the stairs, sandwiching the gun between them.

When it went off, the noise sounded like a muffled pop, but Molly felt the hard reverberation against her ribs. She felt something wet seeping down her robe. She saw the look of horror in Terrenzio's eyes.

Then she heard a gasping noise. She thought it was coming from the back of his throat. His head jerked sideways, and she felt as if he was making one last attempt to push her off him.

Well, she wasn't budging. Not yet. Not till he closed his eyes for good. Not till she was really sure that it was over. She was just going to keep him pinned down as his strength ebbed out of him.

He didn't frighten her anymore. Not now. In fact, she felt so relaxed she would have closed her own eyes if his hadn't still been darting around so wildly. That was so weird, his eyes darting around like that when the rest of him was so still.

Her head sank onto his hard, flat chest. But that was okay; he wasn't going anywhere. It was over. And she felt drained, so tired, she didn't know if she had the strength to reach for the phone and call the cops. Not to worry . . . she would call the cops in a minute.

38

Tommy was quiet in the passenger seat beside her as she drove along Montgomery Avenue towards Belinda's house, and glancing at his glum face, Kate's chest tightened.

She wondered if he always looked so unhappy on his way to Belinda's house. Usually, Belinda came to pick him up, and Tommy had always seemed cheerful enough as he left the house. But today Belinda had called and asked Kate to drop Tommy off. She was getting things ready for a party—a barbecue—and was running late.

"I was hoping she'd forget about me," Tommy muttered as they pulled up in front of Belinda's house. "I don't want to go to the stupid barbecue. I wanted to stay with you and Mike."

Kate patted his hand. "At least you got your ride on the bike. That was fun, wasn't it?" she said. "It was nice of Mike to stop by so early for you."

More than nice, thought Kate. She had been surprised to see him speed up their driveway before breakfast, considering how late it had been when he'd dropped her off after they'd spent the rest of the previous day and evening quizzing Molly Heskell's Channel Seven colleagues and her sister, Vickie.

It was Mike who'd reminded her that Tommy was still waiting for *his* ride. "I'll come by, tomorrow, if you like," he'd suggested casually.

"It would have to be early," she'd warned him. "He's usually out of the house by ten."

Now, Kate nudged her son playfully in the ribs. "Come on, you'll have fun," she said as he remained sitting stubbornly in his seat. "It's such a beautiful day, I'm sure you'll be able to swim in the pool, too."

"Yeah, but I'll have to babysit the brat."

"Tommy!"

"Well, she is a brat."

"She's your half-sister, honey," Kate pointed out, faking an enthusiasm for Tommy's second family that she didn't really feel.

"Yeah, but when I have to look out for her, she always does things she's not supposed to."

Kate laughed. "Four-year-olds are like that. You can always go to Belinda and tell her if you feel you can't handle it."

"Yeah, if Belinda is there."

Kate took a deep breath. "What do you mean, if Belinda is there? Of course, she'll be there."

Tommy shook his head. "Remember the evening she took me to their house from school? You know, before they went away to the shore."

"Yes?"

"Well, she and Ivo went out across the street to their friends, and I had to watch Celine."

"You didn't tell me that."

Tommy shrugged.

"Wasn't the nanny there?"

"Yeah. But she kind of disappeared into her room."

"Oh, Tommy." Kate put her hand around his shoulder. "Well, Belinda's not going anywhere today. She's got guests coming here. Come on, I'll walk you in."

Belinda's house was on a quiet leafy lane in Bryn Mawr. Kate had seen it from the outside when she'd dropped Tommy off once before. There was a large square front lawn shaded by two giant oaks, but the house had seemed dark and uninviting. Watching Tommy walk through the big dark mahogany doors she had felt as if the house was swallowing him up.

Today, though, with the sun streaming through the golden-red branches and balloons strung over the mailbox and at the door, it looked brighter and more cheerful. The door stood open, and Kate walked into the foyer with Tommy and then followed him into the kitchen, where sliding doors led to a deck and then into the backyard. In the kitchen, a young, dark-haired girl stood at the counter, placing what looked like miniature quiches onto a baking tray. She turned and smiled at Kate.

"Please." She pointed out through the sliding glass doors. "Mrs. Basualdo is outside."

"Great!" Tommy's face suddenly brightened. "Celli's in the pool. I'll go and change."

Kate smiled as he hurried off through a doorway, clutching his overnight bag. She stepped out onto the deck and found herself staring at the little girl in the shallow end of the pool. She was startled to see the child was totally naked except for a pair of bright yellow water wings.

Just then she heard her name being called and saw Belinda walking towards her from the side yard, waving. The flash of blood-red nails and dangling silver bracelets on her wrists diverted Kate's attention for a moment but as Belinda approached, Kate nodded towards the pool and said, "Do you know your daughter's lost her bathing suit?"

Belinda's laugh pealed out. "Celli doesn't have a bathing suit. It's much healthier for her to run naked, don't you think? In Rio everyone goes naked, even on the public beaches."

"Well, I'm not sure—" Kate hesitated, wanting to ask if Celli was going to be running around naked when Belinda's guests arrived. But Belinda didn't let her finish. Instead she linked her arm chummily through Kate's. "Come, let's go inside. Do you have a moment to talk?"

Kate glanced at her watch, fighting her urge to leave quickly. Mike had promised to wait for her back at her house, suggesting they go out for a leisurely brunch. Although she'd hesitated at first, thinking about the mass of notes she had to transfer to her computer files, she had quickly discarded the idea of working. She was looking forward to brunch with Mike. She wondered what Belinda wanted to talk about as she stepped through atrium doors into what appeared to be Ivo's study.

There was a desk by the window and built-in book-shelves lined the room. A couch stood against one wall facing a coffee table laden with glossy magazines spread out in a fanlike effect. Kate noticed that many of them were expensive art magazines. On one shelf stood a sculpture of a nude reclining woman, and a picture that hung over the couch depicted a circle of naked women clustered round a giant oak tree. No doubt all this art was considered healthy, too, Kate thought wryly.

Belinda motioned for Kate to sit on the couch. Nervously, Kate smoothed down her long, flowing floral-print skirt. It was a tad more frothy and feminine than most of the outfits in her wardrobe and she wondered idly if the thought of Mike's visit had subconsciously influenced her choice when she'd dressed that morning. She brushed the thought aside quickly and waited for Belinda to speak.

"I'm not quite sure how to start." Belinda played with a long silver drop earring. "But I suppose the best way is to just blurt it out, so I'm asking that you consider us having some sort of joint custody arrangement for Tommy."

"Joint custody." Kate echoed the words, playing for time as her stomach churned. "Meaning?"

"Well, I thought we could do it so that he spends one week with you, one with me. Alternating, I mean. Or two with you and two with me. I'm open to suggestions."

That's big of you, Kate thought, her stomach churning more furiously. Dear God, this was exactly as Maysie had predicted it would be. Before long, Belinda would have Tommy back for good.

She took a deep breath, reminding herself that this was not about her personal feelings.

"I don't know, Belinda," she said quietly. "It doesn't sound like a good idea to me. Bouncing between two homes isn't very good for a child. I'm sure it would be very disruptive and unsettling for Tommy."

Belinda came and perched on the edge of the coffee table in front of her. "I think you should have a longer think about it. Don't just dismiss it. Tommy could only benefit. And, I really would like to have your agreement. We've managed to sort things out between ourselves nicely so far."

Kate looked at her sharply, wondering if there was an implied threat in her words even though Belinda, evidently, didn't want to voice the words court or custody battle. Kate didn't want to either. But it seemed she was going to have to consider that possibility now. She was going to have to put her foot down somewhere, otherwise Belinda would just run roughshod over her.

"Please try to understand, Kate," Belinda continued. "I know it was wrong of me to leave him five years ago, but I want to make up for it now. I want to get to know my little boy again. You know, weekends are fine but I'd like to meet him off the schoolbus, help him with his homework, and just sit around in the evenings playing Monopoly or Scattergories with him. You know, doing ordinary things families do when they're together all the time . . ."

"I understand that," Kate said, when what she really wanted to say was: Well, you had your chance but you walked out on it five years ago. She knew it was a harsh and uncompromising thought, and she understood that people made mistakes, but walking out on a child without a backwards glance was more than a mistake in Kate's book. It was a crime. And only Belinda would benefit from the arrangement she was suggesting. Not Tommy.

"I understand," Kate repeated. "But I can't agree to something that would ultimately do Tommy more harm than good. A child has to have stability, Belinda. He's got it at the moment. Don't turn him into a yo-yo."

Belinda straightened up abruptly. "You're not being reasonable, Kate," she flung back. "I'm Tommy's natural mother and I want to see more of my son. I told you I didn't want to upset anybody, and I've been very careful about that but you're being very stubborn." She paused for an audible intake of breath.

"Whatever I did in the past, I was young and stupid back then. Now I can offer Tommy a complete family. Not only am I his natural mother but he'd have a father here, and a half-sister. That's more normal than living with a guardian and an elderly grandmother. Please think it over."

Kate got to her feet slowly. She considered telling Belinda about Tommy's family tree project, when only a week before he had printed her name in the box next to Steve's. She had gently pointed out that perhaps he should print Belinda's name in there.

Tommy had grunted, his head bent over his work. Then, he'd looked up at her and asked, "So, how do you spell your last name, Mom? The one you had before you got married."

But she couldn't be that heartless. It was enough that she'd gleaned an idea of what she was up against. Belinda would no doubt argue that she could provide Tommy with a normal family life. *And I just might have a court-appointed social worker come and visit the household,* thought Kate. *Maybe all this nudity works just fine in Rio, but this is the Main Line.*

Belinda mistook her silence for reconsideration. "I know we're going to work this out, for Tommy's sake," she said, leading the way to the front door.

Oh yes, Kate thought as she stepped out of the house. *I'm sure we will. But not till I've spoken to the best, most expensive family attorney I can find.*

She drove home, lost in thought. The exchange with Belinda had shaken and depressed her but she cheered herself with the thought that at least Tommy had been happy and smiling, splashing around in the pool when she'd left the house.

As she turned into her own driveway, she was surprised to see Mike pacing on the porch. He came hurrying down the steps as she pulled up, and opened the passenger-side door as soon as she stopped.

"I was going to give you five more minutes," he said, his face set in a somber expression. "I just got beeped. Let's get going," he said, sliding into the seat beside her.

"Where to?" Kate revved the engine.

"Downtown Philly. Molly Heskell's just turned up."

"She turned herself in?"

"Not exactly." Mike grimaced. "She's dead."

39

She drove at a steady sixty-five mph all the way into the city. Mike had an address in the Italian Market area but little more information.

"Harry took the call," he told her as they sped towards the address he'd noted. He stared at the scrap of paper. "Some guy by the name of Terrenzio called it in."

"He found her body?"

"Harry said it was difficult to understand what the guy was saying but it seems this Terrenzio worked a late shift at Seven. Heskell was at his house."

She slowed as they drove down Washington Avenue. "Look for Second, then it's the third on the right," Mike directed her. He paused. "It sounds about right. She was at Seven late on Thursday night. Probably hooked up with him then."

"That must be him," Kate said, pointing to a big man sitting huddled in a big leather coat on the doorstep of the end house on the street. She pulled up behind a gray car that she recognized as Harry's Chevy. "Looks like Harry's inside."

As she and Mike walked up the path towards Terrenzio, she noticed a splatter of vomit by the side of the step. Terrenzio, himself, was shaking so hard he looked as if he was in the throes of an epileptic seizure. His face was white. A bruise on his head stood out in sharp relief to his pallor. There were blood smudges on his chin and left cheek. As Kate and Mike stopped beside him, he stood up and opened his coat to reveal blood-sodden clothing underneath. "She went for me. She threw herself at me and the gun went off. I couldn't get up. I couldn't get her off me."

Mike put a steadying hand on Terrenzio's arm. "Okay, calm down. We're going to take a look inside."

Terrenzio shrank back. "Don't make me go in there. I can't go in there. She's lying right inside the door." He clutched his stomach. "I tried to stop her." He sank down on the front stoop again, gulping for air.

Mike walked up the three steps and pushed open the front door. Kate followed him into the tiny foyer space where Molly Heskell's body lay in a pool of dark red blood that had spread over the light wood floorboards and soaked into the pink robe she was wearing.

Harry nodded, acknowledging her and Mike as they walked in. "She's dead, all right," he said to Mike. "I've called for Art Johnson. It'll be easier to keep a lid on this if he deals with it. I'll just have to square it away with the city later." Sighing audibly he stepped towards the open door and beckoned to Terrenzio.

"We have to talk. Do you want to stay here? Or come back inside?"

Terrenzio looked apprehensive but got to his feet, still trembling as if he had no control over any muscle in his body. He had to step over Molly Heskell's outstretched leg to get into the house but Kate saw the conscious effort he made not to look down. She and Harry and Mike followed him through the small living room to the kitchen at the back of the house, where he pulled out a chair at the square formica-topped table and sank down.

A strange sound came from his throat, as if he was trying to stifle huge sobs, and he hurriedly wiped his mouth with the back of his hand. Kate noticed an ugly red burn mark on his hand.

"Take your time, Mr. Terrenzio." Harry pulled up another chair. "Start at the beginning. You said Ms. Heskell was in the newsroom when you arrived at Channel Seven on Thursday night?"

Terrenzio nodded. "I work the late shift mostly. I transcribe tapes and stuff like that." He gulped. "She was waiting for me when I came in. She said she was in trouble. She said she didn't know what to do."

"You were good friends?"

"We weren't the best of friends, but I knew her well enough. I was surprised to see her because she'd quit the day before. So, I asked her what was wrong. She looked very pale, and she seemed very upset and anxious."

Kate caught the exchange of glances between Mike and Harry.

"So, what happened then?" Harry prodded gently.

Terrenzio's hands shook, and his glance darted over Harry's shoulder. "This is going to get me into trouble, isn't it? I shouldn't have let her stay here. But she asked me if I could help her." He looked down at his hands. "She told me that the police wanted to interview her. She said she didn't want to go back to her own house. She just needed a couple of days to think. What could I do?"

Lewis looked from Harry to Mike with a pleading look.

"Why do you think she asked you for help?" Mike cut in, evidently puzzled that Molly Heskell had turned to someone who seemed such a nobody.

Terrenzio looked down at his hands as his face flushed a bright red. "I don't know. I was there, and she . . . she knew I'd been in trouble myself. It was a while back," he added quickly.

"What kind of trouble?" Mike asked.

Terrenzio coughed nervously. "I served thirty months for assault. I—it was a fight with my girlfriend. I'd been drinking . . ."

"Go on, what happened next?" Harry prompted him to continue with the story.

Terrenzio drew his thumbnail across the table. "I didn't see what was wrong with letting her come here. I mean, I didn't want to get into trouble myself. But it wasn't like you guys said you wanted to arrest her. It wasn't till I saw the papers on Saturday." He shook his head. "I mean this morning. It was this morning, wasn't it? Well, when I saw the papers, I realized then it would be serious. So I tried to persuade her to turn herself in. I even said I'd go with her."

He paused and buried his head in his hands. "I told her it

would be okay." He glanced up, rubbing his eyes. "I showed her the papers. I said she'd just be making things worse for herself."

"Did Molly Heskell admit or confess that she killed Emma Kane?"

Terrenzio put his face into his hands.

"Come on," Mike urged him. "You can't protect her anymore. Where did she get the gun? Was it your gun?"

"No." He shook his head.

"So, come on, if it's not your gun, she must have brought it with her."

He nodded. "She had it in that—" He broke off and drew his hand across his stomach. "She was wearing a purse on a belt. I didn't know she had a gun in there."

Mike stepped from the doorway where he'd been standing, sat down, and leaned across the table. "Mr. Terrenzio, this isn't a time for misguided loyalty. Molly Heskell is dead. You can't hurt her or help her by keeping quiet."

And we've got a murder investigation to wrap, he looked as if he wanted to add, thought Kate.

Terrenzio took a deep breath then exhaled slowly. "She said she didn't know what had happened. She said she couldn't remember going to Emma Kane's house." He turned his pale face to Harry. "She said she'd been taking some kind of pills."

"But she had a gun with her?" Harry reminded him.

"I didn't know that then."

"So, what happened when you showed her the newspapers?"

Terrenzio shuddered. "She started crying and I tried to calm her down. I told her the best thing would be if we went to the police. I said everyone would understand that she was sick."

"And?" Mike prodded impatiently.

"She finally calmed down a bit. She said she didn't want to get me into trouble. She said she'd think about it but she wanted to take a shower and wash her hair. So, I said fine."

Kate saw Mike staring at the burn mark on Terrenzio's hand. "Go on, Mr. Terrenzio."

"Well, she was in there a very long time with the water

running, so I knocked on the door and she told me to go away. Then I heard her scream 'No! No!' just like that and I heard a banging noise, so I opened the door and she'd pulled the shower curtain rod off the wall."

Terrenzio paused. "I have to get a glass of water."

"I'll get it," Kate offered and went to the sink just as Art Johnson appeared at the front door. He let himself in and acknowledged Harry with a little wave.

"What was she doing?" Harry drew Terrenzio's attention back to the conversation.

Terrenzio cleared his throat. "She looked so angry, so wild, and she came at me, just yelling 'No! No!' I wasn't prepared for her and when she shoved me, I went right in the tub and she went tearing down the stairs."

Kate handed him the glass of water. Terrenzio took a sip and then brought his hand to his mouth as if trying to stop himself from gagging.

"Is that how you burned your hand?" Mike broke the silence around the table.

Terrenzio glanced down at the burn mark as if seeing it for the first time. His eyes widened. "I guess. The water was still running. I must have knocked the lever when she shoved me." He looked as if he was going to cry. "She was at the front door screaming that she was going to shoot herself and kill me. She said everyone was against her, she had no friends left. That's when I saw the gun in her hand."

"What did you do?"

"I started to walk downstairs—"

"While she was pointing the gun at you?" Mike interjected in surprise.

Terrenzio shook his head. "She wasn't pointing it at me. She was waving it around and crying. I wasn't sure she even noticed me, she was so upset. But just as I got to the bottom she suddenly came rushing at me, kicking at me." A little gurgling sound came out of Terrenzio's mouth. "I tried to grab the gun, but she had her fingers locked around it, and then it went off."

Terrenzio's fist went to his mouth. "She was on top of me and I heard this gurgling sound and then all this stuff ran out of her mouth, and there was blood all over me."

Mike stared at Harry, then at Kate as Terrenzio laid his head down on the table and started sobbing uncontrollably.

Harry put his hand on the man's shoulder. "Okay, take it easy." He got to his feet and went to join Art Johnson in the living room. Kate saw him crouch down and pick up the gun, lying beside Molly's body, hooking his little finger gingerly through the trigger guard.

Kate followed Mike into the living room and stared absently as Art Johnson got to work. She saw Harry sizing up the position of the body at the foot of the stairs, glancing upwards to the second floor landing. Then he took the stairs two at a time, disappearing for a few minutes. When he returned into view he had a purse dangling from his index finger.

Kate walked out of the front door to sit on the stoop in the fresh air.

It took a while for Art Johnson to examine and remove Molly Heskell's body. He did not have to inform Harry that Molly Heskell had died as a result of a gunshot wound. "Point-blank range." He nodded. Kate heard him say something about bruising on the fingers. "I'll let you have the rest later."

Johnson motioned to his assistant to zip up the body bag. And then they were gone. Kate wandered back into the house where Mike was, again, sitting across the table from Lewis Terrenzio. Harry joined the group a moment later.

"Mr. Terrenzio, I'd like to keep this incident under wraps for a little while," Harry said. "There are things we'd like to check out before we release any statements. I'd appreciate it if you didn't say anything to anyone."

Terrenzio sat bolt upright in his chair, a shocked look on his face. "Detective, believe me, I won't say a word. I'd rather my name was kept out of this." He looked at Harry, beseechingly. "It would be a nightmare to have cameras and reporters descending here." He looked embarrassed. "I know I did the wrong thing. I should have . . . Am I going to be in trouble over this?"

Harry stared at him, looking pensive. "We need to check a few other things out," he said without answering. "And we may need to come back here."

Terrenzio raised himself to his feet. It looked like a major effort. "I'll be here. I'm not going anywhere." He shook his head, glancing towards his front door. "Will it be okay if I . . . if I clean up in here?"

Harry looked nonplussed for a moment, then nodded. "Sure. You go ahead."

Kate waited till they were all on the sidewalk before she said: "Did you see the look on his face when you hesitated? When he thought he was going to have to leave that blood-stain on the floor?"

Mike laughed softly, nodding back at the house. "I bet he's already got the scrubbing brush and Clorox out."

"He wouldn't use Clorox on a wood floor," Kate pointed out, bantering. It was a reaction to the tension of the last couple of hours.

Mike shrugged. "Whatever. But he'll be scrubbing at that stain all night. Did you see how neat everything was in the kitchen and that little plaque above the sink: A place for everything and everything in its place? I think there's something a little strange about Mr. Terrenzio—" He broke off and stared over Kate's shoulder.

She turned around as a short, stocky, old woman approached them. She held her hands to her face. "What happened? Is Louie all right?"

She looked genuinely concerned and Kate smiled at her. "Mr. Terrenzio's fine."

"Good. Good." The woman nodded. "I was afraid when I saw all the cars here. He's such a good man." She gave them a half smile. "Always brings me my newspaper in the mornings. Such a good neighbor."

As she walked back up the street, Mike looked pensive. "I wonder," he said softly. He turned to Harry. "I'm not sure about Terrenzio at all. I just got this feeling when he was talking about Heskell in the bathroom and how she freaked out. I'm thinking to myself, maybe he tried to sneak in a quick grope before she turned herself in. There's just something a little off about the story."

Harry grunted. "Maybe. But we'll see what ballistics turns up on the gun. If it's registered to Sam Packer *and* it turns out to be the murder weapon, I'm not sure there'll be much point quizzing him on what happened in the bathroom." He sighed. "I'd better go talk to Packer."

Kate knew he wasn't inviting her along. She reached into her pocket for her car keys, noticing a small dark stain on the hem of her skirt as she did so. It looked suspiciously like blood, and the image of Molly Heskell lying in a pool of it on Terrenzio's floor popped into her head. It was hard to reconcile the stiff, lifeless body with the attractive, energetic reporter she'd seen on the TV screen. It was not like looking at Emma Kane. Molly Heskell had been Kate's age. She didn't envy Harry the task of breaking the news to Sam Packer.

She glanced at Mike. "Are you going with Harry?"

He didn't answer but continued staring pensively at Terrenzio's front door. "It could be Terrenzio hasn't given us the whole story," he said finally. "Maybe he was involved in the whole thing with Heskell before Thursday night."

"You think maybe he was there on the night?" Kate asked.

"Could be." Mike shrugged. "Or maybe she asked him for some helpful hints prior to doing the deed. He has a record. She apparently knew that. And maybe it was her idea to turn herself in, and Terrenzio's the one who didn't like the sound of that."

"Good point," Harry agreed. "It'd be a more plausible explanation for Heskell's freaking out with the gun."

"You don't think he killed her to stop her turning herself in, do you?" Kate asked, surprised, as she tried to reconcile the idea with the pathetic image of Terrenzio vomiting over his front doorstep.

"I'm not going to rule it out." Harry shook his head. "But I can't say I buy the idea that he did it intentionally. I don't get the impression that he's that hardbitten or he'd have disposed of her body instead of calling us. But there may be something there."

Mike nodded. "I'll run him through the computer. See what turns up on our Mr. Terrenzio before we write him off."

40

Saturday evening, Langhorne, Pennsylvania

Where the hell was Gabriella? What on earth was keeping her? Gloria Rossiter glanced at her watch, and then out of her living room window. The gray Cougar was parked at the curb. That awful man was back.

She felt a stab of anxiety. When Gabriella had called a couple of hours ago, Gloria had told her that the reporter and that awful photographer had gone.

"But I think they'll be back," she'd said, sensing that her daughter might jump at the excuse of not having to drive home. "They did that the other night, too. Disappeared for a while, then they were back the next morning. You have to talk to them, Gabriella."

"Okay, Mother, I'll be leaving here as soon as I'm done with the five o'clock newsbrief." Gabriella had sounded weary, as if she hadn't slept for a week. Gloria knew that her daughter worked hard, and sometimes she felt selfish pleading with Gabriella to come and visit. But this time Gloria really needed her. After all, it was Gabriella who'd brought this on her.

Gloria glanced at her watch again, her annoyance bubbling up inside her. It was almost eight. Gabriella could have been here by now, if she'd really stepped on it. She wondered if she could pour herself a little Scotch. She'd had a teeny drink around six but had put away the bottle, knowing Gabriella would be angry if she thought Gloria had been drinking all evening. Now, she wondered if another small one could really hurt—and it was so selfish of Gabby to keep her waiting.

She noticed it had started to rain, and she turned away from the window and wandered into the kitchen. She opened the cabinet and looked at her bottle of Cutty Sark. Then she brought the bottle out and stood it on the counter. She hesitated just a moment before unscrewing the top and pouring a finger into a heavy glass. She sniffed the liquid and brought it to her lips just as the doorbell rang, startling her, and making her bang the glass down guiltily on the counter.

The reporter was standing at the door, his collar up against the rain. "Mrs. Rossiter, I'm really sorry to barge in on you like this."

Gloria moved to close the door but Lester Franks wedged his foot inside it. "Please don't do that, Mrs. Rossiter. Please just give me one chance, just so that I can tell my boss I actually spoke to you. If I do that and you tell me definitely you won't speak to me, I'll leave and I won't bother you again." A big drop of rain fell from the porch onto his head. "Mrs. Rossiter, I'm pleading with you. My job's on the line here."

Gloria stared at his face. Then nodded. Gabriella would be home any minute, anyway. "Okay. But just for a minute. Gabriella's going to be home soon."

They stood awkwardly in the hallway, then Gloria beckoned for the reporter to walk through into the kitchen. What the hell, she thought. Gabriella should have been here. How does she expect me to cope with this?

She saw Lester Franks eyeing the glass of Scotch and she felt she had no alternative but to offer him one, too. "I was just having a predinner cocktail." She smiled awkwardly at the reporter.

"Bless you, Mrs. Rossiter. After sitting out there in the cold, this will do me the world of good. My favorite brand, too."

She poured him a decent measure and then topped up her own glass and sat down uneasily on the edge of her kitchen chair.

Lester Franks raised his glass. "I really appreciate this. You know I wouldn't do this if it were up to me. I told my editor that you don't want to know about any interviews, but he said to stay here at least until I get the chance to put the offer to you."

"So go ahead, make the offer, Mr. Franks, but then you'll have to finish up and go."

He took a sip of the Scotch and beamed. Gloria sipped her Scotch and felt the heat hit her stomach. That was so much better already. Now she felt she could handle Lester Franks.

He took a long swallow of his drink and she could tell he felt instantly warmed by it, too. He smiled at her and said: "I don't even know if your daughter passed on the message, but I was authorized to offer you ten thousand dollars for an exclusive interview about your affair with Ben Grant."

Gloria grinned. "Ten thousand dollars, Mr. Franks? That's a lot of money."

He sipped and shook his head. "Not for an exclusive."

Gloria was beginning to feel a little more confident. He didn't seem so bad. "But you'd be wasting your money, Mr. Franks."

He grinned at her. "Don't you think the story of your summer affair with the young unknown Ben Grant is worth that much?"

Gloria responded to a sudden temptation of being mischievous. "I didn't say it was an affair." She saw Lester Franks slide forward in his chair. She cleared her throat. "Gabriella didn't say it was an affair, either."

Lester Franks sat back again. "Okay, not an affair."

Gloria tapped the tabletop with her short fingernails. "Definitely not an affair." She surveyed the reporter's face over her glass. "Please don't ask me any more, Mr. Franks."

"I'm sorry. It's just that, well, our editors are tough on us. They get to sit behind their desks and we're the ones that have to stand out in the rain. How am I going to convince them that you turned down ten thousand dollars?"

Gloria shook her head. "I don't need the money. Gabriella is a good daughter and she looks after me. I have everything I want."

"Everything?"

"Well, sometimes I think it would be nice if I saw a little more of her. I'd rather see her than have the money. But I know she's so busy."

Lester smiled at her. "You sound exactly like my own mom, Mrs. Rossiter. She always says to me, 'Lester, I don't need the money. I'd rather see you.' Of course, Mom doesn't even realize how the cost of things has skyrocketed. I have most of her bills sent to me."

"You do?" Gloria took another sip and thought that Lester Franks, up close, looked like a nice young man. "How often do you visit with your mother?"

"About twice a month. I try to, anyway, but sometimes this job has me travelling all over. It's tough. And, if I don't produce . . ." Lester paused and drew a finger across his throat. "The bosses at the *Enquirer* don't mess around."

Gloria stared at him wide-eyed. "But they wouldn't fire you for not getting an interview, would they? Good Lord, you've tried hard enough on this one." Gloria hesitated and poured some more Scotch into her own glass. "If you like, I could call your editor."

Lester Franks laughed and leaned forward across the table. "Thanks for the offer, Mrs. Rossiter. You really are a sweetheart. It might help but I know what he'd say to me. He'd say, 'Franks, how do you think we're going to fill the two pages with that?' "

Gloria leaned back in her chair and her elbow slipped off the edge of the table so that Scotch slopped out onto the front of her blouse. "I could tell him that it's really not the story he thinks it is. I could tell him it would only fill a half page, anyway." She giggled.

Lester nodded. "I know, you already said it wasn't an affair. That's okay." He reached for the bottle and topped up Gloria's glass.

"Thank you." She picked up the glass. He was a polite young man, too. "I mean, I—"

Lester leaned forward again and touched her arm. "Please don't say any more, Mrs. Rossiter. I can see it's painful for you. You must have been heartbroken when you discovered you were pregnant and didn't know where to reach him."

Gloria stared into her glass. "It wasn't like that, Lester."

She glanced at her watch but couldn't focus on the little hands. So, she looked up at the clock on the kitchen wall. "It was—"

"I can guess," he cut in. "You said it wasn't an affair, so I'm thinking probably a one-night stand? Is that why you're embarrassed to talk about it? No, it's okay. I understand."

Gloria let her eyes meet his. A one-night stand! Dear God, she couldn't let him walk away thinking it was a one-night stand. How the hell would that make her look? Boy, was she angry with Gabriella for putting her in this horrible position.

"Mrs. Rossiter, please don't concern yourself any more about this. I can see that after all these years you still feel embarrassed. Isn't that right?"

Gloria stared at him again, her eyes widening. A little warning signal penetrated the fog in her head. What was it Gabriella had said about them twisting her words? No, she couldn't let him do that.

She tried to focus on Lester Franks' glass. "No, it wasn't like that either, Lester . . ." She broke off.

"It wasn't a one-night stand?" Lester's eyes widened. "Oh, Mrs. Rossiter, I am so sorry. I just didn't understand where this was leading. I've been so obtuse. You mean he forced— Ben Grant raped you?"

"No!" Gloria cried out, alarmed. "No! You don't understand."

"Then help me, please, Gloria. Now I don't know what to think."

She took another look at the kitchen clock. Maybe she should just tell Lester Franks the truth. This was just getting worse. By the time he left, God knows what he'd be thinking about her.

He leaned across the table and patted her hand. "You know what, Gloria. Enough of this. I can see I'm just upsetting you more. Finish up that drink and we'll stop this nonsense. I've put you through enough tonight and you've been very good. I owe you dinner. Come on, let's forget about the story and just go and get a nice plate of pasta and maybe a drop of wine."

Well, she did feel hungry. She had been hoping that her

daughter might suggest dinner out, but Gabriella wasn't here and Lester Franks was, and he'd promised not to talk about Ben Grant anymore.

She stumbled getting to her feet. "I know a good Italian restaurant not too far from here." She smiled awkwardly at him. "They have a proper wine list, too."

By the time she got her coat, Lester was holding the front door open for her.

41

The house was quiet when Gabriella let herself in, and she stood for a moment in the narrow hallway breathing in the familiar combination of odors: stale smoke not quite masked by the Plug-Ins air fresheners.

"Mother," she called out softly. There was a shaft of light coming from the kitchen but no greeting by way of response. Gabriella thought her mother had sounded a little tipsy when she'd called earlier. Evidently Gloria had ignored the plea to lay off the booze for the rest of the day. Gabriella sighed to herself and walked down the hallway towards the light. No doubt she'd find her mother head down on the kitchen table.

She had no doubt, either, that Gloria would point the finger of blame at her daughter: "You said you'd be here by seven-thirty."

Yes, she had, but she had not known at the time that she'd be delayed leaving the newsroom because of Molly Heskell. The newswire stories that had been coming out of Philadelphia all day had indicated that Molly was still missing and she had delivered the five o'clock newsbrief with that information. But not wanting to leave without knowing the latest, she'd suggested to the producer that he call the cops in Lower Merion.

It had taken a while for him to come up with nothing. "She's still missing, so far as I can gather," he told her. "They say they have nothing to add to the statement they made yesterday."

She'd thought about Molly on her drive down the turnpike, feeling sorry for her former colleague but surmising that Molly had somehow contributed to her own woes. Molly had wanted it all: the job in New York, Jack Kane, and a baby. She had wanted everything too quickly. That had been her mistake and Gabriella could understand that. She'd once made the same mistake. But she had learned from hers. And Jack obviously had learned from his. He had learned, anyway, to be a little more discreet about his entanglements.

"Mother?" Gabriella stopped in the kitchen doorway. The room was empty, but a half-full bottle of Cutty Sark stood on the table. Had her mother actually made it to bed before passing out? Before polishing off her daily fifth? That would be novel, Gabriella thought, wondering about the two empty glasses on the table as she walked through to peek into the dining room. Then she retraced her steps down the hallway to the front parlor, as her mother called the living room. But there was no sign of Gloria in there either.

Gabriella opened the door leading downstairs. Her mother rarely used that part of the house. Even though Gabriella had converted the basement into a fabulous media room, Gloria made only occasional forays downstairs to the huge deep freezer she'd insisted Gabriella install in the small kitchenette. "I've got to have somewhere to store supplies," Gloria had whined. "In case we have those bad snowstorms again." Gabriella had found this mildly amusing since most of her mother's meals came in liquid form.

But she hurried down now with a sense of foreboding, picturing her mother lying passed out by the deep freezer. The room was empty, though.

Gabriella walked to the wet bar in the corner of the media room, and retrieving a small key from the top of a picture frame, opened the cabinet where she kept her own bottles of good, expensive liquor. She poured herself a small Johnny Walker Black and sipped it, idly scanning the walls and shelves that displayed framed copies of newspaper and magazine articles about her. Two shelves above the large screen TV held the dubs of all the major TV series and reports she'd produced at Channel Seven.

She took another sip of her drink, focusing on the spine of the first cassette. Titled "Philadelphia After Dark," it had been a silly, glitzy three-parter about the city's nightlife, produced with nothing more in mind than providing titillation during the November sweeps. It was almost a year since she'd worked on that series—her first at Seven—and it would have been best forgotten, she thought, except that it had marked a turning point in her life: The series had brought her to Jack's attention.

Until then, he'd had little to say to her. But on the Friday night before sweeps week, he'd walked into the editing room to ask her if the series would be finished on time.

"Are you worried your new reporter won't come through?" she'd asked, immediately adding, "I plan on working through the weekend."

He'd smiled and turned to leave but had then hesitated at the door, standing there for a moment longer to watch her working with Scott, the editor. She had felt his eyes on her, but when she turned to face him, he was staring hard at the monitor.

"If you're around the newsroom this weekend, I'll have part one finished tomorrow morning," she said.

Jack Kane had smiled. "I'd like to see it. Unfortunately, I'm housebound tomorrow."

"Sounds like something you're not looking forward to?"

Jack Kane shrugged. "My wife's redecorating. Again. So I have to be on hand to supervise the work."

Gabriella raised an eyebrow.

Then Jack had grinned at her. "Emma loves to redecorate but the smell of paint gives her a headache, so when the decorators move in, she moves out." He paused. "I'll have plenty of time on my hands, though. Why don't you send the dubs over? I'd like to see them. The news desk has my address."

Gabriella had turned back to stare at the editing screen, trying to cover the rush of blood to her face. But she couldn't focus on her story. Her thoughts were on Jack Kane. The spark between them had been instant and electrifying. She knew she could not be mistaken about it. She'd had plenty of come-ons in her time, and Jack standing there with that look in his eye, telling her he wanted to see her series, telling her that his wife was out of town and all but writing down his address for her . . . well, how much more direct could he be?

He'd thrown the ball in her court and she had run with it, although she remembered worrying about it all the way out to his house that weekend.

Naturally, it had been a needless worry, Gabriella recalled, putting her glass down on the wet bar as she suddenly became aware of noises upstairs. She hurried up and stood in the hallway, staring in bemusement as her mother stumbled in through the door followed by a man that Gabriella instantly recognized as the reporter who'd accosted her outside the lingerie boutique.

Gloria and Lester both stopped in their tracks when they realized that Gabriella was watching them.

"Hi, sweetie." Gloria giggled suddenly. "You were late, so Lester invited me out to dinner. We had a very nice time."

The hairs on the back of Gabriella's neck prickled as Lester, sheepishly holding her mother by the arm, led her into the family room and helped her onto the brown corduroy recliner.

He straightened up as Gloria collapsed in the chair and then stepped forward towards Gabriella. He held out his hand. "We meet again."

Gabriella ignored the extended hand.

But Lester didn't seem fazed by it. "Your mother and I just had a very nice dinner together." He grinned. "And a really good little chat."

Something about the way he said "good little chat" made Gabriella hesitate about telling him to get out.

"A good little chat, Lester? About what?" Her voice sounded cool but she wondered if the reporter could detect her sudden fear.

Lester was still grinning at her. "About your father."

"About my father?" Gabriella wished she could stop echoing the reporter's words.

"Yes. About your father."

Gabriella's stomach churned abruptly. The emphasis he put on the last two words together with the challenging look in his eyes told her all she needed to know. She did not need him to elaborate further. Her mother had obviously spilled the whole story.

"I told you I was going to get the story, Gabriella." Lester's voice was soft but she heard the underlying menace in it. Then he smirked. "I just never imagined it would be so-o-o good. Jeez, what a great week I've had."

"Really." Gabriella felt her throat tighten.

"Yeah, really." He eyed her with a triumphant glint. "First the scoop on your boss, now you."

"My boss?" There she was echoing him again.

"Yeah." He nodded. Then he shrugged. "Well, maybe it's not that big a deal, not as big as this story, but we've got a picture of him all cozy with that writer, Kate McCusker, at Molly Heskell's house the other day. You know Kate?"

Gabriella blinked. She wanted to ask what he meant by "all cozy." But it really didn't matter for the moment. If she didn't deal with the disaster staring her in the face, nothing much would matter. Behind her she heard Gloria start to snore lightly.

She stared at Lester through narrowed eyes. "We both know my mother was drunk when she spoke to you. How can you use a story given to you by someone who's drunk and befuddled? She'll deny it when she sobers up, you know."

Lester shook his head, reached into his inside coat pocket, and brought out a little audiotape. "She doesn't sound too drunk on this."

Gabriella blinked again and exhaled loudly, her thoughts racing. She wondered if she could buy him off. How much did one of these sleazebag reporters make a year, anyway? Or better still, what if she offered him a job in TV? She had enough clout at WorldMedia—and with Jack—to follow through, and surely he'd at least consider an offer like that. One thing she knew: She couldn't let Lester Franks just stroll out of the house with the audiotape in his pocket.

She smiled hesitantly at him. "You're a better reporter than I gave you credit for, Lester," she said. "But maybe you haven't got the whole picture. Why don't we go downstairs, have a little drink, and talk about this."

"Hey, why not?" Franks agreed amiably. "I wouldn't mind getting a few quotes from you. It would wrap up the story nicely."

42

Saturday night, Philadelphia

Lewis splashed cold water on his face and then took the iodine from the cabinet, dabbing some onto a cotton ball before pressing it to the cuts and the bruise on his face. One of the cuts had opened up while he'd been scrubbing, and he didn't want it to become infected.

His hands shook as he dabbed. They looked white and pruney, and they ached like hell. It had been grueling work, swabbing the floor, and even now it wasn't completely clean. There was still one small bloody patch left, just under the bottom step.

What a mess. What a disaster, he thought. He held onto the sides of the sink, noticing the dark, wet patches that circled under his armpits. The shock of seeing Molly Heskell expire on his floor had been greater than anything he could have imagined. He wished there'd been some other way to get out of the mess without calling the cops. But he'd been too panicked to think about moving her body.

He'd stared at her for long enough wondering if he could bear to touch her, to dress her in her own clothes. He could not dump her naked nor, God forbid, wrapped in the pink robe. He didn't know enough about these things but it seemed that these days cops had ways of tracing everything. It had just all seemed beyond him. And what would he achieve, anyway, if he couldn't leave her taped confession beside the body?

He stuck a Band-Aid on his chin and thought about applying some ice to the bruise on his forehead. He wondered if there was something he could take to control the trembling. Every time he thought about those cops sitting in his kitchen, he started shaking again.

Had they believed his story about Molly freaking out in the bathroom? The younger one had stared at him suspiciously. He looked like the type that might go and check his record. But he'd told them about the conviction and there was no reason for them to dig for details, was there?

He shook his head and tried to erase the worrisome thought. There was no way they could ever actually prove he'd lied. He'd been so careful with the story, changing only a couple of salient facts: the reason that Molly had come to him, the fact that she'd brought the gun, and the reason for her freaking out in the bathroom. They could never trip him up on those three lies. Not now that Molly was dead.

They'd be back, for sure, though, to grill him again. Cops were like that. They had to make you tell the same story over and over again. He touched the cut on his chin, gingerly. He'd have to seal off the studio in the basement before they returned—and he had to get rid of his files and tapes.

His stomach churned at the thought. How could he destroy so much good work? No, it was out of the question. He couldn't do that. The cops didn't work that fast, anyway. They'd have to do ballistics on the gun and an autopsy on Molly Heskell, and he only needed another day's grace. On Monday he could place all his files and tapes in a safe deposit box in the bank.

The worst of this whole sorry mess was that his name was bound to come out eventually. And that meant Jack Kane would hear about it. And Kane would never fall for the story of Molly coming to Lewis for help.

Lewis stepped to the toilet bowl and picked up the toilet seat. The thought of Jack Kane suddenly appearing on his doorstep made his stomach heave violently.

43

Sunday, October 6

Jack Kane would not take no for an answer. His first phone call had woken Kate. The second had caught her coming out of the shower. She had hung up as quickly as she could on both calls, knowing what he was after. Fifteen minutes after the second call, she was a little startled to see his Jaguar sweeping down her driveway.

"There was no need to drive over," she said coolly as he came up the porch steps. "I was going to return your calls after breakfast but I really can't help you, Jack."

He either didn't hear or chose to ignore the note of polite annoyance in her voice—and got right to the point. "I know you've been told not to say anything, Kate, and I realize I may be putting you in a difficult situation, but goddammit, someone should be talking to me! I'm not just a bystander here. Do you really think it's fair I should be getting my information from second- and third-hand sources?"

"What information, Jack?"

"Is it true that Molly's dead?"

"Where did you hear that?" she asked, trying to mask the surprise in her voice.

He threw up his hands. "Come on, Kate, I have friends in this town. They're in the news business. Right now every TV station in Philly is working on a hot tip that Molly Heskell was shot last night. The one person I can't reach is Sam Packer." He shook his head in a gesture of frustration. "What the hell is going on?"

Kate sighed and paced along the porch. Obviously Harry and Mike had not been as successful as they'd hoped in keeping Molly's shooting under wraps. Art Johnson would not have talked, but it was impossible to keep news like this from leaking out. The main news organizations made it their business to maintain contacts and sources in key places like the coroner's office.

"Well, Kate," Jack prodded. "You're not falling over yourself to deny it. So, I guess it must be true." He sank down suddenly on the top porch step. "Is the rest of it true, too? The cops found her with the murder weapon?"

"The gun was Sam Packer's .38," Kate said. Then, realizing that it was silly to be evasive when evidently the word on this had also been leaked, she added, "It *was* the murder weapon, Jack. Ballistics confirmed it late last night. The police are going to issue a full statement today, and I'm sure they'll fill you in on everything."

Jack Kane stared at her through narrowed eyes. Tired eyes that seemed blank and lifeless, thought Kate. "Would you like a cup of coffee?" she asked.

He brushed off her offer, getting to his feet. "It's not coffee I want, Kate. I need answers. This just doesn't make sense."

She wondered if it would make any more sense if she told him about the additional twist in the investigation. Harry had been leaving the station the previous evening when Stan Nixon, the realtor who'd found Anna Mae Whitman's body, had walked in to see him. Apparently he had suddenly remembered that the mystery woman client who had looked at the Kane house on the day of Whitman's death had gotten a parking ticket outside the realty offices that morning.

"He said he clear forgot about it until he got a ticket himself this morning." Harry had recounted the story for her and Mike in O'Malley's. "I asked McGrath in Traffic to check on the tickets issued on Dalton that day," he'd added. "Just in case it traces back to Heskell. That would make you happy, wouldn't it, Kate?" He'd turned to Mike. "Kate's had a thing about this woman since day one."

Well, it would tie up all the loose ends, Kate had thought. Even Jack Kane would have to accept Heskell's guilt if it turned out that she had scoped out his house planning cold-blooded murder. But there was really no point in mentioning that now. Jack Kane was unhappy enough with the facts, never mind speculation.

"Please tell me what happened, Kate. How did she die? Was she shot by the cops? Is that why there's all this secrecy?"

His distress was clear, and Kate reflected that this was a very different Jack Kane from the cool executive she'd met on the morning of his wife's murder. This Jack Kane didn't care about displaying his grief, nor was there any doubt about his determination to get answers.

She took a deep breath. "She wasn't shot by anyone, Jack. She was on the run. It seems she . . . she really wasn't well—"

"You're saying she shot herself?" Kane interrupted, punching a fist into the palm of his left hand. "Screw that, Kate. Maybe it's convenient for the cops to pass it off that way but I just can't believe it. I'm sick of hearing she wasn't well. Molly was a very strong lady, Kate." He ran his hand over his hair. "And smart. Not someone who'd dish out a stupid lie about a break-in that she never reported because nothing was stolen, oh, except for the gun, of course. That was so ludicrous I really believed it had to be the truth. And I still—"

"Well." Kate shrugged, interrupting him. "Something like that did happen, in fact. But it happened to someone else. That's probably where Molly heard the story and decided to use it as her own when she had to come up with an—"

"What are you talking about?" Jack Kane broke in harshly.

"I mean one of her colleagues at Seven had a break-in like that. She probably told Molly and—"

"Who was it?"

"Jennifer Reed," Kate said, adding a brief explanation of

how she'd come to know about it. As she spoke she noticed
Jack's face turning pale, and by the time she'd finished it
was closer to a grayish color.

"Was Jennifer actually in the house when this incident
happened?" he asked.

"God, I don't think so." Kate pondered this new thought.
"She didn't say she was."

Jack shook his head. "I don't get it. Someone got into
Jennifer's house, and she didn't report it because it wasn't a
burglary but she moved out within the week. It doesn't add
up, Kate."

That's for sure, thought Kate. She'd thought the same
thing herself at the time. But Jack wasn't waiting for her
answer. He was shaking his head in bemusement, and when
he spoke again his voice was harsh and angry.

"And let's suppose, just for a moment, that Molly was
telling the truth. Then what you've got is two newswomen
from the same TV station who were apparently the victims
of some weird home invasion that they didn't want to
report. And then Emma—who just happens to be married
to a former news director from the same station—is murdered in her own home—" He broke off in midsentence.
"For God's sake, Kate, doesn't that make you think there
might be something else going on here?"

Put that way, Kate couldn't immediately disagree. "But
that's making a big assumption, Jack, and where do you go
with it from here?"

He laughed harshly. "It makes me think that maybe
Molly put it together in exactly the same way, especially
after she realized that something had been taken, and that
it was Sam's gun. Maybe she decided to find it herself, to
track down this intruder. It could be that she found him,
and maybe that's why she's dead."

"Jack! That just can't be."

"Why not, Kate? Maybe she didn't want to go to the
police with this for the same reason she and Jennifer didn't
report the break-ins in the first place. Think about it: There
must have been some good reason. And why not go after
the intruder herself? Molly was an excellent reporter. She
could track down anybody as well as any detective could."

Kate glanced anxiously at Kane, and the tormented look on his face scared her suddenly as he added, "Come with me to Jennifer Reed's, Kate. I've got to know what happened to her and Molly. I've got to know what was going on."

"Stop, Jack." Kate paced away from him, trying to gather her thoughts. Jack had raced ahead, putting together a wild scenario without knowing all the facts.

But to take his scenario to a logical conclusion meant that Lewis Terrenzio had broken into Jennifer's house, then Molly's, stolen Sam Packer's gun, killed Emma and Salerno and then Molly when she'd come looking for him.

And that just didn't make sense, thought Kate. The NCIC printout on Terrenzio had shown that he'd served thirty-two months of a five-year sentence for aggravated assault in Duluth, but that was surely a far cry from the kind of cold-blooded felon that Jack was talking about. If Lewis Terrenzio was responsible for all that, then the last thing he would have done would be to summon the police to his house after killing Molly.

She laid a hand on Jack Kane's arm. "Let it go, Jack. You're not looking at all the facts."

"I haven't been given any facts," he shot back.

Kate chewed her bottom lip, knowing she couldn't let him continue on this road. Finally, she said, "She was on the lam, Jack. She wasn't tracking anyone down. She asked a friend to help her. She was with him. She had Sam's gun with her, the murder weapon, Jack, and she freaked out when she read the police were looking to arrest her. He told us what happened."

There was a long silence between them as he stared at her with incredulity. Then he shook his head. "A friend, Kate? What kind of a friend let her do that? Who was it, Kate? Was it someone from Channel Seven? That's where she went that night."

Kate said nothing.

"Who?" Jack persisted.

"No." She shook her head firmly as visions of Jack Kane slamming up to Terrenzio's door demanding answers danced in her head. "That would be more than my life is worth, Jack. I'm sorry."

"Okay, then just confirm if I'm right." A half smile played on his lips. "Come on, Kate, you know the drill: I'll throw out a bunch of names and when I get to the right one, just walk away . . . hang up."

Yes, she knew that drill. It was one that worked especially well with nervous sources who could always later say, "Who me? I never spoke to Kate McCusker. I hung up on her."

She laughed out loud, and felt herself weakening. But only for a moment. "It really wouldn't help you, Jack. I don't think you'd recognize the name."

He reached into his pocket for his car keys. "Okay, Kate, I don't want to make it difficult for you." He jangled the keys in his hand. "But I still think something here really stinks. Someone went after Jennifer and Molly, and I think whoever it was also killed Emma. There's one solid link between those women—" He broke off, looking uncomfortable. Then he shrugged. "You know about Molly, already . . . well, I had an affair with Jennifer, too."

He let the words hang in the air, then punched a fist into the palm of his hand. "Don't you see, Kate? Everything keeps coming back to me."

"Maybe that's the way it looks. But you can't be serious." She threw him a half smile. "Not if you're implying that this guy was hired by one of your rival conglomerates to frame you for murder—"

"I'm not saying that was the motive here," Jack interrupted. "But it could be someone who just has a personal grudge."

"Don't do this to yourself, Jack," she said softly. "I'm sure you don't even know this guy." *He was in a jail in Duluth when you were at Seven*, she wanted to add but bit back the words. "He's not someone who runs with your crowd."

"Oh?" Jack raised an eyebrow. "That sounds curious."

Kate laughed quickly. "Forget it, Jack. This guy's strictly small time. He's a nobody from Duluth."

There was a short silence between them. Then Jack Kane sighed. "Duluth," he echoed. "I see what you mean."

Kate thought he looked angry and defeated as he walked to his car.

44

K ate thought about Jack Kane as she drove to the police station. It seemed that everything, in the end, came down to someone who was out to get him. Was it a guilty conscience? she wondered. Or some kind of paranoia that automatically afflicted people who reached his level of success?

On the other hand, she had to admit that he had jumped right on the most puzzling aspects of the break-ins. Why had Jennifer not reported an incident that had obviously sent her fleeing from her home? Why had Molly not concocted some simpler explanation for disposing of the gun? She could have just as easily brushed it off by saying she'd dumped it in the Delaware. Either way, Kate knew better than to discount Jack Kane's theory without passing it on to Harry, especially since Jack had pointed to the link between himself and all three women.

She noticed three news satellite vans parked in front of the police station, and a small group of news camera crews standing by the steps to the main doors as she headed from her car into the building.

Neither Harry nor Mike were in the squad room.

"They're in with the chief," Norm Rogers informed her as she sat down at Harry's desk.

"Trouble?" she asked.

"Chief didn't like the press release," he said, handing her a single sheet of paper. She took it and glanced over the few lines:

Police investigating the homicides of Mrs. Emma Kane and Mr. Tony Salerno were called yesterday to the scene of an apparent accidental shooting in which Molly Heskell, a TV journalist, was a fatality. The gun in Ms. Heskell's possession was determined to be the weapon used in the killings of Kane and Salerno.

Kate looked at Rogers. "I can see why. It's not exactly conclusive. It doesn't sound as if the case is closed."

The detective grinned at her. "That's what the chief said. He wants to know what's holding things up." Rogers rolled his eyes. "Montgomery County, that's what's holding things up. Travis apparently isn't totally satisfied."

"Oh?"

"I believe he was unhappy about some new info that came in this morning." Rogers shrugged and Kate laid aside the press release, wondering if the new information had anything to do with Terrenzio. She knew Mike had planned to call the DA's office in Duluth for more information on Lewis Terrenzio. She stared across the room, drumming her fingernails on the desk. Then she pulled a notepad towards her, intending to jot down some notes about her conversation with Jack Kane but was distracted by the ringing of Harry's phone. She reached for it without thinking. "Hello!"

A man's voice on the other end asked for Det. Mike Travis. "This is Simon Selwyn. I'm with the DA's office in Duluth. I'm returning Detective Travis' call."

"Yes, Mr. Selwyn," she said brightly. She looked across the room to the doorway but there was still no sign of Mike or Harry. "I know he was anxious to speak to you." She hesitated. "I thought you might have spoken to him already."

"No." The tone was curt. "I don't even know what this is about."

Kate hesitated again and then immediately decided she could probably handle the call without putting Selwyn on hold to interrupt the chief's meeting. She cleared her throat. "Detective Travis was looking for information about Lewis Terrenzio. All we have at the moment is that he served thirty-two months on an assault charge. I guess that would have been in . . ." She paused, trying to remember the information from the NCIC printout.

"He was sentenced in nineteen ninety-four." Simon Selwyn broke in.

Kate smiled. "That's quite a memory, Mr. Selwyn."

The tone stayed curt and cold. "I don't need the file for this one, detective . . . ?" He waited for her to give him a name.

"Kate McCusker," she said quickly, without correcting his mistake. Something in the clipped cold tone had piqued her interest. Anyway, she figured Mike would be grateful to have the information waiting for him as soon as he returned.

"Well, Detective McCusker, is he in trouble in your neck of the woods?"

"His name came up in an investigation, yes. He told us about the sentence. We're looking for clarification." *Was she impersonating a police officer?* "You said you don't need the file. You remember the case?"

"Why wouldn't I? My girlfriend was the victim of his assault. It was a case that I took a lot of interest in."

"Your girlfriend? He told us she was his girlfriend."

Simon Selwyn laughed abruptly. "His girlfriend! Stefanie? In his dreams, maybe. Or his ranting lunatic fantasy."

"I'm sorry, I'm not following."

"How long do you have, detective?"

Kate glanced across the room again. This was beginning to sound like something Mike was going to be interested in. "Oh I have plenty of time, Mr. Selwyn. Shoot."

Simon Selwyn cleared his throat at the other end of the line. "It's a long story but I'll try to keep it brief, detective."

Kate wished he would stop addressing her as detective.

"Let's see, in ninety-three Terrenzio was on the assignment desk at Channel Five, here in Duluth, and Stefanie had just started there as a reporter." Selwyn paused a moment, as if to gather his thoughts. Then he said, "Anyway, Terrenzio started to show an interest in her, he promised to look out for her on assignments, and started getting friendlier in a rather unwelcome way. It's what you

and I would call harassment, but Stefanie, well, I guess starting out in the business, she was a bit naive and didn't want
to make any waves."

"I'm seeing the picture," Kate assured him, wishing he'd
speed up the story.

"Well, one day he turned up at her apartment and came
on to her, in her words, the way you might if you'd been dating for a while. That's when Stefanie finally wised up, and
that's when it turned ugly."

"He assaulted her?"

"Assault doesn't quite cover it, detective," Selwyn cut in
brusquely. "For eighteen hours he terrorized her and violated her."

"You say violated . . . Do you mean he raped her?" Kate
asked.

Selwyn was quiet at the other end of the line for a
moment before replying. "Not in the technical sense, detective. He apparently had some sort of problem getting it up.
But it might have been better, perhaps, if he had been able
to."

Kate felt her mouth going dry. She tried to imagine how
she'd be reacting if she were a real detective. "What did he
do, Mr. Selwyn?" she asked as firmly as she could.

"He violated her in every other possible way. He used
anything he could lay his hands on . . . for eighteen hours.
Do I need to explain any further?"

"No, I don't think so." Kate took a deep breath. "Was an
assault charge the best you could do?"

There was a short silence at the other end and Kate wondered if she'd said something stupid. Would a real detective
realize that was the only charge that could be brought in a
situation like that?

But then she realized she'd misunderstood the silence.

"We were lucky to get that under the circumstances. He
got to her, you see. Told her he'd deny it all and they'd have
to go to court, and he'd say she agreed to everything. He
said he'd produce pictures of her. He had them, by the way.
Under the pretext of some bullshit line about considering
her for a Fourth of July assignment at the lakes, he'd gotten
her to pose in some skimpy bathing suits. In the end she

wouldn't press charges." Selwyn exhaled loudly. It sounded almost like a groan. "She was topless in one of the pictures."

She wouldn't press charges; they didn't report the break-ins. Kate felt goose bumps erupting along both her arms as her thoughts leaped to Jennifer and Molly. What if Jack had been right? What if Jennifer and Molly were both home at the time of the break-ins?

"Detective McCusker, are you there?" Simon Selwyn's voice interrupted her train of thought.

She gathered herself quickly. "So, how did you manage to make the assault charge stick? Without her pressing charges, I mean."

"He decided to plead guilty."

Kate's eyes narrowed. "I don't follow." She thought she'd detected a hint of a smile in the voice at the other end of the line.

There was another brief silence. "Okay," Selwyn finally said. "But this is just between you and me, detective, all right?"

"Okay."

"I hired a private investigator. Not in my professional capacity, you understand, but I figured if he'd done this to Stefanie, he'd probably done it elsewhere, and as luck would have it, I was right."

Kate glanced across the squad room, her heart beating hard against her ribs. Please, Mike, don't reappear just yet. She couldn't bear it if she didn't get to hear the whole story now.

"Go on, Mr. Selwyn; he had done it before?"

Simon Selwyn laughed. "Oh, yes. But the trump card was the woman he did it to."

"Who?" Kate held her breath.

"It happened in your area, as a matter of fact—"

"In Philadelphia?" she asked, suddenly finding it difficult to get the words out. *Terrenzio had worked in Philadelphia before? When?*

"Do you remember Jessica Savitch, detective? You may be too young to remember but at one time she worked for Channel—"

"Yes," Kate interrupted sharply. "Channel Three. I

remember. But, that was years ago." Kate exhaled loudly. "Are you saying he did the same thing to Jessica Savitch?"

"Not quite the same. Terrenzio was just an intern of some sort back then. He hadn't refined his technique." Selwyn laughed brusquely. "But he apparently scared the shit out of Savitch. It got to the point where he was always hanging out wherever she was. Then she started finding used condoms in her office wastebasket."

"Terrenzio's?"

"That's what she suspected." A pause. "She finally caught him sitting in her chair with his pants around his ankles—"

"I see," Kate interrupted him, struggling to keep her tone professional. "But how did you dig all this up? Savitch is long gone, Mr. Selwyn. I believe she died about fifteen years ago."

There was no mistaking the amusement in Selwyn's voice now. "I hired a crack PI, detective. He found a copy of a complaint she made to her producer, who needed something in writing to fire Terrenzio."

Kate realized she was gripping the phone so tightly that her fingers had turned numb. *Okay, who was the producer, Selwyn? Who fired him?* She wanted to yell down the phone. But the DA was in full flow.

"So, when I finally got a copy of it, I told the little putz he could take his choice, but if he didn't plead guilty to assault and serve time I was going to leak Savitch's statement to the local media. The choice was public humiliation and the certainty that he'd never get another job in TV or some time in the slammer." Selwyn laughed and it was a happier sound this time. "So shoot me," he added. "Unethical maybe but I think the end justified the means." His voice hardened. "I wasn't going to let him just walk away."

Kate nodded into the receiver. "I have no problem with that, Mr. Selwyn. Just one more question, though. Do you remember the name of the producer who fired Terrenzio in Philadelphia?"

"Sure." Selwyn chuckled. "He's the one that gave us a copy of the complaint. He said he'd come to Duluth to testify if we needed him. He was a real stand-up guy."

The goose bumps returned in full force. Kate knew now what was coming before Selwyn added, "A man by the name of Jack Kane. He's an even bigger fish now, of course, but you must have—"

Selwyn stopped in midsentence and Kate realized he'd only just caught on.

"Jesus!" The exclamation was followed by another short pause. "I just read about his wife."

"Yes," Kate said quickly, wanting to wrap up the conversation now. "That's why we're looking at Terrenzio. And I do thank you for your help, Mr. Selwyn," she added, hanging up on him abruptly.

She sat for a moment staring down at her hands, clenching and unclenching her fists as Jack's voice echoed in her head. *Duluth. I see what you mean.* The words slammed back at her with a whole different meaning. Of course. Jack couldn't have failed to put it all together. He'd been looking for a name that fit in with his suspicion that someone with a grudge against him had targeted Emma, Molly, and Jennifer, and no two ways about it, Lewis Terrenzio fit that bill big-time. Jack Kane had nailed him twice.

Kate felt her pulse racing. Could there be any doubt about where he'd driven when he left her house?

She glanced at her watch. It was just over an hour since he'd pulled out of her driveway. Plenty of time for him to track down Terrenzio. More than plenty. A one-minute phone call to any former colleague at Channel Seven would confirm that Terrenzio worked there, and produce an address.

What the hell had she gone and done? She glanced across the room. She had to tell Harry about what had happened. Worse, she was going to have to admit that she'd inadvertently tipped Jack Kane to Terrenzio's identity. If Jack Kane took matters into his own hands, the blame would be all hers. She did not want to begin to think about what Jack might do if he got to Terrenzio.

She jumped to her feet and snatched her purse up off the floor, running for the stairs and down to the parking lot. Her tires screeched as she headed onto the main road though she didn't know why she was driving like a lunatic. Jack had had a good head start. The only thing she could hope for was that she got to Terrenzio's in time to stop Jack from doing something really regrettable.

45

Kate spotted Jack Kane's Jaguar as soon as she turned into Gaskill Lane. It was parked a half block from Lewis Terrenzio's front door, and as Kate slowed on approach she saw that Jack was sitting inside the car.

She pulled up in front of him, jumped out, and ran to the passenger side door. One glance told her that she was not too late. Jack didn't look as if he'd been in any fistfight. He saw her staring at him through the window and beckoned her into the car.

"What are you doing here, Kate?"

She got into the car and slammed the door without answering. Instead she said, "You should have said something, Jack. I know what happened in Duluth. I just spoke to the DA there. You knew I meant Terrenzio as soon as I mentioned the city, didn't you?"

He shook his head. "I suspected it, Kate, but I didn't *know* until Pete Norcross confirmed that Terrenzio was working at Seven—and until after I spoke to Jennifer."

"What did she say?"

Jack Kane laughed. A short hollow laugh. "The break-ins happened, okay. Not just to Molly and Jennifer, either. There were two others." He exhaled loudly. "And they weren't burglaries, that's for sure."

"But what?" Kate asked. "Not rape, surely?"

Jack shook his head. "He forced them to pose for him. He videotaped them."

Kate sighed. "Sounds like his MO," she said quietly.

"And that's why they didn't want to report the incidents, right?"

Jack Kane nodded. "I was right, wasn't I, Kate?" He threw her a quick, pointed glance. "Molly didn't go to him for help. You see that now, don't you?"

Kate took a deep breath. "But you've got to let the police handle this, Jack. You shouldn't be here."

Kane kept his eyes on the street. "Well, I am and they're not. They let him squirm away. Now I'm going to have a go at the little fucker."

Kate suddenly felt afraid. The look on Jack Kane's face was grim and intense—and determined. "I've got to call Harry," she said firmly, reaching for the door handle. "I've got to let them know, Jack."

She saw him stiffen in his seat but in the next moment she realized it was not because of her words but because of something he'd seen in his rearview mirror.

"Go ahead," he said, waving her off with his hand. "Call them. Use the car phone. I've got him first, though."

Kate glanced over her shoulder and saw Lewis Terrenzio walking down the street towards his house. Even as she picked up the car phone and dialed the Lower Merion number she saw Jack's eyes following Terrenzio to his door.

She stared at Jack watching Terrenzio put his key in the latch. She heard Norm Rogers' voice telling her that Harry and Mike were still with the chief.

She saw Jack reaching for the door handle. She heard herself yelling at Rogers, telling him to get Harry and Mike down to Lewis Terrenzio's house immediately, and she didn't give a rat's ass what kind of meeting they were in.

She wondered if that conveyed enough urgency but she couldn't stop to check that Rogers had gotten the message. Jack was already out of the car and she had to sprint across the street to catch up with him as he walked down the path to Terrenzio's front door and pushed the doorbell.

A moment later the door opened a fraction. She saw Terrenzio's face drain of color and then just as he was about to slam the door closed, Jack Kane's foot kicked forward, busting it wide open.

Terrenzio opened his mouth to scream but Jack Kane was

already inside the house, his hands half lifting, half dragging the younger man up by his shoulders.

"You and I are going to talk, Terrenzio, and you'd better not give me any bullshit."

Kate could see terror on Lewis Terrenzio's face.

"I told the cops everything," he screamed.

Jack shoved him backwards into a china cabinet standing against the wall. The force of the push made the cabinet rock forward so that plants and knickknacks fell, crashing to the floor.

"No! Please! Don't!"

"You didn't tell them why Molly came here. You didn't tell them about the videotapes. You didn't tell them she came here looking for a filthy little pervert. You didn't tell them you killed her. You didn't tell them you killed my wife." Jack pushed him again. The cabinet rocked perilously. A potted plant slid off the top shelf and smashed on the wood floor. Ignoring the crashing object, Jack went for Terrenzio again, pinning him against the wall.

Kate stood motionless and helpless, transfixed by Jack Kane's strength and anger, even as Terrenzio's eyes darted wildly, searching for her. "Please do something. Make him let go."

"Talk to me, shithead." Jack shook him, butting his head against the wall. "Me. Not her. Tell me why. Why you did it."

"I didn't do it. I didn't kill anyone. I didn't hurt anyone, I swear." Terrenzio's hands came up in an attempt to shield his face. "Just give me a chance."

Jack Kane loosened his grip on Terrenzio's sweater. "Make it quick, Terrenzio. And make it good because I know what happened. You got to Molly and Jennifer and Janey and Diane. Then you went after Emma, didn't you?"

Jack Kane gave Terrenzio another push, sending him sprawling on the floor, where he lay seemingly stunned while Jack started throwing things off the shelves and opening drawers, flinging everything out onto the floor.

"I didn't do it. I didn't kill your wife." Terrenzio turned to Kate. "Please get the cops——" He broke off, cowering as Kane stepped towards him. With one movement, he had Terrenzio standing on his feet again.

For a moment it looked to Kate as if Jack was going to hit him again. She stepped forward. "Jack! For God's sake, don't do that. You'll kill him." But she knew her pleas were useless in the face of Kane's anger. He wasn't listening. He was staring at the cowering shape where Terrenzio had slid to the floor again.

"You lying sack of shit." Jack turned away from Terrenzio and started throwing things off the shelves again. "Where are they? Where do you keep all your filthy tapes? Am I getting warm . . . hot?" He upturned the coffee table with one sweep of the hand. Then stepped towards Terrenzio again.

Terrenzio screamed, holding his hand to his face where a cut from the previous day had opened up again. "Don't hit me. I didn't kill your wife, I swear. I can prove it."

Jack leaned over Terrenzio. "How?" He made another move towards him. "Talk to me, scumbag."

Terrenzio pointed towards the hall closet. "There's a tape, down there."

"Show me." Jack Kane pushed him towards the closet, then flung open the door, shoving Terrenzio into the doorjamb.

"It's through there, behind the coats. There's a door going down into the basement."

Jack twisted Terrenzio's arm behind his back and shoved him forward into the darkness.

Kate's heart pounded against her ribs. She was afraid for Terrenzio and she was afraid for Jack. She was afraid that Harry wouldn't arrive in time. She wanted Jack to leave this to the police, but there was nothing she could do about that now. She followed the two men down the steps, saw Terrenzio swing open a bricked door, and then she saw the room. It looked like a miniature TV studio.

She felt as if she was in some kind of weird Alice in Wonderland dream, but in the next moment Terrenzio's scream filled the gloomy basement. She hurried into the studio to see Jack twisting his arm and shoving him aside. Then he moved towards the filing cabinets, kicking at the drawers. "Where's the key, Terrenzio?"

"It—I—" Terrenzio motioned with his head to a shelf over a big editing machine.

Jack found the key, unlocked the top drawer, and started throwing cassettes onto the floor, looking at the lettering on the spines as he did so. "Janey," he read and threw the box aside. He picked up another and mouthed something as he looked at the title. He picked up a third. "Kane," he mouthed quietly, opening the box and placing the cassette in the tape deck. "Well, let's take a look at this one."

Terrenzio uttered a sound that seemed like half scream and half moan. He'd curled up into a ball, crouching on the floor. He sounded as if he was having an asthmatic attack. Long wheezing gasps were coming out of his mouth. As Kate stared at the screen she heard music, then Terrenzio's voice as a camera panned a parking lot and then zoomed in on a figure that she recognized immediately as Jack.

"This man is president of WorldMedia News today. His name is Jack Kane."

She glanced behind her as the voice continued. "Tonight we're going to take a look . . ."

She saw Terrenzio cowering. He looked as if he wanted to disappear into the floor. She noticed a fresh bruise welling up on the side of his face.

". . . at the career of a man many know as a starmaker." The picture dissolved to Jennifer Reed at the anchor desk. "But who is better known in inside circles as a star fucker."

The picture dissolved again to Jennifer Reed lying on a big four-poster bed, naked from the waist down, her legs splayed open. The picture dissolved again to a similar pose but a different woman. Kate thought it looked like Molly Heskell.

"These are the women that Jack Kane called his angels."

Kate gasped, staring at Jack Kane's face. He seemed both mesmerized and appalled, as if he couldn't believe that his career had been reduced to a couple of moments in a dirty porn video. Then his eyes narrowed to tiny slits, and she heard him curse as he stepped towards Terrenzio and grabbed him again.

"So, that's what it was all about, you little prick." He thrust the younger man up against the monitors and machines. "All of this just to get even with me. Where did you think you were going with this shit?" He shook Terrenzio. "What about my wife? What did you do to her?"

Terrenzio whimpered and stared longingly towards the doorway. Kate wondered what was taking Harry and Mike so long.

"It's in there, the tape." He pointed to the bottom drawer. Jack flung open the drawer.

"It's under those files." Terrenzio whimpered again as Jack glared at him.

Jack snatched the tape out from under a stack of folders and slid the cassette into the playback machine while Kate eased herself back against the wall and stared at the screen, her eyes narrowing as she tried to define the series of grayish dark images. The most distinct image on the screen was the day and date. She recognized the date as the night of Emma Kane's killing. The time said 20:30. Eight-thirty in the evening, she thought, swallowing nervously as a picture of Emma Kane in her kitchen flashed suddenly onto the screen. Kate was astounded to see the clear image of Emma moving around, walking to her refrigerator, and preparing a snack. Then Tony Salerno walked into the room.

Jack Kane blinked and his face seemed drained of all color. "You were there." He pushed Terrenzio onto the chair by the desk.

"Wait!" Terrenzio screamed. "I've got the killer on this tape." He punched the Fast-forward button and let the tape roll for a while. Then he punched Play again. The screen was filled with just dark grayish mass. Suddenly a flash of light streamed into the picture and then Kate heard the thwump. Her heart skipped a beat. It had sounded too dull for the noise of gunshot, but maybe the audio on the camcorder was not sensitive enough.

"There, look there." Terrenzio pointed as a blurry figure ran into the light of the picture. "That's not me. Why would I make a tape of me killing someone? That's Molly Heskell. Look at her."

Jack blinked and stared harder at the screen. Then he punched the Rewind button to replay the shot, staring at it intently.

Terrenzio struggled to get to his feet. "You know you can get that enhanced. The cops have that sort of equipment, the FBI." His teeth started to chatter as Jack turned on him. "You should have handed this over, you—"

Just then a loud bang upstairs made Jack stop in his tracks. Kate recognized Harry's voice, then Mike's calling out in the living room above them and she ran to the stairs. Without being able to get the words out fast enough, she beckoned them to follow her.

"What the hell's going on here?" Harry asked, staring at Jack Kane.

Jack pointed to Terrenzio. "Ask him."

"What happened to him?" Mike stared at Kate.

"I'm sorry, my fault," Jack Kane spoke up. "He tried to get away. I knew you'd want me to stop him. Ask him why Molly Heskell came here. Ask him what really happened here. Ask him what he was doing at my house on the night Emma was murdered." He paused and waved towards the monitor. "There's plenty of evidence here. You'll be able to put this scum away for life."

Harry and Mike both stared at the gray monitor. "What is that?" Harry finally asked.

Kate pointed to Terrenzio and said: "He taped that outside the Kanes' house on the night of the murder."

"But I didn't do it. I didn't kill her," Terrenzio whined from his chair. "Look. Will you take a look at this?" Before either Harry or Mike could say anything, Terrenzio was at the playback machine punching at the buttons. "Look at this."

Kate stared intently at the screen, as the images were replayed. Again she saw the flash of light, heard the thwump sound, and then the shadowy figure running into the light.

"That's Molly Heskell," Terrenzio shrieked, pointing at the screen. "She saw this tape when she was here. She threw up when she saw it."

Mike stepped towards the monitor and punched at the buttons again, rewinding and then replaying the portion of the tape. He stopped it at the thwump sound. "What's that?" He looked at Terrenzio then at Harry. "That doesn't sound like gunshots to me."

"That's not shots, it's the gun," Terrenzio piped up. "She threw the gun into the trees. It landed on my roof rack—" He broke off as if realizing he'd said too much, and looked towards the door where two uniformed police officers had suddenly appeared.

"So you had the gun?" Mike's voice drew Terrenzio's attention back to him. "You told us a different story yesterday. You said Heskell brought it with her when she came here."

"He's a lying scumbag, that's why," Jack Kane interrupted. "Molly told Sam Packer the truth. She did have a break-in, so did three other Channel Seven newswomen, and that pervert was behind them all. It's all here, all the evidence. Molly came looking for him. She tracked him down."

Mike shook his head, as if trying to make sense of what he was hearing. He glanced at Kate, who nodded to indicate that Jack Kane was right. Then he turned impatiently to Harry and spoke to him in a half whisper. Finally, he looked at Terrenzio again. "So now you're saying that Heskell, if that is Heskell, threw the gun at your car after she killed Emma Kane?"

"Onto my truck," Terrenzio corrected him. "You can take a look, it chipped the paint on the roof." He looked satisfied with himself. But the look faded in the next moment when Harry turned to him and said, "So that story about her freaking out and waving the gun at you was all bullshit?"

Terrenzio screamed. "No! She did freak out." He gulped for air. "It was an accident. I had the gun but she went for me. That's the truth. I told you the truth."

"Yeah, well you're going to have to make it a lot clearer for us," Harry cut in, reaching for the cuffs on his belt. "We're taking you in for the murder of Molly Heskell, for witholding evidence, and for obstruction . . ."

As Harry Mirandized him, Kate noticed Jack brushing off his jacket and moving towards the door. He paused in the doorway, waiting for Harry to finish, and then fixed Terrenzio with an angry glare. "And that isn't Molly Heskell, you dumb fuck," he said before turning and striding to the stairs.

Kate followed him out as Terrenzio was still wailing in

protest and caught up with him on the path outside the house.

"What did you mean? How could you tell if it's Molly or not?"

Jack smiled wearily at her. "If you get the chance, take another look at that backlit silhouette and the hooded top. If that was Molly and she'd tucked all her hair into that hood, well, the way she had it all permed and fluffed, it would have looked the size of a beachball, not so flat and sleek."

"Really?" Kate shook her head in disbelief. She wondered what it would take for Jack Kane to ever believe that Molly Heskell might have shot his wife. "You could tell all that from all that grainy, shadowy stuff? I'm impressed."

Jack Kane shrugged. "You shouldn't be. It's what I do for a living." He paused and then added, "TV is all about pictures and details, Kate. Not just the content of the news but how it looks. Hair, clothes, makeup. It's all part of the package. What's going to distract the viewer, what's going to appeal to the viewer."

For a moment he was silent, staring at Kate as if sizing her up through a lens and judging her possible appeal to viewers. She had a feeling he was about to switch tracks and bring up the subject of her TV show as if now that he'd dealt with one more tiresome personal problem he could get back to business again. But before either of them could say anything, a flurry of movement in Terrenzio's doorway distracted him, and instead he mouthed a quick goodnight to her before walking across the street to his car.

She was still watching his taillights as Mike walked up behind her. "What was all that about?" he asked.

Kate turned to face him. "He was talking about Heskell's hair and the silhouette on that tape"—the words tumbling out quickly—"explaining why it couldn't be her."

Mike laughed. "For once I'm with Mr. Kane." There was a short silence between them before he added, "It can't be Heskell, Kate. I think that's pretty obvious."

"It is?"

"I think so. Never mind all the bullshit about hair and silhouettes, the thing you've got to ask yourself is why would she throw the murder weapon away in the Kanes' backyard? Why dispose of it somewhere she knew it would be found and traced back to her husband and herself?"

"Maybe she didn't realize what she was doing. Maybe she had some sort of blackout that night. Like Packer said, she was on medication, she'd had hallucinations, why not the opposite? It's what she told Terrenzio, if you can believe anything he says." Kate paused. "But we don't need to speculate on all this. You're going to have all the answers when you get that tape cleaned up."

Mike shrugged. "I don't know what they can do with it at the FBI lab, but it's going to take a while, and I'm going to nail this way before then."

The determined tone of his voice told Kate there was more to come. She remembered what Rogers had told her about some new information that Mike had gotten that morning. She stared at him quizzically, suspecting he was about to drop a bombshell on her.

"Well," she said, finally. "It's obvious you're already on a different tack, Mike."

His face creased into a smile. "Have been since this morning, Kate, thanks to you and your hunch about the woman who looked at the Kane house with that realtor. Traffic traced that parking ticket that was issued, and the mystery woman who checked out the Kane house was not Heskell."

Kate sighed. "It didn't have to be. It was just a hunch, Mike. It doesn't have to fit into this case at all."

Mike laughed and put an arm around her, giving her a quick hug. "But it does, Kate. I think it's going to fit quite neatly."

Kate had a feeling she knew what was coming next even as Mike said, "Your touchdown was just called back, Kate. My team's in the lead, again."

46

Kate woke with a start and a chill in her bones. She had fallen asleep on the couch in front of the fire. Now the fire was long dead and she was not only cold but had a painful crick in her neck. She glanced across the room to the digital clock on her VCR and saw that it was almost eight. Down the hall she heard Tommy moving around, getting ready for school. She catapulted off the couch, prompted by a sudden surge of angry disappointment.

She'd fallen asleep waiting for Mike's call. He had promised to call as soon as he and Harry returned from New York. He had expected to be back well before midnight. He intended to wrap things up swiftly, he'd said, now that he was set on the right course again.

Kate had known what was coming the moment Mike had made the crack about the touchdown. She had realized what he was getting at even before he informed her that the parking ticket issued outside Anna Mae Whitman's realty office had been traced through a car rental agency at 30th Street Station—to Gabriella Grant.

"It hardly puts you in the lead," she'd said flatly, convinced that he was suddenly attaching so much importance to the ticket only because Gabriella Grant's name had surfaced again. But Mike had waved off her objections.

"It does now that I know Heskell didn't have the gun in her possession when she arrived at Terrenzio's."

"What does that mean?"

"It means we can consider a whole different scenario."

Mike had laughed at her puzzled expression. "Yeah." He nodded. "Don't you remember that Packer told us when he first asked Molly where the gun was, she said she hadn't touched it? It was only when he showed her it was missing from the nightstand drawer that she came up with the story of the break-in. And we laughed at that because we believed she was on the lam and because we didn't believe that she had actually had a break-in."

"Okay, I'm with you." Kate nodded as he paused to see if she was following.

"Well, she clearly didn't know where it was, and Packer, as he told you and Harry, said that the gun was gone from that drawer before he moved out. So, maybe it was gone before he moved out because someone took it before he moved out."

"And that brings you back to Grant?" Kate shook her head.

Mike had shrugged. "Not yet but I think it will. Look, she worked with Packer, she'd worked with Heskell. I don't think it's beyond the realm of possibility that she visited their house at some time before the murders. The gun could have been gone for weeks before Packer looked for it."

"Well, good luck, detective," Kate had said. "Because you're forgetting one small detail: The time on Terrenzio's tape said eight-thirty when Emma Kane and Salerno were snacking in the kitchen, and like Art said, they were both dead within about an hour of eating that snack. That puts time of death at around nine, nine-thirty, which, if you recall, gives Gabriella Grant a cast-iron alibi. She was home at ten when they delivered from the Chinese restaurant—"

Mike had jumped right in without letting her finish. "No," he said. "That's exactly what sews it all up. When McGrath came through with her name on the parking ticket . . . dammit, Kate, I knew it had to mean something. It just fit in with everything else I had. I just knew that we'd gone wrong with Heskell somewhere. That's why I stopped them from putting out the press release. That's why Harry and I were in with the chief."

"So, what about the alibi?" she persisted.

"There isn't one. That's what took a while to figure out—but I was sure there had to be a hole in it somewhere. You should know, Kate, a cast-iron alibi either means you've been extremely lucky or you've gone to extraordinary lengths to set one up for yourself, like Grant did."

"Yeah, and how did you figure that out?"

Mike laughed. "It was in my notes. Like I said at the time, I thought there was something I should have picked up on in the doorman's reply, and I was right. Remember he said Grant was a long time answering, and then he said, *and also the phone* is ringing several times?"

"And also the phone?" Kate echoed the words he'd emphasized. "Meaning?"

"*And also* meaning *in addition.*" Mike grinned. "Meaning the phone in addition to the intercom. He couldn't get her on the intercom so he tried her on the regular phone. Get it?"

Mike sounded so much like Tommy when he gave her the answer to one of his riddles that Kate laughed out loud. Then she immediately stifled her amusement. Of course she got it. "If you're right about this, and if Grant has call-forwarding, you're saying she didn't have to be in her apartment to answer the phone call. She could have been in California, right?"

"I'll settle for somewhere on the Main Line, even Philly. Maybe she went to a friend's house." Mike had grinned again. "I was arranging a subpoena for her Nynex records when Rogers interrupted us about your call from Terrenzio's." He paused. "I'm glad he did. The one thing I don't think I could have figured out is how come Heskell had the gun when she arrived at Terrenzio's. But, of course, now I know she didn't."

"And, are you planning to arrest Grant on the basis of all this supposition?" Kate had asked tartly.

"No." He shook his head. "I need those phone records first. But Harry and I can pay Ms. Grant another visit." Mike had glanced at his watch. "We're going to head up there now, and in the meantime maybe the damn records will turn up."

And what if they didn't show any call-forwarding on the

night of the murders? Kate had wanted to ask but hadn't. "What about Jack Kane?" she'd asked instead.

"He'll get his turn," Mike had assured her. "But I'd like Grant first. She's going to have to point the finger at him, give us the lowdown on his phone call to her after Emma told him to go piss into the wind. She'll tell us what went down, who suggested what." He'd let out a hearty laugh. "She's not the heroic type. She won't go down alone."

Kate had left for home without raising what she thought was the most obvious question: Why had Jack Kane gone to such lengths to clear Molly Heskell? Why had he stirred things up instead of just being happy that he and Grant were going to get away with it? But it would have been like standing on the tracks to stop a high-speed train. Mike had been on a roll: steaming right ahead to get what he'd wanted from the beginning. Out to nail Grant—and Kane. Together.

Now, as she headed for the shower, she wondered if maybe it had all fallen apart on him after all. Just as all the clues had pointed to Molly Heskell, and wrongly, maybe the same was true for Gabriella Grant. Maybe Mike hadn't called because there'd been nothing to tell.

She showered quickly, then pulled on a pair of jeans and a white turtleneck and combed back her damp hair into a ponytail before calling Harry's number.

There was no answer on his home phone. She tried his beeper, then the unit.

Mike answered the call on the first ring.

"You promised to call," she said without preamble. "What happened, Mike? Did you talk to Grant?"

"She wasn't at WorldMedia. She was on a day off." He paused. "She wasn't at home, either. But we're moving right along."

"You got the phone records?"

"Being faxed right now. And Packer confirmed that Grant visited their home to see Heskell after she came home from the hospital." There was a longer pause on Mike's end of the line, and Kate waited.

"We also got stone solid proof of their affair, Kate. We're bringing in Kane." He sounded as if he suspected that this was a blow to her, but she wasn't going to confirm that for him. First she wanted to know exactly what the stone solid proof was—except she suddenly found she couldn't get the words out. It was only after a short awkward silence that she managed to say, "I'd like to be there."

"I think you should be," Mike responded immediately. "Bring your pencil and notebook. You'll be seeing your police department at its best." He paused again. "Kane's coming in with Brad Warner."

Brad Warner? Kate felt her throat closing up and she muttered a quick "See you" as she hung up. There was no point any longer clinging to hope that she might have been right. Jack Kane had hired Brad Warner—only the best criminal defense attorney in Philadelphia.

She grabbed her purse, checked inside for her tape recorder and fresh batteries, and walked downstairs to the door where the sight of Tommy, already waiting in the driveway for the school bus, lifted her spirits a little. She gave him a big hug.

He grinned mischievously at her. "Mom, do you know why the apple liked the banana?"

"No, why did the apple like the banana?"

"Because it had appeal. Get it, Mom? A . . . peel." He didn't even wait for her to stop laughing before quickly adding, "Belinda's having a birthday party for Celli tomorrow and she invited me. Is it okay if I go?"

"Do you want to go?"

"She's having a magician. And, she's getting a petting zoo in the backyard. She said I can invite one of my friends from school, too. Can I go, Mom? You know I love magic tricks."

Kate stared at him absently. Yeah, and so does Belinda, obviously, she thought. The woman certainly knew all the right buttons to press. If she wanted Tommy on a weeknight she was going to get him, even if it meant hiring a magician for her daughter's fourth birthday.

She kissed Tommy on the cheek. "If Belinda wasn't having a magician would you still want to go?"

He thought about it for a second. "Well, maybe not so much but . . ."

"Of course you can go," she said quickly, ashamed for

putting him on the spot like that. "So long as you get your homework done." She ruffled his hair. "And, I'll try to be home in time today so that we can go out and buy Celli a gift."

"O-kay, Mom!" He grinned. "Thanks."

"You have a great day, sweetheart." She kissed the top of his head then walked to her Jeep, blowing him another kiss as she got into the car. "I love you."

Tommy watched her pull away down the driveway and wondered if he'd done the right thing, asking about Celli's party. Mom had looked sad. Maybe she didn't really want him to go to Belinda's. Maybe he shouldn't have asked. She always said that she missed him on the weekends. And he didn't really want to go to Belinda's every weekend, either. Belinda was okay but she was always talking about when he was a baby and that made him feel weird because he didn't remember those things and he didn't remember her. And he didn't feel the same way about her as he did about Mom, even though he knew that Kate wasn't his real Mom and Belinda was. It was really strange, but he couldn't help his feelings. He wondered if Belinda would go away again soon.

He walked along the driveway, kicking the gravel towards the trees along the path. Maybe he should tell Mom that he'd changed his mind about the party. He didn't want her to think that he was going because he wanted to see Belinda. He was only going because of the magician. But it would probably make her happy if he didn't go. He knew this whole thing with Belinda made her sad. It made his grandmother sad, too. He knew his grandmother didn't like Belinda at all. And that had to mean something because his grandmother had something good to say about everybody including Joey Nevins, who was the biggest nerd in the whole world even if he did have a tennis court in his backyard.

He kicked at the gravel again, sending it in a spray towards the trees. "Touchdown," he mouthed to himself and kicked again, running after the stones to see where they landed. As he raced off the path through the undergrowth, he stumbled and almost went down on his knees. Steadying himself, he stared down to see what had tripped him up. He gave a little gasp. It was something big and soft, something that looked like a body, with white baggy pants on.

He stepped back quickly but almost immediately thrust his shoulders forward again. Nothing to be afraid of. The body wasn't moving. It couldn't hurt him, not if it was dead.

"Cool," he muttered to himself. A body in their own backyard. Mom would really be happy about that. She wouldn't have to go chasing off to write about stuff like this. She could stay right at home for . . .

He crouched down to take a closer look, poking at the white pants, and then frowned.

Rip-off! It wasn't a real body after all. He poked it some more with his foot and brushed the undergrowth off the face to find himself staring at the silly dummy that Mom and Dad had bought to sit guard at the front door. The one they called Ma Kettle. Only she didn't have her wig or hat on, or her dress, just a dirty white undershirt and the baggy white pants. He looked across through the trees to the porch.

Weird, he thought. There was another Ma sitting on the porch. Had his Mom bought a new one?

He stepped back through the trees and onto the path to take a closer look. Then, he walked up the porch steps, staring at the new dummy. This one sure looked newer and younger, and much prettier. This one had big blue eyes.

He jumped back as he saw one of the eyes blink. Then he looked around, embarrassed, expecting to see Mom and Maysie standing on the porch laughing, like they were playing a joke on him. But there was no one there. In the distance, he saw the yellow school bus rumbling down the lane towards the doorway.

Feeling a little braver, he took another step towards her. Was she one of those cool robot dummies? Maybe this one worked on batteries. He was about to go and touch her when suddenly Ma winked at him and raised one finger to her lips. Then the finger crooked as she beckoned him to come to her.

47

Kate stared at the evidence laid out on Harry's desk and had to admit that Mike had done a thorough job. It was all there: the confirmation from the rental agency about Gabriella's car rental on the day Anna Mae Whitman had shown the Kane house, Sam Packer's list of friends and family who had visited Molly after her return from the hospital—with Gabriella's name sandwiched between a Pete Norcross and a Vickie Bowen, the curled fax paper detailing Grant's phone records with a call-forward entry for the night of the murders, and the small square brown box that Harry and Mike had found in Grant's desk after securing a search warrant for her office the previous evening.

She glanced away from the box, which Mike had opened for her to reveal the gilt-edged cards, and picked up the fax copy of Grant's phone record again. The call-forward had been entered alongside a time of 9:52 P.M. on the night of the murders and an exchange with a 215 area code.

"It's a local exchange, all right," Harry pointed out, lighting up a cigar. "Langhorne Manor. That puts us well into the ballpark. With Emma Kane and Salerno dead by nine, or thereabouts, it gives Grant almost an hour to get to Langhorne. Plenty enough time even if she took Roosevelt Boulevard and had to stop at all the red lights."

"Whose number is it, do you know?" Kate asked.

Mike shook his head. "But we will any minute. We're on it, now."

Kate nodded and turned her attention back to the square box of stationery, staring at the thick cream-colored paper with gold-embossed initials at the top. The initials JK and GG were in fancy script and intertwined, and below those there was more fancy gold script. Kate focussed on the words:

> **Gabriella Grant and Jack Kane invite.........**
> **To Share their Very Special Day**
> **At.................................**
> **On...............................**
> **Together At Last.**

She placed the card back in the box and said nothing. She couldn't say anything because the shock was too great. In her time she had met plenty of liars and con men who'd been the best at their game, but Jack Kane had seemed as far removed from that category as her sainted, departed mother. If there was one thing she'd felt she was right about, it was Jack's honesty.

I don't lie. Lying is a sign of weakness, he'd said, and the words had struck a chord with her. Weak was one word she would never have used in any description of Jack Kane. Now she was just as embarrassed by her naïveté as she was shocked by his bare-faced arrogance. He had been so sure he'd get away with it that he and Gabriella had gone ahead with wedding invitations, leaving only the date and place to be filled in after Gabriella got her divorce and they decided it was safe for them to finally make their relationship public. She could not believe her instincts had been so wrong, that she had made such an error in judgment.

"What did Kane say about these?" she asked finally, pointing to the box of wedding invitations. "Did you ask him?"

Harry nodded towards the stairs. "We surely did. That's when he called for his attorney. He's still with him downstairs in the conference room. They're waiting for a third party to show."

"Who?"

Harry shrugged. "Maybe Warner's assistant. He's going to need help with this."

Mike laughed, his eyes still on the fax. "Especially if he thinks he can still maintain there was no relationship."

"Is that what he said?"

Mike laughed again. "That's what Brad Warner said. He asked us if Kane would be off the hook if he could prove there was no relationship."

"That would be a neat trick wouldn't it?" Kate said quietly. "But I don't think even Brad Warner can pull that one out of the bag."

Harry shrugged. "It's not going to stop him from trying. He already told us Kane had never seen the invitations." He laughed and puffed on his cigar. "Like how many bridegrooms get to *see* the invitation before it's mailed out, anyway?"

"He knows Grant is screwed." Mike weighed in. "But he still thinks he can distance himself by sticking to his story. What a piece of work."

Harry's eyes narrowed, and Kate sensed someone standing behind her. When she looked around she recognized Brad Warner. A large, solidly built man, wearing a three-piece suit and polished lace-up shoes.

"Gentlemen, we're ready to make a statement," he announced, looking at Harry, then he glanced at Kate. "Are you Kate McCusker?"

"Yes."

Warner turned to Harry again. "If you've no objections, Mr. Kane asked for Mrs. McCusker to sit in on this meeting."

"For what?" Mike stepped forward in what looked to Kate like an overly protective gesture. "To speak on his behalf? I don't think—"

Warner held up one hand. "Not to speak. Just to listen in. Okay? He knows you've approved for Mrs. McCusker to write the book on this case. He wants her to get the full story, and he doesn't want to waste time repeating it when he's done here." Warner glanced at his watch. "Can we get going, detectives? Mr. Kane wants to be back in New York by three."

Kate stared at Mike, then at Harry, and both looked as taken aback as she was sure she did. Brad Warner had to be bluffing, surely.

48

Jack was already sitting at the long oval table when they trooped into the interview room, and next to him sat a tall, balding man whom Kate estimated to be in his late forties. Jack looked at her when she walked into the room and acknowledged her with a nod and a small smile. He looked exhausted and his face was sunken and pale. He stopped talking to the man at his side as everyone took their seats around the table: Brad Warner sitting down on Jack's other side while she and Mike and Harry sat across the table.

A few more minutes elapsed as glasses of water were poured, and Kate took the opportunity to place her tape recorder on the table and open up her notebook.

Then Brad Warner cleared his throat and began by thanking Harry and Mike for their patience, then introduced the mystery male as Hank Miller, the deputy news director at Channel Three in Philadelphia.

Mike was on his feet immediately. "This isn't acceptable, Mr. Warner. We were under the impression that—"

"Please, detective, bear with me one moment," Warner cut in. "Without Mr. Miller's help there's no way you can understand what you're dealing with here. My client, Mr. Kane, denies, as he has done from the beginning, any involvement in the murder of his wife or Mr. Salerno—" Brad Warner held up a warning hand as Mike attempted to interrupt him again.

"Let me finish, detective. Unless you're prepared to

accept that statement and let my client walk out of here right now, I have to ask you to let us continue with Mr. Miller."

Harry nodded at Mike, who hesitated only a second longer before sitting down again. Warner nodded, glanced down at his yellow legal pad, and adjusted his square-rimmed reading glasses.

"Before I turn the floor over to Mr. Miller let me just set the scene as briefly as I can, and we can start with Jack's first meeting with Hank, just about a year ago, when Jack started looking for someone who might be ready to replace him as news director after he moved to WorldMedia. There was no one at Seven, since Jack's deputy had just resigned, so he took his search outside." Brad Warner looked up from the legal pad and pointed at Hank Miller. "Along comes Hank who seems to have all the right qualifications. He's the news director at a station in Pittsburgh and is ready to move to a bigger market.

"About a week later, when Jack decides to meet with Hank with a view to offering him the job, the executive news producer at Channel Seven happens to mention that he's just hired a reporter by the name of Gabriella Grant from the same Pittsburgh station." Brad Warner paused and picked up his glass of water, taking a sip from it.

Kate waited impatiently for him to continue but guessed he was sipping for dramatic effect. He was a good storyteller, she thought, and probably dynamite in court. It seemed a waste that he was only playing to three people.

Warner put down his glass. "Well, Jack doesn't give this too much thought, but when he finally meets with Hank he mentions that they've just hired a reporter from his station."

Brad Warner stopped, closed his legal pad, and took off his glasses, turning to Hank Miller. "All yours," he said. "Why don't you start by telling us what you told Jack Kane at that meeting."

Kate sat forward in her chair, glancing at what Mike had scribbled on his notepad as he pushed it towards Harry. *This is the guy who had an affair and got Grant pregnant in Pittsburgh,* she read and almost missed Hank Miller's soft-spoken opening.

"I told Jack that I was turning down his offer."

"You didn't want the job?" Brad Warner prompted.

"I did. Very much, but not if Gabriella was going to be working at Seven, too." Hank Miller cleared his throat and smiled nervously. "Not because she wasn't a good reporter. She was, and I told Jack that—" Hank Miller broke off as if he'd lost his place in his script but Brad Warner jumped in immediately to help him out.

"But you were also very honest with Jack, weren't you?"

"Yes." Hank nodded firmly. "I told him about my experience with her, that is, my personal experience with her."

"Excuse me," Mike interrupted, looking at Brad Warner. "I'm afraid I'm not really hearing anything new here. We already know about Mr. Miller's personal experience with Grant. I already heard this story from her husband. I'm not sure where this can be going—"

"This isn't the same story you heard, detective," Brad Warner interrupted him abruptly. "And if you'll let us continue we'll show you where it's going."

Mike glanced at his watch impatiently but leaned back in his chair.

"I didn't come to Philadelphia to bitch about my own problems, detective," Hank said softly. "But I wanted to tell Jack the whole story so that he'd know what he was up against. Kate glanced at her tape recorder to make sure it was running as Miller launched into how he'd met Gabriella when he'd hired her from a radio station in Pittsburgh and how he'd taken an interest in her.

"She was a very hard worker, and very eager to learn everything about TV. She was always there at the TV station, ready to work around the clock. I was there a lot, too, since my wife and I were going through something of a bad patch."

"Okay, Hank." Brad Warner nodded. "We've got the picture. Let's press on to Miss Grant's wedding."

"Yes," Hank grimaced. "She'd been at the TV station about three months when she announced she was getting married to a builder she'd hired to renovate her house. It seemed like a very sudden thing and I was surprised because she'd seemed so wrapped up in her job."

You mean, so wrapped up with you, Kate thought as Hank Miller continued. "But then a couple of weeks later she announced that she was pregnant so I put two and two together, as one would, and assumed the wedding was sudden for obvious reasons. Anyway, she seemed very thrilled about it all for a while but then a couple of strange things happened."

Hank brought a pack of cigarettes out of his pocket and lit one, taking a long drag on it. "Anyway the first really strange thing is that I came home one day to find Gabriella sitting in the kitchen with my wife, Sue. She'd apparently dropped in for a chat to tell Sue how wonderful I was being to her and how kind I was, letting her take things easy because of the baby."

"Why did that seem strange to you?" Brad Warner prompted as Hank Miller took another drag on his cigarette.

The deputy news director exhaled loudly. "Well, it seemed more unkind than strange at first because Gabriella knew—I guess I'd mentioned it to her at some time—that Sue and I had been trying for a baby for about four years. So her visit with Sue struck me as odd right away. And then, over the next few weeks it seemed that whenever and wherever I went out with Sue, Gabriella and her husband would suddenly turn up."

"Like where?" Brad Warner prompted again.

"Restaurants, the mall, the supermarket, the movie theater, even an outdoor concert we went to one day in a park near our house. As a matter of fact, it was a few days after that concert that she came to see me in my office and she said to me, 'Hank, I have to tell Kevin about us. I've tried my best but I can't go on with the pretense.'" Hank Miller enunciated each word and then paused, shaking his head as if trying to erase the memory.

"Those were her exact words. It was like a bolt from the sky. I was speechless. I thought maybe she was upset, out of sorts because of the pregnancy. I thought the best thing would be to give her some time off, so I put her on a paid leave of absence, and I even told her she'd get the anchor position as soon as she came back from maternity leave."

"And she was happy about that?" Brad Warner prodded quietly. Kate found herself looking at Warner with a growing respect. She knew he hadn't had much time to prepare, but he had obviously grasped the whole story. He knew exactly where to prompt, where to ask the most leading questions.

"Oh, yes." Hank Miller nodded. "But that's when the real nightmare started. That's when she started writing notes to my wife and calling her on the phone, telling Sue that I was staying with her just out of pity for her, badgering Sue to let me go so that the baby could have a real, full-time father and so that I could finally be with the woman I truly loved. When Sue tried to slash her wrists, just after I started looking around for another job, Gabriella Grant called her in the hospital and told her that her pathetic attempt to keep me wasn't going to stop us from moving to Philadelphia together. That was just about a week before I got Jack's call about the job offer."

Mike pushed back from the table and got to his feet. "So, what you're saying is that you got Grant pregnant—and in the end she wasn't prepared to let you off the hook, even though she'd snagged some other guy to marry her?"

Hank Miller laughed. "No, that's not it, detective. I wasn't on any hook. I told Gabriella that if she agreed to take a DNA test and it turned out the baby was mine, I'd divorce my wife and marry her."

"And?"

"Well, it became a moot point. A week later she lost the baby. Her husband called in and said she'd had a miscarriage and that she wasn't returning to work. Then I found out why when I met Jack. She'd already gotten the job in Philly. And so I told Jack the whole story."

Mike frowned. "Bottom line, Mr. Miller, what you're saying is that you got involved with Gabriella Grant and it turned into a Fatal Attraction sort of deal, so then you warned Mr. Kane about Gabriella, and you"—Mike turned to face Brad Warner—"think that proves what? That Jack Kane realized Grant was bad news? We're supposed to accept that as proof that Mr. Kane never got involved with Gabriella Grant?"

"You're missing the point, detective," Brad Warner jumped in, and Kate felt a sudden surge of irritation. If Mike was missing the point, so was she and no doubt so was Harry. She supposed one man's fatal attraction could easily turn into another man's fling. She was glad when Mike turned on him and said, "If I'm missing it, it's because you haven't made it."

"Because you haven't let Mr. Miller finish," Warner countered.

Mike sat down again and sighed. "Oh, go ahead."

Hank Miller looked momentarily confused. Then he leaned forward across the table. "The point of all this, detective, is that there was no affair, no relationship, not even a one-night stand between Gabriella Grant and me. The reason I said I'd marry her if a DNA test proved the baby was mine was because I knew there wasn't a chance in hell that it could be. It just was not possible."

Mike exchanged a glance with Harry and raised an eyebrow. Then he turned back to Hank Miller. "Now, you're telling us that you and Gabriella Grant never had a relationship? There was no physical contact between you at all?"

Miller nodded emphatically. "Exactly. A fatal attraction without sex, if you want to characterize it that way. I never touched Gabriella Grant. I have no reason to lie about that. I didn't have to come here this morning."

The silence that followed Hank Miller's vehement denial was deep and long. No one at the table touched a glass of water or lit a cigarette or shuffled papers until Harry leaned his head against the back of his chair, and staring at the ceiling as if seeking inspiration, finally said, "So, there was no affair. Nothing between you, and Gabriella Grant lied to her husband and to your wife?" He sat forward abruptly and faced the trio across the table. "I don't get it. Are you saying she was scamming you? Trying to blackmail you?"

Hank Miller attempted a smile. "No. Not at all. It's sadder than that. So far as she was concerned it was the truth. In her mind, it was all very real."

"You're saying she was fantasizing." Mike laughed abruptly. "You're saying . . . here's this woman who has half the

men in America drooling over her, living in her own fantasy world where you're her object of desire."

Hank Miller shifted in his seat, looking uncomfortable
and embarrassed. "I don't know why she picked on me,
except perhaps because I was her boss. The figure of power
in our little world up there in Pittsburgh." He paused. "And
fantasy isn't the right word, either. Most fantasies are harm-
less because they don't intrude into the real world."

"You sound like a shrink," Harry commented as Hank
Miller sipped some water.

"Maybe I do." He nodded. "I've spoken to enough of
them since this happened. My wife's been in treatment for
a while. As a matter of fact, one of her psychiatrists even
had a name for what Gabriella had done. He said it sounded like erotomania."

"Erotomania?" Mike echoed. "Sounds more like the title
of a bad porn movie."

Hank Miller shrugged. "Well, apparently it's a genuine
clinical disorder. It's listed in diagnostic manuals, too. The
shrink showed me. I don't know if it's a chemical imbalance
or some sort of psychological defect but what I do know is
that it's all to do with delusion and obsession. And that's
definitely what Gabriella's problem was: She convinced
herself that I was in love with her, she believed I wanted to
be with her, and everything else followed from that.
Everything she said and did came from that standpoint."

"Like John Hinckley and Jodie Foster?" Harry asked, his
brow furrowing.

"Not at all." Miller shook his head. "That was almost the
opposite. Hinckley thought he had to shoot the President to
win Jodie Foster's love. In this case Gabriella believed I was
in love with her already." He sat forward in his chair. "It's
more like that woman in Connecticut, the one who keeps
breaking into David Letterman's house claiming she's his
wife."

"But she's as mad as a hatter," Kate suddenly broke in.
"Gabriella Grant isn't anything like that. How could she get
to where she is if she was that nutty?"

Miller shrugged. "There are more extreme and less
extreme cases, I guess." He paused and smiled. "And people

like Gabriella can function extremely well in most areas of their lives except the emotional one. Anyway, television is a world of images and illusion to begin with. You create your own reality even in TV news. You edit it and present it and produce it according to your own biases. It's a perfect place for someone like Gabriella to thrive."

Hank Miller spread his hands out on the table. "I know it's difficult to understand; it's even more difficult to deny. Trust me. It's almost impossible to prove something *hasn't* happened. That's why I understand Jack's predicament. Especially when everything you do, even the most negative things, are turned around and used as proof that you love that person."

"For example?" Mike asked.

"For example," Hank Miller replied. "When I gave her the paid leave of absence, it was because I wanted to get her out of the place and out of my life. But she told her husband it was proof that I cared about her and our baby. She imposed her reality on everyone around her."

Another silence descended around the table. Mike sat shaking his head; Harry looked nonplussed. "It's a bizarre story, Mr. Miller, and I must say I've never heard of anything quite like it." Harry took off his bifocals and wiped them clean with a white handkerchief he took out of his pocket. Then he looked at Jack Kane. "I take it you're saying Gabriella Grant pulled the same stunt with you?"

"I would think that's pretty obvious now, detective," Brad Warner cut in. "You want to know about delusion, just take a look at those wedding invitations."

Not to mention sending out a production assistant for a pregnancy test kit, thought Kate, reflecting that Brad Warner had been right. Without Hank Miller, Jack's denials would have been laughable.

But Harry was evidently not quite satisfied. "But if you knew all this, Mr. Kane, why did you hire her? Why did you bring her to New York with you?"

Kate could tell that Jack was ready to tell his story. He sat forward, his hands clasped on the table in front of him. "First of all, detective, I didn't know that Gabriella's trouble was an actual medical disorder—"

"That's right," Hank Miller interrupted. "I didn't know about that myself at the time I met with Mr. Kane. That was before all my wife's sessions with psychiatrists and therapists."

"But," Jack continued as Miller sat back in his chair again, "I got the general gist of it. Enough to know to stay away from Gabriella Grant. I didn't need that kind of trouble, detective. And, believe me, I got an inkling of what Hank meant very soon after Gabriella arrived at Seven—"

"How's that, Mr. Kane?" Harry interrupted impatiently.

"She turned up at my home on the pretext of bringing some tapes for me to look at. Actually appeared on my doorstep in Gladwyne."

"Was your wife as shocked as you?" Mike asked.

"My wife was away for the weekend, detective. And don't ask me how Gabriella knew that. I may have mentioned it in passing for some reason, but I don't remember. Anyway, I can tell you I made it very clear to her that afternoon that I wasn't interested."

"Well I guess she didn't get the message," Mike jumped in again.

"Oh, but she did," Jack came right back at him. "I told her that afternoon that she had a choice: I told her she had a great future in television but only if she stopped acting like a tramp. I told her it wasn't necessary. I told her I never wanted to see her outside of the office again."

"Tough words." Mike nodded.

"Yes and they seemed to work," Jack responded. "I never even bumped into her in the office after that—not until I announced I was leaving for WorldMedia, and then Gabriella asked me to consider her for a job at the network. At the time I had no reason to say no, and every reason to say yes. She'd done some outstanding work at Seven. I knew she could be an asset."

Jack sighed. "I guess in New York I let my guard down. Except for that one afternoon when she came to the house, she seemed to be a changed person. And I guess I found myself being less standoffish towards her."

"What do you mean by that?" Mike asked.

"Not what you think, detective." Jack gave him a tired

smile. "But I did make sure she was included in various network functions and industry dinners. I wanted her to get out in public and be seen; I wanted to build an image for her."

"Whose idea was it that she move into the same apartment building?"

Jack shrugged. "Mine."

"Well certainly that wasn't very standoffish," Mike commented pointedly.

"But not as bad as it sounds." Jack shook his head. "The building has several company apartments and it's within walking distance of the office. At the time Gabriella was living on the East Side and running up enormous limo bills."

"Pity." Hank Miller returned to the conversation. "That was probably the biggest mistake. That was like sending her a signal, like asking her to move in with you. Now you're living under the same roof, you share the same address. It couldn't get any better for someone like Gabriella."

"But at some level she had to know it wasn't for real, didn't she?" Harry threw the question out.

Hank Miller made a stab at answering, but not very satisfactorily. Who the hell knew? he seemed to be saying. Unless you were in Gabriella's head.

Harry sighed and got to his feet, and Kate could tell he was struggling with the situation. Who wouldn't? she wondered. At least there was an upside for her: She had maintained all along that Jack was telling the truth about Gabriella Grant. And she'd been proved right. At least she knew now that her instincts hadn't failed her. But where did all this leave Harry and Mike and their case? Was all their other evidence going to fall apart the way their stone-solid proof of an affair with Jack had? How deep-seated would Gabriella's delusion have to be for her to actually go out and kill Emma Kane?

Evidently Mike was right on the same track. He turned to Harry. "We're going to need a psychiatric expert to fill us in on this, but I'm guessing an obsession like this doesn't preclude murder. If anything, maybe it's a predictable outcome."

Hank nodded. "It's happened, detective. I believe the

father of the Lennon sisters was killed for that reason. There's no boundaries with obsession. In my case I think Gabriella set out to get rid of Sue by provoking her into a suicide attempt. She may have crossed the line in Jack's case and decided to do the deed herself, especially if she convinced herself the relationship was stalled because of Emma Kane."

Jack buried his head in his hands for a moment. When he looked up his face was the color of paper. "That Monday before Emma was murdered she came to New York to look at the townhouse, and we bumped into Gabriella in the lobby at WorldMedia." He shook his head and reached for the glass of water. "God, that look on Gabriella's face when Emma told her we'd found an absolutely darling house on West Seventy-fifth. I couldn't figure it out. I even looked over my shoulder because I thought she'd seen something terrible out on the street behind me."

Hank Miller nodded knowingly. "She did see something terrible. But it was in her own head, of course. You were going to move out of the apartment building. You were about to move out on her and back in with Emma."

Mike got to his feet again. "Mr. Kane, did Gabriella Grant know that your wife had changed her mind about moving to New York? Did she know you were driving down to the Main Line to resolve the situation?"

"No, of course not. I didn't keep Gabriella appraised of my daily schedule."

"So then so far as Gabriella knew, on that Thursday night Emma was still planning to move to the townhouse in New York?"

Jack Kane nodded unhappily. "Yes."

Mike ran his hands over his hair. "You would have made things a lot simpler for us had you told us all this in the beginning, Mr. Kane."

Jack grimaced. "We only ever spoke once about Gabriella, detective. I know you thought there was something going on, and I suppose there might well have been had I not been warned by Hank." He shrugged. "But the fact is she was a lot more subtle with me than she was with Hank. I must say I even wondered, at one point, if Hank had told me the whole truth."

"But you knew that she'd harassed Mr. Miller's wife to the point of getting her to slash her wrists. Didn't you have the tiniest suspicion?"

Kate studied her fingernails. Enough already, she thought as Jack clenched his fist on the tabletop.

"No, detective," he said very coldly. "She had everything going for her at WorldMedia. I didn't think she needed fantasies to fill her life anymore." He paused. "So far as I knew she'd never made any attempt to contact—or harass—Emma. So, no, I never suspected that she was the one who'd shot two people down in cold blood."

Brad Warner stood up and put a hand on his shoulder. "Come on, Jack, you can't speak for Gabriella Grant." He looked at Harry. "I assume it's all right for my client to leave now, detective?"

Harry waited till Warner had left the room with Jack and Hank Miller, and then without any comment got to his feet, too. Kate switched off her tape recorder and put it away in her purse. Then she followed him and Mike out of the room—only to find Jack Kane waiting for her at the end of the hallway.

"I just wanted to say I was glad to see you there, Kate," he said, smiling for the first time at her. "I didn't think you'd believe the story if you heard it secondhand. I was afraid no one would believe it."

"Tough enough to believe when you're hearing it firsthand." She nodded. "You must be relieved it's over."

"Yes." He nodded. "But I never imagined it would end like this." He paused. "I'll call you, Kate, okay?"

"Sure." She nodded quickly, noticing that Mike was waiting for her at the bottom of the stairs, a pensive look clouding his eyes.

She thought it had something to do with her quick exchange with Jack Kane but he didn't refer to it, and the look vanished as he handed her the note he was holding in his hand. "We traced that Langhorne number to a Gloria Rossiter, Grant's mother," Mike added, walking toward the main doors. "Maybe she knows where her daughter is. They certainly don't know at WorldMedia. According to her assistant she called in sick today. More likely the girl clued her in on our visit yesterday." He held the door open. "Want to check out Mom's place with me?"

"You think I'd pass on an invitation like that?" Kate laughed and glanced at her watch. It was only just after eleven. With luck, maybe she'd make it back in time to take Tommy shopping for Celine's birthday gift.

49

Maysie tried not to show her fear. She knew she had to stay calm for Tommy's sake, but it was difficult while the crazy woman was pacing around her kitchen with the bread knife in her hand.

Maysie had been in the family room lighting a fire in the fireplace when she'd heard the school bus rumbling away down the driveway. She'd seen Kate drive off a few minutes before that, and she'd looked forward to enjoying a quiet cup of tea and her new gardening book in front of a nice cheery fire. The last thing in the world she'd expected was to see anyone in the kitchen, least of all Tommy, standing by the breakfast table with a strange woman dressed in the porch dummy's clothes and holding a bread knife to his throat.

"Just stay calm and neither of you will get hurt," the woman had said. Then she'd ordered Maysie to call Tommy's school to explain his absence. "Be careful what you say," she'd warned Maysie, aiming the tip of the knife at Tommy's face.

Now Maysie stepped closer to her grandson and slipped her hand around his while the woman paced, staring at the pictures on the wall.

Suddenly she flicked at one of Kate's photos with her knife, bringing the frame crashing from the wall to the floor.

"Why are you doing that?" Tommy shouted at her.

Maysie gripped his hand more tightly and shook her head at him as the woman wheeled around and walked back towards them.

"Because your mother's a slut."

Maysie took a deep breath. "You don't have to use language like that in front of him," she said.

The woman laughed and forced Tommy's chin up with the tip of the knife. "What's the matter? Don't you know what a slut is, Tommy? I'll tell you what a slut is: it's a bad woman who messes around with men who don't belong to her."

The thought suddenly occurred to Maysie that this woman had made a terrible mistake. "Kate isn't messing around with anyone," she said, sounding more bold than she felt.

But in the next moment the hope died as the woman laughed in Maysie's face. "Tell it to those porch dummies. I know what I've seen and what I've heard, and Kate McCusker is not going to waltz off with Jack Kane. Not after all the trouble I went to getting rid of his wife."

Maysie's heart sank when she heard the names. This was to do with the murders—and this woman was . . . was she admitting that she'd killed Mrs. Kane? Her mouth suddenly felt very dry.

"Can't you let the boy go?" she asked. "Please, he isn't to blame for anything."

The woman ignored her, pacing to the kitchen drawers and flinging them open one by one. Maysie thought about making a run for it but she would never go without Tommy. Nor could she signal any message to him without the woman catching her. Anyway, she wasn't sure that either she or Tommy could move fast enough to get away, and she didn't want to make this woman any angrier than she already was.

She winced as drawers went crashing to the floor, spilling out knives and forks and other utensils. Then the woman started on the cabinets, opening and slamming the doors.

Finally, it seemed she found what she was looking for in the storage cabinet over the pantry. She turned around with a big fat roll of duct tape in her hand and walked back across the kitchen towards Maysie.

Out of the corner of her eye, Maysie saw Tommy's eyes darting around, and her throat seemed to close up at the thought that he might take a chance on doing something silly.

"Tommy, sit down and be a good boy," she told him as sharply as she could bring herself to do.

The woman glanced around to look at Tommy as she bound Maysie's ankles with the duct tape. "That's right, Tommy," she mimicked. "You be a good boy. Don't do anything silly or I'll have to punish you."

It took her just minutes to bind Maysie's wrists, and then the woman turned to Tommy, binding his ankles and wrists in the same way. Then, she started on his mouth.

"No!" Maysie shouted out. "Please don't do that to him. There's no one around to hear, even if he did scream, which he's not going to, I promise."

The woman ignored her and continued wrapping the duct tape around Tommy's mouth until his face from the nose down was all tape.

Maysie saw Tommy's eyes wide with fear above the tape as he breathed in and out noisily and rapidly. She felt a tear slide down her own cheeks at the thought that she hadn't helped him to get away.

"What are you going to do?" she asked, no longer able to keep her voice calm.

The woman seemed to stare right through her with big, cold, blue eyes. Then she said, "I'm going to teach Kate McCusker a lesson."

"You don't have to do this to us," Maysie pleaded with her. "Why don't you talk to Kate? I think you'll see you're making a big mistake. This is just going to get you in trouble."

The woman smiled and her voice seemed very calm when she replied, "I'm in trouble already. This isn't going to make any difference."

Calmly and methodically, the woman started winding the

duct tape around Maysie's mouth. Then standing back to reassure herself that neither Maysie nor Tommy could move, she headed up the kitchen stairs to Kate's den.

Maysie heard a loud crashing noise, then more banging. It sounded like furniture falling. She thought about Kate's computer and all the other expensive equipment Kate had. She blinked, trying to hide her own distress from Tommy as he flinched with every shuddering crash from upstairs.

Then it was quiet for a moment and Maysie heard her moving down the hallway. Maybe that's all she's going to do, thought Maysie. Maybe that's what she meant by teaching Kate a lesson. So long as she didn't harm Tommy—or Kate—she could wreck the house if it made her feel better, Maysie told herself, and tried not to think about the calm way the woman had admitted "getting rid" of Emma Kane.

She picked up the sound of the woman's footsteps on the main staircase, and then heard doors banging. It sounded as if she was moving around in the laundry room. Maysie closed her eyes and prayed. Off the laundry room was the mud room, where Steve's gun cabinet stood. His guns were still in the locked cabinet.

Suddenly the sound of breaking glass echoed through the house, and Maysie's heart thudded.

A few seconds later the woman walked back into the kitchen. The first thing that Maysie noticed was that she held Steve's service automatic in her hand; the second was the triumphant glint in her eye as she looked at Tommy, then at Maysie.

50

Traffic was heavy on Roosevelt Boulevard as they headed towards Langhorne, and Mike was quiet behind the wheel. Kate thought he looked dejected. She suspected that seeing Jack Kane talk his way out of the police station had hit him harder than he would admit. She knew he had to be wondering if there was a possibility that his case against Gabriella Grant could fall apart in the same way.

"I know you're going to nail Grant," she said quietly, trying to sound encouraging. "You were right about her from the beginning." She threw him a broad smile. "And when you've wrapped all this up, you're going to have to sit down with me so that I can get your thinking on her right from the start. I'm going to need detail like that for the book."

His mood seemed to lighten a little, and he responded with a glance that seemed to say that would be no problem at all. "But I don't know that I'll be able to give you any sort of answer that makes sense," he said. "In the end I expect it'll come down to the same kind of thinking that you had about Kane. *You* were right about *him* from the start. How do you explain that?"

"Gut feeling?" she offered, and then laughed. "By the way that puts us at a tie, detective."

He gave her a tired smile. "Ties suck, Kate. No losers. No winners. And gut feeling isn't going to get me anywhere. If the FBI doesn't come through with an enhancement of that tape placing her at the scene, we don't have any evidence that does. We may not even have enough to charge her."

"Oh, come on." Kate glanced sharply at him. "You placed her at Heskell's house with access to the murder weapon; you've got her in the area at the time of the murders, according to her phone records."

Mike laughed. "Can you imagine what a hotshot like Brad Warner would do with that kind of circumstantial evidence?"

"But she lied, Mike. She lied about being at home in her apartment at the time of the murders. She set up an alibi for herself. There's no way around that."

He shrugged. "I might have agreed with you yesterday but after that performance this morning, I'm not taking anything for granted in this case." He paused and laughed harshly. "Oh, except for one thing, and that is if Grant is ever brought to trial, she'll walk. You watch. Any halfway competent attorney in the public defender's office could get an acquittal on grounds of insanity."

Kate stared at him in surprise. She had never seen him in such a negative mood before. "You can't believe that," she said emphatically. "Insanity, my foot. She was sane enough to set up an alibi for herself. She was sane enough to plan ahead, scope out the house, steal Packer's gun."

"For what?" Mike laughed abruptly. "So that she could kill the wife of a man she *thought* she was having an affair with? Try explaining that one to a jury."

Kate shook her head. "Grant isn't some drooling, witless, mental ward patient. Okay, so maybe the murders were prompted by a delusion, but they were executed by a very cold, sane, calculating mind. If I were a juror I could certainly be made to see that."

He shrugged. "Nice adjectives, Kate. Unfortunately I don't think they're going to get us a conviction for murder."

"Well," Kate said finally, "you know she's guilty and I know it, and I want to go ahead with my book. So you'd better get back on this case, detective, and wrap it up."

She thought she detected a half smile on his lips but then he turned away from her to glance at a street sign. "It should be the next left," he said, slowing down as he approached an intersection.

Langhorne Manor looked like a pleasant neighborhood,

Kate thought, with wide leafy streets and grand, solid-looking stone houses with large front lawns that were set behind low brick walls. She wondered if this was where Gabriella Grant had been raised. She wondered about the mother who had raised her. She was curious about Gloria Rossiter. The *People* article hadn't had one quote from her about her affair with Ben Grant. Nor any picture of the woman. As Mike pulled up in front of the house, and they got out, Kate wondered if Gloria had any idea of the trouble her daughter was in.

They only had to wait a moment before the door was flung open by a small woman wearing a dressing gown and slippers. Her thinning gray hair was tucked into a terrycloth turban.

Mike, badge in hand, started to introduce himself. "We're looking for—"

Gloria Rossiter's shriek interrupted him in midsentence and her face drained of color. "He didn't have to send the police." She leaned against the door. "I told him I haven't seen Lester since Saturday night."

Kate heard footsteps behind them, then a voice: "The trouble is, Mrs. Rossiter, neither has anyone else."

Kate and Mike swiveled around in unison.

"What's going on here?" Mike asked, badge still in hand.

The man stepped forward and peered at it. "I'm Ken Barnes. I'm a photographer with the *Enquirer*, and a colleague of mine was working with me on a story. He spent Saturday evening with Mrs. Rossiter, but we haven't heard from him since. That's very unusual. All I wanted to do was talk to her about it. She keeps hanging up on me."

Mike stared at Gloria Rossiter, who looked confused. Her eyes were blinking rapidly. "All I know is that Gabriella told me they were going to New York. She was going to arrange an interview for Lester at WorldMedia."

"Who did she go to New York with?" Mike asked even as Kate echoed the name Lester.

"Wait, you mean the *Enquirer*, right? You're talking about Lester Franks?" she added.

"Yes, him." Ken Barnes surveyed Kate quizzically, as if her face was familiar to him.

"I'm Kate McCusker," she offered. "Lester spoke to me a week ago. You were working on the Kane murders. What was Lester doing here?"

"No, this was the Ben Grant story," Ken Barnes explained, lowering his voice. "We were trying to get that old biddy to spill the beans about her affair with Grant, the one Gabriella talked about in *People*. Lester got in to talk to her Saturday night, told me to buzz off while he warmed her up. On Saturday night he left a message on my machine saying we're in business. That's the last I heard from him."

"So, did you check all the local bars, Ken?" Kate asked, smiling, and added slyly, "Sounds like a big scoop to me: My Nights of Love with Dead Has-Been. He probably went to celebrate."

Ken Barnes didn't smile in response. "It's deadline day," he said. "And Lester's missing. That's not a laughing matter."

"Well, I'll tell you what, Ken, Detective Travis is here on another matter but if we find Lester drunk under the bed somewhere in there, we'll be sure to call your editor."

She turned her back on Ken Barnes just in time to see Gloria Rossiter slump forward and crumple into a small sad heap in the doorway.

51

Between them they got Gloria to her feet and helped her down the passageway to the back of the house. Off the kitchen a den-type room offered a recliner chair in which they settled Gloria Rossiter.

Mike checked her pulse while Kate went into the kitchen and soaked some paper towels, which she brought back to put on Gloria's forehead.

Gloria gave a little moan and her eyes flickered open. Kate, seeing the bottle of Cutty Sark on the kitchen table, poured a small measure into a glass and held it under Gloria's nose.

The older woman nodded and took the glass, sipping the Scotch. Her eyes opened and focussed on Kate. "Thank you, dear." She sat in the chair, nodding to herself. "That's better. I must have had one of my dizzy spells." She nodded to herself again.

"Let's get on with it," Mike mouthed to Kate. He leaned over Gloria Rossiter. "Is Gabriella here?"

The woman shook her head. "No, dear."

"We'd like to take a look for ourselves."

"Go ahead." Gloria Rossiter nodded. "You think I don't know when my daughter's here and when she's not." She pointed upstairs. "Her room's up there. First on the right."

They left Gloria Rossiter resting in the recliner, and Kate followed Mike who took the stairs two at a time. Gabriella's room overlooked the backyard. A big bay window with a window seat dominated the room. A stack of magazines lay on the seat. They were old magazines, some of them dating back over two years. On the shelves, Kate noticed dolls and stuffed animals, which she assumed were mementoes of Gabriella's childhood. But the closet contained clothes that Gabriella might have worn and discarded in recent years—and the linens on the bed looked expensive and stylish.

It was an interesting room, she thought, looking around more closely after Mike had left to proceed on down the hallway. She took out her notebook to jot down some details. If this was Gabriella Grant's childhood home, these kinds of details would fascinate readers who'd want to know everything about the TV anchorwoman-turned-killer.

A nook contained the window seat. Another nook housed an antique dollhouse. It seemed that Gabriella had enjoyed her dolls as a little girl. About a half dozen of them sat on the padded window seat. They were old-fashioned doll's with cute painted rosebud lips and rosy cheeks. But they'd been well-preserved. Except for one, Kate noticed, which lay in a large wooden doll's crib at one end of the window seat. It was the biggest of all the dolls but it also had the biggest crack in its head and it looked dirty and muddied, like the pink blanket that covered it right up to its chin. It seemed an odd thing to keep, thought Kate. Unless it had been a favorite, of course. She walked across to take a closer look and then realized that Gabriella's mother had followed them upstairs.

Kate turned to her. "Mrs. Rossiter, was that doll a favorite of Gabriella's when she was a little girl?" Kate pointed to the cracked head. "That one in the crib?"

The older woman stepped hesitantly towards the window seat. "Missy? Why no. It was Barbie. Barbie was always Gabriella's favorite when she was a girl."

As Kate jotted down the quote, she saw Gloria Rossiter stepping closer to the doll, still talking. "But I guess she grew out of the Barbies because it was Missy she took to New York."

"You mean recently when she moved to WorldMedia?" Kate asked, and wasn't sure why she felt a sudden tingle run up the back of her neck.

Gloria stared at Kate in bemusement for a moment. Then she shook her head abruptly. "Well, dear, don't pin me down on a date but it was a while ago. I didn't even realize she'd brought her back." Gloria Rossiter stopped talking suddenly and started tutting instead. "My goodness, what did that girl do with her? And would you look at this blankie." Gloria picked up the pink blanket, pointing in disgust at a dirty candy wrapper stuck to the underside. "Where on earth has this been?"

Kate felt the inexplicable little tingle again as she stared at the blanket and the doll with the cracked head. Then suddenly, just as Gloria Rossiter leaned over to pick up the doll, Kate realized why the woman's words had chilled her.

"Don't! Don't touch that, Mrs. Rossiter," she shouted out, forcing the old lady to wheel around, startled. "No, you musn't." Kate strode to the doorway and shouted for Mike.

He returned to the room within seconds, standing aside as Gloria backed out of the room nervously, looking at the doll as if it were a bomb about to explode.

"What's going on? What did you find?"

Kate swallowed nervously. The sight of the doll and the muddied blanket had jogged something in her mind. The stray candy wrapper had prompted a sudden vivid image of the blanket falling to the ground, then being snatched up along with the wrapper. At the same time Sam Packer's words had echoed loudly in her head. *She saw a woman with a baby in the park. In the middle of the night, but when she went running out, there wasn't anyone there.*

Kate took a deep breath now, pointing to the doll and blanket. "Don't laugh, Mike, but I think these are Molly Heskell's hallucinations. Remember Sam Packer told us Molly saw a baby falling out of the swing?"

Mike stepped towards the crib. "This doll?" he asked.

Kate nodded. "Mrs. Rossiter just told me that Gabriella took that doll away to New York with her, and she only just brought it back." Kate cleared her throat nervously. "Maybe this sounds crazy, but is there any way that you could look in the park for that missing chip from the doll's head? Or maybe there's a way to get a match with the mud stain."

Mike shook his head, still staring at the doll. "No," he said quietly. "No, that doesn't sound crazy, Kate. It's something a crime lab should be able to do. But my God, if you're right . . ." He unfolded a plastic bag he'd taken from his pocket.

"If I'm right," Kate jumped in, "wouldn't that prove that Grant tried to drive Heskell crazy, tried to make her look crazy so that no one would believe her?"

Mike grinned at her as the words came tumbling out. "I think what it all might add up to is that Grant set out to frame Heskell. She stole the gun from Molly's house, then tossed it where it would have been found and traced to Molly. She got Heskell's name into the first conversation I ever had with her. And in the meantime, she's setting her up to look crazy, preying on a woman who was already in a fragile state of mind after losing a baby. Hell, if that's not malice aforethought I don't know what is." Mike placed the doll and blanket inside the plastic bag, then threw his arm around Kate. "You're pretty darn good, you know that?" His lips brushed against her cheek, but it was a fleeting touch because just as abruptly, he broke away and left the room, heading downstairs where Gloria Rossiter was sitting in her recliner.

She held an empty glass in her hand, her head drooping on her chest as if she'd fallen asleep. She stirred as they entered the kitchen. Kate took the glass from her hand as Mike crouched down beside the old woman.

"Mrs. Rossiter," he said gently. "We need to ask you a few questions. Can you think back about ten days or so? Back to Thursday night, a weeknight. Gabriella came here, didn't she?"

Gloria Rossiter stared at them, but her eyes were blank. "She was angry."

"She was angry when she arrived that night?"

"No, she was angry when Lester and I got home, Saturday. Gabriella was already here." Gloria Rossiter nodded abruptly.

Mike and Kate stared at each other. "Mrs. Rossiter, we're not talking about this Saturday," Kate prompted her again.

Gloria ignored her as if she hadn't spoken. "Gabriella knew what I'd done. But she shouldn't have put me in that position. I didn't think I'd done anything bad." Her head rose sharply and she stared at Kate. "Do you want to hear the tape? I didn't say anything that wasn't true. I didn't want to say anything but he wormed it out of me."

Kate looked across at Mike and nodded as if to say: Let's bear with her. She was always curious about anything Lester wormed out of his victims.

"It's over there in that drawer." Gloria Rossiter pointed to a china cabinet in the dining area. "It's under the white tablecloths. I was supposed to burn it but I haven't lit a fire yet." She shrugged as Kate retrieved the tape, then pointed to the kitchen. "There's a radio on the counter in there. It plays cassettes."

Kate brought the radio into the den and looked for an outlet, plugged it in and inserted the tape, rewinding it to the beginning. Then she punched the Play button.

A staticky noise filled the room, and what sounded like the clatter of glass and knives.

"We went to dinner. That's at Casita Sol," Gloria offered by way of explanation.

"Lester, I'm not sure I want this on tape." Gloria's voice, slightly slurred, echoed in the room.

Then Lester Franks, in a deep, reassuring voice: "Gloria, I'll switch off whenever you say so, but I'd really like to have something as an explanation for my editor. Just repeat what you told me in the car, that bit about the story not being worth the money."

"Yes, well, I told you that all along."

"You said it wasn't a summer romance, that he took you to dinner on the last night along with the rest of the crew. But after dinner, he took you home, right? You said he kissed you."

"It was just a kiss on the cheek. . . . And . . ."

The sound of ice chinking in a glass.

Lester laughed. It sounded like a phony laugh to Kate. "That sure sounds like a powerful kiss, Gloria. . . ."

Kate saw Mike roll his eyes.

Gloria sounding defensive: "I told you it wasn't worth ten thousand dollars."

"What did he say to you after he kissed you?"

"He wished me luck."

"And what did you say?"

"I told him I would need it. And then I started blabbing and crying."

"Ah." Lester sounded a bit more sincere. "I guess it must have been hard to say good-bye."

"I just started telling him all about my troubles."

Kate could almost see Lester holding his breath.

"I told him about Johnny West, that was the boy I was going with at the time. He worked in the stockroom at West's, the department store in town. He said he was learning the business so he could run it one day."

"You were dating the owner's son?"

There was a silence on the tape broken only by the background chatter in the restaurant.

"What did you say, Gloria?" Lester's voice suddenly sounded sharp, incisive.

"I said, I told Ben Grant I wished things were different. When he walked me up the porch steps I told him I wished it had been him who'd been my first lover, I mean. I told him I wished I'd waited for him, and now it was too late."

"That was very honest of you, Gloria." Lester's voice was soft and gentle, leading Gloria on. "I can understand your situation."

There was a giggling sound on the tape. "He was wicked. Ben Grant was really wicked. He said since I was already, you know, well since I was in trouble, it wouldn't matter if we just . . . just went ahead."

"In trouble?" Lester's voice had risen slightly. "You mean you were already . . ."

"Yes, pregnant with Gabriella. I was already pregnant." Gloria hiccuped, then giggled. "There you have it, Lester. Your editor should be satisfied with that. Aren't you glad you didn't pay me?" She giggled again.

"Let's order, shall we?" Lester's voice was even softer.

A moment's pause, presumably while they looked at menus.

Then Lester spoke again. This time his voice was so soft Kate barely heard what he said but it sounded like: "I understand now why you didn't want to talk. This would come as a shock to Gabriella after all these years believing that Ben Grant was her father." Kate heard the note of excitement in his voice. She could almost hear him thinking out loud . . . She felt sorry for Gloria, who had not realized how easily she'd been led into the trap.

But then Gloria's voice sounded harsh. "Oh no, Lester. Gabriella knows the truth. I had to tell her eventually. I couldn't let her carry on thinking that Ben Grant was her father, mooning over an old playbill and dried flower. I only let her carry on like that until I had worked out how to tell her what a scum her real father was. She was only a little girl at the time. I had to be very gentle."

"Johnny West dumped you?"

Gloria laughed shrilly. "No, Bert Malley dumped me. He conned me first then he dumped me. Johnny West was on a vacation in Europe with his parents. Bert Malley was a fraud, a phony who went around saying he was Johnny

West. He got into trouble for it eventually because he got credit using the West name. They put him in one of those jail hospitals."

There was a sputtering on the tape. Then Lester's voice apologizing. "Excuse me. I guess that went down the wrong way."

Kate shook her head. Went down the wrong way, indeed! She could picture Lester choking—with excitement. Finally he recovered enough breath to ask, "So you told Gabriella all this about her real father. When did you tell her?"

"A while ago."

"After or before the *People* magazine story?"

"Oh gracious, no. I tried to tell her a long time before that. When she was still in school."

"What do you mean, you tried?" Lester's voice was wary now. "You just said you did tell her."

"Well." Gloria sounded confused. "I did tell her, but she never seemed to listen. She told me I was getting confused and addled, because of the drinking, she said. But it was her fault really; she's the one who was confused. But she was always like that, like her father, her real father, I mean. She only ever believed what she wanted to believe."

In her recliner chair, Gloria stirred. "You can switch it off, now. That's all I said. Lester was very nice about it, too. He said he'd wait to talk to Gabriella, to apologize for harassing me."

Kate got to her feet, brushing her hair back off her face. Yeah, right. Lester apologize for getting the scoop of the year. I don't think so.

"I guess Gabriella didn't accept his apology," Kate remarked drily.

Gloria looked confused; her eyes reflected a tinge of fear.

"You said she was angry when you got home."

Gloria nodded. "She told me the next morning. She was very, very angry because she'd warned me that those reporters would get it all out of me. She said she'd had to make a deal with the devil."

"You mean get Lester a job in TV?" Kate tried to suppress a smile. "That's not such a terrible deal. It's better than having that story in the *Enquirer*, believe me." Kate ejected the tape from the cassette player and handed it to Gloria. "Here, you hold onto that."

"It's my fault. All my fault." Gloria's shoulders started to shake.

Kate allowed herself the smile. "Oh come on, Mrs. Rossiter. Lester Franks will be good on TV." Kate put a hand on one trembling shoulder, not adding that Lester's future was already in doubt since Gabriella was about to lose all the clout she'd ever had at WorldMedia. But Gloria seemed to be sobbing harder. "But he's still waiting for Gabriella to pick him up. She said they'd drive to New York together today."

"I wouldn't worry about it," Kate said. "You have the tape. That's the most important thing."

"But I want him to leave. Gabriella said she'd be back for him. I don't want to be alone with him."

Kate faced Mike and made a little whirling motion with her finger at her temple. Gloria was confused now for sure, but she didn't want to leave the woman in distress.

Mike stared at Gloria, impatience written all over his face as he made an attempt to elicit some useful information about Gabriella Grant's whereabouts. "You said they were heading to New York together. Can you tell us what time they left?"

"No!" Gloria's voice rose in a wail. "No. He's still here; he's down in the rec room. I just told you that."

Mike stepped back, looking in the direction Gloria had pointed. "The rec room?" he queried. "Is that in the basement?"

"Down the stairs."

"Okay." He nodded, rolling his eyes. "We still have to check down there, anyway. We'll look for Lester while we're down there."

Kate followed him back into the hallway to a doorway that did indeed open onto stairs leading down to a finished basement. The basement was dark, and they switched on the light.

"Lester!" Kate called out, then suppressed a smile. She looked at Mike and shrugged. "Gloria is definitely out of it."

Mike nodded as Kate picked up one of two glasses standing on the coffee table, sniffed at it. "But Lester was here, that's for sure."

Mike bent down to pick up something that was peeking out from under the sofa. He held it up. It was a lacy bra.

Kate grinned. "I guess Gabriella promised Lester more than just a job."

"Did you find him?" Gloria's voice floated down the stairs.

"He's gone, Mrs. Rossiter. He's not here. You know this is Monday, already." She looked at Mike. Suddenly a lightbulb pinged and went out, making Kate jump and leaving them in a dim glow. "Come on, we've got to go."

"Yes he is." The voice was insistent. "He's in the little kitchen."

"Oh for heaven's sake." Mike strode across the room, pushing open a door at one end. "He's not, Mrs. Rossiter. Honest."

"He's in the kitchen." The singsong note in Gloria's voice suddenly gave Kate an uneasy feeling. But shrugging it off, she followed Mike into the tiny kitchenette.

"Okay, Lester," she called out. "We know you're in here."

"Yeah," Mike caught onto her mood, pointing to the big deep freezer. "We know you're in there, Lester. We're going to count to three."

She couldn't hold back from laughing as he walked towards the freezer and flung the top open.

She heard a loud whoosh of air and thought at first it was the cold rushing out of the open freezer but then she realized the sound had come from Mike.

"Oh, shit!" he said, staring into the freezer. Then he slammed down the lid.

52

Monday evening, October 7

Kate was quiet, wrapped in her own thoughts, when Mike pulled up alongside her Jeep in the parking lot of the police station. The shock of discovering Lester Franks' body had numbed her. The reporter had hardly been one of her closest friends but she'd had enough dealings with him to know that he was not a bad guy at heart, and she could not get the sight of his bloated, bluish-white face out of her mind. Nor could she erase the picture of the stocking tied around his throat. Every time she tried to push the images out of her mind she'd alight on another detail, like Lester's naked, almost hairless chest or the colorful plaid of his boxers. She felt saddened and sickened by the idea of Gabriella Grant feigning seduction, only to end up wrapping one of her stockings around his neck.

"Will you be okay?" Mike asked her as she reached for the door handle. "Maybe I should drive you home?"

"No." Kate shook her head. "I'll be fine." She knew he had work to do, and she knew he was eager to get going. The search for Gabriella was about to become a tri-state manhunt. There were press statements to prepare and APBs and BOLOs to put out.

Finding Lester's body had dissipated any doubts Mike might have had about nailing Gabriella Grant, just as it had quelled any lingering misgivings Kate might have felt about exploiting the anchorwoman's sickness. Now, she wanted to get going, too. She needed to call her agent and start on the outline for her book.

She laid a hand on Mike's arm. "Go, get her, detective, and, don't forget, I'll be waiting to hear all about it."

"You'll be home?"

Kate laughed. "Where else would I be?"

Mike grinned. "Oh, I don't know. In New York, maybe, with your agent or publisher . . . or signing a contract with WorldMedia?"

She recognized the underlying seriousness of the question and decided not to be evasive. She had already made her decision about Jack Kane's offer. Earlier in the day, it had crystallized in one phrase that Jack Kane had used about Gabriella Grant.

I wanted to build an image for her, he'd said as they'd all sat in the conference room at the police station, and while the phrase had echoed in and out of her head all morning, she'd finally realized why it bothered her. She'd realized that's what Jack Kane was all about: building images, reinventing, and creating perfect little packages for mass consumption. Somewhere along the way, it seemed, he usually fell a little bit in love with his creations, and she imagined that could be a heady experience for any woman. But it was not what she wanted for herself. She did not want—or need—to be reinvented and repackaged as Kate McCusker, TV Star.

"I'm not going anywhere, Mike," she said softly. "I'm not signing any TV contracts. I've got a book to write, I've got a son who needs me here, and I'm still waiting for that brunch you cancelled out on."

He glanced at her, raising an eyebrow as if looking for some further explanation. But then, without another word, he leaned over, and cupping her face in his hands, kissed her on the mouth.

Moments later, as she pulled out of the parking lot and headed for home, she found herself wondering how much of her book proposal she'd be able to get down on paper before Mike arrived. She had a feeling it was not going to be a lot. Not if she was going to take the time first to shower, and change into something a little more alluring than the jeans and turtleneck she'd worn all day. She smiled to herself as she pulled around to the back of the house and walked into the dark kitchen. But her smile faded as she snapped on the light and noticed Tommy's backpack on the floor by the kitchen table. It didn't look as if he'd made any start on his homework. And where on earth was Maysie?

Puzzled, she walked across the kitchen, calling out their names as she headed towards the family room where she could see the glow of the flames leaping in the fireplace. Evidently, wherever Maysie and Tommy had gone, they had not been gone long.

She stopped abruptly in the doorway, drawing in her breath sharply at the sight of Gabriella Grant sitting on the raised stone hearth, her back to the flames, garbed in Ma's long, smocklike brown dress.

As Kate shrank back, Gabriella brought her arm up to reveal the gun in her hand. Kate didn't need to look twice to recognize it as the Glock automatic that had belonged to her husband, and her heart slammed against her ribs even as the picture of Tommy's backpack on the kitchen floor leaped into her head.

"Where's my son?" she asked, the calmness of her voice masking the cold fear that suddenly gripped her. "What have you done to him?"

"Relax," the other woman answered. "And come on in. I've been waiting for you. You and I need to chat, first. Come on." She beckoned Kate into the room.

Kate walked towards the fireplace on unsteady legs. Only the strangely comical picture of Gabriella, Glock in hand, dressed in Ma's long plain brown frock, allowed her to keep some measure of control over her anxiety—until Gabriella fixed her with cold, unblinking eyes.

She waved the gun in Kate's face, forcing her to sit down on the floor in front of her. "I don't have a lot of time, so let's not waste it. I know the cops are looking for me. I know they searched my office yesterday. I want to know what's going on."

"Is that why you're here?"

"That's not why I came but we'll get to other business in a moment. First, I want to know what they've got on me."

"And I'm not saying a goddamn thing until you tell me what you've done to my son."

"Oh, for fuck's sake!" Grant tossed her head impatiently. "I didn't hurt him. I wouldn't hurt a child; I'm not stupid. They'd put me away for life for something like that."

Kate stared at her wide-eyed. Did Grant honestly think her words offered any reassurance? Didn't she realize she was facing life behind bars already?

As if reading her thoughts, Gabriella Grant smiled thinly and said: "I don't intend to go to jail for killing Emma Kane."

Kate took a deep breath and told herself to stay calm. "Then maybe you should leave and get going while you can," she said. "I'm expecting one of the detectives here, any moment. Just tell me where my son is—"

Kate stopped in midsentence as Grant's laugh pealed out across the room. "What a quaint idea, but I wasn't talking about running away. Can you see me on the run? Goodness, what kind of a life would that be?" She shook her head. "No, I think it'll be best if I just come clean. Tell the cops exactly what happened. It's not as if I meant to kill Emma Kane. I just went to talk to her. I had to do something. I would have lost my job, you know."

Kate said nothing as Grant continued. "It was that goon's fault. He said Emma was too busy to talk to me. He wouldn't let me near her. He said if I didn't leave he'd push me downstairs. I just panicked, and then Emma came out and saw the gun and started screaming, and I went to pieces." She paused for breath, and stared intently at Kate. "They've got to see that it wasn't my fault."

Kate bit down on her bottom lip, not knowing what Grant expected her to say. She wanted to ask if Grant planned to explain the strangling of Lester Franks as an accident, too, but decided it was wiser not to mention the tabloid reporter. Instead, she looked away, staring down at the rug, allowing her eyes to drift over the mess of Tommy's toys. She picked up a discarded candy wrapper and twisted it in her fingers.

"Well?" Grant said, leaning forward so that the gun hovered dangerously, just inches from Kate's nose. "You can help me out here. You've got an in with the cops. I want to know if they'll listen to my side of the story."

Kate made an effort to keep her face impassive as she realized Grant was serious about palming off the killings as an accident. But was this scenario another delusion? Or was she just spinning a yarn to get out of trouble? Either way, Kate supposed it couldn't hurt to keep talking. If Grant needed a sounding board, the longer Kate could spin this out, the better her chance that Mike would arrive. She cleared her throat, twisting on the candy wrapper nervously. "Well," she began cautiously. "It's the only side they're going to hear, but they may have some difficulty believing you went just to talk. You did take a gun with you, and the police know where it came from. They know you stole it from Molly Heskell's home. That seems to indicate you had some sort of plan."

"Bullshit!" Grant's mouth twisted over the word. "There was no plan, and I didn't steal it. I removed the gun from Molly's nightstand because I was worried about *her*. And the only reason I took it to Jack's house was because if Emma didn't agree to divorce Jack, I was going to use it on myself. If I couldn't persuade Emma to divorce Jack I was going to shoot myself. They can't possibly think I went there to kill her, dear God." Grant gave a little gasp, eyeing Kate as she did so, as if to gauge the effect of her explanation. "Don't tell me they think I planned it?"

Kate tossed the candy wrapper into the fire, and Grant jolted forward, startled by the sudden movement. But she relaxed again as Kate continued. "They know you checked out Emma's home a couple of weeks before the murders. They know you went there—with that realtor."

Grant waved the Glock in the air. "That's meaningless. I was curious about Jack's wife. I didn't do anything that a million other mistresses wouldn't do."

Kate took a deep breath. "The police find it suspicious that the realtor fell down the stairs to her death the same day she was with you."

Grant laughed. "They can find it whatever they want. They'll never be able to pin that one on me."

Kate knew she should leave well enough alone, but her curiosity got the better of her. "But you were with her when she fell, right?"

Grant's eyes narrowed momentarily. "You don't really want me to answer that, do you?" she said softly. "I mean if, and I'm saying *if* I were to tell you that I was there, *if* I were to tell you that she was a very tiresome woman who thought she was so clever because she recognized me, in spite of my wig and dark glasses, and *if* I were to say that maybe I brushed against her on the way down those very dangerous stairs, then I'd have to do something about you, wouldn't I?"

Grant paused but was not really waiting for an answer because then she said, "So, let's just get back to the facts. I want to know what other evidence the cops think they've got."

Kate couldn't focus on the question immediately. The idea that Grant had cold-bloodedly pushed Anna Mae Whitman to her death just because the realtor had recognized her sent a chill snaking up her spine. It was as terrifying as the thought that she had strangled Lester Franks to stop him from exposing her as a liar. How could she dare hope that this woman had had any second thoughts about harming Maysie or Tommy?

"Well?" Grant prodded again, her eyes flickering with amusement as if she was enjoying Kate's discomfort.

Okay, time to take off the gloves, thought Kate with a sudden viciousness. "The cops know all about your phony alibi." She flung the words out. "They know you set it up, ordering a Chinese meal to make it look like you were home at the time of the murders. It's going to be tough to convince them all you planned to do was *talk* to Emma when you went to so much trouble to fake them out."

"I didn't set up an alibi." Grant came right back at her. "I didn't order the meal, my assistant did. I just forgot to cancel it that night. I had other things on my mind, remember?" She paused and stared at Kate with ice-cold blue eyes before her lips twitched into a smirk. "I didn't remember about the food until I got the call at my mom's house." She paused again. "Or are you saying it's some sort of crime to have your calls forwarded? All I did was get the doorman to instruct the delivery boy to leave the bag on the table."

Kate returned the smirk with a half smile. "Making a point, though, of telling him you were stepping into the shower, giving him the impression that you were in the apartment, so that he could later tell that to the police."

"And what should I have told him? Oh by the way, Jose, I'm not really there, and make sure you tell the delivery boy the same thing so that he can have a good nose around and steal anything he has a mind to. No." She shook her head. "If there was any intent to deceive it was limited to the doorman and the delivery boy."

Grant fixed Kate with a pointed look, then let out a loud, exaggerated sigh. "So, what do you think? Think I can make a deal? It was self-defense. It was an accident. I mean, there's no reason for the county to waste time and money on a big murder trial and risk an acquittal. Because that's what's going to happen if I tell my side of it to a jury. It would be much neater my way. The cops could close the case and everyone would be happy."

Kate picked up another candy wrapper off the floor and rolled it in her fingers, wondering how mentally unstable the anchorwoman really was. In spite of her fear, she was fascinated by Grant's incredible interweaving of fantasy and reality. It was like talking to two different women, one totally deluded about her relationship with Jack Kane, talking about her impossible situation as the pregnant Other Woman, talking about going to reason with her lover's wife. The other, a smart, savvy newswoman with a logical, incisive mind that seemed to grasp the reality of her predicament, not to mention the finer points of legalities like premeditation and reasonable doubt.

Kate rolled the hard tiny ball of candy wrapper in her fingers nervously, and as she glanced at the floor, she noticed several other similar little white balls. They were tiny little things and they weren't candy wrappers, she suddenly realized. Tommy called them bang-snaps and used them to scare squirrels and unsuspecting older ladies, like his grandmother, by hurling them down on the porch and hearing them go off with a loud bang. As casually as she could, she reached out to pick up a couple more, wondering what would happen if she tossed them in the fire. But immediately turned her attention back to Grant's outrageous suggestion.

Or maybe not so outrageous, she reflected, recalling

Mike's gloomy prediction. If Grant stuck to her story and explained everything the way she'd just explained it to Kate, for sure, her story would raise doubt. Whether it was doubt about the premeditation of the killings—or doubt about her sanity—Kate wasn't sure. But either way, it wasn't beyond the realms of possibility that Grant might, in the end, evade justice for the murders of Emma Kane and Tony Salerno.

"Anyway, you get the general idea, don't you?" Grant's voice broke the silence. "What I'm saying is, they don't put people like me in jail. Maybe I'll have to spend some time in a hospital somewhere, but wherever they put me, it'll be over in a couple of years, and by that time Jack and I will be able to start over without any hoopla. People forget, you know."

Kate was tempted to ask her who she imagined would forget: Did she mean Jack Kane—or the public? But Gabriella's next words cut the thought dead.

"The only problem is you. I can't stand the thought of being away and you and Jack messing around behind my back. That's why I had to come and resolve this before I turn myself in to the cops."

"Resolve it? There's nothing to resolve. There's nothing going on between me and Jack Kane." Kate rocked forward to distract attention from the sweeping movement of her hand as she gathered up a couple more bang-snaps. "I'm not interested in Jack Kane."

"He's interested in you, though. I saw him in the newsroom with you. I heard about the two of you."

"From?"

"Never mind who." Grant snapped as she raised the Glock, aiming it at Kate.

Kate blinked and drew back. Startled by Grant's sudden change in demeanor, she raised her hands in a useless gesture of self-defense. "Please, don't fool with that gun. This is silly. Shooting me isn't going to resolve anything. It'll make things worse for you. For God's sake—" Kate's words caught momentarily in her throat. "You've got some sort of excuse for what happened at Emma Kane's house, but you couldn't get away with this. If you kill me, or anyone else in this house, they'll put you away for sure."

Grant shook her head, and her voice sounded curiously flat when she spoke this time. "You just don't get it. If you're around, it won't matter what kind of a deal I get. By the time I'm back, it'll be too late for me and Jack." She prodded Kate's shoulder with the gun. "Come on. Stand up."

Kate opened her mouth to protest again but the flatness of Grant's voice and the distant, blank look in her eyes stopped her. She had the feeling that no matter what else she said now, it wouldn't matter. It was as if the rational, logical Gabriella Grant had left the room.

Kate steeled herself. Now or never, she thought, taking a deep breath as she raised herself to her feet. In the very same moment she tossed the bang-snaps into the fire. She saw a spark leap, and then a series of loud popping noises erupted in the room. Hearing Grant's gasp as she turned to see what was happening, Kate pushed off the balls of her feet and flung herself at the other woman, knocking her down, and knocking the gun out of her hand.

But Grant came right back at her, shoving Kate so hard that she grazed her head against the side of the stone hearth. Momentarily stunned, Kate didn't fully register the first shriek. But then she heard the piercing scream, and glancing up, she saw flames leaping from the hem of Ma's old brown dress.

She stared half in horror, half mesmerized by the sight of Gabriella Grant beating at the flames with her hands as she ran shrieking towards the big picture window. As Kate struggled to her feet, Grant flung herself at one of the long, heavy drapes, making an effort to smother the flames by twisting the drape around herself. Even as her hands reached upwards, tugging at the drape to bring it down over herself, the flames leaped to the sheers.

Up on her feet now, Kate started towards her, charging at the draped bundle. She brought Grant crashing to the floor as the flames leaped from the sheers to the drapes framing a side window, and then down to a bundle of old newspapers that she kept stacked near the kindling by the hearth. The paper blazed immediately.

"Where's my son? Where's Maysie?" she shrieked through the heavy drape.

"Upstairs!" Grant's response was immediate. "Upstairs. Please let me go. Let me get out of here."

"Where upstairs?" Kate glanced across as the flames licked towards a fringed lampshade. She gripped Gabriella's head in her hands and shook her, trying to ignore the smoke that was already making her eyes tear. "Where upstairs?" She had to know exactly. The house was too large for her to check every room before the fire spread. She clawed at the drape to uncover Grant's face. "Where are they?" Kate yelled at her. "If they're dead, I'm going to make sure you burn here before you go burn in hell."

She gripped Grant's hair.

"The old lady's room," Grant shrieked once, and then again as Kate slammed her head down to the floor as hard as she could.

She heard a deep, pained groan, but without giving the woman another glance, Kate ran for the door, into the hall, and up the stairs, taking them three at a time.

It felt like she was moving through the kind of thick heavy syrup that Maysie served with her waffles as she ran down the hallway, bursting through Maysie's door to find Tommy and Maysie stretched out on the floor, feet, hands, and mouths bound with thick gray duct tape. Both pairs of eyes blinked and darted in her direction as she stood over them.

She wanted to weep with relief.

Later, Kate would recall that every second had felt like an hour as she'd searched for scissors in Maysie's bathroom cabinets and then hacked away at the tape around Maysie's ankles, and her heart had stopped as her mother-in-law, her feet finally freed, had sagged to the floor momentarily.

"Run," Kate shouted at her, picking up Tommy in her arms and following Maysie down the hallway, through her bedroom and den and down the stairs into the kitchen. The destruction of her den and her computer and office equipment registered only vaguely as she ran down the stairs and through the kitchen to bring Maysie and Tommy out onto the porch.

Sometime between calling the fire department and cutting through the tape that bound Tommy's feet and wrists and mouth, she found herself wondering what had happened to the deranged anchorwoman. She could not imagine that Gabriella Grant had been left too stunned by the blow to her head. She had surely already made her escape from the blazing family room. Either that, or she was dead, thought Kate, hearing the explosion of glass as the force of the fireball shattered the windows on the other side of the house.

Epilogue

K ate stared at the words written across the top of her screen and flexed her fingers. She was coming into the home stretch now, and just as well. Tommy would be home by three, ready to trim the Christmas tree.

She pushed away from her desk and paced across to the windows overlooking the flagstone terrace, then she walked over to the fireplace. A mere flick of the switch had ignited the logs, which were still burning cheerily. No mess, no fuss. She could get used to this, she thought. Just as she could get used to the double Jacuzzi and sauna, and all the other little luxurious touches that she and Mike had found in the guest suite of Jack Kane's mansion.

Jack had been magnanimous. Two days after the fire that had destroyed half of her own house, he had driven down to insist that she and Tommy and Maysie move into the house while her own was being fixed. He had insisted that she treat it like her own home—even after she'd told him she was turning down his offer of a TV job. Even after she'd protested that it was more space than three people could ever use.

"So, invite a friend to stay and keep you company," he'd said in a tone of voice that had suggested he knew there was more than one reason why she'd turned down the job. "You'll be comfortable, Kate. And, you'll be able to finish your book."

Yes, she thought, looking across the room at the white pages already stacked high on the desk. Thanks to Jack—

and the fact that she always copied her files onto diskettes, which she kept in her car along with her laptop—she was about done.

She returned to the desk and glanced over the previous paragraphs where she had left Det. Mike Travis about to get on his bike just minutes after launching the search for Gabriella Grant.

Fatal Delusion was really Gabriella's story, but the last chapter belonged to Mike, and she knew the ending so well she didn't even have to refer to any notes.

Five minutes before the dispatcher received the 911 call about a fire at the McCusker home on Woodland Drive, Mike Travis left Lower Merion police station a worried man. Even though he knew that he and Harry had done everything they could do to launch the search for Gabriella Grant, something still niggled at him. He wondered if in his haste to be with Kate he had left something undone, had missed some vital step.

But, in fact, it was his thoughts about Kate—and Jack Kane—that put him back on track. Revving up his bike, he had suddenly remembered that while detectives had been sent to Gabriella's apartment in New York and again to her mother's home in Langhorne, they had not searched for her in the one home that she surely now regarded as hers. With Jack Kane leaving so swiftly to return to New York, it had not occurred to Mike Travis, or Harry either, to immediately dispatch patrol cars to the empty Kane mansion. But it was worth checking, he thought now, changing direction and heading for the Kane mansion on Cherry Lane.

Though the house appeared dark and empty, he killed his engine outside the front gates and kept to the cover of the trees along the driveway as he made his way to the back of the house. Skirting around the side terraces he stepped onto the flagstone terrace, where he immediately noticed a broken pane of glass in the back door.

It had to be Grant, he thought. Had to be, he told himself as he reached inside the glass pane to open the door. Drawing his gun from his holster he entered the dark kitchen. For a moment, he stood, listening. The house was quiet except for the faint distant hum of something electrical. It sounded as if it was coming from upstairs, and he crept across the kitchen to the hall from where he spotted the faint light spilling out onto the landing outside the master bedroom.

No longer in much doubt about Gabriella Grant's whereabouts, he slipped off his shoes and made his way upstairs. It was only when he reached the bedroom door that he realized what the electrical hum was. He shook his head in disbelief. Gabriella Grant was running the Jacuzzi in the bathroom where she had shot down Emma Kane in cold blood!

He moved cautiously through the darkened bedroom, stumbling over what looked like heaps of clothing. It looked like Gabriella had emptied Emma Kane's closets onto the floor. He padded in his stockinged feet to the dressing room area and glanced through the door.

Indeed, Gabriella Grant was soaking in a tub full of bubbles, humming to herself, her head tossed back against the rim of the tub, her eyes closed. He noticed the Glock lying on the tile surround in the same moment, and took a deep breath as he started towards her. Just inches away, he reached for the automatic even as he prodded her naked shoulder with his own revolver.

Then, with the Glock safely in his hand, he stepped back a pace as Gabriella Grant turned to face him.

"Now, slow and easy, step out of the tub, Grant," he said. "You're under arrest for the murder of Lester Franks."

She surveyed him with calm blue eyes, as if she'd been expecting him to show, and made no move to reach for the thick towel lying on the side of the tub.

Instead, she smiled lazily at him as he stepped back another two paces. "Anything you say, detective. I'm ready to talk," she whispered, rising slowly from the water, like a naked Venus from the waves.

Kate gave a loud sigh and sat back in her chair as she skimmed over her last few lines. She wondered if the reference to Botticelli's *Birth of Venus* was too obscure for the book, but those were the words Mike had used to describe the scene.

"Do you think it makes her sound too sexy and glamorous?" he'd asked as Kate had rolled her eyes.

"No, I think it makes her sound quite deranged," she'd replied.

She had made him give her every detail of Gabriella Grant's arrest. Not that same night because, of course, there had been no time to sit and chat. But the following night—with Maysie dispatched to stay with a friend and Tommy, brave little soul that he'd proved himself to be, escorted happily to stay the night at Belinda's after his half-sister's birthday party—she and Mike had retreated, with her laptop, to the only bedroom in her house that had escaped both fire and water damage.

Sitting cross-legged on the bed, Kate had bombarded Mike with questions about the bizarre encounter in Emma Kane's bathroom. "What on earth do you think was going through her mind? I mean, she was coming onto you, right? Did she imagine she was going to screw her way out of an arrest?"

"Who knows?" Mike had laughed. "I should have called for backup, though. The way her mind works, I'm willing to bet she got out of that tub thinking that I'd come after her because *I* wanted to seduce *her*. She was actually smiling as she walked towards me."

"What did you say to her?"

"I told her I'd just found the body of the last man she'd tried to seduce. That took the smile off her face . . . for about two seconds."

"And then?"

"And then she told me it was Lester's fault. That he had begged her to do a lot of weird, kinky things to him—"

Mike had never finished the sentence because just at that moment Kate's cell phone had rung out shrilly, and she had grabbed for it, only to hear her son's voice echoing on the line.

"Mom?"

She stared into the receiver. "Tommy?"

"Mom, I've got a question for you: What do you do when a kid keeps barfing?"

"Tommy." She smiled, glancing at the clock on the nightstand. Why was her son calling her at midnight with silly riddles? "Why are you up so late? This is no time for jokes; you should be in bed."

"No, Mom, this isn't a joke. This is serious. Celine keeps throwing up and she's very, very hot."

"Well, honey, doesn't Belinda know?"

"Belinda's not here. She and Ivo went to Center City for some big dinner at the hospital. They left right after the birthday party, but I can't get them on the cell phone."

Kate nestled the phone in the crook of her neck as she slipped on her shoes. "What about the nanny, hon?"

Kate had a feeling she knew what he was going to say before she heard the words: "She's out, Mom. It's her night off."

"You're alone?" Out of the corner of her eye, Kate had seen Mike reaching for his jacket. He was already halfway down the stairs as she hung up, telling Tommy they were on their way.

Thank God, it had not taken them very long to get to Belinda's house, where one look at the little girl had prompted Mike to call the paramedics, who arrived at around the same time as Ivo and Belinda.

Kate and Mike had exited the little girl's bedroom with a worried-looking Tommy in tow, and Kate had told her son to get his things so that she could take him home. Belinda had appeared as they were leaving.

"Where are you taking Tommy?" she'd asked, her voice rising to a high pitch.

"Home," Kate had told her firmly. "And what's more, he won't be coming back to stay overnight again."

"Like hell he won't." Belinda had raced down the stairs to the hallway.

"Don't even think about it," Kate had told her. "You can see him weekends at my home. But his nights of working as an unpaid babysitter are over."

Belinda had stood her ground. "You're joking, of course. This was just a mistake."

"Yes, and one too many," Mike had interrupted. "You can take your choice, Mrs. Basualdo." He reached into his pocket for his badge. "You can just go along with whatever Mrs.

McCusker thinks is best, or you can go to court. But if you decide to take this to court, you should know that I'll be there to testify about tonight. You could very well end up losing custody of your daughter, too."

Belinda had looked at Mike and then at his badge as if still not quite sure that he was serious. But then Ivo had stepped in, and ushering all three of them hurriedly to the door, had assured Kate there was no need for any talk about courts.

It was a pity, Kate thought, that she couldn't include that little scene in the book. Mike had been so forceful. So totally determined to stave off any further inroads by Belinda. But there was no place for it. Nor for what had eventually and inevitably followed, when after tucking Tommy into bed, she and Mike had stolen out onto the back porch. Not unless she was going to write an erotic novel.

She smiled to herself and flexed her fingers again. All she had left to do now was the one-page summary. She started typing again:

> After rejecting Gabriella Grant's rough-sex defense, a preliminary hearing ordered the former anchorwoman to stand trial for the murder of Lester Franks. The District Attorney said he would ask for the death penalty after a series of psychiatric evaluations led forensic psychiatrist Annabelle Newton to conclude that while Grant exhibited some classic symptoms of obsessive delusion, only her fear of being exposed as a liar and fraud could be considered a motive in the murder of Lester Franks.

> Subsequently identified in the computer enhancement of Lewis Terrenzio's videotape, Grant was also charged with the murders of Emma Kane and Tony Salerno. The Montgomery County District Attorney refused to consider a plea bargain, stating that when the time came the prosecution intended to produce evidence that Grant had acted with premeditation and malice aforethought.

> Lewis Terrenzio pleaded no contest to four counts of indecent assault and guilty to manslaughter in the death of Molly Heskell. While in custody awaiting sentencing,

he attempted twice to hang himself. Currently he is confined in the infirmary of a maximum-security prison north of Philadelphia.

Jack Kane went on to launch several major shows on the WorldMedia News cable network. Among them was one titled *Psycho*. The anchor of the show was Annabelle Newton, the county forensic psychiatrist who testified at Gabriella Grant's preliminary hearing. The strikingly attractive Ms. Newton quit her job with the county two days after she completed her court appearance. Subsequently, in an interview with *People* magazine, she revealed that Gabriella Grant had threatened to throw acid in her face after hearing that Ms. Newton was going to work at WorldMedia.

Sam Packer returned to Italy to set up a bureau for WorldMedia in Rome.

Harry Holmsby retired after collapsing with an ulcer two months after Gabriella Grant was ordered to stand trial. He was immediately put on a no-fat diet by Maysie McCusker.

Det. Mike Travis . . .

She paused for a moment, then started typing again:

Detective Mike Travis took a short vacation after Gabriella Grant's preliminary hearing. He spent most of that time in bed making wild and passionate love to Kate McCusker.

She stopped typing, suddenly aware that she was not alone. She felt fingers caressing the back of her neck and she grinned as she heard Mike say, "Wow! Are you really going to write that?" His fingers moved to her earlobe.

She highlighted and erased the text. "Of course not." She laughed. "I was just playing."

"So, what are you going to write?"

"I don't know. Something boring like Det. Mike Travis

was promoted to lead investigator at the Montgomery DA's office—and moved into a big house worthy of his new position." She laughed again as his hands found their way under her sweater.

"That's getting more accurate. How about adding: 'and asked Kate McCusker to marry him'?"

"No, too sappy." She shook her head. "Anyway, I can't do that."

"Why not? It's the truth. Or at least it will be as soon as I can get you away from this laptop."

"I know, but if I write that, it's not fair to the reader."

"Not fair to the reader?"

"Well you can't leave them hanging. I can't just leave it at asked. They'll want to know the answer. Did she say yes or no?"

"So go on, type it in. I can't help you with that." His hands cupped her breasts under the sweater. "Or can I?"

Her breath caught in her throat. "I don't know, Mike. This is . . . well, I've got to have some time to think." She sat back and stared at the screen. "I don't have to know the answer now; I'll have time to fill in blanks before the book goes to print."

"When is that?"

"Next May or June."

He laughed softly, his lips nuzzling her ear. "Well in that case, just write what you usually write when you don't know all the facts."

He leaned over her shoulder and started tapping the keys with his right index finger. She watched as he wrote:

Det. Mike Travis was promoted to lead investigator with the Montgomery County DA's office and . . . (FILL) . . .

She raised her face up to his and smiled. "Do you use one finger to type all your reports, too?"

"Yes." He nodded, slipping his left hand in between her thighs. "It keeps them simple and short, and leaves me time to get on with more important things."

Then he punched the Save button and closed her laptop.

Available by mail from

TOR FORGE

CHICAGO BLUES • Hugh Holton
Police Commander Larry Cole returns in his most dangerous case to date when he investigates the murders of two assassins that bear the same M.O. as long-ago, savage, vigilante cases.

KILLER.APP • Barbara D'Amato
"Dazzling in its complexity and chilling in its exposure of how little privacy anyone has...totally mesmerizing."—*Cleveland Plain Dealer*

CAT IN A DIAMOND DAZZLE • Carole Nelson Douglas
The fifth title in Carole Nelson Douglas's Midnight Louie series—"All ailurphiles addicted to Lilian Jackson Braun's "The Cat Who..." mysteries...can latch onto a new *purri*vate eye: Midnight Louie—slinking and sleuthing on his own, a la Mike Hammer."—*Fort Worth Star Telegram*

STRONG AS DEATH • Sharan Newman
The fourth title in Sharan Newman's critically acclaimed Catherine LeVendeur mystery series pits Catherine and her husband in a bizarre game of chance—which may end in Catherine's death.

PLAY IT AGAIN • Stephen Humphrey Bogart
In the classic style of a Bogart and Bacall movie, Stephen Humphrey Bogart delivers a gripping, fast-paced mystery."—*Baltimore Sun*

BLACKENING SONG • Aimée and David Thurlo
The first novel in the Ella Clah series involving ex-FBI agent, Ella Clah, investigating murders on a Navajo Reservation.

Available by mail from

TOR
FORGE